JEWELS IN THE GARDEN OF ENGLAND

Eli Bradbury, the most prosperous brewer in Kent, was determined that his two daughters, Isabella and Lucinda, should marry up in the world.

Pencombe Hall, home of Lord Montford and his sons, nestled in the nearby countryside. Michael was the heir to the estate; Johnnie was his devil-may-care younger brother.

During the long, hot summer of 1901, awaiting embarkation for the war in South Africa, they gathered around the snooker table at Pencombe, brooding over the future of their country and their heritage.

Lucinda was in love with Michael; Isabella was earmarked for Johnnie. But pale, pensive Isabella was quite different from her flame-haired, pleasure-seeking sister. Her dreams ranged far beyond the masculine hush of Pencombe and the click of ivory balls on green baize . . .

HERITAGE

will follow the fortunes of Isabella and her family into the Twentieth Century.

By the same author

Country Enterprise (with Jonathan Ffrench)

HEATHER HAY

Heritage

GRAFTON BOOKS
A Division of the Collins Publishing Group

LONDON GLASGOW
TORONTO SYDNEY AUCKLAND

Grafton Books
A Division of the Collins Publishing Group
8 Grafton Street, London W1X 3LA

A Grafton Paperback Original 1988

ISBN 0-586-20306-0

Printed and bound in Great Britain by
Collins, Glasgow

Set in Bembo

To my family, with love and thanks

Acknowledgements

Whilst the characters in this book are imaginary, the countryside they live in is very real and very beautiful. I was fortunate to work for two years in Penshurst Place, Kent, stately home of Viscount De L'Isle, VC KG. The special atmosphere of this historic house formed the chrysalis from which the Montford family of the book emerged.

I would never have finished *Heritage* without the continued help and encouragement of my husband, Jonathan, and daughter, Joanna. My two young sons, Alexander and Rex, played their part by being good – most of the time. Of course, I must also thank my mother, whose spelling is far better than mine.

I give thanks for the inspiration to take the families of the book out into the wider world that came from Jane Judd, my agent, and for the midnight oil burned by Judith Kendra, my editor.

Finally, I have to thank Barry Hearn, and his Matchroom organization, who brought snooker into the world of television and so clearly demonstrated the drama that is the essence of the game.

Ootacamund, Nilgri Hills, India, 1875

The slow, rhythmic creaking of the punka ruled their lives. They breathed in time with it, a slow restrained form of breathing that made all but the simplest tasks impossible.

Colonel Sir Neville Chamberlain stretched back in his rattan chair, in pride of position on the veranda. His eyes were closed. He was listening to the sound of the game in progress behind him in the Officers' Mess. The hollow roll of the balls on the baize, the strike of wood on ivory. It was like the rest of life at the hill station, a hollow imitation of life in England.

'God damn!' One of the officers had miscued, the sharp edge of stress in his voice spoiling its aristocratic modulation. The young Lord Montford had not reacted well to the heat on the arid plain. Now, in the once longed-for refuge of greenness in the tea plantations, he was finding boredom the final straw.

What they'd needed was a decent skirmish, but it had got too damned hot and nobody had the energy, not even the natives.

The colonel rose slowly from his chair; something had to be done. He straightened his uniform then walked towards the players.

'Right then, chaps. Somebody pass me a cue, what?'

There was a minor commotion amongst the four to be the one with the honour.

'Come on then, what's the game, billiards eh? Let's see how good you are.'

'Yes, sir.' Three voices in polite unison, then came the fourth.

'Yes, billiards,' Montford drawled. 'Damned boring game. Not enough to keep a chap's mind off the bloody heat.'

The colonel's eyebrows rose; this was no way for a subaltern to talk to his superior, but it was hot, devilish hot and one had to make allowances. 'Played a lot of billiards in my time, Montford,' he said, 'in a lot of places. Always found it a good game, along with a Pimm's or something like that, keeps a man feeling human.'

The patrician profile of the young lord came perilously close to a sneer. The colonel pondered the situation; of course, there'd been that scandal, well perhaps not a scandal, but certainly a rumpus: some American adventuress had made a fool of the boy and then made off with the Montford family jewels. That was why the fellow slouching in front of him was out here now. His people had married him off to an eminently suitable English girl. But the American affair had preyed on his mind and at last his wife had threatened to return to her family, taking their small son with her. So he'd been booted overseas to come to terms with his lot.

'You need something to sharpen you up, Montford. Stands out a mile. Now what can we think of?' The colonel was in a benevolent mood, courtesy of an excellent lamb curry vindaloo that he'd had for lunch, and the Bombay duck had been particularly good. So he considered only fleetingly the prospect of sending the man back down on to the plain, and letting him become someone else's problem; no, he could be more constructive than that.

'Look here, gather round the table, chaps, I've had something in mind for a while now. Hey, you!' He gestured at one of the club servants. 'Bring me a dozen or so balls, all you can lay your hands on, chip chip.' He studied the table as he waited. 'The thing is,' he said, 'if you have more balls on the table you can make for a much more complicated game. You've got to create some structure of course, something to follow pretty rigidly, but there's a little trick I'd like to show you. Let's start with this.' He rolled six balls on to the table. 'Right, now, what I'm after is a game where a fellow can use his skill to win against the odds, a way he can manipulate the score, right up to the end. What I have in mind is something like this.' He moved the balls around with his cue, shepherding them into the arrangement he wanted. 'Let's say that I've got these six balls to pot, to clear the table.'

'I say, sir, what's this game then, a version of carom, or pool, or . . .?' Montford was becoming interested, despite himself.

'Not a version of anything, Montford, but a whole new game. Granted we'll have to borrow a bit and improvise as we go along. But it can't be beyond us. After all, we're the regiment!' Not long ago their mess had echoed to the memories of the Mutiny, place-names that sounded like a roll of honour: Lucknow, Delhi, Cawnpore.

'See here, let's imagine as I say, that I'm faced with these six balls. There's been a bit of play already, and I'm quite a few points behind my opponent, more than the tally these balls represent. There has to be a way that I can get him back on to the table, to force him to make foul shots that will increase my score, and this is it. Look at the red in the centre; let's say that's the ball the rules force me to go for next. Now watch.' He took the white cue ball, placed it on the table in front of him, then leaned forwards, easing his portly figure over the edge of the table. He lined up on the white, then struck it firmly and the cue ball collided with the red he'd indicated, both balls setting off in motion. The white ball bounced off the far side of the table before coming to rest. They were now either side of another red ball.

'Right then, Montford, your turn. You use the white to hit the ball that I just did, that's the order of play.'

'But I can't.' Montford leaned over the table, then he

walked round to the far side and bent down to peer across the table. 'It isn't possible to, at least not without hitting the one in the middle first,' he said. His colonel was beaming.

'Exactly, so I'll have those points, thanks very much. Go on, make a stab at it.' Montford did as he was told, striking the wrong ball with the cue ball. 'Splendid, foul shot, points to me. See what I'm getting at?'

They nodded vaguely, because quite honestly they didn't see what he was getting at, but it didn't do to disagree with a colonel.

'Well, it needs a bit more work,' he conceded, seeing their doubt, 'but the essence of the thing is there, and so's the name: it's "snooker",' he said proudly. 'And that little manoeuvre I've just accomplished, getting those points off Montford here, that was him being snookered.'

They smirked at that; it sounded rather vulgar.

In a couple of weeks the young Prince Edward would be arriving on his tour of inspection; that would give the boys something to keep them up to scratch. Meanwhile, they'd work on this snooker thing. It'd take their minds off that Bengal famine business and would be something to take back with them to Blighty. A new game to show the fellows in the clubs in Piccadilly, to prove that those out in India were not the forgotten few. Something to prove that civilization in all its facets was being extended in the outposts of Empire.

Under the inspiration of the gallant colonel, with the application of the gentlemen soldiers of 'Ooty', the new game was devised. It combined the fascination of billiards with the skill of pyramids and the talents of pool. The game was snooker; it changed the habits of nations, the lives of countless men and women.

It was to become part of our Heritage.

Part One

Boyling, like to fire
Spenser

England, 1901

Isabella lay very, very still.

She had learned as a child that the only way to pretend to be asleep without the tell-tale fluttering of her eyelids giving her away was to try to relax by thinking of something nice. An eternal blue sky perhaps or, better still, the past.

First, there was a fleeting view of their home in Yorkshire, its smoke-blackened stone looking welcoming in a street of identical neighbours. In the sienna-coloured photograph that her mind's eye provided, the presence of her mother standing in the small front garden singled out number sixty – and her mother was waiting for her. This had to be a memory from Isabella's early childhood because her mother was rosy-faced, roundly smiling, pretty in her housewifely frock lightened with her favourite blue and white apron.

A high-pitched clang of fire irons made by the maid laying Isabella's bedroom fire sparked her eyes open. The ringing tone had touched a too finely stretched nerve for it jerked her thoughts back to the tram rides, at first an exciting part of a little girl's life and then, as she accompanied her mother on those endless trips to the Infirmary, the clang of the tram's bell became a sound from her nightmares.

She sat up abruptly in bed.

There was no more Yorkshire, no more beloved Mama, no more child Isabella. Yesterday had been her twenty-second birthday; she still felt bloated from the surfeit of rich, sweet pastries and the unaccustomed bubbles of champagne. Papa was a man of wealth, new wealth, and such occasions were now celebrated with unquestionable style in the Bradbury household. Isabella leaned back against her heaped pillows and watched the girl applying enthusiastic bellows to the fire crackling in the duck's nest grate. It was Maude this morning, Maude of the incredibly pale complexion, Maude who had been in service with a titled family before coming to work for the recently arrived Bradbury family eighteen months ago. Maude whose smooth hands were a testimony to the powers of the various creams made from strong-smelling lard that that she was determined Isabella should also use.

Isabella broke the awkward silence in the room. Last night she had rebelled and refused the thick, fat-rich paste on her hands. Maude had taken umbrage and would need careful handling to become even faintly bearable. 'Good morning, Maude. Isn't it a lovely day?'

That was safe ground as the sun was streaming through the recently opened curtains.

'Yes, ma'am.'

Normally Maude thought a 'Miss Bradbury' sufficient. Isabella would have to try harder. 'You know it's very warm for April, Maude. I think I could do without a fire in the mornings now.'

Maude paused, clearly scandalized, in her energetic brushing of a few, unseen specks of coal-dust. 'When I was in service with Lady Dewitt, we had fires every day of the year, winter and summer. Her ladyship used to say that a real lady felt cold in the mornings whatever the weather,' she said.

That was the crux of it. Isabella wasn't a true born lady. She had been born and brought up the daughter of a hard-working North Country man named Eli who had inherited a small brewery business in Kent from his father. Eli had also inherited his father's ability to brew an exceptional beer, but there was more to Eli. From his mother he had learned to dream dreams, dreams of wealth, dreams of splendour. Isabella's mother had worked hard and earnestly to keep her husband's feet firmly on the honest Yorkshire ground. Then she had died and Eli had let his dreams take flight. Unlike the happenings in twopenny novels he did not received a rude awakening. If anything, reality had surpassed his own wildest dreams and dreams, at the very beginning of a new century, could be boundless. So here sat Isabella in her great mahogany bed, waking to a maid laying her fire and about to lay out her clothes. It was a life of richness that would have made her Methodist mother turn in her grave.

Strangest of all for Isabella, town bred, was the silence. Bought at an inconceivable price, the great stone mansion about her prevented the sounds of the surrounding countryside impinging on their newly refined senses.

'Has my father left the house yet?'

'No, ma'am. I understand he's waiting to see Master Johnnie. He's expected at nine, at least that's when your father has ordered breakfast for. Would you like me to bring you up a boiled egg and some toast to keep you going until then?'

'No, I won't have anything, thank you, Maude. I'll wait until breakfast.' She got hurriedly out of bed, to Maude's obvious amusement.

The maid's romantic notions were misplaced. Isabella had felt no heart-filling surge of emotion on hearing that the ever gallant, ever charming Johnnie was gracing them with his presence at the breakfast table. But it was nice to have some company to look forward to, and he was always very successful at lightening the sometimes fraught atmosphere between Isabella and her sister Lucinda.

It was to be a very fine day. Looking out through her bedroom window, Isabella could see over the manicured lawns and far, far out over Kent. So far that she could let herself imagine the very lowest part of sky, where it touched the horizon, was the sea some twenty miles away. The great plain was a verdant patchwork, touched with patches of pink where the blossom was challenging the beauty of the fluffy white clouds that sailed majestically over the endless blue. Isabella could not remember such a perfect spring.

She had an hour to herself before breakfast. She looked into the mirror, and put her hand up to smooth her hair; it was very fine and she wore it in a coil tucked into the nape of her neck. Wisps of fair curls softened her high, intelligent forehead. Her skin was pale, heightening the blue of her eyes that were bright as she looked forward to opening the present Margaret had sent for her birthday. It had arrived by yesterday's post.

The parcel sat squarely on her bedside table, wrapped heavily in brown paper and tantalizingly marked 'Fragile Extreme Care'. She had no idea what it was. But her friendship with Margaret was a link with Yorkshire and as such was forbidden ground in front of Papa. The present was twice as attractive thanks to the necessary secrecy of its existence. Isabella pulled at the covering paper and uncovered a cardboard box. It was unmarked, giving no clues as to the contents. She would have liked to shake the box, to listen to the kind of rattle it made, as if it were a present under the Christmas tree, but remembering the 'Fragile', she set to opening the well-glued seams.

It was unbelievable, remarkable and confounding all at once. A jumble of emotions of which delight was the front runner came over her. It was a box camera. How absolutely like Margaret to think of something that Isabella had secretly wanted, but which she knew would incur her father's displeasure. The appeal of a camera, the joy of owning one lay in being able to photograph friends and family, artistic groupings of wayfarers, perhaps pets. But of course Papa would see it as another damning step against his own especial ideal of feminine gentility. Which was nonsense, because even members of the Royal Family were amateur photographers now. But it was new, modern, words that caused her father to swell with indignation.

The idea of capturing a likeness in an instant was fantastically challenging. There was a booklet with the camera, with drawings to explain how to operate the pull string and when to turn the knob, how it worked and where to send the completed films. It was surprisingly simple. Turning the pages Isabella felt a surge of enthusiasm. She must take photographs of them all, Papa, Lucinda, Johnnie and Michael. She stared for a moment more at the magic box, then made up her mind. She would tell Papa of its existence. She would use it, and he would come round to the idea eventually. Perhaps, though, she would not tell him right away that it came from Margaret, for there was no point in inviting instant wrath from her father.

Margaret Brown, six months older than Isabella, was now ensconced in art school in Glasgow. Isabella almost envied her friend's academic poverty. Margaret was happy in her studies while Isabella's material comforts seemed to present a barrier to any expression of her idealism. Margaret was the embodiment of everything her father detested in women. No, she would have to keep Margaret's generosity hidden for the moment. Generosity that made Isabella pause for a moment. How had Margaret afforded such a gift? There was no new money in her family, everything was a struggle. Isabella was sure the camera must have cost at least four pounds. But there was no letter with the present, only the affectionately signed birthday card, so she would have to wait for enlightenment.

What she needed was an occasion her father would want recorded for posterity. With a smile of victory Isabella realized how fortunate the timing was. She had a scant half an hour to familiarize herself with the camera. She set to with a will. It was wonderful knowing one's father's vanities she thought, with only the very slightest twinge of guilt.

Eli Bradbury made an imposing figure at the head of the breakfast table. His handsome broad face was framed by a magnificent full grey beard, his receding hairline heightened his already considerable forehead. He was distinctly the patriarch.

Only when he spoke was it possible to discern humble origins in the broad vowels, but even these were disappearing. And that was not surprising; since he had become a man of considerable wealth he had little need to speak to the working man. He now flinched bodily from the Northern adage that 'where there's muck there's brass.' To prove his aloofness from mire, the heavily laden drays that pulled out of his new, model factory at Maidstone were splendidly painted. The horses were curry combed to a gleaming perfection and even the leather aprons worn by the drivers were polished freshly each morning.

Eli's secret plans had ranged far, and they were all coming true. He smiled benevolently on the darkly handsome young Johnnie, helping himself to a piled plate of kidneys from the silver-laden sideboard. His smile also passed over Isabella; she was a colourless little thing compared to her sister but it was no matter. Johnnie was the younger son of Lord Montford and he was very conveniently paying a subtle court to Isabella.

It had been arranged between Lord Montford and Eli some three months ago that Lucinda, her father's pride and joy, would become betrothed to Michael, heir to the

Pencombe Estate. The match would be the final jewel in Eli's crown: Lucinda would be a Lady. It was tacitly assumed by the fathers that Isabella and Johnnie would also marry and would live in one of the several fine houses on the estate.

It would be good for Lucinda to have her sister close by when the babies came along. That was something that both his lordship and Eli concurred on very heartily: the Montford line needed a multitude of babies, preferably boys. With the wealth that Lucinda would bring to the estate, hovering perilously on the verge of impoverishment, Pencombe Hall could be restored to magnificence. There were nursery rooms aplenty and they would be full of a bustling, ordered existence. Eli's grandchildren would be born with silver spoons in their mouths. He gave a silent sigh of satisfaction that turned to an audible one of pleasure as Lucinda entered the breakfast room.

'Morning, Papa. Hallo, Johnnie. Isabella, be a dear and choose me some breakfast, I'm much too excited to concentrate.' She walked, smiling, to the head of the table and placed a hearty kiss on her beaming father's cheek.

Johnnie lit up at her arrival and Isabella did not for one moment contemplate not doing as she was asked. That was the thing about Lucinda, she brightened the day for any man within call and heaped work on any woman.

She was very beautiful in a showy sort of way. Her bright auburn curls were pulled back deceptively simply by a wide pale blue ribbon that exactly matched her eyes. The tiny pink rose-buds on her muslin morning dress echoed the pink of her cheeks and the cream fabric complemented the creaminess of her complexion, flawless thanks to Maude's ministrations and Lucinda's parasol that formed a continual barrier between her and any stray rays of sunlight.

'Oh, Papa, wasn't it brilliant yesterday, wasn't it

absolutely brilliant? I do hope when my birthday comes round I can have just the same kind of party, just the same cakes, just the same lovely bubbly champagne. I can, can't I, Papa? Please say I can.'

'But of course, my dear, although I think perhaps that at your next birthday there will be even more to celebrate than the happy passing of another year.'

Lucinda coloured prettily and smiled down at her plate. Johnnie grinned at Isabella who, as always when her sister 'performed' for a visitor, looked quietly flustered, mildly ashamed. Eli's reference to the plan for Johnnie's brother's betrothal to Lucinda on her twenty-fourth birthday set Johnnie off thinking about Isabella. Truth to tell, if he'd been given the choice he would have preferred Lucinda, for he liked his women showy. She might be the most incredibly simpering creature for the benefit of her father, but she was bursting with life and away from parental view always the one who dared. Isabella he wasn't quite so sure about; she was more contained, less willing to pour out her soul, much more of a dark horse. But then he hadn't the first choice; no second son of a belted earl ever does have and Isabella was quite tolerably pretty, and also intelligent, although that was an attribute he only liked to come across in small doses. Most importantly, marriage to Isabella would make life very easy for him. They would live on the estate, newly made prosperous by Lucinda's dowry. Johnnie could hunt with abandon, shoot driven pheasant and fish well-keepered waters on the acres he had known and loved all his life. There would be no more than the normal sisterly bickering between the new Lady Montford and his own wife. Life, in short, would be as perfect as he could wish it, so he smiled his most winning smile, showing off his strong white teeth, at Isabella and she smiled very nicely back. If it wasn't for the comparison thrown up by her sister, Isabella, demurely serene in pale primrose muslin, would have taken his thoughts quite off the reason for his visit.

It was time, however, for him to carry on with the indoctrination of Eli into 'the Country'. Johnnie's father was insistent that his sons should lead the brewer firmly away from any lingering connections with his mucky past and when his lordship intended a thing, it was done.

'Well, sir, when we've finished these quite excellent kidneys perhaps you'd care to come out into the yard and see what I've brought over for you?'

Eli nodded in acceptance. He was as eager as his lordship that Eli Bradbury should become acquainted with the necessary accomplishments of a country gentleman. 'I think the girls should come too, Johnnie. It won't do them any harm to see the dogs, they can keep back out of mischief's way. I'm sure they'll enjoy it.'

Johnnie hastily added a little more education. 'I'm sure it will be quite all right for Lucinda and Isabella to see us unload the hounds, sir.' He paused, having accented the word 'hounds' just enough for Eli to pick up the necessary information. It was the last time he ever referred to any of the tan and white members of the canine breed who were to become a part of his establishment as anything other than 'hounds'.

Lucinda was rosy-cheeked with excitement. She had already had an elegant silk habit made for riding side-saddle. She had been shown the pack of baying hounds that were based at Pencombe. The fact that they, thanks to Montford management, were to have custody of a few couples was a step forwards into the life she longed to live to the full.

Isabella contemplated her companions at breakfast with something approaching amusement. Not long ago the only dog her father had allowed at home was the odd mongrel that had taken his fancy from the half a dozen or

21

so used to guard the brewery yard. In those days if Lucinda came within six feet of one of them she would scream in horror. Now here was her father welcoming a dozen puppies with open arms and Lucinda clearly couldn't wait to follow a pack of similar but grown up hounds as they careered across country in pursuit of a fox.

The stable yard was bursting with life, full of noise where there had hitherto been silence.

For the past eighteen months, since they had moved into Linstone Park, the quadrangle of fine stone buildings had housed only some aged garden furniture kept company during the winter months by some trays of dahlia tubers that the head gardener would not trust to the potting sheds. Now they were being used in a role more in keeping with their original purpose. The dark green stable doors swung back on newly oiled hinges and there was easily room for the hunt van, pulled by two middle-aged hacks, to turn around and be backed towards the doorway.

Johnnie was here, there and everywhere, striding about supervising the reversing, shouting at the groom who was apparently stone deaf and eventually pulling down the tail-gate himself. Just as he was about to undo the picket gates that were the final barrier between the snuffling hounds and their new home, a clatter of hooves on cobbles announced Michael's arrival. They had not expected him.

Lucinda's first sensation was one of fury; she would have worn her best morning dress if she had known he was coming, but she instantly managed an expression of delight. Eli was transparently pleased: both his lordship's sons! Isabella controlled her quick smile of pleasure. Lucinda had told her quite forcibly that smiles did not become her, and, besides, Michael never seemed to notice her much. The heir-apparent to Pencombe was mounted on a splendid tall and well-mannered black mare. The moment Bess entered the confines of the yard she behaved with consummate gentility, whereas any member of the Weald Hunt would tell you that on the field she was a demon, jumping anything and everything with a calculated disdain. Bess was very like her master.

As Michael dismounted, the light breeze in the courtyard ruffled his bright fair hair and he put up an elegantly browned hand to smooth it. As always, he was most correct, greeting first Eli, then Lucinda, Isabella and finally his brother. He did not interfere with Johnnie's continued organization of the hounds, allowing his younger brother a moment of glory; there was a quietness in him as if responsibilities were his constant unseen companions. Not once had Isabella felt she had seen the real Michael who she was convinced must be hidden beneath the layers of culture, breeding and self-discipline. Isabella hid her own feelings but sometimes she longed to be a creature like Lucinda: to be able to wear her heart on her sleeve and have the world treat her as its darling. Johnnie too showed his delight or fleeting annoyances openly on his handsome face. Isabella always hid her tears; she believed Michael hid his joys, for he must truly adore Lucinda. Everyone did.

The moment had come and she had nearly missed it.

'Papa!' Isabella cried with a suddenness that made them all turn and look at her. 'Papa, I have a surprise for you.' There was a sinking feeling in her stomach. How typical of her to have almost let slip the opportunity. She darted into the flower room where she had left the camera, and came back carrying it in front of her. 'I thought how pleased you would be to have a record of all this,' she said, gesturing with her free hand to take in the hounds, the horses, Michael and Johnnie.

On her father's face, disbelief wavered with annoyance.

'But that's a marvellous idea, Issy, can you work it?' Michael held out his hands to take her burden as she turned to beckon the Boots forward with the library ladder she intended to use as a stand.

'I hope so, Michael, I certainly hope so.' And they both laughed.

With a natural artist's eye she posed them. The van to the right, with the horses leading the eye towards the centre of the picture. Then Papa and Michael and Johnnie, with Lucinda standing in front of them, looking ferocious through the lens. The dogs were ranged around their feet, Michael's horse, Bess, stood to the left, facing centre. It was admirable. If only the puppies would keep still.

Isabella held her breath firmly and pulled the string; for an eternity, it seemed, the scene was static, engraved on her mind as she hoped it would be on the film. Then there was noise again and bustle, with Michael insisting that he would take a picture with her in it, if she would show him how. But Lucinda wasn't going to have any of that, and besides, Papa was fretting to get away. He seemed to have accepted the camera as part of the new invasion of hounds into his existence. At last the hounds were locked away. In their last few minutes of freedom in the yard they had paraded their big pawed charm to perfection, even to the ultimate when one of them mistook the deaf groom's boot for a convenient tree. Johnnie had howled with laughter and Lucinda and Isabella had been compelled, for decorum's sake, to turn their heads away.

Lucinda had gazed up into Michael's deep blue eyes at every possible opportunity. Isabella could see her sister aching to take his arm, but such a step would not be right, in Papa's presence, however much he countenanced their forthcoming engagement.

At last Eli said he must leave for his office at the brewery, and that meant he would be gone for the rest of the day. The young people made their goodbyes, Michael and Johnnie professing their intention to depart 'as soon as they'd seen the pups eating up their minced lights'.

Within ten minutes of their father's departure the girls were ordering a picnic hamper from the kitchen, which was in fact already being prepared. The butler, Dove by name, hawk by nature, was a realist. The young people were going to walk off arm-in-arm into the orchards the moment Mr Bradbury left. It had not taken Dove long to work out that his employer's intention was for his two girls to marry the Montford boys. It had been confirmed on the servants' very efficient grapevine that his lordship had decided the Bradbury fortune was preferable to an American one, so the match of the two eldest children would go ahead, and it was in Miss Isabella's best interests to follow her allotted role and marry Mr Johnnie. Dove encouraged this arrangement by every possible means as he had every intention of achieving for himself the coveted position of butler at Pencombe Hall.

Johnnie was strong and capable, with one arm for the hamper, and one for Isabella's waist. On their first walks she had tried to remove the proprietorial arm, but eventually it had become a fixture. He didn't hold her very close; she had the feeling he treated her like a horse thinking about bolting. She was on a gentle but firm rein, a thought which made her smile.

'What are you smiling at, Issy?' he asked.

'Nothing really, just the blossom, the sun and the lambs. Just the beautiful day.' She lifted her face towards the sunlight.

'Heavens, you mustn't do that, you'll brown like a gypsy up here on the ridge. What on earth would Lucinda say?'

'She'd say just what you've said, that I looked like a gypsy, and I expect she'd say some more about how my skin will wrinkle and grow old before I'm thirty and how

25

my children will be born black as coal, dozens of silly things like that.'

'Your children? So you're going to have children are you, Issy? When exactly, may I ask, and how many?' Isabella felt a blush grow from beneath the high neck of her dress, swiftly rising to her cheeks.

'Come on, Johnnie, don't torment. Let's hurry up and catch the others.' She pulled forwards, but he tightened his grip.

'They don't want us with them, Issy, and we don't want to be with them, do we?' He had turned his head to look down at her, his face very close.

Isabella turned away, feeling uncomfortably warm. She was happy with the thought of Johnnie as a brother, at least as a brother-in-law. But further than that she had no intention of committing herself. 'You mustn't go on like this, Johnnie, really.'

'Why not?' His voice was very soft.

'Because, because,' she looked helplessly around for a reason, then suddenly there it was, 'because the others have stopped and are waiting for us. Look, there they are.'

And there just ahead of them, revealed by an alleyway amongst the apple trees, Lucinda and Michael waited, looking back towards them. Johnnie let his arm slip from her waist and she went quickly forwards. Lucinda made a cross little face at her, clearly not wanting their company, but Michael called to his brother.

'Come on Johnnie, you had breakfast twice this morning, and some of us didn't have any; we can't have you disappearing with the hamper.' He smiled at Isabella. He seemed in a very good mood, more relaxed than she usually saw him. It was Lucinda who was having to work at being charming, but her irritation was only just hidden and nothing like deep enough to fool a sister.

★ ★ ★

William Algernon Marmaduke Edgecombe, twelfth Lord Montford, father of Michael and Johnnie, incumbent of Pencombe Hall, its pleasure gardens cross-hatched by yew walks, and of three thousand fertile acres of glorious England, was a man at peace with his world. He was particularly at peace walking his gardens this glorious April morning because his country was at last enthusiastically at war.

He had worried through the last two years, the final year of the nineteenth century and then the first of the twentieth. He had sunk into a dark, unrelenting gloom as England suffered three final awful humiliations at the hands of the Boers, those rag-bag Boers whose very amateur status seemed for a while to guarantee them success.

His lordship allowed his mind to skim fleetingly over the surface of those too recent dismal failures. He hadn't been taken in by the triumphal return of Roberts – it was victory in battle that mattered. Not a trace of the anguish of defeat touched his noble features, nor did the slightest uplift of his iron-grey eyebrows reflect his buoyant mood. His patrician features were those of the true aristocrat, one by breeding and also by choice. His expression was immovable, at once conveying superiority, the aloofness of a creator of men's destiny and that certain patina produced by a uniquely English mixture of persecution at an early age by his peers at school and the fumbling affections of an aged nanny.

The estate staff were quite able to interpret his moods, often even before he knew them himself. That was why Walter, the head gardener, was lurking in the long shrubbery. He had a plan of his own afoot, one that was waiting its opportunity. Being as patriotic as the next man, Walter was aware that under Kitchener the war in Africa was turning a glorious tide. Old war-horses like Lord

Montford could be relied on to rise to the occasion and Walter had a suitable gesture in mind.

'Good morning, Your Lordship.' He doffed his cap; it wasn't quite his place to address his lordship first, but it wouldn't do to miss his opportunity.

'Ah, Walter, busy in the borders are we? Jolly good show, jolly good.' The earl was already in motion, setting off to stride the yew walk leading to the steps up to the parterre in front of the south wall of the Hall.

'If it please Your Lordship?' Walter raised his voice and side-stepped a clump of phlox that was well grown for the time of year. 'If it please Your Lordship, I had a matter I wanted to bring to your consideration.'

His lordship halted, tentatively. Walter had, on occasion, assumed that the gardens were an area for heavy expenditure, but there was nothing his lordship liked less than spending money, even when he had any to hand, which, of recent years, had not been all that often. 'Will it take long, Walter? I can't stop now you know, got a lot to arrange.' He started to edge away.

'It won't take more than a minute of your time, sir. And I think it'll be something you'll think well of.'

His lordship teetered for an instant then stood his ground.

'The thing is, Your Lordship, I've had in mind for some while now the fact that you don't like yellow.'

'I what, don't like yellow? Don't like yellow what?'

'Yellow flowers, Your Lordship. You may not have given it that much thought but I have and it's always the same. If I plant out yellow pansies or put sunflowers at the back of a border or any such, then you get all upset, tell me to take them out. And you've said yourself that you can't understand all the fuss the visitors make about the daffodils in the spring planting; well, they're yellow. It stands out like a sore thumb once you've thought of it.'

His lordship, whilst retaining his aristocratic air of abstraction, was managing to convey a sense of appreciation to his gardener. One thing he did admire was a little self-motivated thought in his staff, especially when it concerned himself. The man was quite right, he did in fact detest yellow flowers; apart from the aesthetics of the thing, they were bug attracters and bugs had no sense of decorum, attacking tender aristocratic skin with unnecessary vigour.

Also, if he allowed his mind to drift back to the dim and distant past, there was the affair of the earwig. As a child, his lordship remembered, he had been a sensitive quiet creature, enjoying the gardens at Pencombe, happy to lose himself amongst the green alleys, the rampant summer flower-beds that contained great spiky dahlias taller than he was himself. It had been the Plantagenet bed that had been his downfall. The vast yellow bed had as centrepiece a great cushion of yellow dahlias, massed tight, the tiny paths between the crammed plants only giving room enough for a weedy seven-year-old to squeeze. And so he had insinuated himself right into the forbidden heart, to sit there silently safe.

Until it began. At first he had scratched at his ear, suddenly itchy, wriggly itchy. Then he had poked at it with a tiny twig; it had itched more, then the buzzing had begun, then it stung and at last in frantic desperation he fled the flower-bed, trampling the juicy green stalks in his flight. He ran for Nanny and safety, but there wasn't any. First there was a scolding, then tales were told and the dreadful ignominy of a spanking from his father, for the dahlias were decimated beyond repair. Through it all the dreadful tickling buzzing went on, through the terrible first night, through the sobbing second, by now with the doctor in attendance on the nearly demented child. For five long days the adults fiddled and tormented him, to no avail, then as suddenly as the buzzing had started, it stopped. One more day and Nanny's hot oil poured into his ear washed out the loathsome creature.

'There,' Nanny had cried in her victory, 'I told them all, and none of them'd believe me. It was an earwig all along, my precious; into your poor little ear he went and wiggled his way right inside. He came from those dahlias I expect; yellow they were, weren't they? That's what they love, these little blighters! Here, look at the pincers on his little head, pet.'

But the little pet hadn't looked, he was rushing away to be sick in a basin, not on the floor, or Nanny would stop being ever so sympathetic.

'Yes,' his lordship concurred with unaccustomed feeling in his voice, 'I hate yellow flowers, Walter. Dig them up, dig them all up and burn them.'

'I had another idea, sir, one with a little profit in it.'

Now his lordship's attention was finally hooked; profit was a word he was discovering, too late, should have featured in his upbringing.

'I had this idea when Mr Bradbury brought his man over to look at the gardens.' Walter was careful not to refer to the Bradbury employee as a gardener; such job descriptions had to be earned, in his book. 'You see, Mr Bradbury was after pointing out how he wanted their gardens made more formal, like. I got to thinking how perhaps what we didn't like might be what they would. What I thought was, if we pointed out to them how yellow makes an instant display, in a new-made garden that is, then we could sell them all the yellow we dig up. There's just time, if I put the men on to it right away; the plants won't take that badly to being moved. And the daffodils down by the river have been in need of splitting for a few years. They could pay us for bulbs and we could

30

use that money to hire in some casual labour. We've not got the staff any more for that kind of job.'

'Ah ha,' his lordship interjected, 'but what about the spaces that these yellow plants leave in the borders, eh? We can't have damned great gaps and I'm not sure I want to invest in new stock.'

'Not at all, sir, not at all. You see, if you remember, I put up those rows of lupins, and delphiniums and the like in the vegetable garden, for cutting for the house. They're all blue and white, as they always are for indoors. Now if I plant those in the borders, with the roses climbing up red behind them then I reckon we'll have the first victory flower walk in England. That'll show we're proud of our boys and get rid of the yellow and get the daffodils thinned, and probably still make a bit to go into the seed fund.' Walter leaned, victorious on his spade, happy and glorious: his victory bed would be the envy of the county, and the man over at Linstone Park had already made it quite clear Mr Bradbury went in for a bit of colour. Well, yellow was colour. If Walter didn't pick up a nice little keg of ale for his ingenuity in getting his lordship to part with a few of his 'specials' then his name wasn't Walter.

Lord Montford sought out his steward in a mood of refined excitement; everything was certainly going well this year, on all fronts. Fronts, the word reminded him of the war. It was time his boys did their bit. There would be a bit of glory going round now; that's what he wanted for the Montford name. He hadn't been too sure for a while, he hadn't wanted them tied up in a fiasco, but there was no better time than the present. The boys had to go to war sometime: the experience would finish their education and victory turned out better fellows than defeat. His sons could lead a small rush of villagers into volunteering in a piece of nicely orchestrated patriotism. It was a coincidence that Walter had brought up Bradbury's name because clearly there would have to be some activity on that score. Michael had better get engaged before going off to war; there was no point in waiting for the girl's birthday now. Everything should be set in motion at once. Fortunately there was no wife for him to consult. Women in general disliked being rushed over such matters, but his lordship was entirely his own master and the Bradbury girl would do as her father told her.

Eli's arrival at the brewery never took his workforce by surprise. Almost the day the new brewery began business, Peter, whose offical job was ratcatcher of the upper floors, was given a more important unofficial task by his mates. The boy had an excellent view of the approach of their lord and master as he made his impressive progression down the High Street, then along the river bank to the yard. Only the men on the moored barges stood a chance of being found smoking a pipe or brewing tea, but the river men counted themselves a breed apart.

This morning Eli was so late that even the most persistent of the cats in Peter's charge was curled up fast asleep, and he was almost dozing himself when the carriage made its appearance on the hill. It was the work of a flurried moment for him to propel the cats back into action with the toe of his boot. Then he yelled down the open stairwell, alerting all three floors below him to the need for that particular form of attention to duty reserved for the old man's visits.

Eli nodded at the doffed caps in the yard. He paused at the great black horses, standing patiently in the shafts of their cart, to give them the customary stroke on their wide, soft noses. The horse on the right was Albert, the other Wellington. Eli liked names chosen for their patriotism.

This pair were the draught horses that pulled the dray

servicing the five pubs closest to the brewery. Always in and out of the yard, they were everyone's favourites, the great feathery hairs on their fetlocks as white as snow and looking as soft as a kitten's fur. The horses that worked on the out-of-town runs had their heels clean-shaven to help cope with the sticky clay mud that bogged down their carts and gave their Kent-born drivers a heaven-sent excuse for a slow round.

'Morning, Eli.'

The bright, loud, man-to-man greeting from behind caused Eli to turn quickly in surprise. This was his kingdom, and he was used to being greeted with deference within the great iron gates.

'If I'd known you were a late starter to the day I would have saved my visit for the afternoon. I've been kicking my heels for over an hour.' The speaker was a young man, broad built and full of health, a countryman with the hands of a farmer and the clothes of a squire. His handsome face wore the assured smile of a self-motivated man, secure in self-belief.

Eli hovered between irritation and admiration. If he had fathered sons, this was the type he would have been proud of, but as a neighbour and business associate he would have preferred a greater sense of deference to himself, older and richer as he undoubtedly was. Eli allowed his greeting to convey the gap that existed between them. 'Cade, isn't it? Thomas Cade, if my memory serves me right.' He allowed a touch of puzzlement to cross his whiskered face, although he knew very well who his visitor was and Thomas knew that the old man was simply marking his territory.

'I've had your buyer out at Reason Hill,' the younger man continued. 'It looks as if we will come to amicable terms over the hop contract for this year, Eli. So you've no need to worry, I've not come to try and twist your arm for a better price. But if you'd be so good as to invite me into your office I have another matter I'd like to bring to your attention.' Thomas raised a well-shaped eyebrow in question.

'Well, I'm very busy this morning, of course, very busy, but if you'll keep it short, I can spare you a few minutes, Thomas.' Eli turned to lead the way to his sanctum. Around him a ginger-whiskered clerk hovered, as if to clear the great man's path. He was a little man with well-brushed but threadbare clothes and too much intelligence in his rat-like eyes for Thomas's liking. He was of a type more suited to the back streets of London than the market town of Maidstone.

The farmer in Thomas looked up for a last glimpse of bright blue sky before he stepped into the dusty, aromatic blackness of the storehouse of the brewery. After a few steps his eyes became adjusted to the dim light allowed by the barred windows. The gloom that spelt money to Eli held no appeal to the younger man, but the money that Eli made by his application to his chosen endeavours did. It was in the pursuit of fortune that Thomas Cade was making calls in town this bright sunny spring morning instead of being out in the fields supervising his workers and adding his own labours to wresting a bit more than a living from the land.

The clerk threw open the door of Eli's office ahead of them, then stepped nimbly aside to let the two men enter.

Eli's office was all that money could make of a dingy space partitioned from the first floor of the factory. This was a floor for storage, where a few remaining hessian hop pockets, sacks as tall and broad as a man, loitered in corners. This was the end of last year's harvest, waiting their turn to add their subtle, heady perfume to the beer brewed in the twin building on the far side of the yard.

A massive mahogany desk occupied almost half the

34

floor space. There was room left for Eli's chair, a great leather-covered throne as befitted his position, and a pair of lesser seats for his visitors. There was nothing for the staff who attended on him; minions were kept standing. The two men seated themselves to their satisfaction, Thomas admitting to himself that this was probably the most expensively furnished office he had sat in this morning in his pursuit of business.

'You said your time was limited, Eli, so I'll come straight to the point. You know me as a farmer, a good one I'm proud to say. You've had two seasons' hops off me now, part of my harvest the back end of the first summer that you started to buy in the Maidstone area, my entire crop last year, and it looks as if you'll have it again this year.' He paused to let Eli nod his head in agreement. 'I've come to let you know that you'll be seeing another part of my enterprise from now on. At least two of the farmers on land surrounding yours have agreed to use my contracting service of steam traction engines this summer. I anticipate that there will be several more locals who fall in along the way. Apart from that I'm booked for work on a dozen other farms within a radius of ten miles. I've sunk a fair amount of capital into machinery and I've trained up men to work it. I aim to provide the most effective force of men and machines on hire in Kent today. Next year I'll have more teams and go further. You built up from small beginnings, Eli, I've heard it said, so you'll appreciate what I'm about.'

Eli sat, impassive, then he spoke in low, measured tones. 'I appreciate you're out to make money, Thomas. What I don't yet appreciate is what you're telling me for, other than from common courtesy of course, but I don't think you're the kind of man to waste too much time on that kind of thing.' Neither was Eli, except when it suited.

'I'm telling you for two reasons. The first is that as your

35

managers go around buying hops, they are going to come across a lot of farmers, more than I can get to, especially now the growth is starting to speed up and I'll have to spend more time on my own land. A word from them to the effect that my service is available will get me enquiries that I can follow up. Also, let's face it, in any year you'll find some farmers too optimistic as to the speed they can get their crop into your store. There'll be times you'll be glad to know someone who can hurry things up, and get the hops in out of the garden, the grain off the field. It'll suit you as well as suit me.'

Eli's grunt was noncommittal. 'And the second reason you're telling me?' he asked.

'The second is because I gather that you and I will be almost related in the near future. You've been in Kent long enough now to know how much store we set on being "cousins" and even the most distant connections count as that.'

'Your intelligence seems to have outstretched mine, Thomas. How exactly are we about to become, as you say, "related"?'

'Ah, now I thought perhaps Montford hadn't mentioned it. I'm Lord Montford's godson, you see, so I'll dance at the wedding, be invited to christenings and no doubt come across you at Christmas at Pencombe.'

'Good God!'

That had taken the wind out of the old man's sails. 'That seems to surprise you, Eli?' Thomas was smiling fixedly now. Eli was transparently put out at a hard-working tenant farmer having ties with the ever noble house of Pencombe, but he recovered quickly.

'No, not surprise, Thomas, nothing of the sort. How about a glass of wine? I always have a little something at this time of day.' He hadn't got where he was by being slow to react. He rang a small brass handbell and the clerk appeared so quickly that it proved he had been waiting just outside the door. This time Eli gave the man a name and Harold, as he was called, scuttled off to reappear only moments later carrying a tray on which he had arranged a bottle of Malmsey, two stemmed glasses and a small dish of biscuits.

The biscuits were dry and the wine overly sweet for Thomas's palate, but they restored the colour to Eli's cheeks and took the edge off the aggravation that niggled in Thomas's stomach at having had to dangle such an obvious bait for the socially ambitious brewer.

Thanks to the sacrifice his mother had made in nursing Lord Montford's young wife through smallpox, his lordship had been prevailed upon to act as sponsor to the Cade's only child. Thomas's mother had inevitably caught the disease herself and, although she recovered, was scarred for life, but Lady Montford had been so weakened by her illness that she survived for just long enough to see her two sons into the care of a tutor and then simply faded away.

Thomas believed it was a duty to his mother's memory to use his godfather's rank to put himself well above the tenant farmer level that had been his father's life-long imprisonment. Thomas intended to rise above it, and in rising would exult in overcoming difficulties, would revel in success, would raise himself to a position where favours were asked of him and were his to dispense. Meanwhile he drank the wine of men like Eli, men who had made their money and now wasted their energies in the centuries-old competition for prestige that surpasses even that for riches.

At the exact moment that Thomas stepped out of the brewery yard, Isabella came face to face with proof of his application. The foursome had walked to the edge of

Linstone land and, turning the corner of a narrow sunken lane, caught sight of a vast infernal machine at the instant it burst into clamorous life. Michael and Johnnie became aristocratically silent at the affront of the noise, Lucinda let out a tiny feminine shriek and clung to Michael, Isabella's hands flew to her ears. Like a neolithic monster it roared its fury, spitting out black clouds over the edge of the foaming white orchards. Smutty, clinging flecks of soot flew at them. The girls turned and fled, taking with them the vivid memory of the tar-stained man with a sweat-streaked red handkerchief tied pirate-like around his forehead and a grinning little boy clambering over the megalith like a monkey. The familiars of the monster had cheered their ridicule at the foursome's elegance, at their disdain and finally at their flight.

The clattering followed them back to Linstone Park, only finally disappearing as they slammed the door behind them. As the sisters fled upstairs to change their soot-smudged dresses the brothers began to plot their campaign. It hadn't taken either of them more than an instant to work out whose damned machine it was. Or the implications of that incredible row on their sport. The land that the machine was working was Pencombe land that fell into their domain. Tenanted it might be, but part of the estate, and as such something that Michael would one day rule over. Johnnie didn't need to throw in his graphic description of the vixen bolting her den leaving the cubs to starve, or the woodcock being scared off their nests leaving their young to fall easy prey to the kestrel, in order to fuel the anger welling in Michael's breast.

Meanwhile Thomas Cade strode the Maidstone streets, coincidentally thinking of the Pencombe boys, congratulating himself that by getting to Eli early he would probably sway Montford on to his side. The boys and their hunting could go to hell, or more appropriately, to the dogs. Montford wanted Michael to marry the brewery money: if Eli's men were going their rounds punting Thomas's steam engines then he wasn't going to jeopardize that relationship by acting dictatorially, not this year at least. And by the end of this summer there would be enough convinced farmers for Thomas to stand up to the hunting interests of the Pencombe set. Smiling at his astuteness he stepped into the Three Compasses, an excellent public house, where he would enjoy a dozen Whitstable oysters before going on to a good helping of steak and kidney pudding. He'd even go so far as to wash it down with a glass of Eli's best; after all a man could do no better than enjoy the beverage his own hops provided.

Eli finished his day's work by dictating to his clerk a memo for his buyers. They were to begin immediately bringing to the notice of hop growers and grain producers, present and prospective suppliers of the brewery, the advantages of the use of traction engines. They were to be informed of the excellent contracting service offered by Thomas Cade and his teams. Any farmer who wished further information could contact Mr Cade through the auspices of the brewery office. Eli particularly like that touch; it would show Lord Montford that Eli Bradbury appreciated the importance of family in the county of Kent.

Whilst, at Pencombe, the affairs of Lucinda's heart were being reorganized without her knowledge, she was at home at Linstone and suffering an acute attack of boredom. She had taken a seat in the drawing room, toyed with a scrap of needlework, flicked the pages of the current fashionable novelette, straightened the folds of her rose-pink dress to her satisfaction, rumpled them, then rearranged them until at last there was only Isabella for entertainment.

'Issy, your having that window thrown wide open is creating a draught.'

'It's doing nothing of the kind, there's hardly a breath of air and it's as mild as can be. Don't be so stuffy. Come over here and sit by me, the view is incredible.' Isabella patted a chair close by her.

She had a small easel carefully propped on her knees, and her watercolours were nicely to hand on a small wine table. Looking out through the open window she could see across the flat, green, short-cut lawn to the first of the apple trees just on the brow of the hill. Then the whole glorious panorama spread out before her. To capture it all on her small canvas was impossible, so she was concentrating on the sky, blue and high with fluffy white clouds.

'Come on, you won't disturb me,' she called again to Lucinda who bounced out of her chair with an angry flounce.

'Disturb you? I should think not. You're becoming the most awful bore, Issy. In fact, everything is just too, too boring. I wish Michael hadn't gone. I wish he spent more time with me rather than his dull old peasants.'

'Lucy!' Isabella nearly dropped her brush with dismay. Lucinda was becoming more and more the lady of the manor; even more so, at times she seemed to think herself mistress of all she surveyed. But it wasn't in the same quiet way that Michael exerted his aura of authority. Lucinda was becoming loud, demanding and, for Isabella, mortifyingly embarrassing. Peasants! Peasants indeed. Isabella had a strong suspicion that Lucinda didn't use that particular description of his tenants in front of Michael. 'Lucy, you really mustn't. What would poor Mama have thought of you giving yourself such airs?'

Lucinda pouted, pushing out her bottom lip at an

aggressive angle that no male was ever allowed to witness. There was no reply she could make to Isabella's remark, so for a few minutes she sat, breathing progressively louder in her irritation. 'Issy, if you don't stop that dreadful painting at once I shall scream.'

Isabella put down her brush to stare critically at her version of spring sky. She was having doubts about it herself. 'Is it really awful, Lucy? I did so want to capture, the . . .' She paused, finding her feelings for the immense beauty of it all impossible to put into words. 'Oh, the majesty of it all. And yet, looking at it now, all I can see is a flat, lifeless sky. You're right, Lucy, it is dreadful, dreadful.'

Suddenly she dashed the brush at the little picture and put savage streaks of brown across it.

'Issy, don't, don't!' Lucinda leaped up in horror. 'I didn't mean the picture was awful, you silly thing. Only that your going on painting it was irritating me. Now you've ruined it. You are a silly creature, Issy, honestly.'

Isabella could feel the tears start up, sharply stinging. She instantly regretted her actions, but it was too late now, for watercolour never conceals a moment's weakness.

'Issy, you're just as bored as me, that's the trouble. I do wish Michael was here, and Johnnie of course,' she added with a smile at her sister.

'You needn't hope Johnnie will come for my amusement I can assure you, Lucy. He's not my great romance, you know, and I shan't fall in love with him simply to suit your planning.'

'If I were you, Issy, I shouldn't be too fussy. It's absolute nonsense to imagine you're going to fall head over heels in love with some handsome stranger. You must just do what's best for you. Johnnie is more than happy to marry you, and you must accept him when he asks you. Then you can live on the estate, and we'll all be great friends and life will be perfect.'

'How dare you, Lucy! How dare you dispose of me like a doll in a china shop. I'm not the idiot you think I am. I'm quite capable of making up my mind for myself.'

'Oh no, we all know you're not an idiot. You're much too clever for your own good.' Lucinda's voice had risen. 'Ladies aren't supposed to be clever. Yes, we can paint a little, sing a little, perhaps even write a little pretty poetry. But we're not meant to be like you, Issy, with all your fine painting, your angelic voice, and, as to poetry, well if you're not writing it then you're reciting it, much too perfectly. As for this business of taking photographs it's just too too much. Papa is not at all pleased. You were very lucky that Michael and Johnnie didn't refuse to pose for you this morning. You're just lucky that it suits someone as nice as Johnnie to marry you. Don't you go throwing it all away or you'll end up on the shelf.' Lucinda's hands had curled themselves into fists and she rested them aggressively on her hips. The girls glared at each other with the instant hatred that only flares in families.

In the sudden silence Maude tapped shortly on the door and threw it open. 'Mr Cade is here to see the master, Miss Lucinda.' The servant girl's eyes were bright, her cheeks flushed, and her expression distracted Lucinda from her fury.

'Mr Cade, and who is he?' she asked.

'He's the farmer at Reason Hill, ma'am.' She added in an undertone, 'Very well thought of in the district.'

Lucinda glanced at her sister for assistance. Presumably this was some respected member of the agricultural community come to pay his respects to Papa. She should send out the message that they were pleased he had called but as Papa was not at home perhaps he would care to call again. But that would mean the afternoon would go back to its earlier state of boredom and she knew that Isabella was itching to point out to her that Michael had been fascinated by the camera.

She hovered for an instant, but then propriety couldn't be offended by an elderly gentleman joining the two daughters of his neighbour for a dish of tea. 'Send him in, Maude, and get us some tea, will you. Just some fruit cake and perhaps a few scones. Don't use the last of the strawberry jam, though; it's Papa's favourite and we shan't have any more until summer.'

Waiting in the black and white marbled hall Thomas surveyed his own reflection in an ornately framed long mirror. He didn't usually feel this nervous about meeting young ladies. The sheaf of advertising pamphlets that he wanted to give Eli could simply have been handed to the maid, but that seemed cowardly. He fingered his cravat, rearranging its folds to best effect.

Maude, still visibly disconcerted, ushered him into the drawing room. He had carefully arranged his expression to enter the formality of the room, but all the same his arrival caused consternation in all its facets to range across Lucinda's face. Isabella allowed herself only a fleeting expression of amusement. Papa would be livid.

In desperation Lucinda turned to Isabella. She wasn't averse to her sister's intelligence now that the situation demanded it.

'Mr Cade. It is Mr Cade, is it not?' Isabella advanced to their guest, her small hand determinedly outstretched. 'I am so sorry that Papa is not at home. My sister and I were about to take tea. Will you join us?'

'I'd be delighted.'

To Thomas's surprise he found the girls not what he had imagined. To begin with the younger sister took control of what was to them apparently an unusual occurence. Lucinda sipped her tea, ate sparingly of a scone and, for some inexplicable reason, sent her sister into a choking fit by admonishing Maude for not having brought the strawberry jam, an error that was speedily rectified. By the time Lucinda had decided to enjoy a slice of fruit cake she was starting to relax. Thomas decided she had a very pretty way of smiling.

Casting around for a topic of conversation, he noticed Isabella's paintbrush and block on the table. 'You paint, do you, Miss Bradbury? It is a very suitable occupation for this lovely weather.'

'Yes, isn't it beautiful,' Isabella replied. 'The colours are all so vivid, much more acute than in town.'

'If you appreciate colour then I suppose you are a follower of William Morris?'

'I am, although we don't have any examples of his work. He is too modern for my father, I'm afraid. Papa does enjoy traditional art though,' she added hastily, 'landscapes and sea scenes.'

Lucinda helped herself to another slice of cake as they talked on. Their discussion led Isabella to describe to him their shattering experience of that morning, when they had come upon the dreadful traction engine.

As Thomas's expression changed, Lucinda leaped up from her chair. 'I've got it! I know who you are now. I remember Michael saying your name. I knew I'd heard it somewhere, Issy.' Lucinda was pink-faced in her excitement. 'Oh my dear,' she continued, 'but we've invited the enemy into our camp. Oh, Issy!' She started to laugh. 'Michael and Johnnie will be furious.' She was giggling enough to make Isabella embarrassed, then suddenly she too realized who this must be.

Isabella turned in surprise to their guest. 'Oh no! You're the machine man, aren't you? Oh, how awful,' but she was smiling as she said it. 'You know, I'm afraid Lucy and

I imagined you must be as dirty as a chimney-sweep and . . .' She blushed, as words failed her.

'Well, I hope you realize your imaginations had run away with you entirely. I'm sorry if you came across one of my machines without warning and it startled you. Perhaps next time I'll take you both and give you a proper show of them. They're something to be proud of, let me tell you. They're the way of the future, and you're going to see the name of Cade emblazoned on hundreds of them before I'm done. As to Michael and Johnnie, well, we used to fight as children and I don't suppose it'll do us much harm to differ again.'

'You know them well, then?' Lucinda asked.

'We were pretty well brought up together until they went away to school and I went to the Grammar. And being his lordship's godson as well as a tenant I go over to Pencombe at Christmas, and for weddings and christenings I expect.' He was staring very forthrightly at Lucinda, who blushed under his gaze.

Isabella thought it was time to steer the conversation to a safer path. 'I wish you could give me an idea what to paint, out here in all this beauty. I really despair of finding a suitable subject, but please don't suggest one of your engines!'

There was silence as Thomas gathered his thoughts – for one used to banter he was feeling strangely at sea – concentrated for a moment, then inspiration struck.

'I have a part of your subject. But you will have to supply a suitable setting. I know a child with the face of an angel and the soul of a little devil who would come out very nicely against a few animals, a puppy or two perhaps. In fact I'll offer you a commission to paint it, for I'm very fond of the little chap and he's game for anything. The angel in his face will disappear before long; it would be good to capture that beauty for posterity.'

45

Isabella felt delight for the first time in ages. He'd taken her seriously, spoken to her as an artist. 'I'd be delighted to accept a commission, Mr Cade, but I'm really not ready for such an act of faith yet. Perhaps one day . . . But I shall paint your "little angel" and you can see if you like it. Although I think I'll put him in another setting than with puppies or kittens. There is a subject I've had in mind for some while that I think will do very well.' Isabella was aglow with enthusiasm, she had something ahead of her, something on which to work, to set her thoughts on, rather than the daily bickering with Lucinda.

Thomas took his leave. The room seemed suddenly empty after his departure; he had exuded a sense of life, of future.

'What a fascinating man,' Isabella said. 'I never expected to find a neighbour who was interested in Morris and the New School.'

Lucinda grimaced. 'You know I can't bear a word of all that artistic nonsense. Although I'll agree that he was interesting in a rather county sort of way. Maude was certainly taken with him. She seemed quite flustered when she showed him in.'

Maude made a noisy entrance as she came in to clear up the tea things. She had overheard Lucinda's comment, and annoyance flushed red up her neck.

By tacit agreement the girls instantly began talking of the new fashion in ladies' dresses. It appeared, courtesy of the *Illustrated London News*, that a display of patriotism was called for and they became quite animated designing an imaginary robe of purple velvet, something neither of them would wear, but it calmed their excited nerves, which seemed necessary, all things considered.

Michael whistled and the black dog looked up, alert. He swung the short malacca cane aggressively at a clump of nettles, already grown high enough to sting above his leather boots. The nettles were an irritation, everything was an irritation these days. He patted the dog's seal-like head, then stooped down to stare into the bottomless eyes. 'You understand, don't you, old boy.' He stroked over the smooth brow, pulling the ears to the dog's delight, setting its tail wagging, brushing on the last dead leaves on the woodland track. 'You're trained like me, but you've a bit of the wild left in you all the same. Bet you'd chase a poacher's terrier off given half a chance.' He stopped stroking then and dropped his voice. 'Bet you'd chase a bitch too, and I don't suppose you'd be too fussy either.'

He stood up suddenly; the dog too leaped to its feet, ready for the off. They walked companionably across the top of the field called Ten Acre, where there was a good chance of putting up some partridge; not that it would do the birds any harm, for Michael didn't take a gun on his evening stroll, much to his father's irritation. Michael had left the house to the usual lecture on how a gentleman at leisure in the country was not dressed without a gun on his arm. But then his father was a great one for killing things. Michael didn't have quite the same urge; even in his great passion, foxhunting, it was the chase he enjoyed, not the kill. Now his father had removed even the thrill of the chase from Michael's love life. Lucinda had been handed to him as neatly trussed and dressed as an Ayles-bury duckling on a silver salver. And, sadly, about as unexcitingly. Now there wasn't even to be a wait until Lucinda's birthday for the betrothal. Johnnie and he were to be packed off to the war and Michael was to be securely chained to his heiress first. Michael didn't consider the reality of the war apart from the distance it would take him from Pencombe, his home that he had loved for so long.

It all hinged on money, or rather, the lack of it.

They had crossed the top of the field now, and were on the edge of Roger Wood. Nothing had taken flight at their passage and now a pair of wood pigeons came wheeling over their heads and into the shelter of the trees, undismayed by man and dog. They were quite intelligent enough to realize he was powerless without a weapon. Smiling at his childishness Michael swung up an arm holding an imaginary gun, 'Bang!' he shouted up into the mild evening sky. 'Bang!', but the birds didn't even bother to change course.

Othello darted forward with a low growl in his throat to stop, immaculately at point, before a cluster of broken reeds skirting the edge of a scrappy pond.

'Come away,' Michael called. 'Come away from there.'

There was no point sending a dab chick scuttling from her nest simply for his amusement. He scuffed his well-polished boots through the woodland debris. He should walk more briskly; he was liverish, that was it. He should plan what to do with the dowry Lucinda was bringing. After all, the Home Farm woodlands were all similar to this one, clogged with dead wood, pathetic remembrances of an earlier age of greatness when a fortune had been spent every year keeping the rides open.

But what was it all for?

After the old man died there'd still be hunting, but not much else. Even Johnnie wasn't a fanatic about driven shoots, so what was the point? At least he hadn't been forced to marry an American bride to refinance the estate. He had a friend from school who'd had to follow that path to restore his family's fortune and look where it had got him. A succession of American relatives stayed at Chiddicombe expecting and receiving hospitality of the sporting kind. The last time they'd met he'd hardly recognized the fat, red-faced blustering earl who had once shared confidences with him in his Harrovian days. Not that it was all that long ago come to that; the past eight years seemed to merge into one to Michael, with few mileposts. Until now. Last year Lucinda had been discovered; or rather, her money, and all that Michael had to do was be sufficiently charming for the estate to be rescued from ignominy. Not that Michael considered their refined poverty as such, but his father was determined to live in the style to which he had never been accustomed, but which he felt was his due.

Othello turned back, sizing up his master's mood. There was a most tempting scent of duck on the water. Michael's thoughts were still elsewhere and so the dog took his chance. He took two quiet, furtive steps into the dark, still water then a steady dog paddle propelled him almost silently, only his black head showing, tipped back, almost flat on the water. Michael saw him then and for an instant would have shouted, but he let the animal have its moment of freedom. There was pretty damn little freedom in the world today.

Michael found a seat on a fallen tree, a once proud beech that now lay greyly magnificent in decay, a prey to beetles. He slowly took out his pipe, and his pouch. There was a solace in the ritual of filling, tamping and lighting. He let the first tentative draught of smoke out with a sigh, thinking how he and Johnnie had become distanced since the plan for the Bradbury girl had come into being. It was inevitable, he supposed, and he didn't really think Johnnie grudged him being the first son, but it was a wedge between them all the same. Meanwhile, Othello had crossed the pond. Pulling himself out on the far bank, he shook himself enthusiastically then darted a quick look across at his master. It told him all was well, so, tail wagging but without his prey, he made his way happily back, around the edge of the pond this time. He stood in front of the man and dropped first to a sitting position, then lay down. He panted softly, his warm breath showing briefly on the cooling evening air, his pink tongue lolling over bright white teeth. The gentle sound of his breathing calmed Michael, and he enjoyed his pipe as dusk filled the shadows of the wood and the sounds of evening creatures formed a nightsong of their own.

After a while Michael rose and stretched; he felt better, refreshed. 'Come on, boy,' he called and they began their walk home, not hurrying, for there was nothing to hurry for, just enjoying each other's company and being part of the gentle death of day.

Tomorrow was for duty, this time was their own.

Had there been a Lady Montford then Isabella would have had someone to wait with. As it was she was left in the stone-cold great hall while her father and his lordship talked to Michael and Lucinda about the settlement. Isabella dutifully peered up to the rafters high above her, which formed the vaulted roof so lovingly described in the guide-book. She made the circuit of exhibits once, peering through the rusty visors of the unpolished suits of armour. She was about to run her gloved hand over an Aubusson tapestry hung in a rather cavalier fashion from a decaying pole, but then thought better of the whiteness of her gloves.

It seemed an age she had waited, and still no one came. With one last glance at the far corner where the party had disappeared up the narrow stone staircase that led to the private apartments, she turned her back on the dust of it all. Her family's money was more than needed, and the first thing it could be spent on was a good spring clean.

She took the narrow path that led from the private gardens of the Hall to the church. It was flanked by a high, well-trimmed yew hedge. A dozen or so feet after leaving the arch-topped gateway in the boundary wall, the path bent sharply to the left, skirting the austere, grey stone family mausoleum watched over by a stern-faced marble angel. Isabella had taken an instant dislike to the sudden dark dankness of the pathway and hurried towards the sanctum of the church. Rounding the bend, her eyes fixed on the uneven, gravelled path, she walked straight into the encompassing embrace of Johnnie's arms.

'Good heavens!' she started with fright. 'I didn't know you were out here. Come to that, I didn't know anyone was here.'

'I can see that,' Johnnie laughed as Isabella stepped back. 'I can see you're frightened of the dark, my little Isabella. And did I ever tell you that your ears are like little sea shells, pretty and pink. Oh my,' he leaned towards her, 'I could eat them, in little tiny bites.'

'Don't do that, don't.' Isabella stepped nimbly sideways to avoid the lunge he seemed about to make. They had started to walk on and were close to the beginning of the village houses, where lace curtains concealed watchers ever alert for scandal from the Hall.

'You must behave, Johnnie,' she scolded, but she was laughing. He really was very sweet, silly but very sweet, and it was much nicer to be out here in the street, in the sunlight, with Johnnie, than back in the dank, narrow path.

Johnnie laughed out loud too and slapped his thigh, thereby convincing the blue-and-white-aproned butcher slowly sharpening his knife in the sparsely stocked window next to the baker, that this must be the heiress's sister, the one marked out for Master Johnnie.

Isabella, in the view of the man-of-meat, was too thin and too pale, and not necessarily good breeding stock. Not that that mattered unless Michael failed with his responsibilities. No, the butcher shook his head slowly in time with the rasp of the whetstone, she didn't look one to plough the fields and scatter, she was more the type to bury her head in a book. Still, the aristocracy were a law unto themselves and Johnnie seemed captivated enough.

Next door, in the bakers, Ruby peered round the fresh baked loaves to get a glimpse of the blond-haired girl who the house staff said was to be Master Johnnie's intended. Well the girl didn't seem that taken with him, not head over heels like, and that was a pity, because Johnnie was as handsome as a spring colt, and deserved a girl who'd love him heart and soul. Ruby was a romantic girl herself. She was two years older than Johnnie and had been one of the village girls who'd set out to catch his elder brother's eye. There'd been a few who had, but no real romances. Ruby would have loved to have been involved in a true-life romance, one where the handsome lord fell madly in love with a village girl, got her with child and then took her off to a secret wedding. But then, the girl would die in childbirth; they always did in the novels that were passed on to her by her elder sister, the one who'd married a tradesman down at Brighton. Her sister did very well, all things considered. Ruby let her thoughts wander and she absentmindedly rubbed her floury hands down her dark skirt.

'Ruby!' her employer's voice came sharply from the back of the shop. He was for ever dinning into her how she should look smart in case any of the visitors to the Hall stepped in. There were instances, he kept telling her, where grand visitors from London had patronized village bakers and that little business had grown into something special. He always told this to Ruby with his wizened face creased with what he imagined was a smile, which showed off his remaining three yellow teeth, two on the bottom, one on the top. Ruby rubbed the flour off her front with her apron. The old man should mind his manners, and mind where he put his hands in the closeness of the bakery

52

out the back, come to that. Ruby sniffed heartily as the young elegant couple walked out of her sight. Well, maybe she would take up her sister's offer after all, and move down to Brighton for a bit, for long enough to find a husband: one perhaps not quite as handsome as Johnnie, but, she hoped, every bit as jolly.

Isabella and Johnnie took the long walk, around the village perimeter, coming back to the park wall with still a good half a mile before they reached the gateway.

'What would you want out of life if you were a girl, Johnnie?' Isabella asked. She had let her bonnet slip back off her head, and a cool breeze played with a scrap of hair that had escaped from her pins.

Johnnie stopped to consider her question. They were beside one of the massive oaks that the guide-book said had been planted before Henry VIII's time, before the King had come riding down from London to court Anne Boleyn at nearby Hever. 'I should want to meet a fine man, of course, one as solid as this,' he said as he beat at the tree with his cane. 'And I should want to give him dozens of bouncing babies.' He paused, seeming at a loss for inspiration.

'Really?' Isabella had disbelief in her voice.

'Well, perhaps not dozens, but several.'

Then they were quite companionably silent looking out over the sheep grazing on the parkland.

But Isabella couldn't leave it there. 'Would that really be all you'd want out of life, Johnnie?'

He furrowed his brow. 'Well, married ladies shouldn't ride to hounds, at least not ones still,' he paused and then grinned, 'in their prime. And I can't stand to see a woman with a gun, they're the wrong shape for it. You should see it if they try and take lessons in the noble art; they're so concerned that their keeper doesn't get his hands on their bits and pieces that it's a miracle they don't shoot the poor fellow.'

'Johnnie!' Isabella's sensitivities were not honestly affected; it was impossible for someone as . . . as what? She thought for a minute: what was it that made it possible for Johnnie to say outrageous things and yet not offend? Then it came to her: he was a child, a grown-up child.

'Hey, I can see the others. Come on,' he said, pulling Isabella away from the tree she was leaning against.

Isabella could see her sister coming round the far corner of the front façade of the house, walking on Michael's arm. It was clear, even from a distance, that all was agreed. Isabella felt a little pang of heartache as she saw the happy couple. She assumed it was a premonition of loneliness, and smiled brightly to hide it as she hurried beside Johnnie who was calling his congratulations although he was too far away to be heard. Lucinda waved a jaunty acknowledgement with her parasol that was carefully disposed to guard her from the sun. The sun! In an instant Isabella was pulling her bonnet forwards, tucking in her loose hair, and slowing to a decorous walk. By the time she reached them to offer her congratulations the brightness had gone from her smile and her eyes held a touch of despair.

The two magpies left their roosts early and flew out on the first eddies of the day to scour their territory. Quarry sighted, they swooped low and then landed heavily on the dew-rich grass, the early morning sun sharpening the black and white of their plumage. Later they could feast on the fledglings that worm-seeking parents left unguarded in their nests, but first there were the discards of the previous night's revels to scavenge.

Not that the unofficial revels had amounted to much, as the few crusts and several empty beer bottles showed. But the sprinkling of tents pitched a day early in the water meadow had attracted a few of the villagers to indulge in a fantasy of forbidden pleasures. The youth of Yalding were never slow to accept the offerings of fate.

There had only been one actual coupling in the long grass, the bent and broken stalks all that remained of the brief, stolen pleasure. Except for a satisfied gleam in the eye of Ham, cowman at Meadow Farm, and the silent prayer being offered to God by Anne, daughter of the miller, that she was not now carrying ripe seed in her belly.

The magpies themselves were providing amusement for at least one of the local community this morning. Timmy had also risen at daybreak and made his way down to the water meadows to see what the early bird could catch. Two magpies, two for joy the rhyme said; hopefully that meant that no busybody would haul him off to school to suffer what education a seven-year-old must. He wanted to be with the men today, to enjoy the pleasures of the chase, the riches of the pickings. Last time there had been hare coursing down by the river he had been given an orange, a whole one. He could almost taste it in his memory.

The sunlight slanting through the poplars struck at the river, flowing low and sluggishly in its bed. Nature had been kind and not filled it to overflowing, for then the coursing would have been moved to higher ground and the magic of it all would have been lost. It was tradition, a new one Timmy had heard said, but a tradition all the same, that if the coursing was held on the river meadows it was a stag affair. No women at all were allowed on what became for a day hallowed ground. His lordship's decree, that no female whatsoever should enter the fields, his lordship's remark that he 'would have none of their rutting on the field of sport' for it disturbed the dogs, was taken by the inhabitants as a compliment to their normal animal instincts, at the same time as a statement that his lordship's own rutting days were over. After all, not a tremor had crossed the aristocratic features at his utterance, while Master Johnnie had grinned and Michael coloured, proving there was still life potential in the Pencombe line.

But Timmy wasn't interested in carnal pursuits, not yet. He followed the beckoning sun to the river's edge, where there was life in and around the bubbling, secret river as it made its way to the far-off sea. A water rat scurried busily from its hole, whiskers gleaming and twitching; it travelled a miniature, well-worn path that skirted the rushes with their feet in the water, then scurried beneath the holes in the bank where the sand martins would swoop for evening flies. The rat stopped briefly to turn its head, scanning the banks and briefly the sky before making the dangerous dash across the open muddy beach where the cattle came down to drink. It was safe. Timmy didn't even reach for the catapult tucked firmly into his back pocket: he was after more pleasures than the rat could provide this morning. At last the rodent reached the warren of holes in the sandy mud around the stone bridge pile.

Timmy slid gently down the river bank, for once in his life careful of his shabby garments. More odd jobs were given to urchins who had made an attempt at cleanliness, that was one of the first lessons he had picked up for himself, while others had told him earlier that odd jobs meant money. He loved the feeling of the cool sticky mud between his toes; he had tied the laces of his shoes together and they were swinging around his neck. His father would laugh when he saw that. His dad didn't mind him not going to the school, and not having a mother meant he was not under continual torment the way a lot of his friends were. He gingerly put his toes into the water. It was cold, not bitingly so, but enough to bring out a gasp of breath that hung on the air like a floating cobweb. The

56

church bells chimed the hour: six o'clock and all's well. Timmy made his way, as cautiously as the rat, to the security of the shadows under the bridge. In the deeper chill he pulled his shabby jacket more tightly around himself. He was first on the field, master of all he surveyed, and he could hear any traffic on the bridge above him, the travellers who would come from Tonbridge, when the rest of the world decided to awake, and still see the activity on the road coming down the hill from Maidstone on the other side of the water. Timmy smiled his slow, delighted smile at the magpies, keeping him company in his wait; two for joy, he thought, then settled back to wait the day.

Further downriver there had been activity for longer than even Timmy had been awake. Activity on the river meadows meant activity on the water and the water was provider of livelihood to a breed of men apart from the landbased farmers. Luke Jones had been about his business for most of the night, but it didn't bother him. He was in his early thirties, fit and healthy, a man who found only a few hours of sleep sufficient and those few hours he managed to fit in at odd hours of the day. He found the night more to his liking, and profit. At ease now in the dim parlour of his waterside cottage, he stretched out slowly, like a cat, his muscles rippling under his brown skin, the stretch reaching up to his face where a wide yawn revealed the strong white teeth he was so proud of. He looked down on his velvet-smooth brown moleskin trousers, which curved round his well-muscled thighs, with satisfaction, he ran his broad hands over the smoothness of his white shirt, ruffled for today's sport. His hand touched for a moment the golden St Christopher hanging round his neck, given to him by his sister Jenny to guard him on his travels.

He smiled at the thought of Jenny. She was of more help to him than any wife could be, and more trustworthy. She knew his business as much as was necessary, and possibly more, but he had never had a moment's anxiety about her loyalty. As for money, well, money would come flooding in after today as well. There were contacts to be made, new and old, all of whom needed the aid of the Jones of the river.

Luke stepped silently through the blue cottage door and out on to the bank. His eyes never bothered much at the change of light to dark; like a water animal, he was instantly aware. A soft splash off to his left was a trout, early awake. If there were flies about this early then it would be a hot day. He looked down the dark alley of the river leading to the village that lay between him and the water meadows where the coursing would take place. Dug into the bank beneath his feet were forty cases of fine brandy, contraband of the very nicest sort. There were gentlemen who'd buy today, and farmers who reckoned they were connoisseurs. No gin selling for Luke Jones. In his finery he was a gentleman of the river and he delighted in running only gentlemen's pleasures.

He stiffened. There, on the edge of the village, was the muffled splash of oars, as different from the trout's splash as day to night. Again, and again the noise, even a hushed man's swearing as a fumble made an oar throw up water, phosphorescent even in the dark. Luke stayed still. If it was trouble it could come to him, and it had to be trouble, for everything else was too well organized.

'Luke! Luke, are you there, damn you?' The voice was low and hoarse with anxiety.

'Quiet!' The river man's hissed instruction that proved his presence to the nocturnal visitor was enough. The man at the oars of the small rowing boat shipped his oars with haste, stepped up on to the bank, and the two men went into the cottage.

Luke turned up the low oil lamp before addressing the well-cloaked visitor. 'Well? What kind of trouble brings you here, John?'

'Trouble for both of us.'

The light showed the newcomer's face, of an age with the river man but with none of his stature or confidence, the face of a man living continually on the edge of anxiety. He raised a hand to rub at his unshaven cheeks, the smoothness of the hand betraying his non-manual occupation. John Winter, clerk to the magistrate, who chose to live on the edges of the fair village of Yalding, the clerk whose knowledge, come across in the course of his work, meant money to Luke and the others of the assorted clan who ran the smugglers' run from the coast at Hastings on through to London.

The clerk continued, his voice growing louder in the security of the cottage. 'There's a body in the boat. A damn fool seaman who thought he could take money off us. He'd worked his way up from the coast, putting pressure on. He'd found out enough of the route to be dangerous. Ned down at Flimwell tipped me off, so I recognized trouble when I saw it. He came to the pub last night and sought me out. We kept him till late, then he got too sure of himself by half.' His eyes were fixed on the oil light, as if he relived the scene in its steady flame.

'He got loud. I'd been giving him plenty of gin to keep him sweet. Then he started on about the list of names he had, and then how we'd all swing for it unless we paid him for his silence.' He faltered to a halt, then with a rush completed his story. 'It was Dusty who went for him, stabbed him in the back. Just one blow it took and he fell to the floor. He thrashed about a bit, then nothing, he'd

59

gone. So we wrapped him in a blanket and put him in the boat. They thought I'd better bring him.'

Yes, thought Luke, they would have sent the clerk. Luke's teeth were clenched so tightly his jaw was aching. If they'd sent anyone else he'd have felled them to the ground for being so damned stupid. But not John, he wouldn't, for John was walking out with Jenny, in a slow, understated sort of way that seemed to Luke to be acceptable for his sister. And the clerk was industrious; with the money he was stacking away he could one day set himself up in business and that would suit Jenny. However much she thought she could live on the river bank forever, life didn't work out that way, as this night's happenings showed only too clearly.

'We'll put the body in the eel trap,' Luke said, and by those words he put himself into jeopardy and he knew it. He was the only one who had legal access to the subterranean vaults that housed the metal grids for the river's eel harvest. Everyone knew that nothing went on in Luke's domain that he was unaware of. But there was nowhere else he could put a body safely for the day, and there was no way he would miss his own attendance at the racing.

The body had started to stiffen already and the effort of carrying it along the bank to the opening to the traps and then down the short dark tunnel that led to the barred door, set Luke sweating. They manhandled the ungainly burden through the doorway and dumped it without ceremony just inside, against the wall, then swiftly closed and bolted the door again.

'Go back home, and get yourself cleaned up, then get on about your business. I'll need you later on, about eleven tonight, and tell Dusty to come too. It's his damned fault,' Luke said. But there'd be no way they could move the body yet, he knew that, to move it now would be to invite discovery.

The clerk hurried to his boat and rowed back to the wooden stage at the edge of the village, and clambered up on to it just as dawn was starting to lighten the sky.

Luke stormed into the cottage. He could smell his own sweat, the sharp acrid smell of fear that had flared briefly at the thought of the noose that awaited the careless.

'Jenny! Jenny!' he shouted. 'Get up, you lazy baggage, and iron me a shirt. Come on, this one stinks,' and he ripped it off with such force that two of the fine mother-of-pearl buttons that he had been so pleased with tore off and rattled on to the wooden floor.

The magpies had not been meant for him this morning.

The Pencombe gentlemen made their journey to the coursing fields in style if not in comfort. Their gold-crested, black-enamelled carriage wore its obvious age as a mark of distinction and the rock-hard springs as an earthly reminder of purgatory.

Inside, the dusty leather seats gave off the peculiar odour of refined decay that made Johnnie desperate for a smoke but a glance at his father, stern-faced as he regarded the passing of his acres, convinced him that he would do better to suffer the pangs of longing for his pipe rather than the pangs of remorse his father would stir in him for defiling the atmosphere.

Lord Montford's concentration was not on the scenery. He was having to face a problem that had threatened for many years. It was the kind of problem that had flared once like an open sore and then been, in the eyes of strangers, healed over. But it had festered beneath the surface and like a tumour was about to spread its malignancy. Like a cancer, the suffering it inflicted was internal in its host. His lordship was staring blindly through the carriage window, aching for relief from his malady, but there is no medicine to relieve a fool and his money who have been parted, unless it is more money, and how does a fool come by that?

Michael looked moodily out at the village they had at last reached. The carriage had joined the crawl of vehicles for the medieval bridge at Yalding. At least in the carriage, so obviously his father's, they would be given right of way and not have to wait while some yokel slowly made his way between the narrow, stone walls at the pace of his oxen team.

There was one saving grace about today's sport, in that there would be no women. Michael's studied charm for his intended was demanding a strain he had never imagined. He glanced over at his brother, debonair as always, and watched in wry amusement as a buxom young woman on the pavement caught Johnnie's attention. The smile that crossed his brother's face required no effort; it was spontaneous, a smile that held delight, anticipation and excitement, the smile of the eager male.

Michael concentrated his own attention on the woman. She was tall for village stock, with well-rounded arms that purposefully held her willow basket firmly up against her front. Above the wicker edge her breasts were neatly covered with a blue cotton print, but proclaimed their essential femininity. And the face was confident; a high brow, swept-up auburn hair. This was a woman to make some man an ideal wife: the inn-keeper perhaps, or a farmer. Then the carriage had its way past and she was no longer in sight. Michael sat back in his seat and caught his brother grinning at him. That was when he realized that his own face had also creased into the predator's appreciation and he raised his eyebrows in query at his brother, who winked slowly. It was the first companionable moment they had shared together in a long time, and it had taken a woman to effect it. As a family the Montfords seemed fated to live by influence from the distaff side.

The front wheels of the carriage reached the bridge and the new metalled sound of iron rims on stone filled their ears just as Lord Montford reached a decision. He would have to ask his sister. There was no alternative. He had been a fool all those years ago and managed to lose the Pencombe family jewels. There had to be at least two reasonable suites to present to Lucinda, one on her betrothal to Michael and another on their marriage. In return for the more than excellent dowry, the Bradburys would expect at least that. He would ask his sister; she was married to that damn fool banker who made money-making look easier than shooting a sitting duck. The man was a social climber. That was why he'd been only too happy to marry Hermione even though she was practically penniless. But he'd done her well, she always looked the part and she'd boasted often enough that her spouse had settled her more than necessarily well. She could rustle up something: emeralds or sapphires perhaps, no need for a multitude of diamonds. And something classic in design, then it would simply be assumed they were family heir-looms. Least said soonest mended.

The twelfth Earl of Pencombe felt the tension fading from his shoulders. There, it hadn't been as bad as all that, and Hermione had never for one moment made him feel less than honourable in his amatory dealings with that dreadful woman in his youth. Well, at least there were no women here today. He returned to his present surround-ings refreshed and ready for his sport.

They were across the river at last and pulling out over to the right on to the water meadows. A respectable cheer greeted their arrival. The horses came to an admirably smooth halt beside the line of dogs and their handlers, ranked ready for inspection. The coachman leaped down to do his duty with the door that creaked only minutely and his lordship stepped out into a bright beautiful morning, full of the scents and sounds of dogs and horses, men and boys. The essentially male cleanliness of it assailed his senses like a draught of fine brandy, and he smiled, which made it an occasion for the record books, the coachman decided. As he walked down the line of dogs, he patted their heads, their profiles were as aristocratic as his own.

Out on to the field of play stalked the owner of all he surveyed, Michael and Johnnie in close attendance. Coursing, sport of gentlemen and kings, promised a fine day out for all the participants, except, of course, the hares.

Timmy had left his hiding-place under the bridge. There was too much excitement abroad now for anyone to bother about dragging a truant back to school.

The first contest was almost set. Both dogs were standing alertly, held firmly on their leashes, back legs quivering with the excitement. Further out in the field the hare cowered in its wicker basket. It might not be killed today; there were times when the hare escaped or the dogs were beaten off it in recognition of its splendid chase, but that was rare and such a fine day deserved a victim's sacrifice. At least that was what Timmy felt, deep inside his budding sportsman's soul.

The quarry was helped tenderly from its temporary home and edged into the false security of a small gorse stand. Then with a cry from the starter, the greyhounds were slipped and the hare was thrust out into the open to be instantly sighted by the dogs. Their tails whipped up in their pursuit, their strides lengthened, then the hare itself showed the power of its long back legs, and stretched out, racing towards the far-distant copse. The dogs raced neck and neck. On an instant the brindle dog forged ahead, its brownish black markings now a blur to the watchers. The hare turned back and away; the brindle had scored once. The cheering in the crowd became a howl, for the brindle was favourite. The dogs checked their run to the new path. The hare was fit and full of the primeval urge for flight. The threesome bolted on their way, then the grey dog received a new surge of energy. Perhaps Timmy's cries propelled it that fraction further as the trio flew by him.

Timmy allied with the underdog. The hare turned again and now the score was even. The crowd went wild, but they were hanging on to their hats; they wouldn't throw them into the air until the result was decided. The hare was tiring and the crowd sensed it. Like an animal the crowd sent up a roar from deep in the throat and the dogs responded with the final lung-bursting run to the death. They were on the hare in a flash, the brindle there by a head, in a rush of tumbling fur and, briefly, blood, but only for a moment as the men ran forwards to pull the tattered remains away. The fur was thick and eating the creature wasn't the idea at all, it was the sport that was the thing.

The crowd broke into a dozen fragments, off to the bookmakers for the lucky ones, off to the gin tents to look for inspiration in the next bout for the others. A chance to meet old and new acquaintances, a chance to do business for some.

Today Luke Jones carried his lists in his head, leaving the meticulously written lists of smuggling business transactions secreted at the cottage. A number of old, trusted customers first to take the bulk of his new consignment of brandy and then a shorter list of new men he wanted to approach. A man who stood still in business might as well admit failure, that was his motto. He thought it must be the rule by which Thomas Cade, tenant farmer at Reason Hill, lived as well. This new set-up of traction engines was proof of that. Luke knew that Cade was aware of the brandy run, but so far he hadn't bought. It was time for that to change. In any case, Cade intended to be a rising star, and one who bought from the run would protect rather than destroy. Mr Cade was high on his list today.

They met, by organized chance, just at the beginning of the second contest. Thomas Cade was on the lookout for business himself. Having just left one potential customer, he was scanning the crowd for another when Luke Jones walked up to him.

'Good day, Mr Cade,' he said.

'Good day.' The greeting was returned, although Cade was clearly going to act as if he didn't know the flamboyant waterman, which he did, at least by sight, and certainly by reputation.

'Good sport so far,' Luke continued. 'Good sport and good company, not much else a man can ask for on a holiday, except perhaps good weather and that's been given us too.'

They stood, looking approvingly out over the sparkling field together: the dogs had been slipped and were off after a new hare; all around them men were rapt in their sport.

Thomas Cade stirred. There was no point in wasting time on such a suitable day for the pursuit of profit. 'A man could ask for a good drink as well,' he said. 'I gather you're just the man to supply it.'

'That I am.' Luke Jones allowed himself a small smile of satisfaction. A new customer would wipe out part of the fury that the thought of the dead man in the eel trap was fuelling in his chest. 'I've one keg to spare this time. If you'd like to try it, then you can order up two or three from the next run. It would help me if you'd collect.' That was a spur of the moment thought. He'd be hard pressed for time in the next couple of days, but he'd have to have this consignment out before the next arrived within the week.

'No, I won't collect. But if I take a fancy to the stuff I'll have four kegs off you.'

Four kegs was good for one order. Well, Jenny would have to do it. She'd run the waggon before and although he didn't like it, she was in no more danger out delivering the stuff than she had been on occasions when her own bed had been on top of a dozen barrels.

The men shook hands and set off in pursuit of more business, just as the second hare of the day succumbed to the inevitable. This time the handlers were slower getting to the mêlée and the lead dog had ripped a back leg off the hare and half-swallowed it. It was choking on the fur and there was a cursing and swearing that attracted the veterinarian from the gin tent. By the time he'd made his addled progress to the scene the dog was down on its side, shivering as if in fever. Its great brown eyes were flecked with red and bright drops of the hare's blood glistened on the quivering muzzle. The handler's hands were streaked with red and his fingers, resting lightly on the rib-cage, sharply visible through the fine thin coat, felt the lack of air, felt the final quiver. More than just the vet made for the gin tent; it was never the hunter that was meant to die, only the hunted.

By mid-morning the gentry and their followers had pulled out food hampers while the villagers fell on quantities of meat pies brought over on trays from the bakery.

There were two certain areas of profit-making today. One was the bookies, who won by skill on a good day or by outrunning the crowd on a bad one. The other was the bakery, where they'd worked all night to stack up pies and cakes and the firm golden spiced biscuits called fairings that a lad might take home to his lass as a token of his affection, and a proof that out of sight had not been truly out of mind.

Timmy had a penny and it bought him a piece of pie almost bigger than he could hold. It was crammed to bursting with good fat pork, seasoned with chopped sage and onion and dripping with stock. Helping drag the dead dog off the course had got him a glass of weak ale, but he hadn't fancied that so he'd traded it with a bigger boy and got a perfect red apple in return. Now all he wanted was a drink of something nice: lemonade would be perfect.

It came into his happy life right on time. The hand that tousled his hair was the hand of a friend. He didn't have to look up to recognize Mr Cade, who of course recognized the boy's need for lemonade, and a bag of boiled sweets as well. Timmy grinned so much that it was hard to stop the pastry bits falling out of his crammed mouth. Thomas Cade grinned nearly as widely as they made a good lunch together sitting on the river bank. It was good of Mr Cade, Timmy knew, for he could have gone and had his lunch with the gentry since he was related in a sort of way. But it made Timmy's day, and Thomas's too, as the sun beat down and the honest smell of sweat mingled with the spilt ale and hot meaty pie.

Later in the afternoon there was a trophy to be presented, a large cup, silvered where polishing hadn't rubbed it off and very precious because of the list of champions-past engraved in copperplate script on its side. His lordship would present it to the victor; he enjoyed that kind of thing.

Thomas timed his visit to his godfather to a nicety. There was always tea served just before the final, deciding race and he strolled into the green space thoughtfully left around his lordship's group by the also-rans.

'Good afternoon, sir, good afternoon, Michael, Johnnie.' Thomas had perfected a way of greeting that conveyed undertones of respect with overtones of his own sense of position.

'Good afternoon,' they each responded in an amiable enough fashion.

If Thomas had called on his godfather an hour earlier his reception would have been very different.

But Eli Bradbury's innocent revelation during the afternoon of his own involvement in the Cade Traction Engines Enterprise had taken the teeth out of his lordship's bite. Michael and Johnnie may have looked less than welcoming, but now neither of them was in a position to curtail the fast-growing venture.

Thomas greeted Eli with the warmth due to a valued benefactor, which was a highlight of Eli's afternoon, as he was still unaware that he had consorted with the enemy.

'Like a scone, Thomas?' Johnnie proffered the plate with little enthusiasm. Pencombe scones were related to rock cakes and Thomas was close enough family to be aware of the fact.

'No thanks, Johnnie. How's your day gone, any decent killings?'

Johnnie, since childhood, had been an enthusiastic betting man, and an habitual loser. It was one trait that he shared with his father. 'Nothing spectacular, except,' he dropped his voice to a whisper, 'the old man lost a packet on the dog that died; something in the rule-books cost it the race. He's pretty peeved.'

They turned in unison to look at the granite-faced earl.

'What's he on in this race?' There was something in Thomas's face as he asked the question that alerted Johnnie.

'He's on Brown Devil, quite heavily I think.'

'What's it worth to fix it then, Johnnie? Do I get a free pardon?' Thomas was happy, he liked to be in the position of doing a bit of bargaining and he knew Michael and Johnnie had heard about his scheme with Eli.

Seeing their conspiratorial huddle Michael came up to join them. 'What's on?'

Three men, who had grown to manhood together,

knew each other well enough to know when a game was on.

Thomas repeated his question. 'What's it worth if I fix it so that your father wins on this one? That'll mean a quiet life for you two, and that's got to be worth quite a lot.'

A quiet life meant that they wouldn't have to go through one of their father's prolonged depressions, when he dredged up undreamed-of grievances and generally made life at Pencombe twice as unbearable as usual. It was up to Michael to decide; he was the elder and Johnnie was happy to leave the terms to his brother. Michael was tempted to turn down the offer, but his fury at Thomas's machines had cooled. In any case they were the way of the future, if it wasn't Thomas who brought them into Kent, someone else would. Their hunting would suffer, but many of the followers were farmers themselves, next year or the one after, they'd all be using engines.

'We'll call off the hounds if you want.' They all knew that meant that Michael would pacify the hunt members who were in full cry against the traction engines. That would be worth money to Thomas.

'How about recommending my services to the Home Farm factor?' Thomas tried.

'Never.' Johnnie shook his head vigorously. They would certainly not agree to those damned noisy machines working under their noses, not that Thomas would have expected them to agree to that anyway. But honour was satisfied.

'I'll just slip off for a moment,' Thomas said and, lifting his hat briefly in the approximate direction of his god-father, he left.

Thomas needed his accomplice, and he was pretty sure he knew where to find him. But it still took a few minutes searching the crowds milling around the tents. He passed

Luke Jones again. This time the waterman was deep in a conversation that was apparently not to his liking. An irritated expression marked his face. Thomas was surprised to recognize the man wheedling beside the waterman. It was the ginger-haired clerk of Eli's, looking hot and uncomfortable and out of place in a rural setting. Thomas had no doubt that the brandy smuggler was being offered an illicit supply of Bradbury beer. It was clear that the offer was being turned down. The thin lips of the clerk suddenly turned back in anger, his thin shoulders hunching aggressively even though Luke Jones towered above him. He was an unsavoury character all right. Eli should look out, thought Thomas, but it wasn't up to him to warn him.

Timmy was getting tired and he still hadn't managed to earn an orange. They cost two pence, beyond his reach, but not beyond his yearning. Golden and round and shiny piled in their wicker basket. A hand reached into the crowd around the vendors and plucked him out.

'Come on, young 'un, time to earn a bob or two.' Thomas had him firmly in his grasp. He bent to look into the face, now streaked with grime and tiredness, but still the bright blue eyes managed to light up with excitement. 'You've got your catapult?'

The boy nodded agreement.

Thomas walked him rapidly around the outskirts of the crowd; he knew exactly where he was making for. The old oak tree was alone now on the upper edge of the meadow. Dark green patches in the lighter grass showed where other trees had once formed a stand, but age had taken its toll, or perhaps they had been felled to make galleons in good King Henry's time. But one tree was all he needed. He picked the boy up and shoved him up to the lowest branch, pushing him firmly in the seat of his thin trousers.

'The brown one's it,' he called up softly. 'Turn the hare twice.'

Timmy nodded in agreement then set to climbing higher. The men holding the leashes were standing ready, the race about to begin, but he needed height to cover the ground. One thing Timmy was very good with was his catapult.

His legs scratched on the rough bark as he climbed and the green growth became sparse, giving little cover. He gained height with the speed of a monkey and twined his legs around the branch beneath him, leaving his hands free to work. The catapult was smooth from use and his hands stroked and caressed his only weapon with love and care. The elastic on it was precious. Thomas had procured it for him long ago. It looked very much like knicker elastic, but Timmy didn't know that; he didn't wear knickers. From his pocket he selected a stone; there were a dozen or so in there, about the size of a wren's eggs, nice rounded ones that would travel straight. Stones big enough to kill a rabbit but small enough to escape notice if need be. A hare was big game to the boy. The missiles would turn but not kill, but then that was the whole object of the attack.

The dogs were off. From his vantage point Timmy could not hear much of the clamour, and the wind was starting to rustle the leaves around him. He would have to take account of the wind. As surely as the longbowman of England who had been his great, great, great grandpapa, he judged the air and the necessary angle of flight.

The brown dog's head was just in the lead. It was making no move to turn the hare but it didn't have to; if the hare turned now the point went to Brown Devil. Timmy held his breath, pulled the stone back against the elastic and let fly. In an instant the hare swerved, almost bounded, to the side. The faint cheer from the crowd made Timmy grin: one to him. The dogs were quickly on the next tack. An older sniper might have allowed the other dog to strike once, just so that no suspicions were aroused, but Timmy's mind travelled in straight channels. He took his weapon once more, pulled back until the elastic hummed, waited for the brown dog's advantage. Then it was gone, faster than sound, the hare jerked round, the dogs collided in a tangle, stopping the hare at the huntsmen's feet. A quick-witted attendant whisked the creature up out of harm's way. A great cheer went up, for the crowd was magnanimous at the end of its holiday.

Timmy shinned down his tree and found himself alone, and saw Thomas striding at speed to the group with the dogs. Timmy ran to catch up, bubbling in his excitement. 'I did it,' he cried, 'I did it.'

Thomas stretched out his hand and thrust something bright and shining at the boy. 'Here you are, Timmy, you earned it fair and square.'

Timmy stopped still, staring down at the shilling that filled his small hand. He felt tears of pride rush into his eyes and thought his heart would burst. For an instant longer he stood still, then he was off at a sprint. He had to catch the man who sold the oranges, and perhaps then he'd buy a whole handful of fairings, and hopefully find his dad, whom he'd avoided all day just in case he got sent off to school. It was so wonderful to be rich.

Thomas was also thinking how good it was to have the odd handful of sovereigns available. So that he could make the grand gesture of buying the brave hare who had given the dogs such a splendid run. He particularly wanted to have it in his possession before anyone thought to have a close look and discovered the two blackening bruises that the couple of well-aimed stones would have inflicted.

His lordship had never been more gracious, the owner of the winning dog declared that night over his victory brandy. But then his lordship, in common with a minority of others at the coursing, had gone home with more in the way of largesse in his pockets than he had set out with, and that was a very rare event indeed.

Jenny Jones sniffed disdainfully as she stood on the dusty pavement. It was ridiculous that women were not allowed to join in the fun. Lord Montford was a woman-hater, but the other men weren't.

She sniffed again and clutched her basket fiercely in front of her. His lordship's carriage rolled slowly past her. She could see his sons eyeing her through the windows but she wasn't going to give them the pleasure of a response. It was a cheek, there was no valid reason for the men to enjoy a day's holiday while the women had to go about their ordinary, mundane tasks. And the struggle in the baker's to get the loaf of bread that sat in the bottom of her basket was disgraceful. The place was crammed to overflowing with pies and buns, and they could hardly be bothered to sell her her usual long loaf. Well, Tom could have bread and cheese for his supper tonight. That would show him that she had more to do than pander to his wants while he had a high old time.

John was in attendance on the magistrate today, or else he would have come to call on her; he wouldn't have wanted to stay for long drinking ale or gin at the tents on the water meadows.

She tried to kindle a spark of enthusiasm at the thought of her beau, but it was hardly the beginnings of a blaze. He was admirably attentive but very, very slow. Jenny lay in her bed on these warm nights and her imaginings took her a lot further than a little gentle hand-holding. John hadn't even kissed her yet, but he was talking of marriage.

At last she managed to cross the street between two carts piled high with farm labourers. They cheered her as she crossed, so she held her head higher; she was above their type and they knew it. She had no errands to keep her in the village and didn't pass anyone worth a gossip. There was nothing for it but to go back to the cottage. She'd already dusted and swept, but there was always something to do.

The uncut cheese Luke had brought back from Maidstone market last week could do with looking at. She stuck in a narrow-bladed knife and pulled out a sliver of the firm curd: it was white, a bright chalky white. Putting her face close to it she sniffed the sharp tang of buttermilk. It would blue nicely given a chance and Luke particularly liked a bit of blue cheese. All that was needed was a week or two in a damp dark place and she was certain that the first threads of colour would start their work. She took the cheese from the cupboard and wrapped it lightly in a piece of boiled linen to protect it from any unsightly moulds. Then, wrapping a shawl loosely around her shoulders, she picked up her burden and set off on her short journey. She had found the key to the padlock in Luke's jacket pocket. At least his absence meant she could go down to the trap without his interfering, and trying to prevent her using it as an extension to her larder.

The key turned easily in the lock, and she pushed the heavy door away from her. She stood still for a few minutes to accustom her eyes to the dark, and then she stepped in to the vaulted space. The dank chill and smell of the river bottom always sent a tremor down her spine. Not a woman's place, Luke said. She scowled at the thought and stepped forwards more firmly.

The cheese should stand high above water level and preferably off the metal slatted floor. There, against the wall, was a pile of goods on which she could stand the cheese. She stretched out to feel the wrapping: fresh sacking, which was ideal. She balanced the cheese carefully. But it would not stay level. Perhaps the barrels were piled higgledy-piggledy.

She lifted the cheese off again, and laid it carefully on the floor; she would have to restack the pile. With a huff of irritation she pulled at the sacking but it was caught somewhere. She bent down closer and pulled again. The sacking gave way abruptly and the heap rolled towards her feet. She took a quick step back, her heels ringing on the metal floor. The bundle unwrapped slowly, uncoiling itself in the gloom. Rigid as it was, the corpse threw out a stiff arm, the finger pointing accusingly at its disturber. Jenny screamed as the head was unveiled, the lips drawn back from the teeth in a death's-head grin.

Luke got home late from his day. The light shone in the cottage window, but to his surprise the door was bolted. He banged loudly with his fist and called out, the drinks he'd enjoyed making his voice loud. There were scrabbling sounds as the bolts were drawn and the latch lifted, then the door swung open and he stepped into the room. He knew the moment he looked into her face. With a mixture of fear and fury, Jenny's eyes told him. They couldn't tell him how she'd struggled to overcome her terror and rewrap the body or how she had shuddered as she did it. But the brother and sister were tied even tighter now and Luke felt a flicker of fear at what might happen to Jenny if he was taken.

The cool church at Boughton-Linstone filled with the sound of the hymn. The clear, high notes ran like a mountain stream through the shafts of sunlight that pierced the stained-glass windows and fell in multicoloured patterns on the flagstoned floor. Isabella gloried in the soaring notes of her solo, then swooped to a depth that made her voice almost a breath. The words she sang with the conviction of innocence.

> And did those feet in ancient times,
> Walk upon England's mountains green.

In her mind's eye, the Christ arisen strode the sweeping, expansive moorland that she had once loved.

The sincerity of her belief touched the congregation in an assortment of ways. For Sam, the engine foreman, it lifted his life for a few moments of vision to the perfect hereafter. His son, Timmy, sitting beside him, wriggled uncomfortably. He did not want to be cooped up in church at all. Thomas Cade enjoyed the voice, felt pleasantly cooled by the clarity of it, slightly ill at ease at Isabella's rapt expression: too much innocence, he felt, for a girl turning into a woman. Lucinda was irritated, as she was whenever her sister's talents singled her out. Eli was the one member of the congregation incensed. His jowls were quivering with indignation, a deep red flush coloured the opulent neck resting so elegantly on his immaculately tied cravat. It was left for Oliver Curworthy, ancient vicar of the parish of Boughton, to enjoy the whole performance as only a man enjoying every day as possibly his last upon this mortal earth could.

The words continued, through the poetry of an artist, to the cleverness of an intellectual. With simple conviction Isabella allowed her voice to fill the air with a sentiment she only partially understood.

> And is Jerusalem builded here,
> Among those dark satanic mills?

Isabella and Sam saw in their mind's eye the hell-fires of Satan being forever driven from this glorious land, this heaven that was their England.

Thomas stirred his memory and glanced quickly at Eli. Of course!

The brewer's apoplexy was clearly visible. Eli knew, as the intellectuals had long known, Blake's immortal words were for the education of mankind. A statement that the industrialists of England were the creators of those dark satanic mills, and a brewery was perilously close, especially when the message was delivered by the brewer's daughter.

Thomas could not control the smile; he struggled but failed. To cover his amusement he looked over at Timmy, who had slumped sideways in his seat on the pew. His legs were too short to allow his uncomfortably shod feet to reach the ground. Thomas knew that the minute the child was allowed the freedom of the churchyard the restraining shoes would be ripped off and ten grubby toes would wriggle in delight at contact once again with the cool, clean earth.

Thomas's eyes slid on past the child, over the aisle to Eli's pew again. Lucinda was watching him, her face expressionless, a perfect oval, perfectly pale against her auburn hair that was severely restrained by a beribboned bonnet of deep pink, the same colour as her dress. As their eyes met, he waited for her gaze to slip away. In company she was distant to him, as if unwilling to communicate on anything other than the most formal level. But now, they were strangely alone in the crowded church and she did not look away. It seemed to Thomas that they shared the look for a long time, although Isabella was still singing the hymn. It was only Eli's sudden change of position that broke the look, and then Thomas found himself staring at the brewer's broad back. When Eli moved again only the side of Lucinda's face was visible, serene in contemplation of her prayer book.

Thomas turned his head slowly to look forward, to

where Oliver, with a painful dignity, was making his slow way to the pulpit. The words of the old man's sermon washed over him, unheard, unappreciated. He did not look at Eli to witness the man leaving his pew in fury, to the intense interest of the congregation. Thomas's thoughts were jumbled, confused, a state of mind unknown to him. He completed the remainder of the service, the ritual kneelings and standings in a half trance. He shook hands with Oliver and muttered his goodbye. He gave no comment as to his appreciation of the sermon, causing the old man's eyebrows to rise in wry amusement. He had expected Thomas to understand where his shafts of righteousness had been fired, but then the farmer was a busy man and presumably had dozed through the erudite argument that had given Oliver such pleasure to compose. That was a pity.

Lucinda and Isabella said their adieus very prettily to the vicar, forming a charming picture in the Norman doorway. Their father was nowhere to be seen outside, but he had his funny ways and neither of them bothered too much about his having taken the carriage the short drive home and leaving them to walk. Lunch would be waiting for their return and Isabella always felt hungry after singing. She looked with eyes newly inspired at the rich, full hedgerows bursting with life and colour.

With a joyful shout of freedom Timmy shot past them, followed closely by his father who doffed his worn hat at the girls and murmured his appreciation of 'Jerusalem'. Isabella could not have been more delighted. Lucinda scuffed her foot then let out a little cry of annoyance. She had marked the toe of her new shoes, which had been sent from London. Now they were spoiled by the unreasonableness of Papa in not leaving them the carriage. She began to march irritably fast towards the house, but to her surprise the carriage was not pulled up in front of the portico. The implication that her father was not there for her to bicker at made her turn on her sister instead.

'I've told you before, you shouldn't tip your head back to sing like that, it shows all your teeth and it's not ladylike.'

Isabella stiffened. She should have expected this. Then, with the instantaneity of a miracle, she saw in her father's absence the opportunity to engineer her own. 'I'm so sorry, Lucinda,' she interrupted with sweetly obvious insincerity. 'I would of course be pleased to listen to your views on my singing, but not now, I'm afraid. I am going out for lunch.' And with a smile she hurried off into the house, making quickly for the kitchen.

She was in luck: the servants had not hurried back from their devotions and she was quite unseen as she took a wicker basket and hastily filled it with her findings in the well-stocked larder. She was especially pleased at coming across a nice, well-cured Bath chap. Oliver had told her more than once that he liked a tasty piece of fat ham, and that would do very nicely. She heard steps and voices down the passageway and she just had time to pick up a napkin to cover her treasures and step hurriedly out through the back door. She had gained the sanctuary of the drying area. The lines were empty of washing as it was Sunday and she ducked to get beneath them without catching her bonnet, then she was through the privet hedge, and on her way to Oliver's rectory. This was the life she enjoyed, sharing her pleasures in conversation and reading with the vicar, while bringing him a simple but nourishing meal. This was how she remembered life being when her mother was alive.

The rectory was a little like the vicar himself, in that it was elderly and leaning at one corner. But unlike its occupant, it had become more beautiful with age, the black timbers mellow against whitewash that had the pearly patina of passing summers. At this season the roses that rambled, pink and yellow, with the intimacy of years, over the age spots, were at the point of bursting into an incomparable magnificence. Each year it seemed impossible that another bloom could squeeze on to the thorny bracts, but each year surpassed the last.

Oliver had surmised that their fecundity was thanks to the proximity of the graveyard and, never one to waste a hint from God, the great provider, he had gradually moved his small vegetable plot closer to the edge of the graves themselves. He felt it only decent to make the move with gradual, almost unseen steps, out of consideration for the feelings of his parishioners. He had once tried to encourage the grazing of the churchyard by a pair of orphan lambs, which would have saved the small bill for the cutting, and he was very partial to lamb, but that had not met with approval; so he had still to rely on the generosity of men like Thomas Cade to supplement his vegetable diet with meat.

His small stipend he spent on books. It was one of his sins and he was aware of it, but he thought that God might perhaps forgive him, especially as his most loved volume was that one book which told the story of creation, and the tale of God's only begotten Son.

Isabella opened the wicket gate at the side of the rectory garden. It saved a short walk to the main, front path and also allowed her to glimpse into the tiny green square at the back of the house, where Oliver at times pottered 'to hide from his parishioners'. She did not see herself as someone he would want to hide from. They had a good relationship, each enjoying the other's company, and each feeling that they did the other good by their companionship.

It was only as she lifted the green weathered dolphin knocker to announce her arrival that she saw Papa's carriage standing at the front gate. She stopped in astonishment. What on earth was her father doing here, and at this time of day? Then, standing very still in her surprise, she heard Eli's voice, deep and round and clearly angry. There was a short pause, and the faintest of sounds convinced her that Oliver must be making a reply. She looked down at the hamper. This would not please her father at all. To invite Oliver to the house to lunch was one thing, but that would be at the master of the house's request. Eli was not one for charity, unless it was of the very visible kind. She would go, but as she edged by the window her father's voice called out.

'Isabella! Isabella!' The window opened, the sun shining at tangents off the leaded lights. Her father thrust his leonine head through the wooden casement. 'What on earth are you doing here?' His eyes dropped to her basket. 'Oh, how silly of me to ask. I beg your pardon, Isabella,' he said sarcastically. 'I had believed you an innocent in this affair, now I see that you are a conspirator.'

Isabella's mouth had dropped open in her surprise. What on earth was he talking about?

'And close your mouth,' her father roared at her. 'Lucinda is quite right, you'll end up looking like a dray horse, all teeth and neigh.'

Isabella felt tears well up. She hated it when her father shouted at her; it was a rare occurrence and all the worse for that when it did happen.

'Come in here,' he instructed.

She turned back to the door, which he flung open before her.

'Sit down,' he thundered, pointing imperiously at a chair dented with an imprint that his own behind had just made. He had no alternative but to stand now, as Oliver had only two chairs, both of them elderly and shabby but with the air of having come originally from good stock; like Oliver himself.

'Isabella was not aware of the meaning that "Jerusalem" has for you, Eli.' The old man's quavering voice was surprisingly strong. 'She sang it purely and simply for the beauty of it and the belief. It does not have to be interpreted as you have done. There is a simple message in it as well.'

But Eli continued to glower down on his daughter. 'She is too full of modern ideas for her own good. I find it only too easy to believe she was aware of the implications all along.'

Isabella was so transparently at sea as to the meaning of his tirade, however, that he had to admit it to himself she had been innocent.

He turned to face her squarely, seeing a portion of her hurt. 'This is your own fault, Isabella, you are too full of artistic nonsense. I would not for one instant have supposed Lucinda to be guilty of what I would see as treachery. But I was prepared to believe that you, with your strange, half-imagined memories of your mother and unhealthy concern with the welfare of others who do not concern you, would have thought to give me a message in this, this . . .' He was clearly in the grip of a strong emotion, beginning to feel upset himself at having misjudged her. 'This way I feel is blasphemy,' and he stopped.

Oliver shifted his position carefully in his chair; it had required a great effort to get to church today.

'Isabella, I owe you an explanation,' Oliver said. 'I did not mean for one moment that you would suffer for your singing today. I can promise you that the simple souls of our congregation will have gone back to their homes uplifted by it.' He paused, to allow a deeper wave of pain to make its passage. 'There is in that hymn another message however, besides that of our fight towards a better world; or rather, not another message, more a well-aimed shaft of light. Your father was the recipient. Not that he is the owner of a dark satanic mill.' He turned to Eli and continued, 'I understand that your brewery is not such a place of despair, Eli, although I have no doubt that some individuals there suffer more than they need in their pursuit of a living. But you are a man in a position of influence, Eli, and as such, I, your vicar, feel duty bound to encourage you on a crusading path. And never forget, Eli, the parable about the rich man and the eye of the needle; the words are written for us all.'

Eli had taken enough. He put out a hand to help Isabella to her feet. 'Isabella has brought you a basket, Oliver.' He lifted the napkin aside for a moment to survey the contents. 'It contains, amongst other niceties, a Bath chap which I am sure you will enjoy.'

Papa too was partial to a Bath chap. Isabella felt a pang of remorse: he did so suffer if anyone tried to tell him what to do.

They left the rectory silently, and made the short journey back to the house in silence. Isabella felt that to speak would have shaken loose the tears that were stinging her eyes. She felt the distance between herself and her father growing unbridgeable. The mother she remembered he seemed to despise. He quashed any remarks she made about the new bright world, the beauty of its art and culture, the openness of its thoughts, and he saw her as a rebel, which she didn't consider herself to be. She wanted him to share her excitements, while he wanted another Lucinda.

There was no breeze to stir the thick, hot air bouncing off the cobbles. The mean terraced houses, with narrow front doors and chipped front steps looked through streaked windows at the children playing marbles on the pavement.

Harold Simpson, clerk to Eli Bradbury, sneered as he approached the little group, intent on their game. He'd never had much fun as a child. There was always someone bigger and better to beat him fairly or steal his rare winnings.

With a shout of victory, the biggest of the boys squatting in the dust shot his opponent's bright, coloured glass ball out on to the road. The children leaped up to their feet to follow the prize. Then stopped suddenly. Harold, quick on his feet as always, had reached it before them. He stooped to pick up the cool, shiny piece of glass and turned it in his fingers.

'A penny for it,' he called to them. 'A penny and its yours.'

But they didn't have a penny.

'Too bad,' he sneered. Pocketing his pickings he walked away with the spring of victory in his step.

He had two more roads to cross before reaching his destination, but there was little traffic in the back streets of the town. There wasn't much money here to attract hawkers, and those lucky enough to be in work wouldn't be back for another hour yet. Harold was superior in his clerk's hours. Still fingering the marble, he rapped with his knuckles on the blue door. The paint was peeling, creased net curtains hung at the windows, but to Harold this was heaven on earth. He could hardly stop himself trembling with excitement.

The door opened, his lips were curling back to smile, then stopped, frozen in shock. It was a man who opened the door to him, a young man. A stranger in carpet slippers, a pipe clamped between his nicotine-stained teeth. Striped trousers, white shirt and red braces put nattily together to highlight the jauntiness of this interloper.

'Wotcher,' the stranger said, around his pipe. 'You must be Harold.' He opened the door wide to let Harold squeeze past him into the narrow hall. 'In you go, I gather you know the way.' He laughed, loudly. Too loudly for the thin walls, and there was an instant muffled banging. That would be Irene next door; she couldn't abide noise.

Harold felt his head spinning, but he walked on into the living room as he'd been told to. There was a bright coloured cloth on the little table in front of the window. It was laid with knives and forks and the condiment set. Harold had brought her that set, three glass bottles with silver-coloured lids and a stand, a present from the trip he'd made with Eli to Margate.

'Sit yourself down, dearie.' It was her voice coming trilling through from the kitchen. 'Won't be a mo', Harry.'

What did it all mean? The room was quite strange in its tidiness: there was none of her clutter, there were even flowers in a vase. He turned round slowly, looking at the changes and came face to face with the stranger again.

'Makes you think, don't it, mate? Makes you see what you can do with a little place like this. Given the money of course, given the money.' And he laughed again.

'Here you are, lovies.' Lavender came into the room, her petite form almost hidden by the piled plates she balanced precariously in front of her. 'A real high tea, Harold. Ooh, you should just see your face.' She hurried to the table. 'Give us a hand, these ruddy plates are hot.' She flashed a grin at the pipe smoker and said, 'Just like the old days. Isn't it wonderful!' She put the last plate down and gave Harold a push towards the table. 'Come on, come on. Get stuck in. It's not every day a girl has her fellow and her prodigal brother to entertain, is it?'

Her brother! It was her brother. Harold could have cried with relief. He sat down quickly enough now and set to eating with a will. For nearly five minutes there was silence, apart from their chewing and swallowing and slurps as the brother drank his tea.

'Oh that was lovely, Arthur, lovely. He did us proud, didn't he, Harry?'

Harold nodded in agreement. It had been a lovely tea, beautiful fried ham, potatoes rich with the fat, a fried egg and even a fried tomato. Lovely.

It was much later, after they'd split a bottle of gin and finished off a fruit cake that Arthur had also provided, that Harold started to realize that Lavender's brother was more interested in Mr Bradbury than politeness required. Now that the surprise had passed, Harold was back to his normal devious way of thinking. It seemed that Arthur had something on his mind. It was very clear that his beautiful, dark-haired, dark-eyed Lavender adored her brother. She kept popping irrelevant details of his life in London into their conversation. Or were they really irrelevant? Harold felt that he was the object of the brother's and sister's scheming. He didn't mind that, as long as the scheming wasn't against him and he didn't think it was. The scheming was aimed at the brewery somehow.

He wouldn't let them realize he was on to them yet. After all, the brother was buttering him up with good food and drink, and Lavender, well, Lavender would do her bit of sweetening later on. There would be looking and touching; most of all Harold liked looking. He wanted to look at Lavender's sweet little body for hours and hours. He liked to look at it in petticoats, in her stockings and drawers. Very, very rarely, if she wanted to please him a lot, he could look at her in the all-together. Harold felt warm with pleasure.

If the brother and sister were scheming then it must be money they were after. Harold wanted money too. He wanted it so that he could show Lavender that she must marry him and lead a fine life. Then there wouldn't only be looking, but having too. She would be his, entirely. He found it hard to swallow, just thinking of it. They started another bottle of gin. He was so excited he didn't notice how easily the juniper-flavoured nectar slipped down. One thing about Arthur, he knew a good bottle of gin.

He woke up stiff and foul-headed as the first light crept round the thin curtains. He felt sick. Arthur was snoring in the armchair; at least Harold had nodded off on the sofa. Where was Lavender? He looked around, twisting his head slowly. Moving it made him feel like he was on a boat, a boat on a choppy sea. She wasn't there. He sat forward slowly; she would be upstairs, lying on her big brass bed. As he started to edge himself up, the springs creaked and Arthur stopped snoring, instantly opening an eye.

'You awake, Harry?'

'Yeh.'

'Come on, I've got something to say to you.'

The men moved quietly around the little room. Harold had lost his shoe and he took a while to find it stuck under the front of the sofa. He hoped Lavender would wake up and come downstairs. But he couldn't hear her move at all. Not even when Arthur ran the cold tap to run water over the back of his neck and rubbed his head vigorously in the coarse kitchen towel. He ran his fingers through his springy hair and grinned at Harold.

'Reckon that'll do. C'm on.'

They went out into the early morning. It was chilly and they pulled their jackets round them and walked fast to get their circulation going. There was more life out on the streets than there had been last night. A stream of workers slamming their front doors on their homes for another day, then dropping their heads to stare at the pavements as they walked so that they could daydream on their way to drudgery. There were precious few greetings exchanged, even among close neighbours. One and all would rather have stayed tucked up in their creaking beds, so what was the point in wishing each other 'Good morning.' It wouldn't be, that was one thing to be certain of: it would be another, ordinary, horrible one.

Harold and Arthur sat down companionably on the bench. At the very edge of the park, they had reached a vantage-point from where they could look down on the happenings on the river in front of the brewery. There was life already astir. A thin line of smoke ran straight up from the galley chimney on a tethered barge. There wasn't a breath of air on the river.

As Arthur fastened his pipe between his teeth a church bell chimed six. That meant Harold had an hour and a half before he must arrive ready for work. He had a brush and comb in a cubby-hole there. There had been other nights when he'd not been home to change. In any case, he'd only worn the shirt he had on now for four days. It was good for another three at least.

Arthur had a way with him. He showed that he appreciated Harold's intelligence; he was obviously impressed at his position as clerk. However, impressed or not, Arthur still managed, bit by bit, to make Harold see that his own thoughts of money-making had been small beer. Very small beer. In a rush of confidences, Harold revealed how furious he'd been at the coursing when the brandy run had refused to take on illicit Bradbury beer. Even as he said it to Arthur he saw for himself how pathetic Luke must have thought him. Beer, well it was a question of pence rather than the sovereigns they dealt in. Harold fell silent and shame started to burn in him. How had he ever thought he could make his fortune that way?

'Too slow,' Arthur said, as if reading his very thoughts, 'too slow by half.'

Then, as insinuating as woodsmoke, Arthur spoke

softly on the morning air. There was a way, he said. A certain way to make them rich. Rich like Midas. With fried breakfasts every morning, and furs for their women. Harold could just see Lavender wrapped up in furs. Arthur had a friend. A grand friend. A man of considerable substance, who wasn't averse to putting a bit of good luck their way. The key to it all was the brewery.

All this friend wanted was some information. He'd pay for that. A few sovereigns to start with. Then he'd put them on to the real big time. Harold owed it to himself, Arthur said, and to Lavender. Dear sweet Lavender, who shouldn't live on that rotten street. She deserved a new villa out by Bearsted and nice, pretty clothes and a girl to help in the house. Harold's mind painted pictures of a life of incomparable bliss. It was easy, said Arthur. He'd be travelling back to London this morning. Harold could start gathering his information today. Hoarding it like a squirrel. Then once a week writing it all down. The figures of the business, the stocks, the bills. Any thoughts that Harold might have as to future plans for the brewery. Harold was to imagine that he was writing a record of the brewery like an instruction book, to show another man how to run one. Then he wouldn't miss out any of the important bits.

Harold nodded, listening intently. He took the address for his correspondence that Arthur handed him. He would not allow himself to imagine the delights that awaited him, not yet.

They parted, shaking hands like the men of business they were. It was just before half past seven. Harold would have to run, but he didn't mind. He wanted to shout and cheer, but he kept it rich inside him and began the day by dedicating himself anew to the pursuit of profit. His own.

Arthur walked back to the terraced house where

Lavender was still in bed. As he climbed the stairs he edged his braces over his shoulders. Lavender was waiting for him.

'My brother,' she squealed in amusement. 'My brother, ooh my eye,' as he slipped under the sheets beside her. 'Just as well you're bleedin' not,' she said as she wriggled down beside him with a sigh.

Lucinda looked thoughtfully at her reflection in the long mirror. The ivory silk of her dress set off the pearl pink of her skin to perfection and made her auburn hair a crown of colour. But her eyes were narrowed in irritation and a thin line had formed on her porcelain forehead.

Michael was being difficult. He would have to change after their marriage. But then after their marriage she would not have to be so subtle in her questioning. She had wanted to know what colour gemstones would be in the family jewels that she would inevitably be given this evening. In her hands she slowly twisted the thin diamond necklet that Papa had chosen as being utterly suitable to have removed by her husband-to-be prior to adorning her lovely neck with the Montford heirlooms. And her neck was very lovely; she turned slightly to appreciate how stalk-like it was for the flower of her face. She would have been pleased at a little more colour on her cheeks, perhaps, but she caught sight in the mirror of Maude hovering behind her. Any artifice Lucinda would add in private; Maude had yet to prove capable of total devotion. Lucinda suspected that the girl still carried tales to the other servants in the house. Well, if she did, then she wouldn't be taken to Pencombe when Lucinda went to take up her residence there.

Lucinda deliberately curved her lips into a smile, opened her eyes very wide: the radiant innocence of her reflection delighted her. Maude could do the honours now and place the diamonds around her neck, and tell her how beautiful she was. Later Michael would perform a similar function. He could scarcely fail to fall madly, head over heels, in love with her all over again. A tiny worm of thought wriggled that possibly 'madly' and 'head over heels' did not quite describe his feeling for her; but that notion she quickly dismissed as nonsense. No one could fail to love her, as a final look in the mirror convinced her.

Michael could be dealt with after the wedding, brought to heel like one of his precious labradors. She turned and swept out in a rustle of silk, leaving the scent of roses to fill her empty room.

Pencombe Hall was ablaze with lights. Every window shone brightly, torches flared at the castle doors thrown wide open in welcome. Carriages pulled to a halt with a flourish to deliver the invited guests in billows of silks and satins, the glorious reds and blues of uniform mixed with the more restrained evening wear of the men who would stay behind. A madcap gaiety breathed life into the usually empty halls. The shrill voices of over-excited ladies reached to the very remotest corners. Music escaped through the leaded windows and trickled up over the battlements in a torrent of delight.

Lucinda stepped forward, her hand resting on her father's arm, aglow with pride. This was all for her, this was her night. Even the sky was studded with diamonds and the air was as soft as silk on her shoulders. She wasn't walking but gliding, and everyone she passed acknowledged her beauty, her success. Michael greeted her with visible humility and Lord Montford actually kissed her cheek. She was introduced to a bony woman swathed in brown velvet with an incredible headpiece of ostrich feathers balanced on greying hair. This was Hermione. Why had Lucinda worried about this meeting when the earl's sister was so obviously instantly captivated, like everyone else? In a glorious dream she was greeted by all, her peers and her minions, but nowhere, nowhere now, were there superiors.

She was on Michael's arm, at the head of the great hall, when the orchestra fell silent and his lordship clapped his hands for attention.

'I beg you raise your glasses,' the old man called, resplendent in the uniform he had worn all those years before in India. 'I give you, Lucinda and Michael, may God bless them.'

The cheer rose higher than the vaulted roof above them and out over the Pencombe acres. Lucinda turned and smiled up at Michael, and he turned his head to look down at her. He was dazzlingly handsome in his close-fitting scarlet uniform, distinguished as that of the Royal West Kent (Queen's Own) Regiment by its dark blue facings. A thrill of pure pleasure made her quiver like a filly foal.

Another clap for silence from her future father-in-law. 'Pray raise your glasses for a toast to our glorious army. I give you,' he held his glass aloft, the old soldier saluting the new, 'the brave young men of England.'

The cheering rang out like the Sunday bells and Lucinda felt tears of pride on her heated cheeks. They would always be linked together in her mind: the glory of England that was hers for ever, and brave, brave Michael who would make her so proud that her heart might burst.

The ceremony of the jewels was to be a private, family affair, so they left the guests enjoying their champagne.

Michael put his arm around Lucinda's waist as they made their way to the billiard room. She was so pale that he was concerned she might faint. Sweet, innocent Michael, Lucinda thought, unaware that it was not the excitement that was inhibiting her breathing, but the tight lacing of her corsets.

The Bradbury sisters had not been in the billiard room

before; it was a late addition to the house, built some eighty years previously. Being on the far side of the public rooms from the main body of the house it was a kind of cul-de-sac, the most private room in the house. Conversations conducted in it were the least likely to be overheard by servants and it had soon become the traditional venue for family occasions requiring privacy. Lucinda hardly noticed her new surroundings, but Isabella felt oddly depressed by its gloom, while being impressed by its grandeur.

The room was magnificent in terms of size and proportion. Dark panelled walls led up to a high vaulted ceiling. The perfume of age-old cigar smoke mingled with the sweetness of dry rot. But it was a room that echoed with emptiness. It was not a snug gentlemen's sanctum, like Eli's room at Linstone. Even the billiard table seemed spartan, despite the multi-coloured arrangement of snooker balls.

Hermione's bewhiskered husband, 'the walrus' as Isabella had secretly named him, let out a cry of amusement. 'Good God! I haven't seen a table like this in heaven knows how long. My God, Hermione, your brother's still living in the Dark Ages.'

'Sssh,' his wife hissed, but far too late for his lordship's sensitivities, as he entered the room to march towards the table, now the centre of their attention.

He lay a veined hand protectively on the baize, feeling the wood beneath it. 'Let me tell you, George,' he said, pausing infinitesimally before the word, 'George'. He disliked calling the man by his Christian name. It implied an intimacy that he certainly did not feel. 'Let me tell you I am proud of this table. It has been in the family for many, many years. It has seen us Montfords come and go. Yes indeed, it has been the dumb participant in many of the pages of our family history.' He was staring down, stroking the surface. For once he was vulnerable: uncalled-for memories were suddenly vivid, as green as yesterday, as green as the cloth.

Eli felt the pause had gone on long enough; this was an evening for celebration not maudlin reminiscing. 'Yes, well,' he started in his heartiest manner, 'I expect Michael will want to have it brought up to date now, won't you Michael?'

Lucinda felt his arm stiffen around her waist.

'You can have a slate put on those legs. No one plays on baize laid on wood any more: too uneven,' Eli continued. 'They're certainly strong enough to stand it.'

He walked forwards as he talked, both he and George bending to survey the acanthus carved legs, which they touched and prodded. Lord Montford was for once totally at one with his sons; it was as if the undertaker had arrived to measure the body before death had occurred.

'They make a very good job of these tables, you know; rubber cushions, new felt, excellent, excellent,' Eli went on, to George's loud agreement.

His lordship stared down at the faint brown stain where his father had spilt a glass of port the night he'd collapsed and died in this very room. And how often as a child had he sneaked in here to stroke the soft cloth, with an ecstasy born of terror, for to be caught was to be punished. The thought suddenly struck him that his sons might well have done the same thing. He looked at each of them in turn. Their young faces prematurely aged above their uniforms, it was, perhaps, a difficult night for them. He hadn't considered that until now.

Hermione came to him, holding out the velvet boxes. He hadn't even seen their contents till now. What did it matter? They were the price for keeping the estate together by using Eli's money; they and his eldest son were the price. He took the boxes she offered, and decided to get this over and then go to bed. He'd had enough festivities for one night; he felt old, suddenly quite old.

Michael's hands trembled almost imperceptibly as he opened the largest box. God only knew what his father had done to fund these baubles. Hermione wouldn't have just given them out of love; George was too sharp a fellow to allow that. The box had an awkward clasp, which he fumbled with for a moment, then it opened. He slowly lifted the layer of bright white tissue. Lying on the snow-bright satin the necklace glowed like ice fire. The gem-stones were of the purest blue he had ever seen, and seemed to dance with life. He lifted the necklace slowly: it was heavy with an intricate white gold setting, a large pear-shaped stone forming the centrepiece, while smaller, matching stones adorned the wrought chain. It was a masterpiece. He looked up at his father, whose aged eyes seemed for a moment to reflect the brightness, but then filmed over.

'It's beautiful.' It was Isabella who said the words, broke the spell, as Michael moved forwards to put it round Lucinda's neck. The necklace had a life of its own as it touched her body. The crystal heart of it hung between her swelling breasts; she felt its touch deep inside. She felt alive, aglow.

'You're beautiful,' Johnnie said, breaking the silence. 'You're as dazzling as the necklace, Lucinda.'

Michael seemed unable to speak, overwhelmed by the occasion.

Isabella came towards her sister and kissed her cheek softly. 'Yes, you are lovely,' she said. 'Michael, you're very lucky. You must take care of her, for all of us.'

Eli watched his future son-in-law as Isabella spoke. The boy was confused: it must be the occasion, or perhaps simply love. Or yet again, perhaps it was the thought of tomorrow and of leaving all this for the reality of war.

Then it was over, and the family rejoined the ball. Michael led Lucinda out on to the empty floor in the centre of their guests, left for them alone. His arm was firm round her waist and he was looking down, so strangely, into her eyes. They began to dance and the dancing seemed like heaven. Lucinda wished it could go on for ever as the other couples joined them on the floor and they circled on the stone-flagged floors of the magnificent house that was to be her home.

The moonlight streamed down from a black, velvet sky touching the rose-covered walls with silver.

Isabella breathed lightly, the air as bubbly as the champagne she'd just sipped to toast Lucinda and Michael. The evening chill touched her bare shoulders making her uneasily aware of their nakedness. She pulled her hand from Johnnie's proprietorial clasp to pull a little of the ruched net up higher to her throat.

'Don't fiddle with it, Issy. You look quite beautiful, you know, out here in the moonlight.' Johnnie was staring out into the dark; he seemed on edge this evening, not quite his usual jolly self.

Issy laughed. 'I see, I need the dark to look beautiful, do I? Thank you very much.'

He turned to look at her. He was barely a couple of inches taller than she, but suddenly he seemed to Isabella to be towering above her. 'Don't tease, Issy. You are beautiful, you know. Beautiful in a strange, remote sort of way.' He reached out and slowly pulled her close, very close, to his chest. Isabella could feel his fingers gripping tightly into her arms. 'It's a night for beauty, Issy, can't you feel it?' His face came down towards hers. She would have turned away, but he put a finger gently under her chin; incredibly she seemed bound by it; where a strong hold would have made her struggle, the featherlight touch held her still.

'Issy, Issy.' Then his lips were on hers, tenderly, fleetingly. She felt the cool hardness of them, then her own lips softened and they moulded to each other. Her eyes had closed, head bent back she felt herself part of the warm night, a creature of abandon. Deeper she slipped into the waking dream, deeper into an ocean of sensation.

Then the kissing stopped, he put his arm tightly around her, and they were hurrying towards the dark, dark shadow of the gatehouse. Johnnie's urgency was in every step; the breeze pulled at Isabella's hair and suddenly the dream was broken.

'Let me go, Johnnie, we must go back in, please.' She struggled an arm free and started to push at him, but this was not the tender Johnnie she knew any more. They had nearly reached the overwhelming darkness of the gatehouse. 'Please, please.' She was struggling in earnest now. 'Johnnie, they'll be looking for us, you know they will.'

'For Christ's sake,' his voice was hoarse, strangled by his own emotion. 'Issy, for Christ's sake, hundreds of men and women in England will be making love tonight, tomorrow we'll be gone. I don't know how many of us will be coming back, Issy. God, I need someone to hold me.' His voice was breaking, he was near to tears. 'Issy, help me.'

In a rush of sympathy Isabella held him close, willing her own strength into him. His face was pressed against her neck, his voice almost buried by her hair that had been shaken loose to fall into a jumble of golden curls. She felt the press of the stone wall against her back, but all her being was now concentrated on dispensing healing balm. 'It's all right, Johnnie, it's all right, you'll come home to us. I know you will.'

His hands were caressing her. Her head dropped back

to let him kiss her neck; she could feel the manhood returning to him; there was no yesterday, no tomorrow. Then suddenly, cutting across them like a knife in the dark, close at hand came a girl's shrill giggle, followed by a man's husky laugh. The girl's laugh had been coarse-pitched: it was the servants at their own play. Johnnie stepped back as if stung, leaving Isabella so suddenly that she nearly fell to the ground, only saved by the wall behind her.

They were aware of the world again, Isabella's hands flew to straightening her dress, and desperately tried to make sense of her tangled hair. Johnnie stood as if turned to stone; the moon moved on its path and the silver light crept round the curve of the gatehouse wall, but Isabella had no time to watch the struggle it illuminated on his face.

'I must find somewhere to straighten my hair, Johnnie.' Her whisper alerted the other couple who had been taking advantage of the dark, and they could hear footsteps slipping away. 'Please, find me somewhere with a mirror. My goodness, I must have lost most of my pins; I must get straight before we go back in.'

His hand shot out suddenly and gripped her so fiercely that she nearly cried out, but the thought of others in the shadows stopped her.

'Don't go back in, Issy. I'll find somewhere better, somewhere private.'

'Don't be silly.' Realism had flooded like a cold sharp shower over her. 'We've been gone long enough for gossip, any longer and they'll send out a search party. You don't really want us to be the laughing-stock of Kent, do you?'

He didn't reply, but he didn't have to: he had let go of her arm and that was assent enough.

They found that the back door to the buttery was

unlocked and Isabella slipped thankfully through it. There was a scrap of mirror hanging on the whitewashed wall for the servant girls to check their hair before going upstairs to serve at family dinners. Fortunately there was no service upstairs this evening so it was a quiet haven for Isabella to survey the damage. Johnnie mounted a sulking guard at the door. He seemed to have regained his normal confidence and was merely acting out his wounded pride. Isabella darted looks at him in the mirror, but he wasn't prepared to meet her gaze. At last, after what seemed an unbearably long time to Isabella, she managed to arrange her hair in a semblance of dignity and she turned to go.

'Will you marry me, Isabella?' Johnnie's face was flushed, he looked almost as if he had been drinking, but it was a different stimulant that had sent the colour rushing to his face.

'Is that really a proposal?'

'Yes.'

Isabella felt suddenly inspired to smile. 'Well, it's not the way I'd imagined it might be. I mean, I had in mind an elegant conservatory, and my beau on his knees, you know.'

Johnnie wasn't answering her smile, so hers wavered.

'You don't want to marry me you know, Johnnie. You don't love me, do you?'

He stood his ground by the door, looking very serious. 'I do, you know, Issy. It might not be what you imagine love to be, but I do, you know.'

It seemed to be quite unreal to Isabella, standing discussing love as if it were the date of the next hunt ball or some other social occasion here, within the oldest part of the castle, where its damp stone sent a chill seeping up through her thin-soled dancing shoes. It didn't seem she could be talking of her own future at all. The total unreality of it decided her.

'I shall not marry you, Johnnie. It wouldn't be right for either of us. Marriage should be based on real love, which if we felt for each other would make it impossible for us to stand here so calmly talking about it. We don't love each other, Johnnie, not like that.' She dropped her eyes suddenly, remembering. 'Out there in the garden we were in love with the night. It was as if we were strangers.' Her voice hardened suddenly. With awful clarity she saw the future she felt he was imagining for them. 'No, I won't marry you, Johnnie, just so you can stable your horses here and hunt the estate, and we'll live at the beck and call of Lucinda.'

Her voice had risen and Johnnie's answer came quickly. 'That's it, isn't it? It's Lucinda. You're jealous that she'll be lady of the manor, and you'll be the poor relation. It's nothing to do with me, or what our families want, or how I made you feel out there in the garden. And don't pretend to yourself, Isabella. It was me who broke away first; you were mine for the taking and but for some bloody, interfering whim of God's, you'd be mine right now. I'll go away to my war, and I'll come back, you were right there. But when I do, I'll think very carefully before I offer again. You think about that, Issy. You wanted me as much as I wanted you, but it might have to be you who begs next time.'

He spun on his polished heel and was gone, leaving Isabella shaking. He was right, the realization surged up in her. She would have accepted him, have become part of the passion herself. The cold from the stone walls was eating into her; she took one final glance in the mirror before setting off back to the ballroom. Her face was deadly pale, her nostrils pinched. It was not the face of passion spent. She could say to her father that she had felt unwell and be utterly believed. Now it was becoming true. A wave of nausea passed over her that was close to

101

self-disgust. A well brought up girl like herself should not have feelings like a wanton servant girl.

She slipped silently out through the buttery door, back into the jostle and the noise. She must perform her act well: it was Lucinda's night, hers and Papa's and she did not want to spoil it for either of them.

There was nothing after the ball for Johnnie and Michael except the train to the docks. Their father had gone to bed almost earlier than was polite. He had looked old. Michael had had a fleeting thought that they might never see him again and his grievances against the old man melted in the warmth of filial affection. He'd do his best out there; whatever happened he would remember that the old man loved a bit of glory.

They took their brandies with them as they went back to the billiard room, now returned to sanctity by the intruders' absence. For the brothers it was as hallowed as a church. Its peace as healing. Their play was ritualistic, their movements slow in the dim light; restricted by their uniforms, there was none of the cut and thrust of youth. If there had been family portraits in the room, then many of the men would have sympathized with the dulling of the senses that the drink and the play brought them. They were suspended, timeless.

The door opened quietly, reverentially. Mathew, the butler, was as steeped in tradition as they themselves were. But for once in his ordered life, he had omitted to perform a commission he had been given and as Master Michael would be leaving in the morning, it was one he had to perform now, in the early hours.

Mathew had been lying warm in his bed, running slowly through the events of the evening in his mind, on the border of sleep, when his omission had come to him. He'd had to get up and dress again to fulfil it, but it was a

102

little thing to do for Michael, whom he secretly loved as if the young man were his son.

He cleared his throat to alert the gentlemen to his presence, without actually interrupting them.

Johnnie looked up first, through the cigar smoke haze that hung over their field of play. 'Good God, Mathew, what on earth are you doing up at this hour? Don't tell me that's just arrived?' Johnnie was referring to the brown wrapped parcel Mathew had brought in on his silver tray.

'No, Master Johnnie, this is a parcel for Master Michael. I was asked to deliver it at the end of the ball, but there didn't seem to be the time or place.'

Trust Mathew never to actually say he'd forgotten, Michael smiled at the old man's vanity. 'Well, you can hand it over now then, and get back to bed, providing of course you are going to bed.'

'Yes, Master Michael.' The parcel delivered, the butler left soundlessly. This time he did not bother undressing and getting into bed, but wrapped a blanket around himself and sat up in the chair in his room. After a while he drifted off, to dream of the boys running through the rooms of the great house, children still. It was sad when they had to grow up and go to war, very sad.

Michael opened the parcel. He had known what it was the moment he saw it. He felt touched by the gesture and annoyed that Johnnie was here to see him open it, for he knew that his brother would misunderstand. Inside was Isabella's camera, as well as an article from the *Illustrated London News* which explained that many photographs were being sent back from the war to be interpreted by their magazine artists. Apparently more and more amateurs were using cameras out in Africa.

It was ideal that Michael should have hers, thought Isabella. There were still at least ninety pictures to take with the film. But all the same, she doubted if Johnnie would understand, however much he'd made it plain he wasn't interested in the camera.

She was quite right. He didn't understand at all.

'Don't go straight to bed, Issy. Come and talk to me.' Lucinda sat hunched up on the end of her bed. Her voice was high with tension, and she sounded close to breaking point.

Isabella was longing for the privacy of her own bedroom, but Lucinda clearly needed her. It wasn't surprising, Isabella thought, for Lucinda had been belle of the ball, and had lost her beau for heaven knows how long, all in the same short evening.

The girls shooed away Maude's ministrations, as neither of them had the energy to answer her questions. So Maude had to go to her narrow bed in the attic with very few facts to tell her fellow girl servants, eagerly awaiting snippets of gossip. Maude, as was her way, invented more than enough to fill their already crowded imaginations.

Isabella fetched a silver-backed brush from the dressing table and took to brushing Lucinda's long auburn hair. It had calmed her sister in childhood and it seemed only natural that it would calm her now. But Lucinda fidgeted beneath the soothing brushstrokes and before Isabella had counted to twenty rhythmic strokes, she had had enough and had left Isabella to look at her own reflection in the mirror. Isabella turned abruptly away. She'd no wish to see her own pinched and tired reflection.

'You're too excited to sleep, Lucy. Why don't you let me send for Maude to get you some hot milk?'

Lucinda spun round, wide-eyed in irritation. 'Damn Maude, damn the hot milk. I just want to talk, Issy, can't you understand that? My God, I just need someone to talk to; that's not too much to ask of you, is it?'

'Don't swear, Lucy, you know Mama hated it.'

'Now just don't bring her into it.' Lucinda was almost spitting in fury as she hurled the word 'her' at Isabella, who was shattered by the ferocity of it.

'Lucy, don't, you know you don't mean to speak like that. You love Mama.'

'She's dead, Issy, dead and long gone, eaten up by worms. I'm alive, oh too alive.' Lucinda hugged her arms around her own body, squeezing tightly. 'I've never been more alive and all you can do is go on about the dead. Leave it alone, Issy, leave me to make my own life. I want to live by my own rules.' She threw herself face down on her great soft bed and sobbed loudly, her shoulders heaving, then she pulled herself up to shout again at Isabella, her face streaked with tears. 'You're so cold, Issy, you don't know what being a woman is really like; no one really knows, except me.'

'That's silly, Lucy, really silly. You're not the only woman whose loved one is going off to the war in the morning. There are hundreds of others and lots of them have got children to think of too.'

'Oh, so now you're going to tell me to think about others, are you, or is it that you're sad for your poor Johnnie? Well, don't for one instant, not one tiny instant, imagine that you're suffering anything like me. I know what love is, Issy, real love, and I would have, I wanted to . . .' There was no one she could tell her pain to. No one who would understand, as Michael had not understood. It was not a sacrifice that she had offered him this evening: she had been longing to give herself to him, to be truly all for him, but he would not accept her. He lived by rules, he said, and his rules forbade that he should take advantage of her. Take advantage!

There in the dust and decay of the billiard room where Michael had taken her for their private goodbye, a gentle kiss. That was all he'd taken. The smell and gloom of the room were jumbled in her mind with the trembling passion she'd felt well up in her. The necklace, heavy between her flushed breasts, had burned like ice. She'd pressed her body so fiercely to his, wishing with all her being to fire Michael with the same burning passion, that the stone had bruised her heated skin. She'd torn it from her neck the moment she'd reached home. Fresh tears started as she remembered too vividly how she had ached to melt into his arms, and she had no one to comfort her, no one at all. So she buried her face deeper in the soft bed and cried again.

Isabella came closer to her, and eventually sat down on the edge of the bed, but Lucinda paid her no attention at all, and just kept on sobbing. Isabella's mind was whirling. She had never for one moment imagined, deep down inside, that Lucinda loved Michael. She didn't believe that Lucinda was capable of the kind of love that Isabella had told Johnnie was her ideal. She stared down at Lucinda still crying. She could understand her excitement: the role of lady of the manor would suit her utterly. She could understand Lucinda's loving glances, her coy delight in Michael's apparent aloofness, at being the chosen one of the heir of Pencombe. But Isabella did not believe her sister capable of a great, all-consuming love, except perhaps for herself.

Eventually Lucinda's shoulders stopped shaking and after a little while she sat up, dabbing at her eyes with a lawn handkerchief. 'You're no good in a crisis, Issy, none at all,' she said accusingly. 'It's a bad failing. You'll have to do better when we're all at Pencombe. Michael is bound to be busy with the estate, and I'll need company. That'll be your responsibility. We'll all have new responsibilities and that will be yours. Be a dear and ring for Maude, I'd like that milk now.'

'But Lucy, it's past four in the morning.'

'Yes, I know, and I really do need my sleep or I'll feel awful tomorrow so do hurry up. And tell Maude to put sugar in it, sometimes she forgets.' Lucinda had recovered her petulance.

There was no point, Isabella knew, in asking her sister to let Maude have even a few hours' uninterrupted sleep. First, the girl had been told to stay up for their return, which had been quite unnecessary: Isabella and Lucinda had taken their own clothes off for many more years than they'd had paid help to do it. Now she was to be dragged out of bed to warm up some milk, and then she'd have to be up with the others at six to get this great house ready and prepared for three people who couldn't possibly use more than a few rooms. All Isabella could do was look her most apologetic to a bedraggled Maude who appeared with her hair tied in rags to take her commands. And all Isabella got for her pains was a venomous glare from the girl, while Lucinda got her glass of hot milk, nicely sugared and with the skin carefully removed from the top.

'Before you go, Issy, you'd better tell me what kind of evening you had. I'm afraid I was much too busy to notice.' Lucinda stirred her milk slowly, then took the spoon and licked at it, like a cat. 'Did Johnnie plight his troth and all that sort of thing?'

Isabella was too tired to pretend. She had meant to construct a carefully-worded explanation for Lucinda, but the words just tumbled out. 'He asked me to marry him, if that's what you mean, and I said no. You must have known I would,' she went on desperately as the look of incredulous disbelief on Lucinda's face turned to puce indignation. 'I can't marry someone I don't love and I don't love Johnnie. He's nice and jolly and all that sort of thing, but I don't love him and I never will, so there's no point in your going on at me.' She had reached the bedroom door and clutched at its handle. Lucinda's eyes

107

were slits; she was in a real rage, the sort Isabella could only flee from.

'You'll marry Johnnie if I have to drag you to the altar by your hair.'

Isabella wrenched the door open, threw one final look over her shoulder and fled down the corridor.

Isabella let the open book fall out of her hands and on to her lap. It was no good, the words danced on the page before her. The poet seemed to have penned the line especially for her, 'July, boyling like to fire,' he had written, and it was.

Through the open window in front of her the sun dazzled on a thousand flowers. The herbaceous border seemed to float in a haze of yellows and reds, and the apple trees beyond were a dark, Elizabethan green, their trunks dappled with grey. It was impossible to stay indoors. Even the coolness of the shadowed room was not enough to tempt her to remain shut away from it all. And the house was so empty. Only the faintest mouse-like noises of the servants, slowly performing their duties, touched the silence.

The only question was whether she should take her sketch pad out into the garden. She would not take the watercolour that was taking shape so well in the privacy of her room. It was becoming a private picture for Isabella, although she had intended at first to give it as a present to Papa. For the prie-dieu chair that formed a focal point of the composition was Mama's very special piece of furniture, and the child lying so pale and delicate, was the best portrait Isabella had so far painted. It made her smile to think of him. Timmy was such an adventurous boy, clambering over the traction engines, missing death a thousand times a day from the great spinning wheels. Yet captured in paint he was an angel. Thomas had found him for her, asleep under the hedge after a morning's work. His brown chubby hands were clutching the edge of his ragged shirt, and Isabella had sketched him quickly, catching the clasp to perfection. In her painting, he held the edge of a coverlet, laid lightly over the child who was so appropriate a subject for the title, 'The Vigil'. The scrap of handkerchief, whose lace border had been so difficult for Isabella, lay on the floor beside the empty chair, and showed where the mother had left, only for an instant, the sleeping child. Isabella breathed in with a tremor. She was so pleased with it, yet the essential poignancy of it upset her; her nerves were very acute. It was probably the heat, and being alone.

She had been alone a lot over the past few weeks. Her solitude had begun the day after the Pencombe boys went off to war. Lucinda and Papa had become inseparable, and their travels continuous, in search of new grandeur for Pencombe. Lucinda had insisted Isabella should remain at home. It was unthinkable, she said, that the house should be left to the servants, which was a ridiculous notion, but Isabella supposed understandable. Lucinda was continually difficult these days, waiting impatiently for the post to arrive each day, and then, on those occasions when a precious letter did appear, she would hurry off to read it in secret. Isabella had no idea how Michael was faring, except that he was well. 'Fine' as Lucinda put it, with bright spots of colour on her cheeks, her head held high as if to dare contradiction.

When Johnnie's letters arrived they were all addressed to Lucinda, and Isabella was told the contents of those, in minute, drawn-out detail. Johnnie was shooting Boers, Johnnie thought the country magnificent. Then one day, Johnnie was injured, a shot in the arm, or 'the wing' as he had put it. Isabella had wanted to write and express her sympathy, but Johnnie was making it clear by his continued correspondence with Lucinda that he was still hurt by her refusal to marry him.

Eventually, Isabella decided to leave her sketching indoors and walked out into the sunlight with only her book of poetry for company. The moment she stepped into the garden she felt uncomfortably hot. She ran a finger around the inside of her high muslin neckline. It felt damp, and her sleeves were much too tight. She could feel the imprint of each and every seam in the fitted bodice rubbing against her over-heated skin. It was no good, she would have to wear something lighter, but what?

Before she could think any further, she caught sight of a dog-cart making its slow way up the rutted lane. It would then pass along the side boundary of the garden, so it must be someone making for the cottages.

She screwed up her eyes to see against the glare. The horse and its burden disappeared for a moment behind the stone dovecot. Then it was for a brief stretch of rutted road in full sight; the driver was flicking at the horse's back with his whip and it shook its head in irritation. It was making a reasonable speed on the rock-hard, pitted ground and did not need any further urging. As if compelled to motion herself by the crack of the whip, she set off across the lawn that was so dry she could feel it crunching beneath her feet.

She went through the wicket gate and out on to the cart track. It was the walk that she and the others had taken when they first saw the traction engine. It seemed strange now that in those days the noise had surprised them. The rolling clatter of the machines at work had become a constant background to summer, part of the heat of it all. She could hear an engine now. There must be one working in the field with the blasted oak. Isabella walked desultorily in the dust. It had worked its way into her flimsy slippers already and was gritty between her toes. If

110

Lucinda were here she would shriek at the sight of her sister in such incongruous footwear. The satin toes that peeped beneath the muslin hem were ridiculous, but Isabella was too hot to conform to decorum.

To cool herself she let her mind wander to a lofty studio, where she imagined herself, paintbrush in hand, loosely smocked, at work on a large newly-started canvas. She applied the brush to her palette. Who would be the subject? As her feet left their patterns in the dust, she drifted further into her waking dream. She could see a vague form, sitting for her in a fine, well-made chair by William Morris, too new for her father's taste, but what Isabella imagined for her ideal sanctum. The features of the man swam slowly into focus. For it was a man; a mist seemed slowly to clear, and of course, it was . . . Isabella stopped with a shock, her heart thundering.

Nonsense, nonsense. She shook her head to shake the stupidity out of it. She hurried forwards. It was not in her heart to imagine that he was there. He was not hers to imagine. With a smile of intense gratitude she saw Thomas ahead of her, leaning over a gate, shirtless, brown as a gypsy. She had no thought for the propriety of greeting him in his undress, being so intensely relieved at finding someone to take her thoughts away from how close she had drifted to treachery.

'Ah, the fair Isabella, and what are you doing straying out of doors on such a beautiful day? You'll end up as brown as I am if you're not careful.' Thomas touched his chest proudly. There was no embarrassment about him that he should appear with hardly any clothes on in front of a lady. But then, why should there be? This was his fiefdom that Isabella was walking into. Papa had very happily rented off their orchards to Thomas, and that meant that walks outside the garden now were walks into Cade's country.

111

Thomas turned away from Isabella to lean on the gate and look out over the land. At the bottom of the hill one of his engines had faltered to an unaccustomed halt. Isabella could just make out the shape of Timmy clambering over it.

'I'm going to walk down past the cottages; you know, the ones at the bottom of the lane. It's shady there so it should be cool.'

Thomas spun round. 'Don't go down there just now, Isabella.' He looked unusually stern and it irritated Isabella, as did the trickle of sweat she could feel running between her breasts.

'What do you mean? Of course I shall go down there. The cottagers may be your workers, but the cottages are ours still. I shall go where I please.'

'You do just that then, Isabella, but don't say I didn't warn you.' Thomas turned back away from her, just as the engine at the bottom of the hill burst into life again, and Timmy slithered off the top of it down to the ground. 'It's about time anyway,' he continued, apparently addressing the cornfield, 'about time that you learned that country living isn't all paintboxes and blue skies.' Then he was silent and Isabella was hurrying away down the lane, damning him under her breath.

The cottages were in a huddle on one side of the lane. They were a jumble of unequal sizes, and where there were only five separate dwellings on the estate plans it seemed that at least eight families lived in them. On the opposite side of the lane a motley collection of wooden huts was home for an assortment of pigs, a couple of dozen scavenging hens and a small flock of immaculate white ducks that waddled away from Isabella's approach. How they maintained their pristine whiteness, when all the human occupants were grimy, and the pigs mud-encrusted, was beyond Isabella's comprehension. The cottages had a deserted air. The men were out in the fields and, today being market day in Maidstone, the women had gone off, laughingly pressed up against each other on the top of an aged cart, bearing their small produce, the sale of which supplemented the men's wages. The only sounds were a few droning bees and a faint snuffling from the hawthorn bushes at the edge of the first cottage.

In incongruous splendour, the dog-cart waited in the dust. The horse, which was little more than a pony in height, had dropped its head to doze in the sun. It was blinkered and did not bother to turn its head at Isabella's approach. She walked up to stroke his nose. 'Hallo, old boy,' she spoke softly, feeling suddenly awkward, the tiny windows placed apparently at random in the tile-hung cottage walls seeming to spy on her.

The horse adjusted its stance slowly, setting up a miniature dust cloud that tickled Isabella's nose. She dabbed at it with her handkerchief, sniffed, but to no avail: she sneezed explosively. The noise in the hawthorn bush stopped instantly. It was as if the world was listening to her. She froze, her hand just resting on the horse's warm, flat face. She realized that she was holding her breath as if she could catch the sounds of life. And there was a faint, alien sound. It could almost have been the traction engine, rhythmic and distant. But there was another quality to it she could not quite recognize, a squeaking, like metal grinding, that would never have been tolerated in Thomas's engines.

The horse moved suddenly beneath her hand, throwing its head up, nostrils distended, alertness spread throughout its body and a shiver ran over its flanks. The suddenness convinced Isabella; she would return home.

As she bent to lift her skirts out of the dust, a movement behind the carriage caught her eye. The horse shied forwards knocking her back. She had just time to throw

113

herself sideways before the nearside wheel swept so close to her that it snagged her dress. She pulled at her skirt in alarm. Then the cause of the horse's fright came horrifyingly into sight and sound. With a Gadarene squeal a pair of mangy, mud-encrusted pigs hobbled into view.

They were obscenely joined, the boar throwing back his tusked, orange head to squeal in fury as his mate, bearing all his weight except that carried by the boar's scrabbling back legs, endeavoured to escape. But the pair were inseparable in their coupling. The sow's low, empty teats banged at the ground as she scrabbled her way forwards, closer and closer to Isabella who was pulling herself back ino the thorny hedge in horror. Drops of spittle flew from the creature's foam-flecked jaws as she shook herself frantically, and still the male on her back squealed in his ecstasy.

With a resounding crash the largest window in the cottages opposite her was flung open. Now high up on the verge where she had clambered, she was almost on a level with the first-floor window from where a shout of fury announced the presence of a man. A man who was pink and swollen like the pig, whose very face seemed snoutlike. His naked form was a mountain of flesh, roll upon roll of porklike flesh formed his centre part. In utter disbelief Isabella's eyes were drawn down to the swollen manhood, and as she covered her mouth to hide the scream he saw her. His eyes gleamed like the boar's, his mouth seemed to overrun with saliva. Then with a grinding of iron bedsprings a girl, little more than a child, appeared at his side, clutching a thin sheet to her nakedness. She was grinning with excitement at the clamour. The man turned his back on Isabella, revealing a bottom as loosely hung as that of the boar which had fallen from its ride in the commotion and was standing shuddering from exertion, as if it had been chilled rather than over-

114

heated. He thrust the girl down from the window and pulled the casement to behind him, but it was too late: Isabella had fled back up the track.

She clutched her skirts up to her, leaving her legs free so that she could run, run. She nearly tripped in one of the deepest ruts and threw out a hand to stop herself. She felt the stone tear into her flesh, but didn't stop or pause; she ran on again as if the Devil was after her. Tears were blurring her view now. She rubbed a dust-covered hand over them to clear her eyes and smeared her face with the blood running freely from the cut. Her hair pulled its way loose, her slippers tore and then she was running to Thomas. He stood for a moment, astonished at the sight of her. Then he ran forwards and she could fall into his arms, hide her burning face against his chest.

'My God,' he kept murmuring as he stroked her hair, soothing her as he would a startled calf, 'my God, I never thought you'd come to harm.'

After she had calmed a little he lifted her in his arms, as effortlessly as if she were a child. He started to carry her back towards her home.

'No,' she cried, when she realized where he was heading. 'Don't let them see me like this, please, please don't let them.'

So he turned his footsteps and walked across the top orchard and carried her into the safety of an empty barn. There was a loose heap of last season's hay in the corner and he laid her gently on it. Then he sat close beside her and went back to stroking her. She cried for a while, and tried to tell him, which was almost impossible, as she could not bear to put it into words. But Thomas knew well enough to fill in the gaps, and he looked grim. At last she rested quietly on his arm.

'There's a stream, nearby,' he said. 'I'll wet a cloth and you can clean up before going home.'

She nodded her assent and he left her.

From where she lay she could see out into the beauty of the day. The air in the timbered barn was cool and dark, and smelled of a warm, dry dust. There was a lingering sweetness from the hay.

It seemed as if she must have dozed, for when Thomas came back she felt calmer. She took the damp cloth, and wiped her face and neck. It seemed natural that she should unbutton the high neck. Then Thomas helped wipe her hand, where the ragged cut had dried to a crusty red. She shivered and he put his arms around her. He smelt of the land, warm and healing. She lifted her face to his, her eyelids trustingly closed. After a moment he bent to kiss her. He was gentle, tender, and she pressed up against him, her lips parting with the ease born newly of desire. He caressed her, slowly at first, then rising to the surging need in her. He stood to undo his belt; it was a last chance for her to change her mind. But as if in a dream she eased herself out of her dress, began loosening her petticoats. He lay down beside her on the straw bed, moved on to her slight form.

The scream that rent the air, shriller and higher than the traction engine's power, froze them. They were apart in an instant, and Thomas was gone. It had been a child's scream, Timmy's, and it had cut short at the very highest pitch of its terror.

Isabella started up. She scrambled into her clothes. It was nothing now what was thought of her, nothing mattered. She dimly heard the engine stop, but the sound was almost smothered, for she was pulling her dress over her head. She dashed to the opening of the barn. But which way. She couldn't see through the orchards, where row upon row of fat mature trees blocked her view.

Then she heard Thomas shout, and she followed it; it was a high, forced shout of a man in need of help,

116

desperate need. She ran down through the rows of trees as if she flew, following his shouts, and then the trees ended abruptly and she was at the edge of the cornfield. She ran on, through the rough-haired wheat that scratched at her legs. The engine ahead of her was a vast silent ominous monster.

She found him, with Timmy clutched, still, in his arms. The child was covered in blood, bright red blood that tangled his hair, streaked his face. Isabella stood very still, then Thomas was telling her to come to him, to take the boy. The child's eyes flew open and he clung whimpering to Thomas who pushed him roughly at Isabella.

'Take him and hold him. For God's sake hold him tightly.'

Isabella threw her arms around the child. He struggled, but with less than his usual strength and she could hold him. She looked anxiously for the source of the blood, then realized suddenly that it was not Timmy's life force that had soaked her dress. She loosened her grip for an instant in her understanding, and the boy sensed it, nearly struggling free. But she knew what her charge was now, and gripped him fiercely.

Two men came running over the field towards them. Thomas's shouts had called more help than hers alone. They glanced briefly at her and then followed their master's shout around to the far side of the engine. Almost instantly, one of them, a big bearded brute of a man, came back. He was retching violently and fell to his knees, shaking his great shaggy head. When he stood up again he muttered an apology before turning back, but he didn't need to apologize to Isabella, for she felt sick enough herself. They rigged a makeshift stretcher from a couple of fresh cut saplings and the rug Timmy used to bring out to the fields. The men gave their shirts to cover their burden, for Timmy's father was no longer recognizable as a man.

They took the remains and the boy back to Reason Hill. The house with such a reasonable name seemed too peaceful to accept the ripped body. Yet it was a gesture Sam would have appreciated, for he had no wife to organize the rites of death for him.

Isabella offered to take the boy back with her. That was later, when the boy had been cleaned and so had she, and that was when Thomas snapped.

'He's not a lapdog, Isabella. He couldn't exist in that ivory tower of yours. And you're too confused for anyone's good let alone your own.'

Isabella had been too tired to argue, but let the words wash over her, like the chilling tide they were.

'You could do whatever you wanted, Isabella. You're beautiful, talented and thanks to your father you'd have a good dowry. But you must choose your way, you can't refuse Johnnie without an alternative.' Isabella was beyond emotion, the blankness of her expression stung Thomas like a goad, urging him to say words he instantly regretted.

'You're a strange creature, half one thing half another. And if we'd made love this afternoon then what would that have done for you? Given you more dreams to dream? I need substance in my woman, Isabella. If you're set on giving yourself to a man, then choose one who can appreciate your talents, but don't for God's sake think it will do for a man like me. I need a woman with fire, Isabella, fire!' He looked so desperate, so close to alien tears that the boy ran to him, and threw his thin arms around him.

Isabella left then; no one cared if she did or didn't. She went back to the great empty house on the hill, with tears dried on her cheeks and a burning shame that matched the burning air hovering on the brink of thunder.

The ebony mirror of the night sky cracked apart, smashed by a jagged fork of light that forced chasms of brilliance in the blackness; thunder bombarded the house, drum roll upon drum roll.

Isabella pressed her knuckles hard against her head, but it was no use. The vicious, spitting electric storm was part of the air she breathed. In the privacy of her bedroom she stripped to her bodice and petticoats as the dense humid air closed in on her, but she could not stand her self-imposed imprisonment. She unlocked the door, threw it open, and ran out on to the landing. Then on, down the wide curving staircase. Another bolt of light flashed across the hall windows, lighting her way as she ran over the black and white tiled floor towards the morning room. The casement doors seemed to crackle with electricity as she pulled them wide open. Another shaft of lightning made the smooth lawn as bright as day. A day where the light was harsh and white and unforgiving.

Unforgiving. As Isabella was unforgiving of herself and of the weakness of her flesh. If it hadn't been for the accident she would have lain with Thomas Cade, given him her virginity.

She ran out wildly on to the stage-lit grass. Great gobbets of warm water rained down upon her from the sky, joining the hot tears running down her cheeks.

The light began to fade as the thunder increased. It poured over her in a great ocean tide of noise, beating her senses to the earth. She turned her face up to the infinity above and the rain hammered down on her. It washed through her blonde hair, pulling it loose from the last restraining pins until it flowed like a golden river down her back. The rain soaked through the thin cotton that she wore, moulding it tightly to her body.

Through it all, the noise, the fear, she could still feel the shame; even as her clothes chilled on her, her cheeks and neck were still aflame with it.

She opened her eyes to glare up, defying God to see her in this world of chaos. But she knew He had seen, He had witnessed her mortification. With all her being she wished it away from her; she wouldn't, couldn't pray, so she must wish.

She held supplicant hands up high to the sky and the water beat down upon her, making even breathing difficult. But the stain in her heart remained, she still saw his face, felt his hot skin touching hers.

A fresh flash, a tearing crash from the orchard and the smell of burning. Then the noise was upon her again, a bombardment of sound like the great traction engines out in the sun-dried fields. The machines that had been the orchestrators of her shame. Their crescendos had compelled her to ignominy, shame and rejection.

Her scream of fury, fury at herself, was lost in the loudest roar of all as, in its turn, the night loosed its fury fully on her. A washing out of the imperfect. The storm had reached its zenith and it took its vengeance upon her.

They found her in the early morning light, the translucent light of dawn that touched the earth with shell pink. The storm was gone now.

She lay, as if asleep, but they couldn't wake her. A sleek cap of wet blonde hair outlined the fine bones of her face before spreading out like seaweed on the still soaked grass. Her underclothes clung to her. Maude lay a modest shawl over her near nakedness before the butler lifted her in his arms to carry her into the house. They sent for the doctor and worried over whether to send for the master; it was a shame the poor girl had no mother they said.

But Isabella was safe for the moment, for all their concern. Her voice had been heard in the clamour of the storm. Senseless to the world still turning, safe within the caverns of her mind, she was calm and quiet at last.

Part Two

But some love England and her honour yet
Tennyson

Transvaal, 1901

Michael ran the back of his hand over his eyes. They were sore, red-rimmed; the grit that flicked up from the sun-scorched tracks and the dry heat itself irritated them. It was all very well for the old hands to say that winter was on its way, that any day now there'd be rain, followed by ice-chilled winds blowing down off the mountains, but for the moment anything cool was beyond imagining. Winter out here, and summer home in England. It was an odd feeling. If he looked up from his camp chair, across the paper-strewn surface of his fold-up desk, towards the wire-festooned perimeter of the camp, he could see the Boer women trying vainly to exist with dignity in their makeshift huts, their sickly children tugging at their faded skirts. But Michael did not look up; he didn't need to, the scene was already engraved forever in his mind. He had to struggle to pay attention to his visitor's words; he wasn't sleeping well and he knew his concentration was slipping.

This was no way for his glorious England to wage war. He'd listened to the reasoned explanations, the whys and wherefores. He understood that the Boer women and children had to be put somewhere after their farms had been razed to the ground. It had been carefully explained that the burning of their homes was the price the Boers had to pay for their own underhand way of fighting. It was well known that the farmsteads sheltered the fighting men, therefore these sanctuaries must be destroyed. The disciplined soldier in Michael had listened to it all, and absorbed it. But the man inside him rebelled. Michael was having to fight that man, he had no intention whatsoever of letting him get the upper hand.

'Do you know the words I hear in my sleep, Michael?' The shabby black of the young chaplain's cassock reminded Michael of the birds, the great black-winged scavengers that had become part of the place. 'They're "Minheer, kom tog heer," terribly polite. You must note it's always "please come here" and of course, "Minheer, gaat tog daar," the "please" again you see. They are very considerate when they ask me to perform the last rites.' He fixed Michael with his haunted eyes. 'I am awake at night a lot as well. The whistles wake me, you know.'

Michael knew very well that the whistles the man referred to were the calls for the body carriers. They were almost continual now, and they woke him too, even though his tent was outside the wire. The women and children were dying with terrifying speed in this dreadful place.

Michael had no idea what to say to steady the man. If his faith in God was not enough to carry him through what was an ordeal for anyone, then perhaps it would be best if he was sent back to ministering to the soldiers. But Michael had been ordered to inspire this unhappy chaplain. Push him back into the fray, his colonel had said. Michael doubted if the trembling wreck he saw in front of him would last another week before breaking down entirely, but they were all under orders.

'I think, chaplain, that the best inspiration I can give you is to remember that you bring the grace of God to these women. Whatever it is that's causing them to die like this, I don't know, but they surely shouldn't be left to face it without all the help a man of God can give them.'

'You think I don't feel that? You think I want to leave them?' The man was crying openly now, tears coursing down his emaciated cheeks. 'I'm so terrified I'll break

126

down,' he continued. 'So terrified I'll say the words hurtling round in my brain. I'm too muddle-headed.' He shook his head savagely. 'I keep hearing the words of the Good Book, scourges, plagues, then I look at these people. They're fine people, Michael, beautiful women, fine handsome children, when they arrive. They're proud of themselves, proud of their men. Then you watch them start to change. To begin with the pride stays. In a few, a very few, it's there to the end, but for most it's a slide into despair. They become objects of abject misery. And the numbers of deaths now are simply appalling. I've seen whole families die on the very same day: a mother, two or three children. I had one family this morning, Michael; the mother went first, struggling to stay for her children, but she hadn't the strength. She left two girls, tiny, wasted little creatures they were. The eleven-year-old went first, then the eight-year-old.' He slumped forwards in his seat, dropping his head on to his hands. 'I held that little girl's hand when she cried out for her mother. I would have given anything, Michael, anything, I would have cast my soul into eternal damnation for that poor little girl to have her mother for those last dreadful minutes. Here, I've talked about them as poor, wasted creatures, look at this. This is how I first met them eight weeks ago.' With a trembling hand he held out the photograph to Michael.

Michael didn't want to take it. He was too emotionally involved already, he knew it, he could feel it. He'd come out inspired to do his duty, to give his father the satisfaction of a son doing his best for his country. He hadn't expected to come to this.

'I don't know what you think I can do to help you, Simon. I can only follow orders, the same as you must. We're pawns in a game that we don't know the half of. I think you'd better keep your photograph.'

'We're not game pieces, Michael, we're men.' Simon

stood up, a new fragile vitality filling his sparse frame. 'If you won't take the picture, then I'll find something else to convince you. I'll go back, Michael. There aren't many men for whom I'd go back, but you're one of them. As for your superior officers, and most of your contemporaries come to that, they're damned, damned to hell and I wouldn't lift my little finger to help them, not if St Peter himself asked me.'

Michael stood up as the chaplain left. He walked to the tent doorway to watch the slight figure make its way back through the wire-encrusted perimeter gates. He felt sick at the pit of his stomach.

The note from Johnnie arrived at midday. It was brief and to the point.

Despite rumours to the contrary, I am not dead. Merely winged.
Johnnie

There wasn't much doing, so Michael was able to ride over to his brother's unit shortly after lunch. There had been a few days of inactivity so he wondered how Johnnie had managed to get himself wounded. He wasn't left in doubt for long; Johnnie's activities were the toast of the brigade.

'Come to see the wounded hero, have you?' asked one of the devil-may-care young officers who formed part of Johnnie's entourage as he came up to hold Michael's horse while he dismounted. A necessary courtesy because an impromptu game of polo was throwing up the dust and inspiring any horse or pony worth its oats to kick up its heels as well.

'Yes, I have. Thanks.' Michael handed over the reins; the young idiot could find somewhere to tether it. Michael disliked the flippancy of this particular set. They were only a couple of years younger than him, but he felt they were an alien generation. 'Where is he?' he asked.

'He's in his tent, believe it or not. Only don't look worried, he's not that bad. But the doc got pretty mad when he found him mounted and about to take part in this shindig. Actually up on a pony, do you see? So he gave him a draught of something to tame him down a bit. He's gone quite gaga, lying like a lilly. Still he could probably do with a rest, what with his gallivanting out to stir up the enemy and all that.'

Michael walked slowly over to the indicated tent. Why his brother had to keep the company of fools was totally beyond him. He lifted the flap and looked in. Johnnie was lying full stretch on his camp bed. There was another empty bed with kit neatly folded on it. For a moment Michael thought his brother was asleep and he almost turned away, but then a drowsy voice called to him.

'Hallo, old man, nice of you to drop in.'

Michael walked into the stuffy dimness, looking for something to sit on. He saw Johnnie's tuck trunk, familiar from their schooldays. It was strange to see it here. 'How on earth did you manage to get this out here?' Michael had his own gear in kit-bags.

'Oh, a chum brought it out. I'd left it at his house one hols, years and years ago. Said he thought this was the ideal time to give it back. Bit of an ass really. It wasn't worth the passage.'

Bit of an ass, yes, Michael expected he was. He glanced quickly at his brother's left arm which was wrapped in bandages and tied up in a sling. He couldn't look too hard, or Johnnie might notice. It wasn't done to fuss. 'Thanks for the note,' Michael said. 'Actually, I hadn't heard anything before that, I'd no idea at all.'

'Oh,' Johnnie sounded disappointed, 'Everyone here

was buzzing with it, so I thought you might be . . . might . . . well, I thought I'd just let you know.'

Michael nodded his head. He didn't feel that he had much to say. The jolly clamour of the polo match outside made him feel suspended, unreal. It was very different to his own quarters, close to the camp and the sounds of suffering.

The tent flap opened, letting in a new wave of hot, dusty air, and Johnnie coughed.

'So sorry,' the newcomer cried, his clothes proclaiming him instantly as a polo player. 'Hate to interrupt and all that, but could you be an angel and move, sir?' He fell on his knees beside the somewhat startled Michael and began to rummage under Johnnie's bed. 'Where have you put them, you idiot? Come on, old chap, the game's held up, where the hell are they?' He rummaged some more, this time sticking his head and shoulders under Johnnie's bed. 'Bloody hell.' His voice came out muffled. 'What on earth are these under here for?' With a scrabbling he re-emerged dragging his find, a pile of battered felt hats.

Michael looked down in growing fury. He knew what they were of course.

Johnnie hauled himself up to a sitting position. 'They're mine, old man, shove 'em back, will you? Gerald's got my sticks already so you'll have to borrow someone else's.'

The visitor left and Johnnie turned to Michael, 'Just as well I'd already lent some blighter mine; he's a devil at breaking them.' His words tailed off as he looked at the fury on Michael's face.

His brother was white and pinched with rage. He watched Michael reach down to pick up a hat from the top of the pile that had been pulled from under the bed. 'They're Boers', aren't they?' Michael clipped the words, his lips pressed into a thin, narrow line. 'They're Boers' hats. By God, you've taken them as trophies, have you? You bloody little savage.' Johnnie was amazed, he'd never seen Michael this angry, never. 'You've shot the poor bastards, and you want a tally I suppose!' He was quivering with anger, almost unable to speak.

Johnnie replied, 'Yes, they're Boers' hats, all right. What of it? This is war, old man, whatever else you may like to think. I got them for the old man. We're not fighting the fuzzy wuzzies, or I would have taken him back a handful of spears; I thought this was a decent alternative.'

Michael threw the hat down on to the floor. 'It's a filthy business this, Johnnie, a foul dirty business, and there's a lot more to it than meets the eye.' He walked abruptly towards the tent flap, pulling it back to let light flood in. 'You're sick anyway, so you might well get sent home. That would be the best thing.'

'No, it wouldn't, Michael. Don't you act so dictatorial with me. It's my left arm they got. I can still ride and shoot. And I damned well will. I don't suppose it will please you one little bit to know how we add up our scores, old man, but you're going to hear it. We've got a system, you see. We count our Boers as we would duck: one point for a sitter, two for one up a tree and three for one in flight, on horseback that is. I'm leading at the moment, you know. I've got forty-eight. That's how I got this little souvenir, yesterday evening. I want my half century; there's a fair bit of money bet on it. So I went out with a couple of pals for a little duck hunting, you understand. Unfortunately, one of the devils managed to wing me, so I'm stuck on forty-eight, but it won't be for long. I'll be up on my feet again tomorrow.' His defiance flushed angrily on his pain-lined face.

Michael didn't say a word. He bent down and picked up every one of the dented, dusty felt hats, checking under the bed that there were no more. It was a considerable pile

131

he held. He looked around for something to put them in, then saw the chest and opened it. There were a few shirts, some books and letters inside. He tipped them on to the floor then dropped the hats inside. He fastened the buckles then heaved it up on to his shoulder. Without a backward glance he left the tent.

A soldier was holding his horse. The man assisted him up into the saddle, then passed him up the trunk. It was bulky and awkward and he sawed on the reins as the horse shook its head. It hadn't been treated like this by Michael before and it set off at a jerky canter. They made an uncomfortable ride to the camp.

'Miserable bastard,' muttered the soldier who'd helped Michael mount. He knew who the officer was; he wasn't a bright young spark like his brother. He'd have swapped a joke or two, but not that one, with a face as stiff as wood, and without a word of thanks.

Michael set fire to the trunk and its contents. It didn't take much to get it burning, everything was so dry. A small crowd of children came to peer through the wire at the strange little bonfire, then they were shooed away by the guards.

As Michael stood staring down at the pitiful ashes, the remnants of some thirty-odd fighting men, Simon came towards him. He had with him a Boer woman. Michael looked up at her and for a moment a spark leaped into his eyes, then it faded. She had for an instant reminded him of someone, a friend at home. Her hair was fair and her eyes very blue, but that was all really, for her face was not the one that had sprung to mind. In front of him was a woman who had suffered, who was in the midst of suffering. But there was pride in her eyes, pride in her bearing. She was probably of an age with Michael, but he felt she was an eternity removed from him.

'This is Mrs Verboert, Michael,' Simon said. 'She would

132

like to speak to you; she has some news for you from home.'

'Good afternoon, Captain,' she said. Her accent was soft, warmer than that of the other women he'd heard calling to their children. 'You will be surprised to have news from home via the camp, ya?' She indicated the sprawling mass behind with a hand that was reddened, chapped with unaccustomed hard work. Michael realized she was very new at fending for herself. 'I have a letter here.' She pulled a crumpled piece of paper from a pocket hidden in the folds of her skirt. 'I am afraid it has been handled many times; it is rather a ray of hope to us, you see. Here, I will read you the part that concerns you.' She held the paper up closer to her eyes.

'This letter is from Margaret Brown. Here, this is the passage that will interest you.' She folded the paper, then handed it to him: Michael was only to be allowed to read the portion that concerned him.

He read slowly, carefully; any letters here were precious, anything that called up memories of home.

A very dear friend of mine, Isabella Bradbury, has written to me that her sister's fiancé and his brother are sent to South Africa. They are the sons of Lord Montford. Isabella says that if there is difficulty in getting letters to England, she feels sure they will help, especially Michael, who is the elder, and always very concerned to see fair play. She also says to send her best wishes to them both, and that her sister Lucinda is very well and very busy preparing for the wedding.

He lowered the paper and looked, almost unseeing, at the woman.

'You are to be married then, Captain? I hope you will be very happy; marriage is a precious state.' Her eyes had filled very suddenly, but the tears did not fall; she was obviously determined that they should not.

133

Michael pulled his drifting thoughts together. 'What does the bit about fair play mean?' he asked.

'I must explain that this letter came from London, from, as I have said, Margaret Brown, a friend of Isabella Bradbury clearly, but also a friend to us all here. Those in authority here do not really wish us to communicate with England. Margaret is one of the women who are pleading our cause in London. You see, all women have a kindred feeling for children and very, very many poor little souls here are being called to God before their time.'

'Amen,' said Simon.

'Do you have children, Mrs Verboert?' Michael asked.

'Yes, Captain, I have a dear daughter Emily, who is four years old and a son Louis who is only eighteen months.'

They were silent then; there was too much to say and yet nothing that could be said. After a long time, Michael said, 'Do you have a letter I can send, or is there anything I can do for you?'

A tired smile crossed the woman's face. 'Is there anything you can do? My dear Captain, there is a world out there to tell. We women are feeble creatures. Indeed, here we grow feebler every day. I would not ask that you should help me and mine; that would be the greatest insult to all the other women in there who must carry on the struggle to their last breath. No, there is nothing you can do here that will make any more difference than a stone dropped in the greatest pond. You are a lord's son, Captain, the eldest, so one day you will be a lord yourself. Tell your peers what they do to us, ask them if they really mean to make us suffer. Great men should not want to see the children of their enemies cast down.

'I must go back. I have left my children for too long already, and Louis has a nasty cough. Be our champion, Captain, fight for us, we cannot fight for ourselves.' She put the letter very carefully back in her pocket, then slowly, deliberately folded her arms. It was as if she had to do something to stop her hands from clenching into helpless fists. 'I shall pray for you, Captain,' she said and then turned and walked back to the desolate camp.

Simon did not follow her at once. He paused a moment to look at the man whose soul he was trying to save, then followed the woman.

It was another week before the film from the camera Michael had been lent by Isabella was ready. He had taken all the shots, the ninety or so that were left, and then given it to a fellow officer who was being sent on an errand to Johannesburg. There was a man there who could develop it. Michael looked through the photographs, the first he had ever taken. About half of them were smudged, the subject matter almost impossible to decipher, but several were surprisingly good, mainly ones of the children: pathetic, painful, evocative.

Isabella's attempts were better than his. The one she had taken of the hounds in the yard at Linstone was excellent. Michael looked at the pups with the first smile that had crossed his face that week. There was Johnnie and Eli, the groom and Lucinda. My God, Lucinda. He sat very, very still. A Lucinda he had never seen before had been caught by the camera: her lower lip jutted, her eyes were small, venomous.

He was still sitting with the photograph crumpled in his hand when Simon came into the tent.

'Michael, I feel you might like to know . . . that is, I feel I should tell you . . .' He sank on to the camp bed, his shoulders shaking. 'Mrs Verboert did not tell you the other day that both her children were ill. Well, in the last two days she has lost them both. I thought, I thought that

135

the daughter would last a little longer, a few more days perhaps. But she didn't make the night.'

'My God!' Michael was on his feet. 'I shall go to her. I . . . I must be able to do something.'

The man of the cloth put his hand out to hold Michael's jacket. 'There is nothing you can do in there for the poor woman, nothing she would want you to do. She won't last long herself, Michael, for she has the wasting disease. You know what she asked of you. Do it for all of them. There are hundreds of little Louis, hundreds of Emilys. There are more and more women and children arriving every day, being crammed into this prison; do it for them. Go out and tell the truth at home in England. You must stop this, Michael; you must stop it for the sake of us all.'

The Honourable Michael, son and heir of Lord Montford, left South Africa two weeks after the death of Mrs Verboert. His commanding officer chose to interpret his impassioned pleas for the care of the camp women and children as proof of his deteriorated mental state. He was sent back to England on the sick list but, truthfully, he did not care. He was a man with a mission: to change the hearts of England.

Linstone

'Issy, Issy, oh please, wake up, Issy.' Lucinda squeezed the pale hand for at least the hundredth time that morning. Not a flicker of movement on her sister's alabaster face answered her.

Lucinda had no tears left any more. She'd cried for two solid days and then there simply hadn't been any more tears to cry. Now, a week after they had come home to find Issy lying still in her bed, like the living dead, every emotion possible had been gone through and only desperation remained. The bedroom smelt unpleasant, a mixture of the foul beef tea they trickled, drop by drop, over Issy's still lips, and the carbolic soap with which the room was disinfected every day. Lucinda scrubbed the smell off her face and hands every time she left the sick room, but it still clung to her clothes. It had become the smell of hopelessness.

Lucinda laid the hand down gently on the bedclothes. She stood up, uncertain whether to stay or go. But the nurse had gone to take a rest in her room; perhaps she would stay another ten minutes or so. She wandered over to the window. The weather had changed suddenly, and was cool, damp and lifeless. Their view was cut down by a grey mist that clung to the land. It was so deadly dull. There hadn't been a letter from Michael or Johnnie this week. Nothing to break the interminable gloom. She looked over at the bed. Isabella was wasting away despite it all; she was going to leave them, then there would be no happy foursome at Pencombe, no sister to perform Lucy's bidding, and Johnnie would marry a stranger. It was ridiculous, such a waste of all her plans.

Enough! She darted across the room. There was no one here but the pair of them. She knew Issy, she knew what she needed. She reached out and held the skinny arms, squeezing hard as she hauled the sleeping form up off the pillows. 'Wake up! Wake up!' she shrieked in the marble ear. 'Don't be so selfish. Wake up, Issy, wake up, damn you!' Lucinda shook her with all her might.

Isabella's head lolled back, the lips parting in a parody of laughter.

But she wouldn't give up. 'Wake up, damn you, Issy!' She let go of a lifeless arm and hit, with all her might, across her sister's face. 'Wake up! Wake up!' she screamed; another slap, a red flush showed her hand print, vivid on the white cheek. 'Wake up!'

The door crashed open and the nurse, her cap perched crazily on her head, came running in, just as Isabella, half-supported by the hysterical Lucinda, opened her eyes. She opened them wide, staring as if in terror. Then, as intelligence flooded back into her expression, she sat forward, her body curling in convulsive spasm.

The nurse ran to her charge, delight writing new lines on her creased face. 'It's a miracle, it's a miracle,' she cried. It was. All the thoughts the nurse had had about having to leave in a day or two when the girl died were gone in an instant. There would be a good few weeks' work here now, and there was no better job than in the houses of the newly rich, where a sick child well looked after meant the nurse was fêted like a queen.

Isabella lay in bed for another week, weak as a kitten on plumped-up cushions. She was cajoled into taking beef tea and cool consommés until at last being decreed fit enough to take a lightly boiled egg for her lunch. It was heaven.

Afterwards she drifted off into the first dreamless sleep she had enjoyed since her illness.

That was what they called it, her illness. Her father and Dr Groake muttered about it, thinking they were outside her hearing. But she caught enough: the comments about nerve fever, exhaustion, her being highly strung. She knew what they were about, and they were right in a fashion. She had become far too highly strung, living on her nerves and her emotions. What was it Thomas had said? She could cope with his words now, for they were true, she saw that for herself. She was neither one thing nor the other. She would have to change and no one could do anything except herself.

The decison, she found, was easy. She must leave the emotions to Lucinda, who could flaunt them and cope with them. She must become a creature of common sense. She would discard art; her painting she now saw as shallow, a meaningless pastime. She would look for a reason in life. Something to do. Something worthwhile.

Lavender dropped her head over the chamber pot and groaned with the agony of it all. She could feel her lank, greasy hair sticking to her flushed skin. It had been the same for the past three mornings.

It was at least five minutes since the last wave of nausea. She was probably past it now. She shuffled forwards on her bottom to the edge of the bed. Very carefully she slid her legs out of the blanket and down on to the floor. It was chilly under her warm toes. She shivered and clutched her dressing gown to her, but as she pulled it round her shoulders she suddenly realized her breasts were hard, full. She put her hands up to them in astonishment. They were swollen and painful to touch.

She sat down on the bed with a thump. She should have known. All that fuss she'd made about the whelks; it hadn't been them at all. She should have known. As for the other, monthly clue to her state, well, it hadn't arrived, but then that was nothing new; she'd never been one to be regular.

She stared down, unseeing, for quite a while. Then she stood up, and after a few tentative steps to make sure that the sickness didn't come back, she walked purposefully downstairs. In the tiny kitchen, cluttered with the remains of the bread and cheese she had eaten the night before, she lit the fire, brewed a pot of tea, put some dripping on a slice of bread and then walked slowly back to bed with her breakfast.

Lavender Biggs had some thinking to do. She didn't see the answer being in mother's ruin and a touch of something more specific; she'd seen enough young girls harm themselves trying that. And she certainly wasn't going to let some old hag go to work on her with a knitting needle. She shivered at the thought and pulled a shawl off the end of the bed to wrap round her shoulders.

The tea and bread put new life into her. That's what she had – new life springing in her. She'd made her way in life with men, and men were funny about babies: it took them one way or the other. Arthur, for example, would disappear without a backward glance, she knew the type. But Harold, old rat-face, how about him? Lavender rubbed her tummy fondly. Her life was going to take a change, she could see it quite clearly, and the first change would be . . .

Every morning of the week after she was allowed downstairs, Isabella had woken to the same sinking sensation of alarm. Time, like a great consuming monster, stretched ahead of her. Another day to fill and nothing to fill it. And she had started waking much too early: from first light consciousness retook possession of her. But in a way it

140

was a relief, for her dreams were jumbled, cluttered with the debris of her past.

Eli always left early for the brewery on Friday mornings. That left the biggest hurdle of them all: breakfast alone with Lucinda. And today was Friday.

'Issy, I would like you to paint me a picture, a nice dainty little one, about seven inches by five. In blues and pinks, with perhaps a little grey. It will have to be ready for framing in three weeks.' There, thought Lucinda complacently, that's given her something to do, something to stop her mooning about.

'I'm very sorry, Lucy, I don't really feel like painting at the moment.' Isabella had no appetite; she simply played with the boiled egg she had chosen as the least daunting breakfast.

'Well, perhaps you'll feel like it when you've started. I really do need the picture, you know; there's a space just begging for it.'

As the request was for pink and blue that must mean it was intended for Michael and Lucinda's bedroom. It was being redecorated, and had to be perfect, down to the minutest details. It was an honour for Isabella to be asked to contribute, which just proved the depth of Lucinda's concern.

'Will you do it then, Issy?'

Isabella started in her chair, her mind had drifted off on its own. She'd forgotten all about her sister's request already. 'No, I won't.'

'Well, what will you do then?' Lucinda was flushed with annoyance. It made her look over-heated in her maroon morning dress. 'I'm absolutely exhausted trying to think of things to inspire you. Of course,' she added maliciously, 'I expect if you had your camera you'd feel inspired to take some photographs.' It was the first time she had referred to that. 'As you haven't, you'll have to take your pick of all the traditional pastimes you're so good at. Unless of course you feel like going out for a spin.'

The bicycles that Lucinda had brought back from London for them were still in their brown paper over-wrapping. Lucinda's own enthusiasm for them had waned, but anything was better than this awful atmosphere of desperation that drifted over in waves from her sister. Lucinda had so much to occupy her own mind that she would have been happy for Isabella to have simply disappeared off the face of the earth for a little while. Just long enough for Lucinda to get things organized as she wanted at Pencombe, then she'd be quite happy for Isabella to reappear. The old Isabella, that is, not this taut-faced stranger.

'I think I would quite like to try the bicycle, Lucy,' Isabella said hesitantly.

Lucinda was amazed. 'What, really?'

'Well, yes, I think so. Shall we go now?' Isabella stood up as she spoke.

Dove moved quickly to open the door for her, and Lucinda followed her sister out of the room. She gave Dove a sideways smile of victory. He was delighted; the Pencombe job was as good as in his pocket.

They took the bicycles out on to the drive. Seen close to they looked a little alarming, at least Lucinda thought so, even though they were not penny-farthings. They were more modern, their wheels were nearly the same size, and the handlebars quite in proportion. She looked down at her dress in some confusion. It was very full – what on earth could she do with it?

Isabella seemed to be having no such qualms. She was wearing a simpler dress in any case, of a soft forget-me-not blue lawn. She put one leg over the bicycle and very efficiently folded the bulk of her skirt on to her lap. Then, with a look of intense concentration, she put a foot on a pedal, took a deep breath, held it and then lifting her other foot quickly from the ground pushed hard down on the second pedal. She was moving. With alarming speed the drive swept past her.

Suddenly she was happy. 'It's wonderful, wonderful . . . come on, Lucy, oh!' She had skidded to a halt, but apart from scuff marks on the gravel there was no damage. She was still standing, and she had travelled at least twenty yards. Twenty yards of brilliant, exhilarating freedom. Isabella breathed deeply. She felt alive for the first time in so very long. She looked up at the heavily laden chestnut trees bordering the drive and smiled; she looked out at the orchards, ripening fruit gleaming in the sun, and her smile widened; she looked up at the vast blue sky above her and laughed out loud for joy.

'You're a genius, Lucy, an absolute genius. Come on, it's not that hard.' And she was off again, almost wobbling more than the first time, but bravely trying a turn with the handlebars. She didn't really notice Lucinda going indoors to change her dress, and it seemed no time at all until a cry of victory heralded her sister's own advance on wheels. Dove had come out to help her balance to begin with and now he was running alongside the teetering bike and the triumphant Lucinda. His place, he thought breathlessly with the increasing pace, his place at Pencombe was most definitely assured.

By Monday, the girls felt proficient enough to venture further afield. They had cycled on all the local roads and lanes during the weekend. Now, Isabella announced that they should take a picnic and see how far they could go. Lucinda agreed on condition that, however far they went, they left themselves enough energy to get home.

Inevitably they took the road south. The long sweeping hill was such an invitation. The road was narrow in places and there were rutted stretches that slowed them down, but in the main they swept down, like birds in flight, the wind pulling through their hair, the trees rushing past. They were nearly at the bottom when they came to the bend. Isabella was in the lead. She turned to call back to Lucinda, then glanced in front of her. To her horror, a wide, slow cart filled the road ahead. She pulled frantically on the brakes, shouting out to Lucinda to do the same. The front wheel of her bicycle wobbled violently, the handlebars twisted and bucked like a live thing, and she lost her foothold on the pedals. She was heading for a collision, then suddenly she had steered to the side. There was a gap, a slim one, but she was juddering to a halt in it and with a screech Lucinda came to a skidding stop behind her.

'You damned fools, you could have been killed!' The woman's voice from the cart beside them was a shock. Isabella hadn't noticed it was a woman driving the cart. 'You want to thank God that I was driving and keeping my eyes on the road, or there wouldn't have been any room for you at all, and you want to add a prayer for the fact it's Brownie in the shafts and not anything with more spirit, or we'd all be upside down under the cart.' She was about their own age. She was obviously shaken and had had a fright, but curiosity was getting the better of it.

'What's it like careering down hills on a bicycle, then? When you're not frightening ordinary mortals out of their wits, that is.'

Isabella decided that their saviour was pleasant although a little strange, for she was full-blown compared to them: there was no demureness in her bearing. Lucinda took an instant dislike to her, but then she always did to anyone or anything that might compete with her.

'It's absolutely splendid.' Isabella was glad her voice wasn't shaking too much. 'Except for the last little bit, that is. I thought I was going to crash, and that wasn't very nice at all. I am sorry. Is your cart damaged?' She looked over to the other side, where the vehicle seemed to be wedged against the rough stone bank.

'No, it's fine, this stretch is too narrow anyway. I said so to Thomas the other day, but he's too mean to give up a piece of his field to widen it.' She smiled, obviously pleased at saying the man's name. Isabella felt a shiver down her spine.

'Thomas?' came Lucinda's voice from behind her. 'You must mean Thomas Cade. It's his land here, isn't it?'

'Yes, that's right, Thomas Cade. Do you know him?'

'We are shortly to become cousins by marriage.' Lucinda's voice was becoming very much that of the grande dame, and the atmosphere, hitherto so charming, was becoming strained.

'You must be Lucy then.' Isabella could feel her sister stiffen.

'Lucinda Bradbury, yes that's right, I am. And who are you?'

'I'm Jenny Jones. I don't suppose Thomas has talked to you of me, has he?

'No.' Lucinda's shortness was verging on rudeness.

'No, I thought not. Still, I expect he will before long. Now if you'll excuse me, I'm off up to Reason Hill.'

Isabella whispered the words, 'Reason Hill?'

'Yes, that's right. I'm giving a hand with young Timmy. He's a bit of a handful since his father died. You knew about that, did you?' She turned her frank, inquisitive look on both the girls, then she added, 'But of course you know. You're Issy, aren't you? Thomas told me you were there.'

It was cold in the lane, Isabella hadn't noticed until now. She shuddered.

They parted, Isabella and Lucinda finishing their ride down the hill more carefully, Jenny clicking her tongue to hurry up the pony in the shafts. So they were the Bradbury girls? She thought she might quite like a bicycle herself. She'd ask her brother Luke. She wasn't quite in a position to ask Thomas Cade, not yet.

Harold took the pin out of the cork. He selected the biggest, blackest winkle from the bowl and with a dexterity born of practice flipped off the black, lacquered seal that protected the shellfish from the air. Then he stuck the pin into the wormlike flesh and, slowly twisting, drew it from its shell home. Beautiful. In one whole piece the succulent morsel appeared. He dipped it into the pool of malt vinegar on his plate then took a bite of the buttered brown bread. He swilled his mouth with brown ale. The mixture of flavours – the iodine from the sea, the malty goodness of the land in his drink – were working a transformation on him.

He'd come to Lavender's feeling low. It was all very well this information garnering, but it was slow. When he'd been building his own castles in the air, they'd been achieved more quickly; the reality of it seemed to be different.

'Have a few more, Harold, I know they're your favourites. There were cockles too, nice fat ones from Leigh on Sea, but I knows you don't like them, so I didn't bother.'

'But you like them, Lavender. You should have got some for yourself. Harold belched gently. He was feeling much, much better.

'P'raps we could go to Leigh one day, Harold? For a holiday like. P'raps we could go for a week?'

'Harold's eyes bulged with surprise. He'd like nothing more than to get Lavender away with him for a week. 'When d'you fancy then, girl?' he asked.

'Oh, I don't know, Harold. P'raps . . .' she paused coyly, 'p'raps on our honeymoon, I thought?'

Harold dropped his winkle pin. 'Lavender! Lavender!'

146

he cried. He was round the table in an instant, down on his knees in front of her. 'Lavender, say you mean it, say you'll marry me, really and truly. I'd do anything for you, you know that. Oh my love, my darling.' He clutched her hand and was smothering it with kisses. She could feel his ginger whiskers, like a mangy cat, rubbing on her skin.

''Course, I'll marry you my dear, you knew that all along.'

Harold was beside himself; he leaped up off his knees. 'Come on, let's go out and celebrate. We've got to tell the world. Oh, Lavender, I can't tell you what this means to me.'

'No, no, we don't want to go out.' Lavender pulled him down towards her again. 'There's other things we can do, other private things. Now we're engaged, like.' She reached up to him, slipping her fingers through the buttons of his shirt. She could feel his vest. 'Come on.' She smiled and stood to lead the way.

Harold was trembling in his excitement.

She held out her hand to him, twining her fingers round his. 'Come on, my dear,' she said, as siren-like she moved ahead of him, up the narrow stairs.

Harold felt he was swimming. His head was hot and he was swelling up with pride. She was going to be his, really, truly, his at last. The little room smelt fresh, of roses; there was a bowl full of blooms on the tiny polished table. The bed was turned down, ready for them, the sheets inviting and white.

'I got it ready for us, my dear, all ready you see. And there's something else as well.' From its hiding-place down by the bed she brought out the green glass bottle.

God, it was just as well. Harold wiped the sweat from his brow with his sleeve, he could do with a drink. Now it had really come to it, he felt a cold rush of fear; it was

147

all so unexpected. He would have been more prepared with a bit of warning.

'Here you are, my lovely, have a little nip.'

He took a deep draught. She was slowly, very slowly taking off her clothes for him. That was what he liked. To watch. But now, now there was something else for him to do.

'Go on, my luvvy; it's good stuff, yer know, really good.' Lavender had a reason in her actions. She wanted him good and squiffy when 'it' happened, then there wouldn't be any fuss about her not being a virgin. She'd say she was and how it had hurt and all that afterwards. How would he remember? It was nice and planned, how Lavender liked it. 'Come on, dearie, your turn now.' She'd stripped down to her drawers.

Harold would have liked to sit back and look; he was quite comfy where he was on the chair. But no, Lavender was beckoning him towards her. He moved in slow motion. The buttons of his shirt seemed to stick, he fumbled to open them. He wished suddenly he'd worn his other, cleaner underwear. But it was too late now. He stumbled getting out of his trousers, and the braces tangled round his legs.

'Come on, my lovely.' Lavender was reaching for him, pulling him towards her. A flash of surprise crossed her face. There was nothing, nothing at all, to show for all her titillation.

'Come to me.' She had a careful line to tread between the innocent she wanted him to think she was, and the practised harlot she was going to have to be to help him get it up at all.

'Can't I just sit back there and look at you?' he asked plaintively.

'Of course you can, my darling. I'll do anything you want now, anything.' She rolled her eyes when she said 'anything'; it was the biggest come-on she'd ever had to give.

Harold sat back in his chair. He sat and looked, and smiled like a thin Cheshire cat. She'd never thought to check before, never felt her eyes drawn to see how bursting he was with desire, but then that wasn't surprising as she didn't fancy him.

Much, much later, she got him into bed beside her. But it was only to sleep. She couldn't kick him out into the street after all that guff earlier. But what the hell was she to do? She'd only wanted him on top of her to be able to claim he was the father of her child, and now where had she got? He was impotent, and all her plans were ruined.

For the very first time since leaving Yorkshire, Eli wished he could put the clock back.

He fixed his eyes on the door that had just closed behind his clerk, but he wasn't seeing the rippled glass panes in their wooden frame. He was concentrating on an inanimate object to try and slow his whirling mind. The balance sheet figures Harold had brought in lay discarded on the desk. He knew what they would tell him: he had far too much money out on grain and hops, bought and paid for and as yet unprocessed. Much of the produce was still on the farms, not even in his warehouse.

He should never have spent so much time in London with Lucinda, but the days had just slipped by. There was still so much to do.

He needed a brewery manager. He allowed himself the thought at last. It was a relief to admit it. He couldn't let his chance to live life the way he wanted to slip by him. He sat up abruptly in his chair. There was no time to lose, no time for lounging about. He would set the affair in motion at once.

149

'Harold,' he shouted. Raising his voice gave vent to his pent-up emotions. 'Harold!'

The door opened as the shout still hung on the air. For an instant, Eli considered if the clerk could do the job. He certainly knew the business and it would save another new wage on the payroll. But, no, of course not; the brewery had slipped perilously near the edge in the past few weeks, and the man had been here all along. The right sort would have kept his master more informed and looked to his interests. Eli chose to ignore the fact that he would not for one instant have listened to the clerk, and that the man knew it.

Harold had no idea how close he came at that instant to pursuing a life of managerial dignity. It was a pity that his shirt was on the last of its seven days' hard wear. If Eli had scrutinized his employee on the next day, the smarter image might just have swayed him in Harold's favour. That would have saved them both a great deal of trouble.

'I want to put an advertisement in the *Messenger*. Take it down, will you, Harold?' Eli straightened his cravat carefully. This was a big step for him. 'Applicants are invited to apply for the position of manager. I think we'll have a new line there. No, I change my mind. Head it . . .' Harold's pen scratched furiously on his notepad. He was boiling inside, seething; how dare the old bugger! 'Right now, head it "Bradbury's Brewery", then underneath just put the word "manager", then "applications are invited for this prestigious post". Put the usual stuff about only experienced people need apply etc. etc., and that applications should be addressed to this office. Run it round to the paper yourself, will you? I want it put in a prominent position, mind they do that. This is an important advertisement, make sure they treat it as such. And come to think of it,' said Eli as he toyed briefly with his watch chain, 'you'd better have it put in the London *Times* as well. I'm not sure there'll be anyone in Maidstone who can handle a job of this importance.'

Harold's pen had kept up with the dictation, writing in a flurry of madness. He couldn't manage to speak, but he nodded his head and left the room. He would have fallen back against the door – he was desperate for air; his fury was consuming it in great draughts – but Eli would see him through the glass. So he stumbled, almost blind with pent-up rage, down the twisting stair and out into the yard. He leaned back against the hard brick wall. He was shaking like a leaf. He could taste iron in his mouth; he had never been in such a passion. Passion – he almost thought of Lavender, but his mind slid away from her. To have been manager would have provided a life of luxury for her. Now there was only one way. He clutched the advertisement draft tightly in his fist and he took the first staggering steps across the yard. There was only one way now. He'd show the old devil, he'd bring him to his knees.

At that very moment Lavender was thinking of Harold. She was standing on her doorstep, closing her front door carefully to check the lock had caught.

'Morning,' she cried to Irene next door, who was peering round the curtains. She gave her neighbour the benefit of her very brightest smile. The old crone's face crumpled. Lavender didn't know if it was a smile or a curse, but it didn't matter. Today was going to be a good one, Lavender knew it.

It wasn't very far to the brewery, not when she was so excited, thinking of her little subterfuge. The only problem she might have would be getting past Harold. She hadn't worked it out yet, but something would turn up, she just knew it. Lavender slowed her steps as she came near the brewery gates. She wanted to look ladylike,

151

special. She certainly looked special; the eyes that the draymen made at her proved that. They thought she looked a treat in her pale rose frills, and she was so dainty.

Eli's gaze had followed that of the men. And stayed. What a pretty little thing, like a painted doll. Lavender was unsure what to do next. She knew it must be Eli Bradbury standing beside the great iron gates, so obviously admiring her. But what next? She couldn't just stop walking, so her short steps took her to the towpath. The barges were moored alongside, swaying gently as the wind caught them, ruffling the feathers of a swan on the water. Lavender continued. She could feel his eyes following her; she willed him to come after her. The breeze was tugging lightly at her parasol.

It was so easy, the touch of genius. She just let go her hold. The tiny, pink-frilled flower of satin floated up and away from her, its trim handle as light as a stalk. It bumped on to the barge and she held her breath for an instant; she didn't want it to stop there, that was too easy. 'Oh! Oh!' she cried, and then, to her great delight, the wind obliged her yet again and lifted it up once more, sending it scudding across the surface of the water, upside down. The parasol floated serenely.

'Oh, no,' she cried, 'oh dear,' and turned to her right where, of course, she saw Eli hurrying to her rescue.

'Here, here, lend a hand.' Eli was magnificently in command. 'Come along, you there, use a boathook, can't you?' He'd run along the river bank, king of his castle, just the right person to rescue a damsel in distress.

The young boatman who had come up on deck to see the cause of the commotion didn't mind a bit of larking about for the girls, but he had no intention of getting himself wet in the process. Clutching his boathook, he leaned out, but nowhere near far enough for Eli's inflamed sense of gallantry. The master of the brewery was remarkably light on his feet for a man of mature years and was on to the narrow boat in a twinkling.

'Further, come on, damn you.' Eli was becoming agitated, the breeze was ruffling the frills on his quarry, and he had a premonition it was about to take flight.

'Come on, damn you.' He pushed the reluctant rescuer to lean further over the water. With his final, most hearty shove he propelled the boatman over the edge.

The man went in head first, still clutching his pole. He emerged almost instantly in a flurry of brown foam, swearing like a trooper.

'None of that, none of that in front of the lady!' cried Eli, who was very quick to notice that the boatman was in water up to his chest, but with his feet firmly on the river bed. 'Go on then, go on after it.'

'I can't,' wailed the waterlogged, reluctant rescuer. 'It gets deep out there.' He gestured towards the centre of the canal, where floated the pink object of Eli's desires.

'Well, swim then, damn it!'

'I can't, I can't, not with all me clothes on.'

'Five guineas if you fetch it. There you are, that's a reward for you, five guineas.' Eli was nearly jumping on the deck in his eagerness. The boatman still wavered, looking pathetically out at the quarry.

With a splatter of bare feet on the decking the boy dashed past Eli. He nearly had his employer in the canal, he was so quick. With a spectacularly bad dive the boy was in the water. He surfaced, shaking his head like a dog to clear the sodden hair from his eyes, then he was off, head held as high as he possibly could above the water. In a frantic dog-paddle the boy advanced. The wind, capricious as always, gave the parasol a little nudge away from him.

The cheer from the bank made Eli turn round. Half of his workforce was ranged along the bank; Eli's offer of five guineas had pulled them all out of their listening places. Eli flushed with pleasure. That dear little creature whose romantic token he was rescuing was clearly overcome with delight and was clapping her dainty hands in rapture. He turned back quickly as a cheer heralded the boy's success. There! Brave boy!

Peter was greeted as the conquering hero. Eli bestowed the largesse in his dripping hand, his mates clustered round him. There'd be a free drink if they played their cards right. And Lavender, well, Lavender was the delight of them all. It was only right and proper that she should walk off on the old man's arm, lucky old devil. Still, it had broken the afternoon up a treat.

When Harold slunk back into the office no one bothered to tell him of the excitements. He wasn't the sort to share a laugh, and if they told him then Peter would have to stand him a drink as well, which would be a pity, since Harold was nobody's favourite.

Lavender and her benefactor strolled amicably along the canal bank. Eli had placed his well-manicured, broad hand over her little, white gloved one. He breathed the refreshing air coming off the water like a new man. That was just how he felt, renewed. He'd been so long organizing his family's fortunes that he'd forgotten himself. He needed a little admiration, a little charm, a little dalliance. The word 'dalliance' had drifted very gently into his mind. 'And what were you doing down at my brewery, mm? Come to see the horses, had you? Or come to meet a friend?' Eli didn't for one moment imagine that his last question was anywhere near the mark.

He had no idea that the becoming blush on Lavender's pretty cheeks, the one he supposed he himself the cause of, was occasioned by her fleeting thought that he might have guessed.

'Oh no.' She was managing her vowels pretty nicely, as

she thought he probably liked a bit of gentility. 'I just wandered there. I've got so little to do now, you see.' She lowered her eyes most invitingly.

'Why is that?' asked Eli, duty bound to enquire.

'Well, since my poor dear husband died, you see, I've no one to keep house for, except myself. And there wasn't that much money, all things considered, so I'm only in a little tiny place. Today was the first day out of my mourning clothes. I just wanted to get out of the house. You can understand that, can't you?'

'Oh yes,' agreed Eli wholeheartedly, 'I understand perfectly.' And he did. So perfectly that when the first slight drops of rain began, he called a cab for them. They drove out of town and up on to the heath by Tovil. It was a touch bleak outside, but cosy and warm in the cab's interior. Eli called out to the driver that he could take a stroll, or have a drink at an inn; or anything his heart desired, in fact, thanks to the sovereign that his fare had just tipped him. Eli explained that they just wanted a little peace and quiet.

That was six sovereigns the afternoon had cost Eli so far. But he got his money's worth.

They managed very well, considering the narrowness of the leather seat and Eli's not inconsiderable bulk. Lavender lay back very decorously, her skirts piled high and foaming round her waist, Eli balanced rather dangerously on one knee, but he didn't notice the pain in his knee or how he got the bruise on his thigh that turned so purple afterwards. Eli was in heaven, where he hadn't been since his wife had died. Lavender was perfect; a widow, not a virgin, a woman in need of solace like himself. The cab driver had a quiet smoke sheltering from the drizzle under a hawthorn tree. The cab was bouncing merrily on its springs, but the horses carried on grazing happily. It wasn't the first time their fare had been more than usually profitable thanks to a bit of love in the air, and he didn't suppose it would be the last.

When the cab had been still for a few minutes, he approached it, whistling loudly and untunefully. He mounted to his seat, took up the reins and called out, 'Ready for the off, guv?'

The girl's voice answered; the old boy was probably still puffed. 'Right you are, cock, we're for a slap-up dinner now. Where's good?'

'Pub or hotel?'

'Ow!' cried Lavender, 'a hotel please, we're celebrating.' She gave Eli's arm the nicest little squeeze.

He sat back, more at peace with the world than he'd been in months. What a sweet little creature, a sweet, sweet little creature. He looked appreciatively down on her, as she beamed her happiness back. Lavender had done it, sorted out her little problem just right. Soon, not too soon, but soon all the same, it wouldn't be her little problem, it would be her little bit of splendid news.

Isabella lifted the letter up again from her desk. Margaret hadn't written for weeks and now she could understand why. Politics! It was unbelievable. Margaret had always been an independent, impulsive girl. But Isabella had thought that her friend's independence related to her beloved art. Now, out of the blue, this. She read the letter again.

My dear Isabella,

You must not reproach me for being a poor correspondent. Your friend has been very, very busy on your behalf as well as her own. On behalf of all we women in fact. You will be impressed – at least you ought to be – to learn that I am now a fully paid up member of the Women's Liberal Federation. The words 'paid up' remind me. My sudden access to money, which bought your camera, an identical one for me and paid my subscription to the aforesaid, was thanks to my having the inspiration to sell all my artist's paraphernalia. Wasn't I surprised at how much I was worth! I was very fortunate to find a fellow member of the fellowship who was intent on inspiring her invalid son to paint. She happily bought everything I had and I, even more happily, pocketed my small fortune. Of course, there is nothing left of it now, so in pursuit of further affluence I am giving art lessons to small, fairly innocuous, but very messy children, again infants of fellowship members. It is wonderful to find so many new friends, all willing and eager to help each other.

I must stop rambling. I have a vast number of pamphlets to deliver before the meeting tonight. I should not be stealing time to write to you at all. But I had to tell you of our decision, and to tell you to start to study the newspapers very earnestly. Read everything you can about the camps that the Boer women and children are being put into, after they have been dispossessed of their homes. You must become involved, Isabella. You will see from the enclosed snippet our decision – we are not the first to make it, and please God not the last. However difficult it is for you (because of you know who), you must do something. Everyone must.

I have been chosen to write to the Boer women, assuring them of our sympathies with their hardships. The authorities seem to view this natural reaction of ours as something close to treason. They are making communication into and out of the camps as difficult as they can. Do you have any influential friends in your new well-connected life who may help us?

I shall write again as soon as I can. Have you taken any photographs yet? I almost forgot. I am intending, as soon as I can, to buy a chemical camera. Their definition is superb, and I shall look very elegant with singed eyebrows!

Your friend, Margaret

The enclosed newspaper cutting was from a May edition of the *Manchester Guardian*. It reported on a meeting of the Women's Liberal Federation, where the ladies had decided, for the time being, to concentrate their efforts on the conduct of the Boer War rather than on women's suffrage.

Isabella stared blankly into space. The word 'suffrage' would make her father have a seizure. He, of course, was the 'you know who' Margaret referred to. And the war her father saw as another glorious example of Empire in action, whatever it cost.

Loyalty was a difficult thing for Isabella. To whom did she owe it most? Her father, her sister who was another true believer in British might, or did Isabella owe it to herself, to inclinations that could take her at least a part of the way Margaret was going?

Well, she knew Michael and Johnnie who were out in Africa with the army. The Montford family was certainly influential. Perhaps they could do something. At least, Michael might. Johnnie was obviously still not speaking to her and to ask for help in Isabella's name would be to invite a definite refusal. But, Michael, he was different.

She thought for a moment, then took up her pen.

Dear Margaret, she wrote.

The courtyard in front of the elegant hotel was almost overflowing with carriages. Afternoon tea at the Savoy was apparently a magnet for American visitors to London. As Hermione stepped down from her cab the twang of transatlantic accents was even louder than the cabbies' strident cockney. Once through the foyer, crowded with comings and goings, all was miraculously calmed. As she was decorously ushered into the tea room Hermione recognized Betsy at once. It was a shock, after all these years; it must be thirty at least. And there she sat, still so very clearly Betsy McLintoch. Of couse, that wasn't her name now, she'd been married twice and her surname was Macaul now.

Hermione put her hand up uncertainly to straighten her hat. It was broad, swathed in silk, the latest fashion. She had a feeling Betsy would find it difficult to recognize her.

Hermione herself sometimes wondered who the grey-haired, unremarkable old lady was who stared out of the mirror at her every morning.

'Hermione! Hermione!' Betsy was on her feet, coming towards her. Seen close to, the years had not really passed her by. 'Hermione, it's so good to see you, after all this time.' She took both her visitor's hands in her own. 'I can't tell you what this means to me. I know we wrote to each other – I thought you were very brave to do that, Hermione – but I never honestly believed we would meet again. I really, really am so happy. Come on, let's sit down and you can tell me all your news, and I shall tell you mine, and . . . oh, isn't it so good to be together again?'

Hermione could only nod her head in agreement. She felt the sting of tears and it was a long time since she'd felt such a strong emotion. She and Betsy had been very close once; Hermione hadn't really had such an intimate confidante since. How they'd changed! She looked down at their hands: hers and her friend's were the hands of old women, rich old women, pampered, cared for, heavily ringed but still dry, with paper-thin skin only kept from cracking by expensive creams.

Betsy interpreted the look. 'Funny isn't it, Hermione? Some days I don't feel much different from when we were girls together, then something makes me realize. Usually it's something to do with the children, remarks their friends make; some of Mark's contemporaries have even gotten married. There are babies, and some of my own contemporaries are grandmothers. My, when I think how carefree we used to be.

The pastries came, overflowing with cream, deluged with chocolate. Betsy reached out to pour the tea.

'It's a pity you never had children, Hermione; they can be a great consolation as the years go by. They bring their troubles too, but I'm very glad I have them, very glad indeed. Mind you, I think you look a good five years younger than me; perhaps the children took more of a toll than I thought!' Betsy was laughing happily. She'd seen the hurt on Hermione's face at the talk of children; now she'd wiped it away with her little white lie.

'Are we going to talk about William, or are we going to ignore his existence?' Hermione surprised herself by asking the question, which had popped out around a mouthful of cream éclair.

It was Betsy's turn to look uncomfortable. 'I suppose you're right to bring him up,' she said. 'We ought to make a clear-cut decision.' She looked suddenly very American, capable and firm-minded, quite unBritish. 'We never really referred to him in our letters, did we, Hermione? Just as I never really wrote to you about why it all happened. I never told you, and you never asked. I have no idea what William told you. His letters were so very, very bitter. Then your first letter came, after the death of my father. You can have no idea how grateful I was.' Betsy looked up at her friend. 'Those times were desperately difficult; no one who hasn't lived through that sort of thing can possibly imagine how difficult. I wrote to William, you know, three long letters. Each one trying to explain to him what had happened. He never answered. Oh, I got a few more notes from him, but they weren't answers, they were just more about what he thought of me. It was all pretty terrible.'

She paused to take a lace handkerchief from her bag. 'No, no, don't look like that, Hermione, I'm not going to cry, your English weather just makes me sniff a little. Here, do have another cake. They're so good; no one in Chicago makes them quite like this. I wouldn't say that to just anyone, you know Hermione; I am very proud of my country, but I guess I can let London lay claim to the best cream cakes.' She reached out and patted Hermione's hand on the table. Her friend's concern was touching. 'Would you let me explain it all to you, Hermione? I think I would like to.'

'Yes, if you want to, Betsy. But you don't have to, you know; it was all a long time ago.' Hermione sipped her tea. She would like to know. She'd always sympathized with her brother, but he did tend to over-react and she'd never quite known the exact truth.

'Well, here goes. Of course you must know that the main thing was that I took the jewels with me? It was while I was up in London, having a fitting for my wedding dress, that I got this urgent, desperately urgent, message to come home, that there had been a disaster. William wasn't with me, he was off hunting with the Quorn. I was so worried that I just gathered up everything and ran. I didn't even think about having them, not at first that is. I left messages everywhere for William, but he'd moved on, gone to hunt somewhere else, and I simply couldn't get hold of him. I left notes saying that I'd had to go home at once, that I'd write and explain everything as soon as I could.' Betsy paused for a moment, her thoughts running ahead of her words. 'The moment I docked in New York I heard about the terrible Chicago fire. I didn't know about it until then, I just thought there had been an accident in the family or something. The train across country seemed so slow, it was just awful. Everyone I met seemed to have some new story of the disaster; the fire had raged for days, thousands of buildings had been destroyed. By the time I reached Illinois I was convinced that my whole family must have been wiped out. I was in a pretty bad state. We were lucky, though. We'd lost everything, as all our money had been tied up in the offices that were burnt down, but the family was safe. Safe from the fire, that is.'

Hermione beckoned for some more tea. Betsy was looking frail; the memories were not good for her.

'Only a few days after I'd got back home,' she continued, 'my father had a seizure. We were all there, my mother, my brothers and my father, at the table. Father stood up suddenly, kind of choking, then fell down on to the floor. It was horrible. The boys carried him up to bed. We got a doctor in, and he said it was the shock of losing his money really. The reality of the fire he could cope with, but not the fact that we were pretty near penniless. The next morning a letter arrived from William. I was upset, I just cried over it and my brother Bill took it away from me and read it. He showed it to Dick and they went wild. I'm afraid your brother had put a whole lot of thought into my sudden departure, Hermione, and none of it was nice.' Betsy looked over at her friend. 'He accused me of having staged the whole thing. Us meeting, even our falling in love, so that I could steal his family jewels. That's how he put it, Hermione, steal. I couldn't believe it. I'd been expecting to go back to England. I knew I'd have to stay a while longer in Chicago, but I'd never meant not to go back to William. And there he was with his mind already made up, hating me.

'My God, I'd no idea.' But if Hermione allowed herself to think of it, she should have had an idea; she knew that William rushed his fences.

'I wrote back straight away. I don't think William could even have read it, though. A few weeks went by – I don't remember much about them; I was pining I guess – then Bill and Dick went off to see a lawyer. There was a lot of questioning, they insisted on seeing all the letters William had ever written to me. I had them, I still have, come to that. Eventually the lawyers said that the jewellery was mine. We had been officially engaged, I'd been given it as a present and William, they decided, had broken the engagement with those awful letters. I think the lawyer wrote to England asking if there was a possibility of a reconciliation. I know that nothing was done for a few more weeks while they waited on a communication from William's lawyers. Then my brothers came to me. They said it had been legally proved that the jewellery was mine to dispose of. They said that if they sold it they could refinance their company. Chicago was being rebuilt out of the ashes already. We are a nation of achievers, you know, Hermione. They said that if I agreed it would help Papa who couldn't stand another attack. So, of course, I said yes. What else could I do? Anyway, the boys did very well, very well indeed. Pa lived out his remaining months in comfort and was really proud of them. When he died I wrote for the last time to William saying that although I no longer had the jewellery, I would have liked to send him the money we'd raised on it. We were doing well enough by then to afford that. I don't think you'd have been very proud of William right then, Hermione. I could understand some of his behaviour, when he thought I'd run away from him, but not that long afterwards. He was very bitter. Of course he wouldn't take the money, which was very stupid. I know now that he's not what you'd call wealthy. What's your good old-fashioned saying, "Pride comes before a fall"?'

Hermione realized she'd underestimated the change that time had wrought in Betsy. This was a formidable lady sitting opposite her now. It suddenly occurred to her that the suggestion of meeting was not simply to chat over old times. There was something else motivating Betsy. The past history had only been to set the scene. What was next?

There was a flurry of new arrivals in the salon.

'Ah,' Betsy was on her feet in an instant, 'here you are, dears, come on. Adele, say hallo to Hermione, Mrs

163

Bullstone, that is, and Mark, and finally David.' Betsy flourished in the company of her family. Her daughter Adele was a real American beauty, brightly vivacious, dressed impeccably in dark blue and white, wearing a hat with nautical echoes that set off her brown curls. The boys shone with New World elegance: Mark, the eldest, with dark straight hair, was tall and slim, his brother David a shade shorter with the bouncy hair of his sister. They were a handsome family. A formidable source of energy. At once the room came to life as there was a great moving of chairs, the ladies' tea was cleared and a whole new one appeared. Hermione sat in a daze at the organizational ability displayed by each and every member of the family.

'What a shame your father can't be here with us,' Betsy said to her assembled offspring.

There was a pause which it seemed only natural for Hermione to fill with her question. 'Is your husband here in England with you then, Betsy?'

'Oh yes, dear,' Betsy answered. 'I thought you knew. He's with George at this very minute. Yes, that's right,' she added to Hermione's astonished look, 'he's with your George. They've been involved in some business together for quite a while. That was one of the reasons for our trip.'

'Only one of them, Ma,' put in Adele. 'The most important reason, Aunt Hermione is – oh, I may call you aunt, mayn't I? We've all heard about you for so long I feel I must. The real reason is to find me a husband. What I want,' the efficient Adele continued as she took off her lace gloves so that she could tick her requirements off on her fingers, 'what I want is a handsome Englishman, with a title, a lord I think. I want him to have lots of rolling fields and woods and things and I want him to have a castle. A really, nice charming sort of castle where we can

164

stay when we're not touring the Continent and that sort of thing.'

'I think you'd better add money to that list, my dear,' her new aunt added in a faint voice, 'that kind of lifestyle is expensive, even in England.'

'Oh, he needn't have money, Auntie, I've got plenty of that myself. We're here to buy me a husband, aren't we, boys?' She grinned at her brothers. 'I know just what I want and they're going to get it for me.'

The assembled Americans were mightily amused at Hermione's expression; it was just too quaint for words.

The scene in the Pencombe billiard room could have been painted by Rembrandt. It was a study in classic aristocratic pose.

'Have you any idea what you are doing to the family name?' Lord Montford had drawn himself up to his full height, his face expressionless in his fury. Michael was standing as close to attention as an English officer ever can. Even though he had now discarded, for ever, his country's uniform. 'Have you any idea what the talk will be, eh?' his father continued. 'My God, it will be all over town by now. I shall be cut everywhere, by everyone. Good grief, I just can't get over this. You're the last person I would have expected this sort of thing from, the very last.'

Michael waited to reply until his father had slowly lowered himself on to a ladder-backed side chair. Even talking of his shame made the old man shake. 'Perhaps it would help if you told me what you meant by "this sort of thing", sir.'

'What? You dare to talk to me, do you? Don't think I intend carrying on any kind of dialogue with you. I know your sort. By God, to think I've nurtured a viper in my bosom, all these years. You didn't even have the courtesy to let me know you'd returned to England. All the attention that's been lavished on you, all the hours I've spent, my God.' His lordship was spluttering; clearly he was in danger of losing his power of speech.

Michael wanted to leave. This was intolerable, but there had to be some attempt at reconciliation. Apart from anything else, Michael knew his father would take years to forgive an affront, and he didn't think they had that long. The old man had changed a lot in the time that Michael had been away. And that wasn't all that had changed. Here, in the billiard room that had once been their sanctuary, all was becoming bright and new and alien; Bradbury money had been at work.

Lord Montford couldn't keep still. He got to his feet and turned away from his son to walk to the windows. Dull panes let in only a little of the outside light; out there somewhere there would be sunshine. In here, with the smell of varnish on the walls, the new vivid green cloth folded reverentially waiting to be laid on the new slate bed that now topped the old table, it was as if it were all in a dream.

'There is only one honourable way out of this.' He didn't call Michael by his name, he couldn't. 'You know what you must do.'

Michael felt the revulsion strike him. He thought he would be physically sick. This was unreal, quite unreal. 'I hope that I don't understand what you mean, sir. I think,' Michael said, groping for words, 'I think this has all got quite out of hand.'

His father spun round to face him, his face suffused with blood. He was livid. 'Out of hand? Out of hand, you degenerate?' He hurled the words. 'No one in this family, no one, has ever acted a coward as you have done. First you're sent home, not a scratch on you, not a mark. Fatigue, nervous exhaustion they say; that's bad enough, by God. But we might have survived that ignominy, given time. Then what? Then what indeed? A letter from the War Office, asking me if I am aware of the carryings-on of my son. Asking me, no, not asking me, damn it, telling me to control you from harassing them. By God, if you weren't my son you'd be on charges of sedition by now. The Boers are the enemy and as that they'll be treated, men, women and children. Now,' he paused, a kind of mad reason lighting his face, 'now you will do me the honour of taking the only step open to you. It would have been better for us all, if I hadn't had to ask you. Go on, get out of my sight.' He turned his back.

Michael stood for a moment longer, then turned and left. He went to the gun room and took down a ratter. It was a simple, single-barrelled gun. He didn't need anything more impressive. He took one cartridge from the box and loaded it.

He walked out into the afternoon light. It was almost autumn; he could see it in the touch of brown at the edges of the horse chestnut leaves topping the courtyard wall. He walked out through the east gate. There was no one about. Eli's team of gardeners were hard at work creating a new fountain in the centre of the west lawn. The brewery money was being poured into and over Pencombe.

Othello came padding round from the stables, but Michael ignored him. He didn't want the dog's company today. The retriever sat down disconsolately on the gravel. He waited until his master had cleared the drive, then set off on a walk of his own across the fields.

Michael wandered out towards the lake. He did not have any particular route in mind, he was just wandering, as his mind was wandering. It was all still so unreal. The very greenness mocked him. He saw in it tones of Africa. When the rooks cried he fancied it was the children calling as they played in the camp. He had said little, he thought.

Certainly not as much as he had felt in his heart. But it had been enough to send regimental arrows of righteousness winging to his father. He had reacted to the parental summons and abandoned London at once. Where was the champion that Mrs Verboert had called to in him? Not in the puzzled, lost soul following the dictates of his father – a father from a generation without pity.

He walked down to the lake's edge. It was a deep, rippled blue. Like watered silk. Lucinda had a dress like that. Lucinda. He had not felt up to meeting her after his return. He tried to remember her the way she'd looked that evening at the ball and half closed his eyes to summon up her face, but the hard image of Isabella's photograph crowded in and then was jostled by the painful pride of Mrs Verboert. He remembered her blue eyes, her fair hair, which had reminded him then of a friend at home.

'Hey, hey you! Get on out of it!'

The cry made him look up. It had come from behind the copse away to his left.

'Hey! Hey!'

He started to walk towards the shouting. There were sheep in the field and he could see they were running, a scattering of late lambs among them.

'Hey, you bastard, stop that. I'll get . . .'

Michael suddenly remembered Othello and started to run. Like running in a dream he was too slow, always and for ever too slow.

The crash of the shot stopped him for an instant. Then he started on again, this time walking; the scene would be waiting for him.

The sheep had run into a huddle. Lying on the ground in front of them a lamb lay limply, panting, its eyes black and wide with fright, tufts of loose wool pulled from its flank. Othello was lying spread out on his side, his head a tattered mass of blood and bone where the shot had taken

168

him. Over him the sun-burned farmer stood, muttering in his satisfaction. He carried a gun very similar to Michael's, a working gun. He looked up.

'Ah, Mr Michael, sorry, sir, but he'd done it for the last time. I've seen him at it before, now just you look.' The man gestured to the lamb.

But Michael didn't stop at the words, he just carried on walking to the dog. He stooped down and reached out a hand. For a moment he couldn't touch the still warm body, then he laid his gun slowly and carefully down on the grass. He lifted the dog in his arms. Its poor head lolled down. The farmer looked sadly at the man and his dog, but he'd done right. He looked with compassion and not with contrition.

Michael walked back slowly. By the time he got to the billiard room the blood had stopped making a trail. His father was where he had left him. 'Father.'

The old man spun round. He'd heard the shot; this was the last voice he'd thought to hear.

'Is this what you wanted?' Michael lay the dog down gently on the slate-topped table. 'Is this what you wanted for me?'

Lord Montford walked slowly towards him and put out hesitant arms; he had never embraced his son. There were tears on the withered cheeks, tears of anguish that even his aristocratic soul had not been able to prevent. 'God forgive me, God forgive me,' he said as he slumped forward in his son's strong arms.

Dove brought Isabella the parcel with an obsequiousness that made her want to kick him. He was her sister's lapdog, he made that perfectly plain. Services for Isabella he performed with condescension lightly veiled by a creeping charm as befitted the heir-apparent to butlerdom at Pencombe.

The box-shaped parcel had been posted from London. Michael must have given it to someone coming home. She very nearly didn't open it at all. The camera was too much part of the past. Then she smiled at herself for being so ridiculous, laid down her book and started to unwrap the package. Besides, there might be a note from Michael. Lucinda was being so odd about imparting any information whatsoever about her fiancé's welfare in South Africa that Isabella was eager for news. She looked in vain for his handwriting. But she did notice something, or rather two things, which made her think she might now have a clue as to Lucinda's behaviour.

Enclosed with the camera was the first photograph that Isabella had taken. She was pleased with the clarity of it. The horses were perfect, as were most of the hounds. There were two separate fuzzy areas where there'd been movement, but the overall effect was surprisingly good for a beginner. Her father was magnificent. She hadn't looked closely at him in a long time, she suddenly realized. His wealth suited him, he had expanded. Johnnie was smiling and looking over towards a hound, one of the blurred ones. Michael was looking frankly, openly, straight into the lens of the camera. Isabella caught her breath; she'd never seen him before quite like that, unguarded, without reserve. It was as if he was looking right at her, into her eyes. Lucinda was also looking right at Isabella. She was, quite clearly, furious. The expression of pure selfishness was one Isabella knew well. But Michael wouldn't. He must have been horrified. Looking at them, almost side by side, they did not make an ideal match.

She laid the photograph down hesitantly. She couldn't show Lucinda; she'd never be forgiven. She picked it up again quickly. She tore it across and across, through the tell-tale likeness of Lucinda. By accident, Michael's face

170

remained whole. It looked up at her from the heap of pieces. She slipped it into her book. She couldn't bring herself to rip it up.

The other photograph produced no such dilemmas. She knew at once what she had to do with it. It was Timmy and his father, standing together in front of a traction engine. Unfortunately it wasn't quite as clear as her first shot, but it was a good likeness of the man and his son. Timmy should have it. She would take it to him herself. It was mid-afternoon and the men would be out gathering in the harvest. If anyone was at home at Reason Hill, it wouldn't be the master of the house. She still didn't feel up to facing Thomas.

It was a delightful ride. Isabella took the lane that ran along the top of the ridge. The bicycle had given her freedom. The sun beat down from a high sky, and she was thankful she was wearing the wide straw hat. The hedgerows were crowded with blackberries, black, red and green. There were even white flowers still on them. She suddenly thought how like a family the plant was. The different ages, living and growing together. Eventually some would die. But there would be new birth next year. Her thoughts touching on death was not accidental. Her friend Oliver was slipping away fast. He was so tender, gentle in his belief. He tried to communicate his own, overwhelming trust in the hereafter to her. He had no fear of going, only concern that those left behind should not suffer. But she would suffer, she knew that, however much she read the lessons he advised and found a kind of comfort in the thought that the house of God had many rooms and Oliver was simply moving to another. All that aside, it would hurt to be without a friend; without his consolation.

The bicycle lurched alarmingly over the sun-dried track. The trees on either side of her were heavy with fruit.

Some of the other orchards had been stripped already. These were fine cooking apples weighing down the boughs. They'd keep till after Christmas. She would ask the cook to make sure to have some for their store.

She rode right up to the front steps of the house. The view over the weald was almost hidden by the heat haze. She looked down, startled for a moment, then saw that the tugging at her skirts was a tortoiseshell cat brushing up against her. It looked up with a plaintive yowl.

'Hallo, puss; what's the matter then?' she said.

It pushed itself up on its back legs to rub its face against her stroking hand. It pushed so authoritatively that she could feel the sharp white teeth as its lips parted.

'Oooh, you cross little puss. Not getting enough fussing are you?' She stooped down to obey the cat's apparent desires and stroked the back it arched for her.

'It's cross because no one's here to pet it, right enough. I don't hold with house cats.'

Isabella looked up, surprised by the voice. It was the woman she and Lucinda had met in the lane, the day they'd nearly had the accident with the wagon. 'Hallo. I didn't expect to see you here.' Isabella was smiling, but her smile wasn't returned.

'And why not? I'm here every day, rain or shine. That polished door knocker that you would have announced yourself on, that's thanks to my hard work. You'd have been hard put to find it before that. Green and tarnished it was. But I don't suppose you've come to look over my housekeeping, so what can I do for you?'

Isabella was sad the woman was so aggressive. She had liked her when they'd met before. But while Jenny had been prepared to like an Isabella who she gathered had been frightened off by Thomas, she didn't like one who called on him.

'It was Timmy I came to see,' Isabella said.

172

'He's out at the fields. With Thomas.'

'Oh,' Isabella coloured. 'I knew Thomas wouldn't be at home. I didn't want to see him.'

So it was true then. Jenny relaxed imperceptibly. 'They'll come back together,' she said.

Then she looked again at the girl. There was nothing wrong with her really, and Jenny did get lonely when the men were away all day. 'Why don't you come in for a cup of tea,' she relented. 'Perhaps I can sort out whatever you wanted to see Timmy for. And,' she smiled, 'you can amuse that dratted cat. It knows I don't like it, and winds in and out of my feet all day. It's a relief to get home to Yalding in the evenings sometimes. Though I must say everything else here is very nice.'

Isabella was very pleased. She too felt lonely. The thought of a cup of tea in pleasant company was comforting, and Jenny, now that she had gathered Isabella was not competing for Thomas's affections, was very friendly. They took their tea in the garden, in the shade of the yew tree where it was pleasantly cool. Birds were everywhere, singing, chirruping. There were so many that the cat ignored them, over-faced. After jumping up on to Isabella's lap it turned itself round in circles for a while, kneading with its paws to check the softness of its intended bed. Then it lay, curled up. Within minutes it was apparently asleep, purring contentedly. Jenny relaxed totally, freed of her feline persecutor.

They talked about a lot of things: the harvest, the weather, the hare coursing that they hadn't been allowed to watch. Then Isabella gave the photograph into Jenny's keeping, asking her to judge the right moment to give it to Timmy. Jenny flushed with pleasure at the responsibility. It was an honour, she said. She'd make sure the little chap didn't get upset by it. It was good that he'd have the photograph to help him remember his dad.

173

Then they talked about the war. Jenny hadn't heard of the activities of women like Margaret. Isabella saw her chance and launched into winning a new convert for the cause. She gave a skilful précis of the articles she had read, the newspaper columns that were beginning to express concern on conditions in the camps. Jenny showed a quick, bright mind. She was instantly compassionate for the cause of the children, scandalized at their plight and that of their mothers. Talking about it fired Isabella further.

To her own amazement she revealed to an admiring Jenny that she was thinking of going to Africa herself, as a volunteer nurse for the camps. Isabella only found out herself, as she spoke the words, how committed she was becoming. But it was true. She had no ties on her, not when Lucinda's wedding was over and done. Her father would be involved enough with the brewery and Pencombe Hall. She must lead her own life, do as her own morals dictated. She knew she must talk to Oliver about it; soon, before he was no longer there to advise her. She left Jenny and Reason Hill inspired with a sense of purpose. There was a reason for life: she didn't need to be an observer, she could be a doer.

She rode the bicycle back determinedly, oblivious of the scenery, her mind intent on its new path.

Jenny cleared the supper things from the table. It had been a simple meal: she had no time for fancy cooking now that she worked at Reason Hill during the day. She was glad for an excuse to be able to stand up, to move away from John's plaintive gaze. Her brother's scowling she didn't mind a bit, but her ex-beau's mooning was driving her mad; as was the fact that John had not actually been told he was an ex-beau. She would have to face up to it some time. But, for the moment at least, their conversation this evening was far removed from her love life: the eel trap still held the sailor's body and kept them in mortal peril.

'You can't persuade him off this idea?' Luke asked his visitor.

'Me? Persuade the magistrate? No one can persuade him to do anything, least of all me. He thinks he's God Almighty over everyone in his employ. Come to that, if he does carry on like this, he will have the power of God over all of us.'

This time the 'us' did not refer to the local magistrate's small workforce, but to the smuggling run that the two of them were part of.

'I'll tell you,' John continued, 'if he publishes that pamphlet he's going to have every man and his dog up in arms against us. It's crammed full of murder and violence. He's up to convincing the valley that not a soul can sleep safe in their beds at night while the run goes on.'

'He's clever, all right. Someone'll talk. Money's one thing: you might get an odd informer that way; but convince them we're a bunch of murdering cut-throats intent on their lives and their women and they'll be cackling like a wagon-load of old hens.' Tom leaned back in his chair. 'Bring us a bottle, Jenny.'

She hustled about, getting out glasses and putting the bottle of brandy on a tray. The number of glasses she brought spoke volumes.

'Good night,' Luke said coldly to her. He would deal with his sister in private, in the morning.

John stood and looked down despairingly at the glasses. It was the first time in his memory that Jenny hadn't stayed and joined them for at least one drink. She loved to be with the men, to be involved. She was telling him, as clearly as she dared, that their days were over. 'Good night, Jenny,' he said sadly.

'Have a drink, John.' Luke was furious, he had enough

on his mind without Jenny proving troublesome. She was as excited as a spring filly and he didn't for one moment suppose that Thomas Cade had marriage in mind. 'Have you got a copy of the draft?'

'No, I don't dare make one now. He's forever getting it out to add new acts he's dredged up, new tales he's wheedled from old men who should know better. I actually had the paper in my hands this morning, ready to take a chance and copy it down, when he came storming in to add some more. He seemed to believe me when I said I was reading it through to check the place names were written correctly. But he's suspicious of everyone just now. He sees himself making a great coup in rounding us up. He wants to move up to London, and this is his great chance to make a name for himself. God, I wish he'd chosen another way.'

'You're not alone there.' Luke stared moodily down into his glass; the amber liquid that normally soothed was burning in his throat, like a rope burn he thought with a grim smile. He had the feeling that the odds were stacking against him.

'So what was your lord and master's stroke of genius this morning?'

'Oh, you'll appreciate this one, Luke, it's his best so far.' John held out his glass for a refill; he needed it. He couldn't have the girl he wanted, and now it looked as if they'd have to close the run and he wouldn't even be able to amass the small fortune he had planned. 'He's added the story of a smuggling run that went wrong. It all happened over a hundred years ago, but he doesn't say that. The main gang was from Hawkhurst and that makes it local enough to stir up opinion against us. It began as a perfectly normal transaction by our lights. They contracted with a skipper at Rye for a boat and put a buyer of theirs aboard with gold to buy tea and brandy on Guernsey. They invested some five hundred pounds. They intended to offload at Christchurch Bay, so a Hampshire run became involved too. On the way back from the island, their vessel was stopped by the Revenue. All the men escaped but the boat and its cargo was towed into Poole, and offloaded into the Customs House there. The Hawkhurst representative, Perrin his name was, took instructions from his group, then met up again with the men from Hampshire. They made an agreement, signed and sealed, to support each other in rescuing their property by a raid on the Customs House. So far, all quite unexciting.'

'I don't know about that, I'm not sure any of our members would put their names to storming a Customs House,' Luke laughed.

'Anyway,' John continued, 'each of the men received some 135 pounds weight of tea from the raid, so it was a fair venture. Their problems began on the way home. Passing through Fordingbridge, one of the smugglers was recognized by a man called Chater who was given a bag of tea for old times' sake. The Revenue had got very excited at the raid and a reward of five hundred pounds was offered for information leading to the smugglers' arrest. Chater didn't go after the money, but he did talk to his friends and neighbours. That talk was heard, his smuggler acquaintance was put in gaol and Chater instructed to bear witness. Any man with half an eye can see that it was the stupidity of the Revenue that was responsible for what happened next.' John held his glass out again. Talking was thirsty work, or was it the reference to men of their own ilk being uncovered?

'The Revenue provided Chater with an escort to the JP where his testimony was required. The escort they chose was an old codger they sometimes employed to rummage vessels. A witness against a run, Luke, he should have been guarded by half a dozen militia at least, to be safe.

177

But just the two men had to make their route across country. They stopped for food at the White Hart Inn at Rowlands Castle. The landlady was no friend of the Revenue and sent for a pair from the local gang to question the travellers. They got them fuddled with drink and everything was revealed. They beat both men up, tortured them and buried the Revenue man in a foxearth, while he was still alive.'

'They were drunk,' Tom said.

'Oh probably, but that doesn't affect the power of the story. I don't suppose the Revenue man cared if they were drunk or sober.' John stopped talking. His was a very difficult dual role to play, close to law and close to lawlessness. Then he continued. 'They still had Chater. They took him back and chained him in an outhouse. Eventually they threw him down a well and stoned him to death. It makes powerful reading.' Luke banged his glass down on to the table. 'Damn that bloody miller. Damn him.'

John agreed in silence. Until the murder of the sailor there had been no killing on their stretch of the run. It had been important to them in keeping the locals on their side. But for the higher profits made thanks to evading the excise tax, and the essential secrecy of their activities, they were businessmen pure and simple.

'You've still got the body well dug in?' John asked.

'Not well enough for my liking. We'll have to do something with it. There must be someone who saw the bastard snooping around the village. If he just disappears off the face of the earth there'll be talk.'

'There is.' John had saved the biggest blow till last. 'The man's activities had been watched by the Excise. They've traced him as far as Flimwell.'

'God damn.' The glass broke in Luke's grasp, he'd squeezed it so hard in his rage. He slumped forwards in his chair. He had to think, he had to do something. Something to break the web he could sense being spun around him.

Luke changed into his best moleskin trousers with a grim smile. The last time he had dressed like this he had also been intending to meet with Thomas Cade. That interview had been conducted in a civilized fashion, a part of business completed by relative strangers. Now Luke no longer felt a stranger to the farmer. Jenny filled the house with her prattle about the man. About his fine farm, his ways with the men, his manner with Timmy. But Luke was more concerned with the man's ways with women, and his manners, in particular, with Jenny.

There was a silence in the waterside cottage that a few weeks ago would have been rare at midday. Now, with Jenny working at Reason Hill, Luke was getting used to his own company at lunch times. Getting used to it, but not enjoying it. His simple food eaten, he went out to the stable.

He walked past Brownie, dozing in her stall. For today's visit, he had felt it necessary to hire in some decent blood. His mare was fine for pulling the cart, or if needs be a few miles of sluggish transport under saddle, but that was the limit of her abilities. So he had hired himself a hunter. Fortunately at this time of year they came cheap. In another month, with the cubbing begun, he'd have had to pay upwards of three sovereigns for the day. He had better use for his money, especially now that they were cutting the brandy run's activities to the bone. He shouldn't have been foolish enough to spend his gold on Jenny's bicycle, either. That just made it easier for her to leave the cottage.

His way to the Maidstone road took him through the village. He surveyed the cottages from an unaccustomed height: seventeen hands at least, the ostler had said. It was certainly an impressive position from which to view the world, and also a considerable way to fall. Luke took a firmer grip on the reins as they veered round to approach the bridge. A horse that was hired out should have decent manners, he hoped, but he wished that he'd just used Brownie after all.

The waterman's growing nervousness communicated its way down the reins to the mouth of his mount, sensitive despite its continual change of riders. In fact, it was only very recently that Redwing had come so far down in the equine world as to be out for hire. That fall from grace had something to do with the shattered leg that his ex-owner was still nursing, the leg that had been so badly broken when the horse took fright at a high loaded waggon like the one waiting its turn to cross on the far side of the bridge opposite Luke.

He rode with his stirrups long, his hard calf muscles well in contact with the horse's side. Redwing shivered, a long thrilling shudder that ran through his coat, starting at his crested stallion's neck and ending at his flowing tail. The tail raised up, a sign that the distended nostrils scented danger.

They were on the bridge itself now, between the stone walls, the newly shod hooves echoing on the hollowness. Luke pulled on the reins to bring the head towards him, shortening the creature's neck to keep it in hand. From a fast jerky walk it was spasmodically breaking into a trot that Luke was discouraging with savage, downward jabs on the reins. He did not want to look a fool on his home territory. If he could have spared a glance he would have seen the bakers gathered at the bakehouse doorway to watch.

Nearing the centre of the bridge he had the reins as short as was humanly possible. His arm muscles were aching with the effort of keeping the horse in hand. The animal's weight was pulled right back on to its hind-quarters. It seemed to the watchers inevitable that it should rear and then bolt with or without its rider.

The hay wagon filled Redwing's vision: he had no intention whatsoever of passing it. But Luke's legs were of corded muscle and the tighter they gripped in their determination to act as an anchor, the more the trained mind of the horse was forced to go onwards, whilst the sight ahead encouraged retreat. The compromise set horse and rider crabbing, sideways but ever forwards, towards the far side. Luke's vision was briefly spoilt by the sweat dripping from his forehead.

If he was thrown here, or worse, if the horse fell, he was a dead man. A flood of calm, icy desperation filled him. There was no way but past the wagon. To turn would be to beg for a fall. The bridge was shiny with use, and there was no purchase for flying hooves.

The sudden stillness in the saddle unnerved the animal further, removing its power of independent thought. Struggling to shake its head free of the cutting bit and the tight restraining reins, it still inched forwards. They were only feet now from the end of the bridge. Luke bent his mount's head under and down, while he squeezed with all the strength in his legs. The animal coughed convulsively, almost pulling him over its head with the full power of its arched neck muscles. They were alongside the wooden sides, the green, fresh hay looming up above them. Luke had pulled the creature's head tight round, away from the obstacle. It was impossible for it to see the load, and it continued forwards in a straight line thanks to the power of its rider's legs.

They were past! He felt the anxiety drain from him in a flash; the open road was ahead of them. Just then the wagon driver, with nothing to amuse him now the mettlesome horse had crossed, flicked his oxen into action with his whip. The crack caught horse and rider unprepared. Redwing recovered first – which was why the talk in the public house that night was all about how Luke Jones had left the village, run away with by the fine horse he'd hired for the day; and not about how he'd managed to cross the notoriously difficult bridge with a horse that had been sold cheap, as it had all but killed its previous master.

Jenny might have guessed it.

She caught sight of her brother approaching through the orchards and bustled Timmy in through the kitchen door. So that was what Luke's preoccupied air had been all about this morning. Damn! She wished herself anywhere but at Reason Hill. She was creating a comfortable home in the once bachelor establishment, but she wasn't yet sure of her ground.

Damn! It would be the one day this week that Thomas had kept indoors all day. There had been a continual coming and going of his labourers; it was the final run-in to the grain harvest and plans were being laid. She had only seen Thomas briefly at lunch; apart from that her sole companion had been Timmy, and of course the cat. It wound its way through her legs as she crossed the kitchen to get the flat iron down from the shelf. She would make a start on the shirts that were piled up high in the basket. She banged the iron down on the range to heat.

Timmy was looking oddly at her, puzzled by their sudden rush indoors. He had been quite happy peeling the apples sitting out in the sun. It wasn't so much fun in the shade of the kitchen. But it still beat school. The beauty of it was that no one could even threaten him with it. It was still holiday time and the day was his own, and Thomas's and now Jenny's and of course his friend the cat's. He bent down to stroke Victoria. Jenny didn't think it proper to

182

call a cat after a queen, but Timmy thought it was all right. After all she was a very special puss, a proper house one, none of your scavenging round the barns for this tortoiseshell beauty. Timmy had a suspicion that Jenny didn't really like cats, but she never said anything. The funny thing was that Victoria never got between Timmy's feet or tangled up in Thomas's.

It was the first time Luke had been up at the house. It was handsome enough, red brick and red tile. A fine yew tree gave shade to a flat lawn that overlooked the view. A rustic bench provided a suitable seat for the master of the house to survey his acres. There was a neat vegetable garden and a scattering of roses. But it was far from water, up here, on the very top of the ridge. There wasn't even a glint from the valley below; the river had dropped so low in its banks as to be smothered by the enveloping green. Luke felt alienated. This was strange country to him.

Thomas had watched the last few hundred yards of his visitor's approach. His desk in the farm office window was specifically placed to oversee the farm track. He had had enough time to work out the reason for the visit. And to take in the horse's heaving sides, the lather staining its flanks. Thomas did not think well of a man who was heavy-handed with his horses or, indeed, a brother who was heavy-handed with his sister as he anticipated the waterman was about to be. In Thomas's book the woman was old enough to know her own mind. He went to open the door himself. It would compromise all of them if Jenny went.

'Good morning, Mr Jones.'

'Mr Cade.' Luke dismounted stiffly. The mad career uphill had taken the wind out of the beast, and most of the wind out of its rider.

'And to what do I owe the pleasure of this visit?'

'Whether you feel it's a pleasure or not had better wait until after I've had my say.'

'I'm just trying to be civil, Mr Jones, nothing more. Will you come in?'

The farmer led the way back to the office, Luke taking note of the substantial oak chest in the hall, the tall clock with the painted face that chimed two o'clock just as they passed. There was an old turkey rug on the wooden floor. The smell of beeswax hung on the air and there were late roses in a blue and white bowl on the window sill. He recognized his sister's homely touch and it gave new fuel to his anger.

They sat, Thomas at his desk, Luke in the supplicant seat. Thomas had no intention of making this easy so he sat silently, waiting for his visitor to begin.

'I have no doubt that you are aware of the talk?' Luke began. Now he wished he'd planned this out. His host was obviously well practised at intimidating callers.

'Talk, Mr Jones? And what talk is this?'

'Look here!' Luke banged his clenched fist on the arm of the chair, and tried not to wince; the reins had cut in deep. 'You know damn well what I'm here about. It's up to you to make an honest woman of my sister.'

Colour rushed into Thomas's face and he felt a surge of irrational anger. 'An honest woman? An honest woman of Jenny? That's how you interpret all this, is it? You've a low mind I can tell you. Your sister's come to help with the boy, to make what was a shell of a house into a home for the child, and you see it that she needs making an honest woman of. God help you, if you see evil in everything!'

Luke clutched the arms of the chair fiercely. His words were being turned about. What he felt for his sister, and the good name she had enjoyed, was being twisted. 'There is no need for you to bring the boy into it. I've nothing to

184

say about Jenny's feelings for the child. She's welcome to darn his socks and mend his shirts. That's not what I'm here about.'

'So you complain about her doing my washing and mending, I suppose. Many an honest woman has earned an honest shilling by performing that service for a man. And yes, by God, by cleaning my house and feeding me and the boy.'

'That's not what I'm here about.'

'Then what is it? What gossip is it that the village is agog about?'

There was no talk in the village, at least none that Luke had heard, but only in his head. Voices, insistent voices, that told him Jenny had thrown away her chances of marriage with John, tossed him on the dung heap. There had to be an alternative. Luke couldn't take the responsibility for her for ever. 'They say,' Luke took a gulp of air, 'they say she is your woman.'

Thomas was on his feet in an instant. 'That's a damned lie, an insult to her, and an insult to me, by God. If I can't be trusted with a housekeeper in my home, with the boy as well mind, the boy living with me day in day out, then what the hell's it all coming to? And you, you, Luke Jones, what do you believe?' Thomas had bent down; their faces were belligerently close, both flushed red with anger.

'I believe, I believe . . .' But Luke couldn't finish, couldn't bear to finish the thoughts that muddled in his head. He wanted her safely wed, that was all, so that he could put all his thoughts and energies to his own business. He had far too much on his mind right now.

'I believe, I believe,' he started again and then something snapped. He smashed his fist up into the face above him. Thomas staggered back, blood gushing from his nose. Luke jumped up, pushing the chair away. They were locked in a fighters' embrace in an instant. Thomas

185

struggled, blinded by pain and fury, sure his nose was broken. Luke's bile surged, bitterness flooding through him.

The door opened suddenly, thrown wide by Jenny who'd rushed in at the sound of smashing furniture. Close on her heels Timmy came peering round the door. The boy saw the blood, running freely. With a tiny whimper he fell to the floor in a dead faint.

'Stop it! Stop it!' Jenny screamed. 'It's Timmy. Stop it! Please.' She'd fallen to her knees beside the ashen-faced boy. 'It's the blood,' she said as she loosened the boy's shirt. 'He was sick when I cut myself in the kitchen the other day.'

The men had stopped their struggle. They stood above her, breathing heavily. As she talked, trying to cover her own desperate concern, she undid the child's belt buckle. His breathing was very, very faint. She turned frantically to Luke, 'Help him, help him.' Her brother bent down and turned up a marble white eyelid.

'Rub his hands, Jenny.' Thomas too was kneeling by the boy and began gently to slap the child's cheeks.

'Talk to him, Thomas,' Jenny said. 'It's your voice'll get through.'

Thomas talked, talked as he'd never talked to Timmy before, told him he loved him, told him he had a home here for ever, that Reason Hill would be his one day. A flush of rose crossed Timmy's forehead as he stirred, then struggled in their grip. His eyes fluttered open. They widened at the blood now dried on Thomas's face, close to his own. Then he smiled. He'd never realized before how much Thomas cared for him. He grinned shyly at them all, unaware, in his childishness, of how much Thomas had meant by his words.

★ ★ ★

Another letter from Margaret. Isabella was almost unwilling to open it. Oliver had been too weak for her to talk to about her plans. He'd slipped gently out of this world into the next, leaving her sad and lonely.

She left the letter until after dinner. She had found the last one disconcerting, to say the least. She was still applying herself to sifting the news with a more specific attention to the war. But to go further would require a commitment that she was not yet able to give and, despite her determination when she had spoken to Jenny, one that she was not yet honestly prepared to make.

'My dear Isabella,' it began as always. Then Isabella looked more closely. It had been written from an address in London! She read on.

Have you written to me since your letter with news of Lucinda's forthcoming marriage? I have not been at home to receive letters for several weeks and I am moving so quickly from one house to another here that nothing can catch me up. I sent the Montford names as you suggested. But have not yet heard if they were able, or indeed willing, to help.

My activities here are as a representative of the Women's Liberal Federation in Manchester. I have been in London for three weeks, and have attended a great variety of meetings and spoken to an immense number of women. Last night I was invited to a meeting of the women's branch of the South African Conciliation Committee at the Queen's Hall. There were women from all over Britain. It is wonderful how we are pulling together, thrilling to be a part of it. We passed a number of resolutions and if it wasn't two o'clock in the morning, and I wasn't writing by the light of a very small candle, I would tell you them all. But it will have to be brief – I cannot write in the dark! So, in short, we were unanimous in condemning this unhappy war and this government's policy that has already cost our country more than 20,000 poor souls. Isn't that an awful figure? There were also details of the cost, in money terms, that you would imagine would make any man think twice, even if they are heartless enough to see the soldiers simply as numbers in a book. We ended with a momentous resolution expressing

187

our sympathy with the women of the Transvaal and Orange Free State and expressing our deep regret at the action of our government. What do you think of that? It was splendid, a great joining together of womanhood. I felt so proud, Isabella. I wish you had been there. Why aren't you? You *MUST* join us.

I have tried to arrange a visit to you in Kent, but I do not see at the moment that it will be possible. I will try my utmost, though, and then we can talk and talk, and I shall persuade you.

Take care, and read all you can. The papers are going to be full of this. Try as the government will to restrict our freedom of speech, there are thousands of people who want to know more, men as well as women, I am sure.

Your friend, Margaret

It was certainly as well that Isabella had decided to read it in private. The thought that Margaret might at any instant appear was extraordinary. Especially a Margaret who sounded militant in her cause. Isabella's father had long ago forbidden the friendship. In those days it had been simply because he disapproved of Margaret's pretensions to the new art, and of her lax, bohemian parents, as he saw them. This time, he'd probably try and have her committed for insanity!

George quite deliberately shifted the half-smoked cigar from the left-hand corner of his mouth to the right. It was a gesture he performed when he was very, very pleased.

The information he held in his hands would be worth a considerable amount of money, and altogether this had the makings of a very good day. George Bullstone, at work in his office in Lombard Street in the heart of the City of London, was a very different individual from George, husband of Hermione, at home in Belgravia and sometimes at the country estate. Here, surrounded by the polished mahogany panelled walls, the marbled floors, the immaculately suited clerks, he was a man apart. George had created for himself an image of the successful man of finance, albeit not a member of one of the larger city institutions, but a person of substance, a man to have with one, rather than against.

It was in the position of antagonist that he had forced his niche. A natural-born predator, George could smell rich pickings where another man wouldn't catch a whiff. Take the Bradbury brewery for instance. Brewing made kings, and sensible kings kept king-makers alongside them. Eli Bradbury was unsupported in his role, therefore he was easy meat. Harold's neat clerkly hand made the valuable inside information, which George was paying a pittance for, look almost legal. The most interesting column of figures was the one for monies paid out, for raw materials as yet unprocessed. Particularly when it was added to the column for amounts owed to the brewery. Bradbury was being stretched. The fact that George would shortly be lunching with a partner of the bank that handled Eli's account was no coincidence.

Hermione had added to her husband's pot of pleasure over breakfast this morning. Apparently she would be lunching out herself today. With Lucinda and her father. Lucinda, Hermione said, was scouring London in the pursuit of expensive delights to heap upon Pencombe. Hermione had rattled on about the lovely Lucinda and the plans afoot for Chinese silk hangings for the drawing-room walls. She was also searching for the ultimate in fashionable lighting for the billiard room. Lucinda did so want to have a fitment similar to the one she had seen at Woburn Park, stately home of the Duke of Bedford and his family. At George's raised eyebrows his wife had hastened to explain that Lucinda had not actually been invited to the great house on a social occasion, but had visited on a conducted tour. George had been relieved; they themselves had not been invited as guests to Woburn yet, although all things would happen with time, and money. Being a City man George had no illusions at all as to what made the world go round. The main motivating force was money: it always had been and it always would be. It helped to have connections in the 'right' places. Hermione had most definitely been an asset to him, all things being considered. But without money a man was nothing, as Hermione's idiot brother had at last to accept. It was ironic that in choosing Eli Bradbury as his source of funds the viscount had brought another sacrificial lamb to George's altar; but it would all turn out satisfactorily in the end: for George, that is.

George had a good reason for lunching at the Savoy, but he felt slightly uneasy there all the same, as he was used to the hallowed hush of his clubs. Here there was a remarkable coming and going. His luncheon guest did not seem to notice, however.

'I say, George, these gulls' eggs are pretty good. Why don't you change your mind and join me?' Samuel Gregory, partner in one of the City's best known banking institutions, looked at George with pale eyes that matched the mottled eggs on his dish quite remarkably.

'No, no, I find a thin soup at luncheon suits me very well.' George's smile was not a genuine one. He liked gulls' eggs, all manner of eggs, in fact, but they tended to bind. George Bullstone had problems with his bowels.

'Excellent wine if I may say so, George, excellent.' The banker swilled down another glass of Pouilly Fuissé '94. True to his profession, he was extracting the full value of his lunch.

'Better than beer; Bradbury beer that is, eh?' George had put on his dashing, whisker-bristling, man-of-intrigue look, that thrilled Samuel to the core. He'd passed the odd hint on to George before and done very well out of it, privately, that is; this was a question of feathering his own nest. Meanwhile he was keeping an eye out for the bank's position. By keeping it out of trouble he would add a little more kudos to his reputation.

'Ah yes, beer. Yes, I'm afraid beer isn't exactly in fashion with us at the moment. Balances are what matter to us in the long run, of course. When we took this particular account there was a good, healthy working balance. Allied to the capital position it was considered something of a coup.' Indeed, Samuel had earned a pat on the back for obtaining Eli's account, and enjoyed the brewer's hospitality. But one must move with the times. 'You say we may be advised to keep a close eye on things, George?'

George paused for a moment before replying. The waiter was performing dexterously with a Dover sole. Most waiters in London's top eating establishments were spies, George knew that very well. He had several in his own pay.

'I think you may be advised to do more than just keep an eye, Samuel.' He smiled around a mouthful of the succulent fish. 'If I were you, I would start shortening my reins.'

'Really, as bad as that? I must say I admire you for keeping your ear so close to the ground. I hadn't heard a whisper.'

George smiled down at his plate. That wasn't surprising, since there hadn't been one to hear before he had started it, himself, moments before. They had reached a very amicable dessert. Samuel, having filled himself on a blood rich Chateaubriand following his sole, was managing only a dish of strawberries. George, who had nibbled at the edges of a ragout, was ladling down Cabinet Pudding. He had to fill up on something; a man's inner workings were a sure sign of his success. The more chaotic they were, the more a man was getting on in the world.

'Well, well, what a surprise to see you here, George!'

The handsome, silver-haired gentleman who loomed over their lunch table spoke with the full, rolling pride of a natural born American. He'd taken his own lunch in his suite at the hotel. George had said the most auspicious time to deal with a prospective source of finance was after they had eaten, and eaten well. George was rather pleased that Randolf Macaul in his search for sterling had agreed to foot their lunch. The wine bill alone was going to be considerable. But it had done its job. Samuel stood up to welcome the visitor to their table. He glowed at the remarkable service that liberally applied dollars had inspired. Of course he would accept a brandy, and a cigar.

Finally, sitting back with a sigh of pleasure, George put the magnificent Havana straight into the right-hand corner of his mouth. He could see the fat commission he was going to get from Macaul already tucked into his safe. It could snuggle up to the deeds of the brewery, alongside . . . George's beam of pleasure deepened. But he did not allow himself to finish the connection. He was at heart a very secretive soul. He distrusted even himself with thoughts of the total coup he was constructing.

It had taken three days of interviews for Eli to find the ideal man for the job. There'd been three close contenders who'd eventually been whittled down to two by the third's inadvertent admission that he had a sickly wife. Eli didn't need a man whose mind wasn't firmly on the job. The final two had been difficult to fault. Both men of experience, whose entire endeavour would be dedicated to their employer. Eli had been very close to tossing a coin to decide when he had a brainwave. At the final interview he offered both men a sample of the best of Bradbury beer, his Partner's Ale. It brought about the first divergence in their approach. One quaffed his ale with the ease of habit

192

and smacked his lips in appreciation. The other sipped it contemplatively, pronounced it excellent and then clearly had to force himself to finish the pint. That made the choice easy. Eli didn't encourage a man to drink more than his fair share, but then a man who couldn't sup his ale wasn't much of an advertisement for a brewery.

The successful applicant was Michael Nesbitt, soon to be ex-floor manager of an East London brewery. He'd have more responsibility at Bradbury's, which was in all ways a bigger business, which was why he wanted the job. He was ambitious. Eli had the man's curriculum vitae copied out neatly by Harold who, unseen in his cubbyhole office, swore eternal hatred of Nesbitt over every immaculately formed word.

It was that pristine testament that Eli now had amongst the sheaf of papers to take to the bank. He had felt the need to do it all at once: a new overall manager, and a new, expanded financial facility. He'd stayed up late for a week working on his figures. It wasn't that they needed falsifying; not at all, just a little judicious editing and there was no law against that. At least, not one that Eli knew of. Eli sat back in the train and glowed. Thank God it was all over. At last he'd be really free to dedicate himself to Lucinda and her plans. They would make Pencombe Hall into a showplace. But it would take a firm hand – Eli's. Lucinda was very good at coming up with ideas, but it had to be a man of experience to carry them out.

Samuel Eustace Gregory, banker, smiled thinly at the figures on his desk. He'd taken the brewer's account against his finer instincts, distrusting the man's northernness. Inevitably, he was about to be proved right. Damned outsiders always went wrong in the City.

Eli arrived flushed with bonhomie. 'Good morning, good morning.' He bustled into the bank exuding confidence. And why not? He felt on top of the world. 'Good to see you, Samuel. I must say it seems a very long time since I was here last. Still, a lot of water has passed under my particular bridge since then, yes indeed. You'll have heard my daughter Lucinda is marrying Pencombe, the heir to it that is, the Honourable Michael?'

'We have noticed the bills drawn on your account that point to such an occurrence, yes.' Samuel was his most banker-like. His wife called it his salmon face, with its hooked upper lip, and oily, expressionless eyes.

'Really? You pay that much attention to my account, do you, Samuel? I must say I'm flattered. Now, down to business.' He delved into his capacious leather case. 'I have some notes here you might like. Just a formality of course, but we men of business like to be seen to be doing our bit, mm?'

Eli was finding the going a bit heavy. He should have taken the banker to lunch first; it would have loosened him up a bit. Still, they were a fishy lot. He handed the file over the desk. 'You'll find a curriculum vitae on my new manager there as well. Excellent fellow, just what the brewery needs. If you just give me any papers I have to sign, then we can get off to lunch. I thought we'd go somewhere really special. I've booked already.' Eli's words ran down under the banker's stare.

Samuel had laid the file down, unopened, on his desk. 'What exactly did you think you might have to sign, Mr Bradbury?'

'What? Well, I thought perhaps there'd be something, but do my existing arrangements cover it? I'd be delighted if they did.' Eli was getting flustered, and the 'Mr' hadn't escaped him for a minute. He'd have to concentrate.

Samuel continued. 'I am rather at a loss as to what this visit is about.'

'Nonsense,' Eli's blood pressure rose with a surge. 'You know perfectly well why I'm here, Samuel. I simply want to extend my working facility and agree next year's financing for the Bradbury expansion. That's straightforward enough. It's only natural; at this time of the year every brewery is a bit stretched, at least every brewery that pays its suppliers on time.'

'Stretched?' Samuel looked astonished. 'Stretched? But that is a word very rarely used in banking circles, Mr Bradbury. In an exalted organization such as this,' he waved an arm to indicate the halls of reverence, 'it is not used at all. I would also point out that the affairs of your suppliers are no concern of ours. If it has compromised you to pay them, then you should not have done it. You owe a duty to the bank first. We took your account on the understanding that yours was a wealthy business, based on high-value capital assets, with a well managed cash flow. Such has not been the case, and the situation seems to be worsening.' Samuel paused for breath.

'The position of the bank is that, as a concession, we will allow you one calendar month to rearrange your affairs, Mr Bradbury.'

Eli had subsided like a burst balloon.

'At the end of the month we will review the situation. Obviously, in all our interests, we hope that you will have been able to show a marked improvement in your position. We shall at that time further require detailed plans for continued improvement. If this is not done, then we shall close your accounts. You may wish in the meantime to make alternative banking arrangements. In any case, we shall have to debit your account with the increased charges that are being incurred owing to the time and effort necessary in keeping it under close scrutiny.' He looked down at his immaculately manicured hands. 'We have moved fifty thousand pounds deposited in the account marked Pencombe into your brewery working account. The balance on that deposit account now stands at sixty thousand seven hundred and forty-seven pounds twelve shillings and four pence. Your working facility is now some ten thousand pounds in credit. We are unwilling for that account to go overdrawn during the month we have discussed. Should there be any likelihood of it doing so we will further debit the Pencombe account. If necessary we shall then transfer funds from your recently established family trust.'

'This is monstrous!' Eli nearly shouted the words.

'It is not monstrous, Mr Bradbury, it is simply good banking practice. You signed documents at the outset of our connection which, amongst other things, give us the power to move funds between accounts as we see fit. You should appreciate, Mr Bradbury, a bank is not a charitable institution, and its reputation must remain inviolate. Your actions have embarrassed us. We are being extremely civil in allowing you this month of grace.'

Eli jumped to his feet. 'One month; right, Mr Gregory, one month it is. But just you listen to me. I made a fortune when you were still drooling round your mother's skirts. Don't think a pompous little ass like you is going to bring down the Bradbury empire. Good day to you.' And he strode out.

'Empire? Empire by jove!' Samuel said to the empty room as he stood up and swept back his thin hair. 'Mother's skirts; God, it makes you sick. Chaps like that weren't even brought up by a nanny.'

Whinnying contentedly he took himself off to Wheeler's as Eli gave the cabbie an extra sovereign to gallop for the station. He'd got to get back to the brewery, back to work.

The hotel manager was very circumspect. Coming across his quarry in the foyer, he coughed softly, deferentially, into his tight-balled fist to announce himself, and then made his request. 'I wonder if I could just have a brief word, Mr Macaul?'

Randolf Macaul didn't know it, but this was the approach reserved by the Savoy staff for their best spending, often American, customers who sometimes required a guiding hand towards a suitable sense of decorum.

'Yes, sure, anything you say, boy.' Randolf quite liked the man.

'I hope you are enjoying your stay in London, Mr Macaul. If there are any more arrangements we can make, theatre tickets, trips to the country, anything at all, you have only to ask.' The manager paused but Randolf just waited; he knew soft soap when he heard it. 'I wondered if you might like us to provide a guide for your sons? Sometimes we find our overseas visitors like to employ a young Englishman, someone close to their sons' own age, to escort them of an evening. It is always difficult for strangers in any town to get the best of things.'

Still Randolf waited. He was being quite effective by his silence. The manager had to resort to stratagem two.

'Perhaps it would be simpler if you accompanied me up to your sons' room for a minute, sir?'

Randolf nodded. He had an idea the boys had begun to enjoy themselves. At least they'd stopped going on about wanting to go home and were never in for supper. That suited Randolf as he liked Betsy and Adele's company to himself. They were having a great time; they'd been to Drury Lane for the theatre, to the ballet, and they were going to the opera at Covent Garden. It was great that the boys were getting more into the swing of things. These happy thoughts had taken him up to the third floor where, a few doors away from his own suite, his sons' door was guarded by an hotel under-manager. Randolf raised his eyebrows, they were bringing in the reinforcements. At a sign from his superior, the young man unlocked the door. Very quietly, the three of them entered the room.

It was almost dark, the curtains still pulled tight although it was nearly midday. When his eyes had adjusted to the light, Randolf followed the manager's gaze. There were two beds in the room. The boys liked to share; they did at home, even though there were a dozen bedrooms in the house. They liked to talk on into the night and they'd clearly been amusing themselves well into the night on this occasion. There were several empty champagne bottles, most of them lying on their sides, one upturned in the aspidistra pot. The table bore the remains of a feast. Empty lobster shells, cracked oysters and assorted other delectables perfumed the air like a miniature Billingsgate.

The young Americans themselves were in their beds. Mark slept, face downwards, clad only in an evening shirt. His bottom, nicely rounded and pink as a baby's, glowed in the twilight. His right arm was flung out over a female form wrapped tight in a sheet, a nubile naked arm and one breast uncovered. David, on the other bed, was more decorous in that he was covered with a blanket. He lay flat on his back, snoring louder than a buffalo. Across the foot of his bed a girl lay draped, wearing a black lace-trimmed corset and stockings and suspenders. Randolf smiled in appreciation: she was a little beauty. He admired his sleeping sons for a little longer, then he noticed the others. On the floor between the beds slept two more girls, curled up, their hair tousled. They were quite, quite naked. Randolf fought down a grin. They were his sons, all right!

The visitors left the room and walked in silence to an alcove at the end of the corridor. The manager was very good at his job. There was no expression on his face whatsoever, except polite attention. He didn't even show the envy he felt.

'I do think, sir,' he said, 'that an escort may be the

answer. There are only a few rules we keep to here, you see. One of them is that we do not allow the visitations of gaiety girls. I'm afraid the particular company your sons have with them falls into that category.' From his own experience the manager knew two of the girls very well indeed. 'The other thing is, that in deference to the ladies in the building, I think it would be a good idea if your sons occupied separate rooms. Or at least,' he smiled, 'were seen to occupy them.'

Randolf had a fleeting urge to buy the hotel. That would show the creep. But reconsidering, he had other plans for his investments in England. And the boys did need a bit of pulling in hand. It wouldn't harm them to cool down a bit. 'I'll take the adjoining suite,' he said. 'Have it ready for the boys when they wake up. And I'd like them to have their sleep out, so make sure it's prepared quietly. I'll think about your offer of an escort and let you know. Meanwhile,' he put his hand into his pocket for his wallet, 'spread a little of this around. I like to oil the wheels, boy, oil the wheels.'

He walked back towards his own suite. He felt a passing pang for pleasures he had now grown out of. They would all go to Covent Garden tonight, all of them. The boys could be taught to appreciate a little culture for a change. That never did anyone any harm. And presumably there would be no opposition to the occasional opera singer being entertained in their illustrious suites; no, probably none at all.

It was George Bullstone who had the bright idea.

Having no sons himself he was prepared to put his thwarted paternal energies into sorting out the Macaul boys. Their father might be prepared for them to bucket round town, but George knew the system better. They would have to learn to be circumspect and be taught to run their social life by the rules.

It was that thought of 'rules' that gave him the idea. In his own youth, when he hadn't been whoring, he'd been gaming. At least, that was how he liked to look back on it. Although in truth, he'd been so busy making money that there hadn't been that much time for either. Which was why, not many years ago, in an effort to make up for his unmisspent youth, he'd set out on a progression of tutelage. The most satisfactory lessons had been those given to him by a dapper, professional player at one of the lesser known London clubs. The man had been a wizard at his game, and a master at imparting his talents to others. The game had been snooker, and George had become hooked for life. That was just what those boys needed: an interest to dilute their interest in things carnal, an alternative pursuit for the night hours.

Randolf was not quite so sure that George's suggestion would encourage his sons to enjoy entertainments vertical rather than horizontal, but it was, as he said, worth a shot.

The Curzon Street Club boasted the inevitable heavy chandeliers, the thick red, fitted carpets and the lush draped curtains of a London gentleman's gaming club.

Mark and David were here on sufferance. They'd decided to go along with Pa's advice for one visit, at the most two. In any case, they knew him well enough: he'd forget about their evil ways in a week or so. And they knew full well that he did not see their ways as evil at all, but it amused him to pretend that he did. They were a pretty close family, all for one and all that stuff.

'This,' the professional, resplendent in his spearmint green and rose-pink striped satin waistcoat assured them, 'is a billiard table.'

Mark nudged his brother surreptitiously. It was a pool table, any idiot could see that.

'On this table,' their mentor continued, 'we can play billiards or snooker. The difference in the games is in the number of balls and the rules. The cues and balls themselves are interchangeable. I gather from Mr Bullstone that you gentlemen wish to partake of coaching in the game of snooker?'

Randolf answered the affirmative for them. His sons' faces were remarkably similar when they sulked, he realized.

'Well, that's right and understandable,' the tutor continued, 'because it's the game that all those who matter are playing now. But there is one big problem about my coaching you gents.' To their surprise he put down his cue and proceeded rather slowly to light a cigarette. 'You see, I like and admire Mr Bullstone; he's a proper gentleman, and he picked up the game better than anyone I've taught before or since. Now, he did so well because he came to me determined to learn. He didn't put any defences up against me, if you see what I mean. He just watched, listened and then practised and I would say he's one of the best amateur players of the game today.'

All the Macaul men looked amazedly at George, who was blushing with pride.

'Now the problem is,' John continued, 'that I'm not so new at being a coach to gentlemen any more. I've had hundreds through my hands. It doesn't matter to me that much how they fare, as long as they're reasonably competent, that is. Mr Bullstone, here, comes in and asks me as a special favour to coach you two youngsters. More than that, to really polish you up, make you something special. Oh yes, he offered me a nice bonus if I succeed and all that sort of thing, but money's never excited me . . . So what have we got? We've got me who isn't really that inspired, we've got you two who look as if you'd

201

much rather be off with the girlies. And we've still got good old Mr Bullstone who knows better than anyone how important a talent like this can be to a gentleman.'

'Important?' The interruption was Randolf's.

'Yes,' George answered him, 'damned important, I can tell you. It's got me places I wouldn't have been asked otherwise. It's a talent that picks a man out of a crowd of dinner guests and gets him invited on to other influential houses. It's done me no end of good in my business. That's why I suggested it, Randolf. Apart from occupying the boys' time, it's a great social asset, and in this country that means it can be a great money earner.'

'Okay.' It was Mark who walked towards the table first, then his brother followed. 'We'll give it a crack. But there's one condition.' He looked very like his father when he laid down the law. 'I don't want any snide, clever remarks if my brother and I get a name wrong. You may think we speak the same language – but we're Americans. Okay?'

'Right,' said John, ushering them around his domain. 'This table that we're going to play snooker on is an English billiard table, and that has nothing to do with trying to confuse foreigners or the like, it just is called a billiard table. Right? It has eight legs, and measures twelve feet by six feet one and a half inches. It has a slate bed, covered with a billiard cloth in which the nap runs from the bottom of the table to the spot end at the top. There are six pockets, one at each corner and one in the centre of each long side as you can see. There are rubber cushions around the inside edge of the table; the edge of that cushion slopes towards the base so that the balls only ever come in contact with a thin strip of the rubber. Have a good look at it, gents, lean over, peer underneath. Get to know the table as well as you would want to know a battlefield.'

David was on his hands and knees, looking underneath,

when he began to get interested. 'Back home a billiard table has no pockets, and a pool table does,' he called up.

'That's carom billiards you're referring to, Mr Macaul Jnr, and yes, your pool table has pockets like this, but it's a different size,' John said.

'What size is a pool table exactly, then? Ours at home is a lot smaller than this.'

'Pool, which, by the by, is called pocket billiards in England, is played on tables exactly half as wide as they are long. The standard sizes are four by eight feet, four and a half by nine, and for championships, five and a half by eleven,' John supplied.

'There is another meaning for pocket billiards, of course,' George chipped in. 'It's the name for a pastime indulged in by the younger players of the game, boys of about thirteen or fourteen. When they're lounging about with time to kill, hands in their pockets, nothing to do. Then they play it, if you get my drift.' He put his hands in his pockets and fumbled energetically with his low-slung cluster. 'Ball game, if you get my meaning,' he laughed.

Randolf roared his approval and patted George on the back. He was a damned good fellow. 'Champagne, champagne, old man,' he cried. 'Come on, let's buckle down to this, men.' He put his arms around both his sons. 'I get the feeling I might just get to like this English scene, after all. Come on, chip chip, got to learn to play the game before we catch your sister her lord, what!'

They applied themselves to their sport. By early morning, the boys were fluent in the fundamentals of the game. They were playing with fifteen red balls, six colours and one white. A stroke by Randolf had them all informed that since 1898 it was a foul to shove the ball with the cue, rather than strike it. John was full of the history of his sport. While demonstrating to them the correct technique for chalking the tip of their cues he imparted the information that, in years gone by, gentlemen pushed their cues into plaster ceilings for the same service. He showed them, with remarkable dexterity, how the chalk gave the cue adhesion to the ball, so that it could strike off centre. He took a small cue, never chalked in its life, to demonstrate how impossible it was to impart the essential spin of the expert, known as 'side' or 'English' in American parlance, without chalk, and the boys tried it. George further enlivened the proceedings by telling of a recent infamous episode in London society when a gentleman, desperate to win, resorted to the expedient of peppering his chalk, which he then blew into his opponent's eyes.

It had been an excellent evening, the boys decided. They would return tomorrow, and the girls in the chorus line would be bereft of their company.

Lucinda's face was very set as they made the journey from Linstone to Pencombe. To find out that Michael had come back from the war, and was staying in London without contacting her, had been mortifying. Eli said nothing, he was as stern-faced as his daughter. Isabella sat huddled close to the window and tried to concentrate on the rich, fruit-laden orchards that lined their route. She seemed to be the only one who'd felt any pity whatsoever for Michael. Perhaps having Margaret's letters had something to do with that. But surely, even without a certain understanding of what had affected Michael so badly, Lucinda could have taken his side.

As they drew up at the Hall the sky was overcast and there was a storm on the horizon. The butler came out to usher them in. His lordship was in the billiard room, he said. Isabella drew a deep breath. Obviously Michael's father was expecting a tempestuous interview.

Michael and Johnnie were both there. Lord Montford had both his sons in England thanks to the slow mending of Johnnie's wound. Young men of good family were sent home with a problem like that, while commoner stock were sent to the front. They were standing, one either side of their father, who was sitting in a winged armchair on the new Aubusson carpet gracing the floor between the table and the window. There were several other new, soft upholstered chairs in the room, thanks to Lucinda's determination to 'soften' the atmosphere. Lord Montford had a rug draped over his knees. He looked very poorly.

There was an awkward silence that Eli broke. 'I'm sorry to see you like this, William. Have you a doctor in attendance?' He looked vaguely around the room, as if expecting to find one loitering in the shadows.

'My father is well cared for,' Michael said. 'I am afraid that he has taken my actions badly. It has affected his health. I didn't intend that.'

Lucinda stood up quickly to face him. 'Then perhaps you would be good enough to explain to us all what you did intend.'

'Very well. Although I believe you all know my motives, I will say them again. What I saw in Africa changed my life. I can't accept that we should inflict needless suffering on women and children. I intended, or rather I intend, to bring their desperate plight to the attention of the people of this country. I do not believe that we wish, as a nation, to be responsible for a slaughter of innocents. I cannot believe that anyone in this room would wish that. I won't be bound by convention anymore. I must be able to pursue the cause I believe in.'

'We are at war, my boy,' Eli said. 'Sad things happen in wars. It is part of the pattern of things.'

They were silent again, as Lucinda looked round at each of them. Her eyes were bright with anger. When she spoke it was to Michael again and with venom in her voice.

'There are thousands of men out there, Michael, literally thousands. None of them have seen fit to come blundering home, ruining a family's good name, casting a slur on its glory. Why did it have to be you? Why you?' Her voice had risen.

'I take it as an honour to be the one who was chosen,' Michael said very simply.

Johnnie stirred. Standing was making his arm ache; it hadn't really mended yet.

'Michael believes his cause is right, you know, Lucy,' Johnnie said. 'You're not going to get round him on that. I think there are other things we have to consider though.'

'Such as?' Lucinda said.

'Such as,' Michael said, 'if you intend to go on with the marriage.'

Isabella gasped. She had never thought this would happen. Lucinda was shocked too, stunned into silence.

Most affected though was Eli. 'Go on with it? My God! I've sunk thousands in this place already,' he said. 'There's no way we're not going ahead with it. We've got to make the best of a bad job. And the bad job is the mess you've made of it so far. You'll have to get down to sorting it out. I'm sorry, Michael, but I cannot allow you to carry on like this any longer. You must accept that I've acted in all good faith, but it's not just down to emotions now: there's money concerned.'

Michael was as pale as stone, his cheek muscles were raised, clearly defined under his taut skin. He had never in his life had to work so hard not to say the words revolving round in his brain. It was too much. He laid a hand gently on his father's shoulder then walked through them all, out of the room. He had to get away for a while, he needed some air.

It was Johnnie who took control. 'Would you like to sit down, sir?' he said to Eli. 'I think you and my father will have to deal with this.'

'Thank you,' Eli said. 'Thank you.' He was very upset. It had never crossed his mind that the marriage might not go ahead. He was thinking of all the money that had been spent already, with nothing solid in return. He suddenly realized he had been very foolish.

Johnnie turned to Isabella, 'Would you like to sit down too, Issy?'

'No, I'll go out, I think. I'm not involved, so it will be easier if I go.'

Lucinda and Johnnie watched her leave. Then their fathers started to talk, but before long it became clear that the presence of the younger generation was hindering Lord Montford. He was too tired for an audience. Lucinda rose and Johnnie went out with her. They had some things they needed to discuss in private anyway.

Isabella made for the river. She needed something to look at to take her mind off it all. It was so sad. Michael had looked torn, and he must be being pulled apart by duty to Lucinda on one hand and by his other duty, as he saw it, to those poor souls in Africa. She walked down the long yew walk. Even here there was evidence of the money that her father had been spending. There were new flagstones, a new perfection that hadn't been here last summer. Ahead of her the wooden gate in the boundary wall was closed. Reaching it she turned the iron ring handle and pulled the heavy door open. To her surprise, Michael was only a few feet away from her.

'Hallo,' he said, obviously surprised to see her. 'I thought you'd all still be indoors.'

'No, our fathers are talking, so I thought I'd be in the way. I needed some air, too.' She smiled. She did so want to help him. He looked very pale and drawn.

'I don't suppose you'd better be seen talking to me. I'm the enemy, I'm afraid,' he said.

'I don't mind. I'm usually cast in that role myself. Why don't you keep me company? I thought I'd walk along the river for a little way.'

He turned and walked beside her. It didn't seem to matter that they didn't have much to say. The river gurgled throatily and that was noise enough in the stillness. A kingfisher darted out over the water, hovered for an instant then flashed away as instantly as it had appeared. There were dragonflies, too, adding vibrant colour to the crowded greens. It was damp close to the water, which was a relief, for the day was extremely hot and sultry. They walked as far as the river bank path went, then turned at the stile that led to the fields.

Walking back towards the house their silence deepened. Whatever was going on behind those thick stone walls affected all their lives. At the gate they stopped.

Michael took her hand in his and looked down at it, an artist's hand, sensitive. 'Thank you,' he said softly to her, then lifted her fingers to his lips. He walked on through the gate, towards the house, by himself.

Isabella stood still for a while, then raised her hand to her eyes to wipe away the tears.

Eli was growing more and more annoyed. But he must keep his temper; to lose it would be disastrous. They were all now back in the billiard room and were trying to come to some reasonable agreement. However, Lucinda had refused to sit down; she was like a caged wild animal. She had taken her stand beside the billiard table, her eyes shining unnaturally brightly. Eli suspected she was only being silent while she stoked up her fury to its utmost. Johnnie was standing with his back to them, looking out through the windows. Lord Montford was sitting in his habitual high-backed chair, and Michael stood in front of the empty fireplace, seemingly at bay, confronting them.

'I think the first and most important thing,' Michael said, 'is for you all to appreciate that I will not stop. It does not matter what you say, I'm afraid. I was brought up to do my duty, to serve others. All those codes of conduct that you instilled into me, sir, I accept them to the letter; it is simply that I interpret their application differently to you.' He was looking earnestly at his father. 'I am honestly sorry that my actions are hurting you. I can only hope that eventually you will appreciate how I feel, and see that my leaving the army was utterly essential. I am obeying a call to duty. It may not be the same as you want for me, but it is the one I believe in. Nothing will change my mind, nothing at all.'

'What if I said I couldn't marry a coward,' Lucinda cried, 'that I couldn't bear to link my name with a man who has disgraced himself!'

'It is your choice, Lucinda, if the marriage goes ahead or not. I've already said that.'

'Then it shall go ahead, but on my terms, Michael.' She was nearly beside herself with fury. Reaching out she picked up the two red balls that had been left on the green baize. For an instant Johnnie thought she was going to hurl them, but then she rolled them, very quickly, one after another across the table, their hollow rumbling seeming very loud.

Michael's temper was rising, too. Eli could see it in the compulsive tightening of the young man's jaw.

'You're not the one to tell me what to do, Lucinda. In fact, there is no longer anyone to tell me what to do.' He had laid the stress on 'tell'. 'I listen to my father, because I respect him, and then it is for me to judge how to act on his advice. I am a grown man and accountable to no one but myself and my God.'

'Accountable, accountable, that's a good word. You should try accounting how much of my father's money has already been spent here. You owe him a duty even if you're not prepared to admit it.'

'Lucinda!' Eli thundered. This had gone far enough. 'That will do. You must calm down; nothing will come out of this. Now! Everyone must calm down.'

Lucinda's eyes narrowed to slits. 'Calm down, calm down, should I? I'll calm down, when Michael's come to heel like those idiotic dogs he's so mad about, when he treats me with the respect I deserve. It's my name he's prepared to drag down with his; my name, I'll remind you.'

Johnnie walked across the room suddenly, calling out loudly that he would order some tea. He'd been on the point of leaping to Lucinda's assistance, but that probably wouldn't have done her any good at all. He was convinced she was right. His brother was set to make an ass of himself over these damn Boers. Let someone else act the big hero in their cause, or, better still, let them remain out of sight and out of mind.

He had no intention of summoning tea. It was up to him to further his own part of the Pencombe scheme as well as he could. Lucinda and he had discussed it. Isabella must be made to see reason.

He closed the library door quietly behind him. He couldn't see her at first, but walking further into the centre of the room he could see around the bookshelves and into the alcove where she was sitting. 'Isabella!'

She looked up, startled, both by his entrance and by a distant roll of thunder. 'Hallo, Johnnie. Is it all over? Have they sorted things out?'

He came up to perch beside her on the arm of the chaise. 'No, it's worse, if anything. It'll take an almighty row to clear it, I expect. A bit like this storm's needed to clear the air.' He looked over her shoulder at the book in her hands. '*Vanity Fair*, is it? I should think that's the first time that book's ever been read. It's not quite required reading in this house.'

Isabella looked up at him. She felt vaguely unnerved with him sitting, almost predator-like, above her. 'And what is required reading for you, then?' she asked.

'Oh, warlike stuff, you know the sort of things, campaigns and sieges. The victorious types of siege, that is. We're believers in victory in this family. At least,' his thoughts flashed back to the billiard room, 'we are most of the time, when we're not led astray by a pretty face.'

'A pretty face? You mean Lucinda's? How has she led – '

Johnnie jumped to his feet and interrupted her, laughing coarsely. 'Oh no, not our Lucinda. But Michael's head was turned by some pretty little Boer wife; it was all over the camp after he left. God knows what he saw in her, and I don't think she can even have been all that clean; it's not exactly Buck House in those damn camps, you know.'

Isabella felt sick. Johnnie had a side to him she'd never seen before.

'Poor old Michael was sent quite gaga by the woman. Terrible shame and all that, but really he should give up his protestations now. Just like you should give up, Issy.' He came to a sudden halt in front of her. 'The time has come, Issy,' he said, 'for us to make a declaration.'

'A declaration, a declaration of what?' Isabella started to get up. She felt trapped in the alcove; it was no longer a place of refuge.

Johnnie shot out a hand and grasped her arm firmly. He pushed her back down on to the seat. 'Now, don't try and escape. You know perfectly well I mean a declaration of our own forthcoming marriage. There's too much nonsense being spouted about. We must give a lead and calmly, rationally, do the right thing.'

Isabella was rubbing her wrist. It hurt. 'Will you please let me up, Johnnie?' she said. 'I would like to go out of the room.'

'You damned well won't.' There was a crackle of lightning very close to the house; the light flickered briefly around them. 'You'd better do it the easy way, Issy. Just agree like a good girl. Our announcement will take the heat off in there.' He jerked his head back towards the far-off billiard room.

'If you don't let me up, Johnnie, I shall scream.' Isabella said it very quietly, but she meant it utterly. Johnnie had become a stranger, a flushed, agitated stranger who frightened her.

'Oh go on, Issy, scream your head off. There's no one about to hear you at this time of day. They are all off in the public rooms on the other side of the house. You see, you should know the system here better; you will when we're married.' He leaned over her, his face twisted, leering.

'I'll never marry you, Johnnie, never.' She spoke up firmly, above the thunder, as more lightning shot its unnatural glow across them.

'You will, you know, Issy. Lucinda and I have sorted it all out. Everything's set. As I said, you do it the easy or the hard way. It doesn't matter to me.'

'You can drag me to the altar between you if you want, but you'll never make me say yes. I promise you that, I never will.'

Johnnie leaped towards her throwing himself heavily on to her. The warm smell of wine made her realize he'd drunk too much at lunch.

'All right, Issy, you've asked for it. It's the hard way for you all right.' With one hand he grabbed both her wrists, twisting them together. His free hand pushed her head back, flat against the arm of the chair. 'Damn me,' he

212

cried. The thunder roared around the house. 'I'm glad you chose this way, Issy. I want you, I always have, but never as much as now.'

Then he was upon her. His kiss was brutal, his mouth hard, as he forced his tongue between her teeth. Her neck was arching back and she couldn't breathe. She heard the ripping of the muslin before she felt the dress tear. He was pulling frantically at the fabric and she heaved her body up against him to force him away. His hand was on her breast, squeezing and kneading. Isabella was moaning in pain. She twisted her head away trying to call for help, but he jerked her back towards him again, forcing his lips brutally down on hers once more. She tasted blood as her lip split. His breathing was louder than the rolling thunder in her ears, but to Johnnie the roaring, rising tide of noise was his own passion. He forced his knee between her thighs, but the full skirts were in his way. He let go of her wrists to pull them up and she clawed at him. She hit out, screamed, suddenly free of his mouth at last.

Then hands clutched at her; she fought them off. 'Issy, Issy, for Christ's sake,' the voice called. It wasn't Johnnie, it wasn't Johnnie.

She fell against her rescuer with a sob, shaking as if in a fever. As Michael held her against him, she felt her naked skin against his jacket. 'God!' she cried, 'God, please, please, help me, Michael.'

'It's all right, all right, he won't touch you again, I swear it.' He was smoothing her hair back from her eyes. She felt faint, but he held her close again. 'Get her a shawl, Johnnie, get her something, anything.' His voice was clipped, he was keeping his fury in control.

There was a rustling as Johnnie got up from the floor where his brother had hurled him. He slunk off to fetch a wrap from the hall. When he returned he had straightened himself pretty well. He walked towards them, his eyes glittering with hate.

Michael put his hand out for the wrap. 'If you go near her again, Johnnie, I'll kill you.' There was no question of his sincerity.

'I shall go near her, as you put it, on our wedding night. She'll learn her lesson then. But don't worry, brother dear,' Johnnie sneered, 'I won't upset your sensitivities again by attempting conquest in these hallowed halls.' He backed out of the room with a mocking bow.

'He's drunk,' Isabella whispered. She was wrapping the shawl around her. It didn't stop her shaking.

'Not drunk enough to excuse that. Nothing could, ever.' Michael seemed to be looking into a far distance, then he pulled himself together with a start. 'I can't stay, your sister's run off somewhere and we can't find her. It's a hell of a storm. She must be found. Issy, do you hear me?' He bent down to look into her eyes.

'Yes, yes, I hear you,' she whispered. She was calming a little now. 'But please,' a fresh shiver ran through her, 'please don't leave him alone to come back to me. Take him with you.'

Michael looked again at her, a look that seemed to give her strength. 'Of course,' he said, then with a little smile he was gone and she sat down, well away from the alcove, to cry the tears she needed.

Lucinda ran out of the room. She couldn't stand another second of it.

Pride! Pride! Her heart would burst with tortured pride. Michael could ruin it all, the glory, the splendour, the future she'd mapped out for them. She could kill him, squeeze the life from him with her small hands, such was the force of fury welling within her as she ran along the

214

stone-floored corridor. She stumbled on the hem of her dress and careered against the wall, knocking the breath from her for an instant. Then with a quick backwards look she was off again. She must escape, escape the clutches of mediocrity, the compromise she could scream at. Shame, dishonour and her father cautioning reason.

She could kill them, kill them all.

She ran blindly out into the courtyard. The rain was falling in torrents, astonishingly cold on her fever-hot skin. She stood for a moment, then, catching up her skirts, ran on to the stables. There was no one, not a servant, a menial, not even a dog out in the accursed rain. She peered in at a stable. Michael's horse twisted her head round from the corner she was facing, trying to escape the barrage of noise from the heavens. Her eyes were rolling, streaked with red. The mare was too tall for Lucinda to handle. She darted along, checking two more stables before she found the pretty dappled grey snorting at the door, tossing its head against the electricity in the air but coming towards her in its greediness. She usually brought it sugar.

She had to rush back to the tack room for a saddle and bridle. Her gown was ruined by the continual downpour.

The saddle seemed incredibly heavy and awkward and the grey began to prance round in its box and roll its eyes. The mistress might not care about the thunder but the horse did. At a lightning crackle it side-stepped smartly away from her and the saddle crashed on to the ground.

'Damn, you stupid, damned animal, damn.' But then Lucinda stopped and stood quite still. The beast was flattening its ears, pawing at the straw on the floor. She had no intention of being kicked to death here, ignominiously soaked to the skin. She deliberately calmed her voice to soothe the animal, and after a few minutes she tried the saddle again. By the time he was tacked up, the lightning seemed to be right over them. The rain, if it was possible, was falling even more heavily. Lucinda waited for a pause then dragged the reluctant creature out into the yard. Her destination was the mounting block. She got there just as the thunder began a new peal. Fear made the horse freeze for a moment; that was enough, then Lucinda was on its back, her skirts pulled up high to her knees. The lightning sparkled, and with a vicious clatter on the cobbles they were off, out of the yard and on to the road through the village. Unseen.

She let the horse have its head. There was a long, steep hill to climb out of the valley where the village nestled and by the time they neared the crest it was tiring. It was still galloping headlong, and she couldn't have stopped it if she'd wanted, but at least they were covering the ground. There were ten miles to Linstone and home.

The rain that fell covered the roads and fields, then drained into the network of ditches that were quickly full. The water ran down, for ever downwards into the valleys. All the valleys led eventually into the river. The first to suffer were the new-born water rats. Pink and naked they drowned in their fur-lined river bank nests that were safe for normal summer rains, but flooded with a surge. The late chicks of the water martins suffered a similar fate.

Then the river began in earnest. There were sheep whose water-sodden fleeces weighed them down so that they couldn't outrun the water. There was the publican's goat that had been tethered apparently out of harm's way. But the hungry waters reached out for it, as it bleated frantically, cavorting on the very end of its chain, and then went under in a flurry of foam.

Lucinda ached all over by the time she'd passed through Tonbridge. It was the halfway stage of her journey. Her legs were chaffed from the wet saddle against her skin, and her hands were blistering from the reins. As her temperature cooled her fury solidified. She had time on

216

her journey to reason through the chaos of the past few days. Finding Michael was back in England and had not contacted her, as any fiancé should, then learning of his desertion. The army might not call it that but she thought they would have had it been another man's son, and not a viscount's.

The water was some six inches deep on the road now, and the horse only kept on its path by following the guideline of the hedges that stood up above the water. Lucinda didn't take notice of the sky, the road or the flooded fields. In any case there was very little definition: it was a water world. And she was as wet as any of it. Now the animal was dejected, its head hung low. It hardly bothered to flinch at new assaults of lightning while Lucinda disdained to take notice of them at all. Pictures of Michael kept crowding through her mind. He wasn't the man he could be; he should be much, much stronger. But more than Michael, it was herself she thought of. It was unfair: she was a woman any man would want yet he treated her like a nobody, merely with what she now saw as a polite attention, and latterly not even with consideration.

The horse stumbled suddenly, dropping nearly on to its knees in an unseen pothole. She pulled hard on the reins to stop herself falling, and somehow they stayed together. The near fall made her notice her surroundings. With a start of alarm she realized the roads were totally awash. The bridge, she thought, if she could just get across that then the road was uphill. Linstone could never be flooded. She looked around for possible shelter in case she couldn't make the last mile to the bridge. There was a tumbledown cottage, made more desolate by the torrents pouring over its roof and no doubt through it. Lucinda kicked hard at her mount's sides. Damn it, she had no intention of spending a night in some hovel. She'd make the bridge, she knew she would.

Just as Lucinda urged her horse on, Michael was mounting Bess. They'd searched everywhere in the house and out-buildings and couldn't find Lucinda. Now they had to get out and over the low bridge that led out of the village before it was covered by the raging water. It was nearly too high already. Keeping an eye on Johnnie had cost him time. Why the hell hadn't he thought to check the stables first? The little grey was gone; he should have thought to look earlier. But he had too much on his mind, too much. Damn Johnnie, damn him to hell.

Bess was throwing her head about, nearly frantic with the storm; she was too highly strung for this kind of job, but she'd cover ground quicker than anything else, and Lucinda had to be trying to make for Linstone. He had to reach her before the flood did.

'Stand back, stand back!' he cried to Eli who was too close to the kicking hooves. 'Johnnie's to stay with you. Don't let him out of your sight, you hear me?'

Eli nodded his head; he was soaked to the skin, as they all were. He had no idea why he was to mount a guard on the boy, but he'd do it with his utmost endeavour. The only hope for Lucinda now was Michael. Eli would follow his instructions to the last letter, whatever they were.

The mare was slipping on the cobbles, which were all but awash. The lead-lined gutters were channelling oceans of water from the vast slate roofs and it ran loudly in the drains and cisterns.

'Hold up, damn you.' Michael pulled the reins up sharply as a vicious crackle made Bess slew away from the archway and he jabbed hard into her side. He used the whip on her to keep her going on, towards the narrow neck of stone that just showed above the torrent. She fought him every inch of the way, but they were almost there. Then only twenty feet from them a jagged fork of fury stabbed down from the sky and pierced the very core of the great elm. The tree staggered like a man struck through by a lance. Bess threw her head up for one final, desperate time. There was no way Michael could stop her. She leaped upon her back legs, twisting and turning to get away and he was thrown, landing full-length on the mud of the bank. He saw her leg crumple as she fell, cracking loudly too, like the tearing, ripping tree. The waters closed over the last escape. They were marooned at Pencombe. Michael had all the time in the world now to put poor, heaving Bess out of her misery.

Lucinda had reached Yalding and the junction of the rivers. The houses were shuttered with sacks of mud and earth at the doors as the water swirled up and over their steps. The horse was trembling; she thought it might well be close to going down, but it would have to last out. She turned left, off the road through the village to the bridge approach. Her breathing was shallow, the fear primitive, undenying. The roar of the water was terrifying; it galloped like herds of fierce white horses. Carried high on its back were uprooted trees, smashed barrels and all the debris of streets and fields. Her eyes were hypnotically drawn into and along with it. The rushing flood drowned all but the loudest rolls of thunder.

She shook her head. This was no time to give up. The water was up to the horse's fetlocks on the approach, but there was a clear island of cobbles above the waters at the crown of the bridge. Lucinda fixed her eyes on that. The bridge could not possibly be swept away, she told herself. It had stood for the last four hundred years; why should it give way now? The horse was too tired to resist her and it stumbled forwards through the surge, and then she had gained the centre point. She dared not look on either side of her.

Horse and rider went slowly down into the waters on the Linstone side as a glimmer of hope warmed her. They were nearly there, nearly. The bridge suddenly shook violently and with a resounding crash a great chunk of parapet behind them was carried away by the branches of a mighty tree, trophy of the flood. They were so nearly there. The hooves touched the firm ground beyond the bridge at the very instant the banks burst. The waters came for their prey with a howl of victory.

Maude sniffed loudly. She was warm huddled up by the vast iron range in the bleak old kitchen, but it wasn't like being at home; she almost wished she hadn't been at Pencombe when it had all happened. Although, in some ways, she admitted to herself, it was nice being so important. The personal servant of the missing Lucinda, she was being treated with something close to awe by Chrissie, the girl who'd been brought in from the village to help with the extra workload that Isabella and Eli's staying had put upon the servants.

'I saw them meself, in the church,' Chrissie said. Her voice was thick, snuffling. She had a cold in the head, but it hadn't stopped her from going to matins that morning; there was too much to see. Maude, meanwhile, had stayed in bed; she wasn't up to being looked at by a lot of nosy villagers.

'Yes,' the girl continued, 'your Miss Isabella looked a right sight. She'd got a scarf pulled up round her mouth and a veil over her eyes, not that it hides how red they are. Funny though, she kept as far away as she could get from Master Johnnie. You would have thought she'd want to cuddle right up, wouldn't you? He never looked at her once, just glowered at the poor vicar right through the service. And Master Michael, well he looks as if he's seen a ghost right enough. I reckon he must think your lady's a goner.'

Maude leaned closer to the range. She was unhappy. She hadn't been fond of Lucinda, but she had admired her and messages had now come through that Lucinda had not reached her home but was gone two days and nights without a trace.

'What about Mr Bradbury?' Maude asked.

'The father, you mean? He's like stone, just like a figure carved in marble. Terrible grief, terrible.' The girl's voice thrilled with it all. 'They're finding a lot of nasty things, now the waters are goin' down. There's a dead cow, down by the bridge, fat fit to bursting. And she's not the only one the waters took. That farmer, Thomas Cade, he was from over your way, wasn't he?'

Maude stirred herself out of her apathy. 'Mr Cade,' she said, 'what about him, then?'

'Oh, he's gone all right. Last seen with a load of bullocks trying to get them off a flood island. Silly bugger!'

Maude sank even deeper into her shawls. She felt the sting of tears, as the picture of a dead man kept forcing its way into her mind: he'd be all swollen, like that cow, fit to burst. She didn't like it, didn't like it at all. She reached up her sleeve for a handkerchief, and blew her nose loudly.

'Upsets you, does it?' asked Chrissie. 'Not surprised. I hear he was a fine figure of a man. Like a cup of tea would you, dear?'

Maude nodded weakly. She wished she was back home away from this silly girl who wasn't a real servant at all.

Isabella had hardly left her room at Pencombe and spent her time sitting on the end of the lumpy bed, trying not to think about Lucinda. It was no good. All morning, her sister's face and voice kept darting up at her. Surely, she was too quick to be among the dead.

Suddenly she heard a clatter on the gravel and, looking out of her bedroom window, saw a young lad, sixteen or thereabouts, a yeoman's son by appearance, wearing a leather jerkin and mud-splattered thigh-high boots.

'Mr Bradbury, it is Mr Bradbury, isn't it?' he asked, as Eli came out of the house. Jumping down off his pony, which like its rider was streaked with the bright brown of river silt, he said, 'I'm Saul Solomons. My father farms down at Nettlestead. You buy some of our grain, Mr Bradbury, sir.'

'Yes, yes, I know.' Eli was testy. 'What do you want?'

'My father says will you come over to us, sir? I'll lead the way.'

Eli had turned deathly pale. He had convinced himself there would be no news to face until he had reached Linstone Park. Isabella's stomach contracted violently; it was hard to ask the question.

'What is it? Have they found her?' Eli said.

'No, sir, at least not by the time I'd left.'

'Then what . . .?'

'It's the horse, sir, they've found the grey. It was down by the lock. Must have been swept down from Yalding; that's where they reckon she tried to cross, isn't it? There's talk she was seen riding on into the village just before the banks went.'

'The horse is dead?' Eli asked, his eyes glazed. He felt so cold, so very cold.

'Oh yes, sir. It had caught fast up against the lock gates when the run was on, we reckon. It's pretty bashed about anyhow. It floated up this morning; well, it would, it's the air, see, it . . .'

'That's enough, thank you, Saul. We'll follow you as

222

you say. Come along, Isabella, we mustn't keep the young man waiting. It's good of him to come for us.'

Neither of them looked out of the carriage windows. For one frantic moment Isabella had thought of peering, looking here and there. Perhaps she would be the one to find Lucinda, where no one else could. But then the thought of the poor animal trapped up against the lock gates stopped her. She wasn't going to see Lucinda out there: she couldn't see through river water.

Eli had something to concentrate on: his own emotion. He must control himself, must hold on.

The Nettlestead lock was further upriver than the Nettlestead bridge that had been damaged, like the one at Yalding, by the flood. There were great gaps in its parapets like broken teeth in an old man's mouth. The fields on either side of the river were littered with vast tangled tresses of straw and hay. They'd made an effort to drag the dead livestock out of the way under the hedge. The field on the Tonbridge side always got the biggest part of that grim harvest. The horse alone was still lying close to the river bank. It was a Pencombe animal, property of a lord, so they accorded it the respect of not throwing it with common men's debris. Eli didn't want Isabella to get down from the coach, but she insisted. She had to see the place where Lucinda might be.

The horse was grossly swollen. There was a great jagged lump of flesh missing from its shoulder, and the legs themselves were gashed, as if it had been whipped. The flesh showed fish white where the water had leached the blood. There were flies buzzing around the head, clustering blue and green to feed around its gaping teeth. The boy Saul flicked vainly away at them. His father was an older, thicker version of his son, very kind and considerate. Eli seemed to spend a lot of time thanking him for being so kind.

223

All the while, Isabella's eyes were fixed on the lock. The doors reared up out of the water, black and forbidding. Around their feet the water swirled and bubbled, topped with a thick brown scum that covered the tell-tale shapes of debris brought down by the flood. Beneath that fetid water, Lucinda might lie, floating with the current. Isabella walked back to the carriage with the taste of bitter bile in her mouth. Her father stumbled on the step, barking his shin painfully on the edge of the door.

'Damn!' he shouted, 'damn!' and he sat on the floor of the carriage as they jolted their way home, tears pouring down his face like the tears of a child in pain.

Part Three

The old order changeth, yielding place to new,
And God fulfils himself in many ways
                                        Tennyson

England, 1901

Luke had waited for this for several days. He had hidden his impatience as the sun had spent the necessary long weeks baking the earth rock hard in preparation for the great event. He had felt a deep thrill of excitement at the sight of the massed battalions of cloud that had heralded the advent of the heavy rainstorms. Now the expected flood had come and he was almost, almost but not quite, afraid of it, for water was truly his element.

The house at Reason Hill was safe, too high above the valley for the flood to touch, so Jenny had come to play her part in protecting her brother's cottage. She had taken roost in the upper floor, where all their decent furniture and portable possessions had been hauled, so that the two small rooms were crammed like a victualler's. Even the chickens were there, imprisoned in clucking umbrage; she had no intention of losing them to the river. Outside the cottage, lapping hungrily at the blue door, the waters raged. Her brother was out on the water, but that excited more than frightened her. And she knew what he must be planning to do out there. He had something to dispose of and he wouldn't be the only one taking advantage of the flood to do that.

The coracle was so light that it bobbed on the water, so immaterial to the surge that it was left to scurry across the pools gushing out over the fields that bordered the river. Luke believed fiercely in the spirit of the waters. He knew there was a great elemental life force that dictated this wet, unbounded power and that by casting himself flimsily afloat, he would not offend that power. Other men who put their trust in firm, well-built clinker boats would turn turtle and be drowned, where Luke, a true believer, was left about his business. Not that he tempted fate too far by venturing near the flood race itself. Neither man nor beast should face that.

The body from the eel trap weighed the little vessel down and made it unaccustomedly sluggish, but, all the same, he was making a good pace, going with the water as he was. He wanted to get below the lock gates. Then the body would float downstream to Maidstone waters. By then it would be well enough punished by the flood to cover the fact that it was already partially decomposed. The rot of death was filling Luke's nostrils. He would be glad when it was over.

The roaring, throbbing waters covered the sound of the first scream, but not the second. It soared like the cry of a curlew, high and mournful, almost without hope. Then it came again and he realized it was a woman's voice he heard. The coracle bobbed frantically for a moment as his inattention caused it to drift too close to the race. He straightened it with the single oar he wielded. He half-stood, turning his head slowly to scan the full hundred yards width of water, ready to catch the direction, when it came again.

There! There!

He stood to his full height, feet well astride for balance. The cry came from the far side of the water. He saw the grey of the horse first and its mad, tossing head; he could hear its screams now, he was so close. They were held by a tree, an aged oak that had shadowed the pool beneath Owen's meadow. The flood had undermined the bank, loosening the roots to send it toppling head first into the river, its branches reaching out, almost bridging the entire width. The horse was held, like a pinned moth, by the force of the waters against the trunk. The girl was clutch-

228

ing frantically at its tail, with only her head above water. As she raised herself up to shriek again a wave smashed over her, and she disappeared in a welter of foam. Then it was past and she was still there. Luke was battling with the current now to stay abreast. He had his own affairs to see to; he couldn't stop to help. In any case she would be gone soon. Another smother of water covered the auburn hair; this could be the end. But no, she was still there, gasping for air. She caught sight of him then and her head twisted round as she shouted at him. Hope put renewed life into her struggles. If she hadn't seen him he might have gone on, but humanity is a strange bond. There was no choice now. He lifted an arm in acknowledgement and then put his mind to the job in hand. He had to get back upriver and lighten the vessel.

Off to his right there was a narrow island spit standing up above the waters, where years ago there had been a vain attempt to dam the floods of the water meadow. He steered hard towards it. The waters were carrying him downriver and he had been swept out of the girl's sight, but still he could hear her calling him. He grounded hard and nearly tipped over, but he was out in a second, only ankle deep in water. He dragged the body out, heaving it awkwardly over the flimsy gunwales. The sacking was putrid but there was no time for the niceties. He dragged it to the highest part of the low island. He could only hope it would wait on him; the waters shouldn't go much higher.

He heaved the coracle up and over, on to his back, and then he started to run upriver. He heard the renewed vigour of the girl's cries as she caught sight of him. She'd got guts all right. He ran on, then water surged up round his knees, as the level of the land dropped away, but he still reckoned he wasn't high enough upriver. If he got swept past the tree he'd have the devil's own job to get out of the race and back to try again and she'd definitely be gone by then. As if to prove how little time he had, there was an ominous rumble even louder than the flood's roar as a wedge of bank beside the last clinging roots of the tree slid down into the waters. If the tree went before he got to her she'd have had it anyway.

He strode on into the rising water, fighting the fierce undertow, whose tug nearly had him over. He pushed on until it was heaving round his thighs and then suddenly he couldn't stand at all. He threw himself over frantically and ended up head over heels in the bottom of the wildly tossing boat. He struggled to his feet and stuck the oar hard down into the waters. It gave him a tentative grip on the bottom, and steadied him enough to take his sightings. Then, with a vast heaving push, he shot himself out towards the centre of the maelstrom. He stabbed the oar time and time again down into the bubbling, frothing madness, but it was the river that dictated his passage; he was now in the hands of its gods. He flew over the waters, hurtling with terrifying speed towards the tree that loomed ever closer, ever higher above him.

The final disintegration of the river bank saved him from being smashed to pieces against his goal. Just before he reached it, the tree slewed violently downriver, and he crashed obliquely into the tangled branches. The jarring shock knocked the breath from him, but even in his daze, he knew there was no time. He was downwater of the girl, but so close they could almost touch – so close. He stretched his hand out, inching towards her. Her breath was coming in great sobs, but there was still desperate determination in her eyes and they willed him on. He was leaning right out of the boat now, so nearly there, when the tree lurched again. She looked full into his eyes and then she turned, let go of her only hold on safety and lunged towards him. The tide threw her at him, and he

230

stumbled back, clutching her frantically in his arms. Reeling with the shock of collision, Luke slipped half out of the craft, but a crashing wave threw him back into its fragile safety.

With a rending, tearing, tortured keening, the tree twisted right around, slowly at first, then terrifyingly fast. The full, open river, implacable in its fury, was revealed ahead of them. They were tangled in the last of the topmost branches, and clutched each other as their world careered around. The horse shot past them, propelled out into the madness; a final flurry of kicking legs and it was gone. It would be their turn to be discarded next, and still the tree turned, majestically bearing them onwards, careless of their mortality. There were prayers on Luke's lips, prayers he'd long forgotten. There was a final, bone-jarring lurch and they were spun out, thrown away from the clutching branches that a moment before they'd thought a sanctuary, and now were twisting down into the river bed. The coracle spun around, shooting wildly forwards with the currents and then with a convulsive shudder their crazy passage ceased.

They'd been expelled, cast off by the waters, and they drifted haphazardly on the great flood pool spreading over the lower river meadow.

Thomas Cade had a wide vocabulary and he was putting to good use all of the vulgar words it contained. Around him in the barn twenty or so heifers milled nervously. There was no fodder for them – none for him, come to that – and they were cut off from civilization by the flood waters. It was a damned stupid situation to have got into, and he only had himself to blame. He should have left them to their fate and saved himself. Now, he had no idea how long they'd be stuck here, but the rain still thundering on the roof showed no sign of letting up.

He hauled himself up to the hay loft, empty now and hopeless for the livestock, but at least it was out of the way of being trampled. The beasts were becoming more and more agitated, but there was nowhere else for them to go. The water was right up to the closed doors. Another foot higher and it would cover the barn floor; then there'd be real pandemonium and somehow he'd have to open the door and let them career off to drown. He felt sick with the situation, sick with himself at not having been hard enough to abandon them earlier. After a while, the drumming on the roof lulled him into a doze. He woke with a start when the noise stopped; the silence seemed very loud.

He peered down into the dusty darkness of the barn again. The animals were quieter, only the occasional beast tossing its head about with wild eyes. He wasn't going to chance going down there amongst them for a look outside though; he didn't fancy getting gored. They might only be youngsters, but they carried a good six inches of horn already. The roof of the barn was in good repair. There was the odd rivulet of rainwater trickling underneath a crookedly hung tile and along a beam, but there were no holes. It was a pity to spoil its perfection, but it had to be done. Thomas took off his jacket, almost dry now, and wrapped it around his arm. Then he pushed against a wooden batten. It was surprisingly stubborn to break. But eventually, with a reluctant splintering, it gave way. He gave another shove, a couple of rows of tiles clattered down the roof and an oblong of daylight appeared. The sky was pearl grey, still streaked with angry charcoal smudges, but the worst was over, he could see that. He pulled away another row of tiles, shoving them out of his way and hearing them slide to land with a splash. At least that told him how high the water was, still right up to his eyrie. Normally this barn was on a hillock, surrounded by fields that sloped off down towards the river. Now, it was on an island. He stepped forwards, sticking his head and shoulders into the open space he had made for himself. Prepared though he was, he still drew in his breath at the sight. There was water as far as he could see.

Thomas had lived his nearly thirty years close to the river that ruled this valley and never had he seen such a flood. From his vantage point the course of the river itself was clearly marked by the white frothing passage it cut through the vast lake that stretched as far as the eye could see. He turned slowly. There were clumps of treetops making deep green islets in the distance. Another barn further down the valley had only its roof showing above the water. The cattle had begun a plaintive mooing, urged by their empty bellies.

He was about to step back into his shelter when he saw the coracle. It was some couple of hundred yards away from him, floating gently on the slow, eddying waters. There were two people in it. He shouted at once, although they might well still be too far off to hear him. He shouted again and a rustle and flapping answered him as a brace of ducks flew up and wheeled around in front of him. They had been close up to the barn doors, out of his sight. The birds alerted the occupants of the little boat. The man sat up and with the aid of an oar, began to propel the vessel towards the building.

He knew who she was the moment he saw her hair, its reddish glints defying the greyness of the elements. She had seen him now and knelt up in the boat, leaning her body towards him. She felt that she had created him in her mind, made him, standing there waiting for her. The man with the oar moved sluggishly, slowly, almost unwillingly it seemed. It was as if she alone propelled the boat towards him over the water, by the sheer force of her will. Thomas hadn't known until that instant what she meant to him. Hers was the force, bringing them together; here was the

233

woman he needed. Like the flooding tide itself the knowledge grew and his love washed over him.

Luke Jones brought them up to the front of the barn. Thomas yelled down for them to back off and not to try to open the doors until he got down as they would be trampled by the cattle. He clambered down again amongst the animals. It was wet and treacherous with slippery mud underfoot now as the water had risen those last few inches to flood over the floor. There was no help for it, they'd have to go.

'Stand back, stand back!' he shouted, then ran to the door. He'd reckoned he wouldn't have much time, and he'd been right. At the sight of daylight the beasts went berserk. They twisted and turned, jostled each other and kicked out to be the first into the open air. Then the leaders saw the water and frantically tried to stop, but the stampede behind was forcing them on. A leading heifer, her soft warm coat a delicate brown and white splattered with green-tinged mud, slipped and went over, rolling on her side. Her legs vainly thrashed at the water whilst the others trampled her underfoot. As her head was forced under another fell, and another. Several of the beasts were swimming now, way out of their depth, their eyes rolling, their nostrils distended in panic. Then, all at once, the barn was empty, the waters still, the cattle gone.

Luke waited until the way was clear, then he brought the coracle close in and handed Lucinda into the barn's temporary safety. She fell into Thomas's arms. This was the miracle she'd prayed for. She clutched the big, strong maleness of him, a man of infinite strength. She was soaking wet, shivering with cold and with the aftermath of terror, but she smiled, and then she laughed, and he laughed too, as they clutched each other.

As evening came to them, Luke had left, to return with a sturdier craft in the morning and Lucinda and Thomas had time to be alone together. More alone than Lucinda had ever dreamed it possible for a man and a woman to be.

She looked steadily into Thomas's eyes as he reached out to take her by the shoulders. The only sound in the loft was their breathing, as he started to pull her slowly, almost imperceptibly, towards him and a surging, aching power began to well inside her. She pushed aside the thoughts that tried to break in, memories of Michael, her future at Pencombe. She was throwing it all away, willingly, eagerly, for the ultimate, achievable love that every fibre of her body was urging her into accepting here, now. She trembled as her tightly corseted breasts touched against Thomas's shirt. Dedicated to his tutelage she closed her eyes to feel every minute sensation, her nipples hardening, a pulse throbbing in her throat. As the pressure of his body increased the rivulets of sensation ran down, down to her stomach creating an empty longing, then down again and suddenly her legs felt weak.

Still he did not let them kiss. He waited to feel the change in her, the moment when her body moulded against him. She began to push against the rising urge in him, accepting the new hardness of his manhood, then he bent his face to hers; her lips were parting, her tongue a pink, trembling tip. This was the only way to make Lucinda his and keep her, to chain her to him by the fulfilment of her body, to make it his power that awakened and brought her to release. As their lips met he had one last fleeting thought: she brought with her Eli, his money and his power; the thought made him smile and their teeth touched, a tiny jarring that reached every pulsing nerve in Lucinda's body.

He was strong with her, running his hands over the outlines of her body. Over the uplifted breasts, the yielding waist and then pushing her down to the rough wooden floor, pulling her skirts up, his face held in her hands, he covered her with kisses. She could feel the fabric of the final silken barrier tangled round her knees. She quivered at the roughness of his hands on the smooth skin of her thighs; it was so new, so powerful, overwhelming. Her longing matched the rising surge of his lust. She cried out as he entered her, the sharp pain of it surprising her, but like a goad, urging her on. With his broad hands on her hips he moved her in the perfect rhythm. Lucinda knew now what victory was, what was power and freedom: it was all within her, this was what she'd been created for. He urged her faster, faster, there were no kisses now, nothing but pure sensation. Higher, higher they flew, rushing to a climax she did not know existed. Soaring, flying, touching infinity then falling back to earth, to the dusty barn, to the man heavy on top of her.

She opened her eyes wide to see the roof above them, turned her head to look into the dim corners. She wanted to drink it all in, hold it in her mind to savour. This was her first time, her very first, and this was the place. Thomas lay still. He wanted her to speak first, to make her commitment in the aftermath. He was drained yet whole, tired but ready to race.

She stirred beneath him. 'Again,' she murmured. He turned his head to catch the word. 'Again!' And then she laughed, a rich warm laugh that bubbled in her throat. Thomas took her hands in his, stretched her arms back above her head, pressing them down on the floor. She was his captive, his most willing slave. He put his mouth on hers, probing gently at first, then fiercely, the male dominant as she answered him, every move echoing his, arousing him again to possess and be possessed.

Maude had her chair pulled up to the well-scrubbed kitchen table, her elbows resting in the empty half shells of a fresh lemon and a paste of lard and elderflower water covering her hands and neck. Her face glistened with a thin film of honey and the faint smell of egg white hung around her newly washed hair. Dove sat belching gently over his brown ale while Emmy, the cook, rocked in her chair, in pride of place, tucked up close to the black polished stove. It should have been a peaceful evening below stairs at Linstone. The kitchen window was wide open to catch the welcome breeze at the end of a long, hot day and the song of a lovesick blackbird provided a gentle music. But the atmosphere in the room was one of confused dejection. At one fell swoop, their dreams had been shattered.

No Lucinda at Pencombe meant no Dove, no Maude there either. Emily, while not wishing to move with them and leave her family, who lived close to Linstone, had been looking forward to a lighter workload when they had all gone – even though some who envied her said she was sinfully under-employed already.

Maude closed her eyes to try and concentrate. She was trying hard to work out what was for the best. As Mr Dove had quashed her immediate instinctive reaction to the news, she was now trying to work out other possibilities; but try as she might, her thoughts kept coming back to her first feelings. They should tell the master what they'd heard. She opened her eyes still convinced that she was right.

The butler was looking at her fixedly. 'Don't you go doing anything hasty,' he said to her.

'I don't never do nothing hasty,' she snapped back. It was all very well him telling her what and what not to do, but he hadn't come up with an idea himself yet, she noticed.

Emily maintained her placid rocking to and fro, to and fro. It could drive a man to drink, that squeaking, thought Dove as he took a good draught of his ale.

'We've got to tell right enough. If we're first with the news, then it'll be to our credit, and not to someone else's. But the question is, who do we tell?' Dove joined in with the cook's rhythm by swaying to and fro on his carpet-slippered feet. 'Now,' he continued, 'Maude's all for telling the master, but there's one fact she's overlooked. The master's going to be none too happy about this. And whoever takes him the news is going to be tainted for him. You still want to go to him, Maude?'

'Oh, no, not me. You're not going to get me to be the one to tell him. I think it's your place, Mr Dove, don't you, Emily? It's only right. You're always telling us how you're the head of the staff, so it's only right.'

Emily didn't nod in agreement. She didn't want to fall out with anyone; she liked a quiet life.

'What you don't seem to understand, Maude,' her superior continued, with the patience of Job, 'is that I can't possibly tell anyone. It's beneath my position to carry tittle-tattle. No, it's not on, definitely not the ticket. But, it is up to me to organize the running of the household, as you so rightly remind me, and in that capacity I have made my decision.' He walked round the table, the one where Emily prepared her pies, peeled her apples, where they themselves ate, the very hub of their lives.

'Here's what you have to do now, little Maude,' he said. Dove had been about to pat her on the shoulder, but on second thoughts decided better of the gesture. 'You've got your way to make in this 'ere world, same as I've got mine. You'll have to make up to Miss Isabella now. She's a simple soul really, just needs a bit of coaxing along and she'll be eating out of your hand. And you won't be alone either,' he added quickly, to placate the girl's look of horror. She didn't like Miss Prissy Boots. 'I shall do my bit to bring her into the fold. She'll have to give up her airy-fairy ideas and come down to earth with a bump. Old

Bradbury's not going to let the Pencombe business slip away from him; he's spent too much time on it already for that. Soon as the hoo-hah has quietened down a bit he'll be over there, quick as you like, and it'll be Isabella they're putting in as the new lady of the house. Just you mark my words. Tomorrow, Maude, you'll begin tomorrow, putting what I've just said into practice. And you'll begin by telling what we know to Miss Isabella.'

Maude thought for a moment before replying, but she'd seen the reason in Dove's argument. There was nothing for it but to agree. 'That'll put the cat among the pigeons all right,' she said. 'Isabella'll probably faint right away, like she did before.'

'Isabella won't throw no faint. She's more like to throw a fit when she finds out who's involved though. I'm looking forward to tomorrow, I'll tell you that. It's going to be a right old rumpus. Just thinking of it's got my appetite up again. You got any more of that apple pie, Emmy? And a spoonful of your damson cheese with it, if you please. Maude! Wipe that disgusting mess off your hands and get me another glass of ale, and don't scowl, girl, it'll give you wrinkles.' He laughed at her trying to smooth the lines off her funny, skinny face. 'Tell you what, you can both have a glass with me, and we'll drink to success.'

'Here we are then, ladies,' he said a little later, when all their glasses were charged, 'I give you,' he raised his drink, 'Isabella!'

'Isabella,' intoned Maude, with all the fervour of the newly converted.

'Isabella,' joined in Emily.

'May God bless her,' continued Dove, 'and all who sail in her.' And they all collapsed with laughter.

* * *

Maude added the finishing touch to the neatly laid tray of early morning tea by placing an Abernethy biscuit on the saucer. She opened the door to the bedroom quietly and placed the small, marquetry tray on the chest of drawers. Then she walked soundlessly over the thick Indian carpet to draw back the curtains. The scent of autumn was already indoors; it had crept around the heavy hangings and a smell of woodsmoke mingled with the last, dusty green of summer's end.

Isabella stirred. She had slept only fitfully until dawn and then drifted at last into a deep sleep, untroubled by dreams. 'What time is it?' she mumbled. Her eyes were heavy with sleep as she sat up fumbling for a handkerchief under the pillows.

'Seven, ma'am.'

Isabella suddenly sat very still. She wasn't normally woken until eight. 'What's happened, is there any news?'

Maude took a deep breath. This, as far as she was concerned, was it. 'In a manner of speaking, ma'am. That is . . .'

'Go on, go on.' Isabella couldn't wait, she had to know now.

'The thing is, there is news, but not how you'd expect it. And,' the girl allowed a ghost of a smile to colour her cheeks, 'it's not what you've expected.'

'You mean she's all right, Lucinda's all right, they've found her?' Isabella was pushing back the tangled bed-clothes. She had to get up, get dressed.

'She's safe, if that's what you mean, ma'am, the flood didn't get her.'

Isabella cried a 'thank God', but Maude wasn't going to be interrupted now.

'Miss Lucinda's safe from drowning, but she's not coming back here. At least,' Maude looked to the ceiling for inspiration, 'she's quite local, it's not as if she's far away.'

'For heaven's sake, what are you going on about, Maude? Where is she, what's all this about?'

'She's up at Reason Hill with Mr Cade. She's been with him since that Friday. It's as if, as if, as if they're man and wife, if you get my meaning.'

Isabella did, and sat back on her bed in astonishment. 'Mr Cade, Mr Thomas Cade?' she asked, but she didn't need the answer, she felt it already. 'Does my father know?'

'Not yet, ma'am.'

'Then I must tell him.' But she made no move to rise. What on earth could she say to him? How would she start? Even Maude had found the revelation awkward.

'I don't think you'll have to, ma'am,' Maude said. She came closer to Isabella; this was her chance to become a confidante. 'We've heard that your father's to be told this morning. I'd let others break the news if I was you.'

'We? Who's this "we"?'

'Well, us in the house; come to that the villagers, everyone except you and your father. It's been known about for two, maybe three days. Mind you,' Maude added quickly, as Isabella looked up at her furiously, 'they didn't tell us house staff till yesterday afternoon. But the villagers will be on his side, see; a lot of them work on his farm.'

'But why hasn't Lucinda let us know? I don't understand,' but as Isabella slowly voiced her doubts, understanding began to dawn. There was one way to ensure a marriage: Johnnie had been at pains to make that clear to her.

'It's by her choice too, ma'am,' Maude added.

'Yes.' It would be, wouldn't it? Isabella could see, suddenly, how the two of them would get on. It would be a formidable match. God help her father if he tried to stand in their way.

'You can help me dress,' she said to Maude, who felt her tension fly away in an instant. She'd done it right, Dove would be pleased.

It was at that very moment, as she delved into the drawers for Isabella's underclothes, that Maude began to work out a scheme for herself. It was Dove who'd said that Maude had her own life to look out for, and he was right. Maude had had her fancies right enough, Thomas Cade for one. But fancies don't always get a girl what she wants. Dove would do quite nicely. Wife of the butler at the big house at Pencombe; that would suit Maude very well.

She assisted her mistress most carefully with her dressing, and Isabella looked particularly polished as she took her place at breakfast. Her father was totally unaware of the turmoil that surged beneath her sprigged muslin bodice. It was as well that they had fallen into the habit of silence at table, Isabella thought, as she bit into a piece of hot buttered toast. Now she must wait on the timing of others. The thought that kept rushing into her head was that now there was no possibility that Lucinda would marry Michael.

When the note arrived at eleven that morning, it was from Thomas. Eli received it in his study. The wording was short and to the point. 'Your daughter, Lucinda, is safe,' it said. 'We would ask you to come to us at Reason Hill.' It was signed Thomas Cade. The first overwhelming, flooding feeling was relief. She wasn't dead, she wasn't dead. But fury was quick in surfacing at the implication of the use of the pronoun 'we' in the note.

He called for the carriage, and as he ran down the steps towards it Isabella joined him. 'You knew,' he cried, seeing her ready dressed for the visit. He waved the note at her, 'You knew?'

'Only this morning, Papa.'

There wasn't another word between them until they reached the house, then, as they stood side by side at the door of Reason Hill, Eli turned to her. 'You'll not speak to your sister unless I allow it,' he said.

'I'm sorry, Papa,' Isabella said and as the door opened and Thomas and Lucinda stood there, Isabella darted forwards and Lucinda stepped out of her lover's possessive arms to kiss her sister. They were closer in that moment than they'd ever been.

Thomas stood back to usher Eli through into the parlour. Eli ignored Lucinda's plaintive little cry of 'Papa'; she hadn't bothered that he'd suffered all this while. He would construct walls of hate between himself and his favourite daughter.

Compared to Linstone their surroundings were almost humble, but the furniture, although old, was good; and a new atmosphere of warmth prevailed that bemused Isabella. When she'd called here before, to see Timmy, the house had seemed waiting, only half fulfilled; now it was complete. Thomas and Lucinda stood close together, his arm again around her waist. That was it, this was what had been lacking: it was no longer a house but a home.

'Where is Timmy?' Isabella broke the silence.

'He's staying with Jenny. Her brother Luke was the one who saved me.' Even Lucinda's voice seemed to have changed, it was softer, gentler, slower.

'Who the hell is Timmy?' Eli was still standing.

'My adopted son,' said Thomas and a spark of irritation leaped into Lucinda's eyes; she hadn't changed out of all recognition after all. Eli saw a foothold.

'A son? I see, you bring my daughter into a household already populated with family, do you, Mr Cade? You'll

243

do me the service of taking your arm from around her waist. I do not approve of such familiarities.'

'Oh, don't you now, Eli?' Thomas laughed. 'Well, you'll have to get used to it. And any other sort of familiarities I choose to display in my own home, with my own wife.'

'Your wife, your wife? You mean you're married already?' Eli had paled.

'In all but name.' And Lucinda stood beside him, unblushing, unrepenting.

Eli felt a wave of panic. 'Lucinda is engaged to Michael,' he said, 'you know she is. That can't be broken.'

'It can and is, Papa,' Lucinda answered for herself. 'Michael and I were never meant to be, I can see that now. I don't want a man who holds some imaginary ideal more dearly than me, I want one who wants me, and only me. And I have such a man.' She slid her own arm around the man beside her. With Thomas, Lucinda showed a different facet: her vitality shone, her forcefulness became an asset, rather than a destructive liability.

'Why not face it, Eli?' Thomas was calm, in possession of himself, his house and his woman. 'It's a *fait accompli*. Nothing you can do about it, and nothing you should want to do. We'll make good friends, you and I, and good business partners too. Come, Eli, give us your blessing, for we'll marry with or without it. We'll have to, you know,' he continued, 'for the sake of the child.'

'The child?' Eli's head was spinning.

'Sit down, sit down, Eli,' Thomas said to his guest, who abruptly did as he was bid. 'Look, I'm a farmer, Eli,' he continued, 'getting stock's my business. If I didn't know when a mare was ready for covering or a heifer would stand for the bull, then I wouldn't last long at it. Lucinda is carrying my child and we'll be wed as soon as possible. We don't want any more tattle than needs be, and don't worry, this tale won't go much further than the villagers. By the time it's spread abroad, it'll just be a natural matter of two neighbouring estates brought together by marriage.'

'You're a tenant, Thomas, you've no estate to bring.' Eli had almost given in; he'd given up using the 'Mr Cade' unconsciously.

'Only until I buy the farm out, and with you as a father-in-law, Eli, I don't see I'll have much trouble.'

'What? And what about Pencombe?' Eli asked. Although he knew the answer already, his gaze had turned to Isabella. She felt the look and saw Lucinda and Thomas also staring at her. A tiny glow of excitement stirred just below her breastbone.

'Well, it's only natural, isn't it?' Thomas said. 'And you were going there all along, weren't you, Isabella?'

Isabella couldn't answer, she felt light-headed, her cheeks were burning.

'It's all working out for the best, then,' her father said. He could feel a lessening of pressure already. If Pencombe had slipped away he'd be in very dire straits, but with the settlement in hand the bank could be placated. 'I suppose instead of damning Michael I should be blessing him,' he continued. Isabella looked at him, puzzled; and then he enlightened them all.

'The note that he left for me on Monday morning, when he went up to London. It explained it all. He said if Lucinda was found and was prepared to let him out of the engagement, he'd give up the entail. He wants to go into politics or some such nonsense. So Johnnie gets the lot, the title, the estate and now, of course, Isabella.'

They all looked at Isabella, beaming their pleasure, as the world around her crumbled into ruins.

Hermione was enjoying being flustered. Her guest was bright, young, vivacious and asking her for advice, so

Hermione dispensed the tea, set out so charmingly on the Chippendale side table in her mustard panelled morning room, with her usual equanimity overlaid by a liberal helping of animation.

'You know, Adele, you remind me so much of your mother, I just can't get over it. You could almost be her, all those years ago.'

'Don't let Mom hear you say "all those years" like that, Auntie. She's pretty edgy about her age, you know.'

'Is she really?' Hermione asked with the warm concern of the non-afflicted. She herself felt happier now than she had ever done in her youth. But then, she hadn't been that much of a beauty, and she hadn't had much of a marriage portion. To be utterly truthful, she'd had absolutely none of those two commodities so precious to a young girl. But of course, she'd had her family name, and that in the end had been enough. Now, here sat Adele with loads of beauty and pots of money, asking her Aunt Hermione for advice. It was a moment to savour.

'Will you have another éclair, Adele?'

'No, thanks. You know, I'm having a problem with my brothers. I'm afraid they're into this anti Uncle William thing pretty deep.' Adele stressed her use of the 'uncle'; she might not have actually met Lord Montford, but as he was Hermione's brother Adele saw no good reason why she couldn't appropriate him. It was very irritating of Father and the boys to be so awkward; Adele was sure it could be very useful to her to have an earl in her collection.

'Anti William thing, what on earth do you mean?' Hermione was instantly alert. She had no cubs of her own to protect so she was quite maternal about her brother, however much she told herself he didn't deserve it.

'Well, there are all sorts of plots and schemes and things afoot, I know that. I expect you do too?'

But Hermione shook her head. Damn, Adele had really

only come here in the hope of ferreting out what these deals were all about. She'd played her hand now, and looked like getting perilously little in return.

'Well, you do know anyway that my Pa goes wild if I even mention your brother? It's funny because it was all so long ago, but it really stirs him up and of course the boys have just joined in. The maddening thing is . . .' Hermione leaned forward, all the better to hear Adele, but fate decreed that she was not to. At that moment, the downstairs maid came in to announce Michael and, being family, he sailed into the room without hesitation. Into the elegant, bang up-to-date domicile of George and Hermione and into the aura of Adele.

The introductions performed, they sat, all three, partaking of tea. It had been Michael's intention to widen his circle of acquaintances in town, whilst he waited for the Marquess of Salisbury's reply to his request for a meeting where he could bring the South African women's plight further into the open. But this girl was something. The daughter of a very old friend, Hermione had said. Odd that he hadn't met her before, but then Michael had never been one for London. Then, during the conversation it was revealed that Adele had never been in England before. That was truly amazing, Michael thought, as, whilst her accent was charmingly American, she had all the mannerisms of a perfect London lady. And her clothes, well, her clothes were all that money could buy, tempered with a positive knowledge of what suited her deep blue eyes and smooth brown hair. Hermione ate yet another éclair with a queasy sensation in her stomach. This feeling became one of definite unease when George, unbelievably early for him, returned from the office. 'Ah!' he said at the cosy little gathering that met his eyes.

Michael stiffened fractionally in his uncle's presence, but he had come across him several times recently and was beginning to think that George Bullstone wasn't half as bad as he might have been. It was strange how Michael's views on most subjects were altering with his new-found freedom. That was how he viewed his forthcoming removal from the direct line at Pencombe. Freedom from an all-consuming master that had held him in its thrall. He felt differently about his father these days, too. It was easier to see a lot of things with the mists blown away.

'Well, my children,' said George. 'Now, Adele, I expect that if you told your mama you were going out to the theatre this evening with this young man, she'd be over-joyed. On the other hand, if you told your papa, he'd be pretty furious. And you, Michael, if you told your father that you were going out on the town with this young lady, would be lucky not to be horsewhipped.'

Michael looked obligingly astonished.

'But, you would, old man,' George slapped his thigh, so great was his amusement. 'She's *that woman's* daughter, don't you see? Yes, go on, add it all up. Funny to watch him, isn't it, girls? Yes, that's right,' he said to Michael's obvious awakening, 'she's the daughter of your father's very own *bête noire*. I don't suppose he ever even mentioned Betsy's name, did he?'

'No,' said Michael very slowly. He hadn't thought of a connection for an instant. He looked even more keenly at the girl. How fascinating to come across the girl who might, all things being different, have been a sister. Well, that wasn't really how it would have worked out, but it was odd all the same.

'What shall we do then, Hermione?' George continued. 'I can just see these young things are dying to go off out somewhere. Now, I'll tell you what, young Michael,' he dug into his wallet, 'I've a couple of tickets here for a damned good show, damned good, lots of singing, danc-ing, that sort of thing. Now you whisk Adele off somewhere nice for dinner, then on you go. I'll sort out her parents, easy as winking. Go on, go on,' he urged. 'What on earth are the two of you waiting for?'

It seemed rude to Michael to point out that he had other plans for his evening, but it was nothing a hurried line to his club couldn't deal with. As for Adele, she loved anything that smelt of chance, and this was positively gamey.

They went out into the London evening, thrown together as only fate and a benevolent 'uncle' can contrive.

Michael was nervous. It mattered so much to him to be able to make the first step into politics, towards a position of influence. He'd been awake most of the night, sitting up at his desk in his room at the club, preparing for the interview at eleven o'clock. He'd given himself too much time, and now breakfast was only just over and gone. At ease in the reading room, to kill some more time, he'd digested the morning papers along with the kipper, and he was left with nothing to do but worry. He should fix his mind on something else, anything other than the Prime Minister's office and his appointment. The obvious choice was Adele. He'd taken her to yet another show last night. George's manipulations had ensured that they had almost unlimited access to each other's time. Michael quickly lifted his paper up higher in front of him: Arbuthnot Tremens was making his way into the room, and Michael could think of nothing worse than being subjected to a verbal grilling by the nosiest man in London. It was such a waste of time, time that he could be devoting to his cause, and he had to hang around in reading rooms, avoiding idiots like Arbuthnot. This morning had better go well, or else – or else what? But it didn't do to cross bridges until you'd come to them.

Protected by his paper wall, he returned to his

contemplation of Adele. She was a charming girl, witty in a way he almost understood and very, very pretty. Taking her out was a pleasure, but not, he admitted to himself, not an all-consuming joy. There must be something wrong with him. He stared unseeing at the newsprint in front of him. He'd never wanted Lucinda and she was a beauty, now he didn't want Adele; at least he didn't want anything of her other than her occasional company, a pleasant evening to break the monotony of dining in club. There was more to love and marriage, there had to be. Increasingly he was remembering Mrs Verboert, the Boer woman who'd urged him to plead their cause. He thought of her hair and her bright blue eyes that shone like that necklace, the one they'd bought for Lucinda, the one that had arrived in this morning's post, neatly wrapped and accompanied by a note from his ex-fiancée.

There was no more animosity, no more wounded pride. Lucinda's letter had overflowed with her own satisfaction. She was to marry Thomas Cade; in fact, they would probably be married by the time Michael received the letter. And Isabella was to marry Johnnie. As soon as the estate was passed over to him, that is, and the entail broken. But then that was being taken in hand, as Michael knew, for he had spent several hours last week with his family's solicitors discussing what must be done, closeted, on what was probably the last bright day of autumn, in a dingy, dusty room close to Smithfield.

Michael had walked away past the market itself, past the hanging sides of meat, beef from Scotland, pigs from Norfolk. Lambs, he smiled grimly at the thought, lambs from the slaughter. At times, when he allowed himself some self-pity, he felt like a lamb led to the slaughter, sacrificed by his own too tender emotions. He should not have suffered from sensibilities; the emotions of his time were self-belief, self-righteousness. Perhaps he should have been born in an age when men of conscience went on holy crusades. Even as head of the house, he would have been spared for that. Truth to tell, he was not happy at the step he was soon to take. He did not want to leave Pencombe; he loved it, loved the familiar ways. If he allowed himself, he could feel bitter at how fate had contrived it all.

He let his paper fall down on to his lap. So Johnnie was to have Isabella, was he? The girl must have forgotten, or at the very least forgiven, her beloved's attempted rape. Beloved, yes, presumably he was her beloved. It had been the ghost of Isabella in Africa that had inspired him to all of this, that had made him throw up his whole ordered way of life, for what? For a girl who would marry a man given to excess, a man who killed other men for sport.

The voice cut through his thoughts. 'Hallo, old chap, thought it was you, lurking behind that rag. What are you up to then, what's your . . .'

'Bugger off!' Michael had jumped to his feet, flinging the paper down beside him. 'Bugger off, will you?' He stormed out of the reading room, leaving Arbuthnot, monocle dangling in astonishment. A pair of elderly gentlemen who'd been snoozing gently beneath their coverings of *The Times* snorted in disbelief. But neither of them could believe they'd really heard what for one moment they thought they'd heard. Not in these hallowed halls, and not from young Montford. Good God, the young chap was an old Harrovian, wasn't he?

Michael continued his flight from his own thoughts by marching out of the club portals and throwing himself headlong into the business of crossing the road, which at ten o'clock in Piccadilly was no mean challenge. There were other expletives in the air that morning, from the cabbies he caused to heave on their reins and from the butcher's delivery boy he made swerve into the pavement.

But he didn't hear any of it. He was trying quite unsuccessfully to fix his thoughts on Adele, trying to exorcize from his mind those bright blue eyes that sparkled like the necklace, tucked safely in his shirt drawer, but burning in his heart.

'What I should like to impress upon you, sir, is that this interview in itself is a sign of exceptional interest. There are hundreds of applicants for the Prime Minister's time who are put off by letter. Only a mere handful are ever invited to this office.'

'Yes, but I had understood that I was to meet the Prime Minister himself.' Michael sounded petulant, and looked it, as he sat, legs apart in the highly polished visitor's chair in the Prime Minister's Under-Secretary's cramped office. The Under-Secretary was almost on the point of deciding that the preferential treatment being shown to him was misplaced. But he would allow the young man a little longer to prove his worth – if he had any, that is.

'Then I am very sorry if you received the wrong impression on that count, and I can understand your disappointment. But the Prime Minister has indeed read your submission and has asked me to put to you a few further questions and, more importantly, to make one or two comments that he feels may be of help to you.'

Michael held his breath and his tongue. It wasn't the fault of the man on the other side of the desk that he felt so bottled up, so ready to explode. He managed to nod, then he forced himself to say, quite slowly, 'Thank you, thank you for being so understanding. As you say, I am disappointed. But I must not let that stand in the way of further dialogue. Please, please continue.'

Bartholomew Giles, Under-Secretary in the Prime Minister's office smiled to himself. Poor young man, brought up with a silver spoon in his mouth, only too eager now to spit it out, but he'd have to change his manner. Condescension, even in the PM's office, had gone out of fashion long ago.

'The Prime Minister's main concern, and this stems from his own experience, is that members of the aristocracy who wish to become active politicians are all too often led by others. It may seem strange to you, sir, but it is borne out by history that those who were brought up to a position such as yours, heir to large estates, heir to a title, heir indeed to power, albeit of a limited sort, are themselves, once out of their sphere, often easily influenced.'

Michael showed his disbelief. He'd never been led by anyone, other than his father of course. Surely his recent saga in the army proved that. He opened his mouth to make just that case, but was forestalled.

'Before you speak, sir, I would ask you to think again. I am aware that since your decision to abandon your inheritance, you have been living in London. During that time you will, of course, have made many new acquaintances. Truthfully now, are you their natural leader? Or do you go along with the crowd? Is there anyone you can think of who is already manipulating you? It will be in someone's interest to do just that, I can assure you. The only real question is if it has begun already, or if the situation is still awaiting you. Members of Parliament have schemes woven around them continually. It is a rare man who can negotiate them. An even rarer man who has not learned early to exist in the cut and thrust of normal life who can come unsullied into the fray and win.' Giles sat back.

'Rather heroic it all sounds, doesn't it? But actually, underneath it can get pretty sordid. That's what the Prime Minister is particularly anxious to avoid. A breath of scandal would blight your cause, you see, and it is a cause that is close to his heart, I believe. But it is one that must be approached with the utmost caution. There is a very narrow line between humanitarianism and softness, but it is one that must never be crossed.'

Michael was thinking frantically. He'd skipped through his chance acquaintances, the Arbuthnots of his world, but his mind had faltered at George, his Uncle George who was making the Adele situation so dreadfully easy. Adele herself, what was her part in all of this? For, of course, the more he thought about it, the more he could see he was being embroiled in something. George was a man who lived to make money. He wasn't a kind, considerate relative out to help Michael enjoy himself. He looked up at the Under-Secretary with a new firmness in his expression.

'I must thank you, I have never looked at life quite that way before. It is, to say the least, illuminating. I can assure you that there is nothing in my recent existence that would compromise my position. However, I must say that I think your warning was timely, in fact probably quite incredibly timely. There will be nothing I shall do in the future that will have the slightest likelihood of jeopardizing my future.'

'Thank you, sir.' The PM had been right after all; there was something different about this one. 'If I can just ask you a few more questions that the Prime Minister would like to have answered?'

The meeting went on for another half an hour. Michael concentrated fully on the questions he was asked, not allowing his mind to wander to the awakening he had just experienced. He had not been slow in learning the first essential lesson of application in politics.

Lavender hadn't heard from Eli since the day he'd rescued her parasol. She'd told him then that she could be contacted through the Red Lion Hotel, and she'd thought that he might want to carry on a little liaison, a gentlemanly affair. But guilt, as Lavender knew, had a habit of conquering all. And he'd obviously got out of the habit of making love since his wife died. It had probably decreased his need; it did in some men. So, it was up to her to start the running again.

She had given her approach a lot of thought and she had a lot of time to think these days, because since their 'engagement' Harold was paying all her bills. She hadn't bothered to try and get him to make love to her since the fiasco, and he obviously hadn't wanted to. It was still a peep show he fancied. The thought of it made her squirm, as she sat embroidering a cheval set for her dressing table. She didn't dare start on baby clothes yet, Harold would be sure to find them, but a great growing maternal urge was willing her on to the tiny caps, mitts and bootees. She wished the next stage was over and done. Her tummy was becoming a round pot. Harold had even laughed at her about it the other evening, told her it was because she was so happy that she was getting fat. She'd got to get Eli all tied up before Harold guessed the truth, or she'd have no income, and soon she'd be so obviously pregnant that there wouldn't be any way she could earn one. She picked out a poppy-red thread to work into the tiny bouquet of flowers on her pattern. It was a pity she had to fend for herself in her condition. No, it was no good. She stabbed the needle firmly into the linen and wound the unused thread around it. She wouldn't be able to settle now until she'd done something positive.

She went through to the narrow hallway.

'Irene!' she shrieked, banging on the wall with her fist, 'Irene!' The old crab could write with a lovely hand, better than Lavender's own spidery crawl. She'd write out a note for the price of a glass of gin and she was as close-mouthed as an oyster.

The wording had to be inviting, mysterious and in

character with Lavender Brown, widow. In the end she decided that it was a case of least said.

'Dear Mr Bradbury,' Irene wrote to her dictation. 'You will remember the happy day we spent together early in the summer. Shortly after that day I went away to the seaside on a holiday for a few weeks. I am now back at home in Maidstone. I have a matter that I would very much appreciate your advice on. As I said I am without many friends here and I do so hope that you will see your way to assisting me. Yours, etc., Lavender Brown.'

Lavender got Irene to read it back to her, and it sounded awful. It was so difficult. Face to face with him, she wouldn't feel tongue-tied at all, but this, this was too difficult. It wasn't as if she was writing to Harold, that would be as easy as pie; perhaps she should just imagine she was writing to him? That was when the idea struck her.

Harold received the note at lunch-time. A kid from the back streets had brought it, sniffing over the envelope with a runny nose. He looked hopefully at Harold for a moment, thinking he might get a penny, but he nearly got a clip on his ear instead, so he sloped away. Harold read the missive nervously. It was the first time he'd ever had a note personally sent to him at his workplace. It seemed like an omen of doom. But there was no clue in the writing; simply a message for him to meet 'a friend' out by the gasworks, at two o'clock this afternoon. There would be, the note said, something to his advantage. It was all very worrying, but perhaps it was the unknown gentleman in London to whom he sent his information? Harold couldn't afford to upset him, not with Lavender to support. And she was eating so much these days, and being finicky about what it was; already the extra his spying brought him was seeming nowhere near enough.

He gave a sigh of vexation. He could almost wish Lavender hadn't said she'd ever agree to marry him, what with all that bed stuff as well. It weighed a lot on his mind these days. He'd have to have another go at it when they were married, but what if he couldn't manage it then? What if he couldn't manage it ever?

He told Eli he'd run out of sealing wax and that he was going up the town to buy some more. The old idiot was so distraught these days, he hardly even noticed what he was told. He spent hours poring over the ledgers, working out new sums on scraps of paper and then crumpling them up and throwing them into the wastepaper basket. Harold carefully collected these jottings and sent them off as a kind of bonus, with his copies of the accounts, to his secret benefactor. It was all quite easy at the moment. What would happen when the new manager turned up next week? They'd see.

As Harold darted off towards the gasworks Lavender slipped out from her vantage point in the pub doorway. She walked nervously towards the brewery. It towered up above her, suddenly dauntingly impressive. The Eli she'd thought of when she'd made her plans was approachable, but she had never bearded him within his den. She was pale with nerves by the time she reached the gates, trembling as she crossed the courtyard. She pulled the brass bell for callers too timidly at first, then gave it a good yank, so that it jangled. Lavender Biggs, she thought fiercely to herself, you're not a girl to give way to nerves; come on, girl, buck up.

'It is, you know,' said Peter, ratcatcher of the upper floors, to his mates. 'I should know, I was the one wot got the five guineas; it's her.'

'And I says it's the one wot's stepping out with old misery guts. It is, you know, I even heard her, it was Harold this and Harold that.'

Then Bill, drayman on the country run, had a stroke of genius. 'Wot,' he said, 'if it's one and the same?' And they all paused, struck dumb by the hysterical thought that man and master might be sharing the same bird.

Eli took a moment to recognize her. 'Why, it's Mrs, Mrs Brown, isn't it? How nice to see you,' and he ushered her to a chair. She was surprised how ruffled he looked; not the dapper, smooth gentleman he'd been a few short weeks ago, more like a worried owl. 'Would you like some tea? Oh dear, I'm sorry, my clerk's popped out for a moment. He won't be long though, we'll have some then, shall we?'

Lavender hoped that she knew for certain Harold would be a lot longer than a moment, but it was an unpleasant reminder of his existence. 'I wonder if I could tempt you into a little walk, Mr Bradbury, just for old-time's sake, you know.'

'I don't think I can, my dear, pressure of business, pressure of business, you know.' He ran his fingers through his hair.

'Sometimes, when I'm really mixed up, like, I find a little walk helps.' She looked her most inviting.

Eli looked at her uncertainly. He couldn't see the wood for the trees; he knew the formula for success was there, somewhere, but even with the Pencombe securities coming in soon, somehow it didn't look right on paper. Then he remembered how good, how clear-headed, he'd felt after their last little walk. He made a decision, the first decisive one he'd made today. Quickly he shuffled his papers into a folder then dropped them into his desk.

'Come on, my dear.' He put an arm out to her. 'I think you're just what I need. Let's go for a walk right enough, how about up on the heath? I'll get a man to call us a cab.'

But he wasn't going to get it as quickly as all that. Lavender had her speech to make first. 'Oh, let's walk into

258

town ourselves and find one. It was so romantic, our last little walk, wasn't it, Eli?' She used his name shyly, tentatively, and it delighted him.

'Whatever you say, my dear,' he agreed, patting her pretty hand.

They walked out across the yard together, Eli pausing on the way to let her pat the horses' noses. He enjoyed showing her off in front of the men. Thank God, he thought, not for the first time, that he had a life of his own well away from Linstone, where he could walk with a little bit of fluff on his arm, and be admired for it.

It was the leisurely stroll across the yard that put Lavender's timing out of kilter. Not that she realized it, for she was so delighted at Eli's reception of her that she had all but forgotten Harold. The clerk came back half running along the lane leading to the brewery. There'd been no one at the gasworks, the whole thing had been a put up job. He suspected Bill, the drayman whose wages he'd docked for perpetually late rounds. Harold had been keeping a weather eye out for the old man; he didn't want to be seen approaching the brewery from the wrong direction for his errand.

He couldn't believe his eyes. It was Lavender. What on earth was she doing? But it couldn't be! Whoever the girl was, she was hanging on the old man's arm as bold as brass. It was Lavender, wasn't it? He peered round his doorway refuge for a better look. He was sure it was. He hid until the couple had walked out on to the towpath, and then he slipped into the yard.

'Oi,' called out Bill, as all the others listened. 'Oi, Harold, you turned pimp now then, as well as weasel, have yer?'

And they all roared with laughter, howled with mirth. The blood pounded in Harold's temples until he thought his head would burst. Someone would pay for this, he vowed, someone would pay dearly.

'I nearly didn't tell you,' Lavender continued. She wasn't looking at Eli, but out over the river as she had been ever since she'd started on her saga. She thought that Eli would react better given a bit of privacy to sort out the expression on his face.

'But then after my friend did that little business with the ring, and she said that it was definitely going to be a boy, well then I got to thinking that it wouldn't be right, not to you, not to the little lad.' She was silent then, letting nature, she hoped, do its work.

Eli was stunned. The last words of all, 'little lad', kept revolving round his head. He'd done so well; all these years he'd been quite content with two daughters, and now he was at the stage of looking towards grandchildren. Good God, according to Thomas he'd already got one on the way. But a little lad of his own . . . he felt almost unmanned by the rush of emotion. And a few moments ago he'd been thinking of Lavender as a 'bit of fluff'. He did some hasty mental gymnastics. She was a simple little thing, there was nothing wrong in that. She was of a type with the girls he'd gone with as a young man back in Yorkshire. They'd all been bright, bouncy, happy young things which was why, when he'd met Martha, who became his wife, he'd been captivated by her quiet ways, her retiring nature. Yet that very nature left so little substance to remember.

Thank goodness Lucinda was in her own establishment. The thought of her and Lavender sharing the same house was beyond belief. But then, even Isabella; he slowed his happy plans. Now, particularly, Isabella had to be considered. Or rather, not her, but the Montfords of whom she would shortly become a part. He let out a sigh of irritation.

260

'What's the matter?' Lavender looked round at him quickly, she'd been so sure he'd be pleased, so sure.

'Oh, it's nothing to do with you, my dear, nothing at all.' He tucked her arm more securely into his own. 'I can't tell you how pleased I am. What a brave little thing you are, even coming to me, face to face, to tell me. Not many women would have done that. No, no, nothing's the matter and nothing's going to be the matter. I'll look after you now. Come, let's go and have some tea at an hotel, and we'll make some plans; perhaps we'll even start pulling a few names out of the family hat for the little chap, shall we? How about an Ernest, or an Edward; that's patriotic too? Oh, Lavender,' he turned to face her, put his arms around her and kissed her very gently on the cheek. 'I think, my dear, you've given me back my youth. How can I ever thank you?'

Lavender bloomed, glowed, in his embrace. Care and protection, it was all she'd ever wanted. The fact she'd thought him like a frazzled old owl swept out of her head. She let her mind drift happily on to the dear little baby's clothes. She, like Eli, had absolute faith in the wedding ring, suspended on a piece of thread, that Irene had happily got revolving clockwise over her bulging navel. She'd embroider a cap in blue, and the christening gown, that would be all white with a cap to match.

They had a decorous tea in the Star and Garter Hotel. Eli told her, very gently and tactfully, that she'd have to go through a bit of polishing before she met the family. On account, he explained, of this connection with the aristocracy. After all, the little boy would have a real Lady as a sister. Lavender came over a bit dizzy at that, although she didn't let on. The old dear, he was actually talking marriage. She'd look after him all right; second childhood, that's what she'd given him.

Eli was all for her staying that very night in the hotel.

He'd take a suite for her, he said. But she didn't think she wanted to arrive like a waif and stray with no baggage. So she said no, thank you very much, dear, but she'd go to her own home tonight and come in style tomorrow. Not that, she admitted, she had that much style to come in. Eli was delving for his wallet in an instant, but she wouldn't take the twenty pounds he tried to press on her. What was the point in spending that much when she could get by very nicely on ten. She'd look after his money for him; after all she was going to be family.

When she got back home and started looking through her things, there really wasn't that much she wanted to take. It was a bit pitiful, she thought, looking at the small heap she'd made on the bed of clothes to keep. There was a much bigger pile of things on the floor that she'd give to Irene tomorrow. That was the sum total of her life so far, and if it wasn't for the scrap of life inside her at this minute, she probably wouldn't have got much further. She felt a twinge of guilt at presenting Eli with another man's son. But she'd do her best to give him one of his own next time, not that he'd ever know the difference. Who knows, once she got in the swing of things she might just make a great big family for him, half a dozen assorted kids; she giggled, there only were two sorts, but he'd know what she meant. As she slowly folded a black woollen shawl with red roses on the border, she started to think about Eli. He was a good man, and good men had been lacking in her life.

Looking after the baby meant eating well, Eli had said at tea when he'd pressed her to take another ham sandwich. So she cut an extra generous hunk of cheese for her supper, and she'd have two slices of bread. Anyway, there was no point in not eating it up, she'd be at the hotel tomorrow. After her bit of what Eli called 'polishing', she'd go to Linstone, to a home where there were servants, a cook and that. She'd probably never have to prepare a meal for herself again. What a lovely thought.

She heard the key turn in the lock and could have kicked herself. She'd meant to get that key off Harold last time he'd stayed the night. It would have been easy to slip it out of his pocket when he was asleep. His footsteps resounded in the hall, and as she heard him come to the kitchen door she turned to him, the bread knife still in her hand – which was just as well.

He was putrid with drink, and the reek of it filled the cubby-hole of a kitchen. His eyes were streaked red, a trickle of saliva ran down his chin. Lavender had lived a bit; she knew murder in a man's eyes, and this was it.

'You bitch, you slut, you fucking rotten whore.' He stepped to come close, but she held up a knife to him and he swayed, but stood still. 'I'll kill you,' he crooned at her, like a mad animal. 'I'll kill you slowly, I'll torment you, I'll make you wish you'd never been born, you miserable – ' his voice was rising to a scream.

'Shut it!' she shouted at him. 'Shut your foul, stinking mouth.'

'I'll kill you, Lavender, I'll rip you apart with my bare hands.'

'You! You!' She spat the words at him. 'It takes more of a man than you are to kill me, mate.' She wielded the knife tantalizingly in front of his eyes. 'Don't you try anything on me. I know you, Harold, I know you through and through, and you're rotten, that's what you are, rotten.'

She lunged towards him suddenly and he took a quick step back, stumbling over the leg of a chair. 'Yeh, go on,' she tormented, 'back off, and sod off too. Out of my way, Harold, and out of my life. I've got better things to do than waste my time on the likes of you.'

Harold was crouching on the floor; he felt sick now, the blood lust draining out of him, its place taken by a great empty, yawning void. 'You've taken all me money,' he yowled. 'I've supported you and you've gone and given yourself to him; it's horrible, horrible,' he wailed.

'Here you are, that's all I've got, now clear off,' she yelled, throwing five golden sovereigns at him, Eli's sovereigns. He grovelled on the floor to find them, cuckold's coins. He looked down, beaten, but she kept the knife well in front of her with the wall behind.

'Go on, go on,' she shouted, 'piss off. And don't you come here no more. Me key, where's me key? Give us it, come on, throw it on the floor.' And he did. 'Piss off!' she yelled again and followed at a distance as he crawled towards the door, and hauled himself up to stand against the frame.

'I'll get you, Lavender.' His voice was suddenly chillingly sober, the slur quite gone. 'I'll get you, don't you kid yourself. And I'll get your fancy man. Don't go planning on a future, Lavender, 'cause you ain't got one.' He laughed.

It was the laugh that made the fear flood through her. She held the knife up in defiance as he left. Then she slammed the door. There wasn't a bolt. Yes, she had the key back now, but what good was that if he broke in through a window during the night? She grabbed her clothes together in a bundle and slipped out the back door, into the yard. Then she nipped next door to Irene's and gave her five bob for a bed for the night. She still had over four pounds to help her arrive at the hotel tomorrow looking like a lady.

She didn't get much sleep that night, but then it wasn't surprising with the bread knife still clutched tightly in her hand. It was time for Lavender Biggs to leave the back streets and no mistake.

★ ★ ★

264

Isabella had taken refuge in the rustic arbour that adorned the leeward wall of the dovecot, at the southernmost corner of the garden. She had turned her chair to face deliberately away from the view over the weald, and had fixed her gaze on a small stand of Scots pines. Behind them the sky was a pale grey wash that made the trees themselves look like black cut-outs. It was a Japanese study in contrasts, the hard outline of the branches softened by a sketchy infilling of the pine needles.

Perhaps if there had never been that momentary thrill of excitement at the thought of Pencombe with Michael, when for an instant she'd thought her father was suggesting that she should take Lucinda's intended place as Michael's wife, it wouldn't be so bad. There! She had let herself admit it now. And that was dangerous, and stupid. Even if that had been her fate, Michael would have been forever thinking of the Boer woman, the one who'd inspired him to create all this chaos. And it was chaos. If he thought that duty was confusing for him, then how much more so it was for Isabella. She would not marry Johnnie, would not, could not. And yet, how could she avoid it?

There had to be an alternative, an alternative for all of them. For Eli, whose money was sunk into Pencombe, for Isabella who would never be allowed to 'go to waste' now that she was her father's sole pawn in the marriage stakes. Thomas and Lucinda obviously saw that with Isabella at Pencombe their path to buying out Reason Hill, and other even more grandiose schemes for tracts of Pencombe land, would be so much easier. But she could never accept Johnnie; now she'd seen what hid beneath the surface she couldn't even bear the thought of him.

A breeze ruffled the top branches of the pines, and a pigeon slipped sideways from its perch, wings spreading wide to sail off on a downdraught. It had no need to clap its wings, but as it turned away from the house, it did so out of sheer bravado.

Even Margaret and her indefatigable pursuit of justice for others seemed shallow to Isabella today. None of them knew how awful the future looked spread out before her. None of them. Thinking those words – 'none of them' – consciously twice, struck a chord in her mind. She'd heard something like that before; what was it? She was eager to clutch at straws, to divert her thoughts just now. Where was it she'd heard those words?

Then she remembered and flushed, suddenly embarrassed. The words had been Lucinda's, that night after the ball at Pencombe. She had cried that none of them suffered like she did, with love, with abandonment. Then she had cried for Michael, now her love was Thomas. Isabella stood up, smoothing her skirts, dusty from the seat that had been unused all summer. How like her sister she must be after all. And Isabella herself had said how selfish those thoughts of Lucinda's were.

She found her father in his study. He smiled at her entrance; he seemed to have been smiling a lot these past couple of days. Well, Isabella thought grimly, she just hoped his smiles weren't too soon.

'Good morning, my dear,' he said. 'I'm sorry I wasn't at breakfast, but I was in the middle of some very important calculations, very important indeed for the brewery. And I'm sure you'll be delighted to know I'm making great strides. Yes, everything seems much, much clearer now.'

'Good, Papa.' Isabella had no idea what he was talking about. Her father had never been in the habit of talking business at home and it was too late for him to start, as far as she was concerned. 'I think, Papa, that it would help me if we went over this Pencombe problem a little.' She had decided against instant, outright refusal; subtlety might be more effective.

'Problem, what problem is that, my dear?' Eli too had worked out his strategy; it was to play 'never heed' to complaints, and carry all before him.

'Well, it's all so sudden, that's part of it, I'm sure. But I am confused. It seems to me, now that Lucinda can't marry Michael, that everything is best dropped, forgotten. I mean,' she hurried her words, turning away from Eli's obvious growing irritation, 'if Lord Montford were to pay you back all the money you've spent there, then the best thing would be for everyone to forget what might have happened, isn't that right?'

'Don't be so stupid, Isabella. Lord Montford hasn't got a penny. Why on earth do you think he agreed to the match in the first place? There's only one way that people like us, people with our roots in the working class, ever get up there, with the aristocracy, that's when one of them has spent all their money and needs ours. It's as simple as that, a business transaction like any other.' Eli realized, fleetingly, he'd never seen it so cut and dried before.

'Oh Papa, I'm sure it can't be as bad as you make out. After all, both Michael and Johnnie went away to school and they've got hunters, and staff, all sorts of things that cost a lot.'

'For God's sake, Issy, leave it alone. I can't bear to hear you sound so stupid. Won't you ever grow up?' He thought of Lavender; she'd got the idea of the value of money right down to her little fingertip. And she'd grasped instantly that he had to marry Isabella to Pencombe to recoup his investment.

'Look here, Issy,' he said, breathing slowly to calm himself down, 'I'm sure it's all a shock to you. You were expecting to marry Johnnie and live in a nice quiet backwater of the estate; now you'll be lady of the manor instead. But that's no bad thing. And your talents will be appreciated; why, an aristocratic young lady as gifted as you are, Issy, you'll be taken up at court, the world will be yours for the asking.'

'I won't be an aristocratic young lady,' she almost shouted, leaning over his desk towards him, scattering his neatly piled papers. She stepped back quickly to stand beside the swivel chair kept for visitors, put her hand on its back and began pushing it, jerkily, to and fro. 'I'll be a brewer's daughter, with, as you yourself just said, my roots in the working classes and there's nothing wrong in that. And it's not right that I ever planned to marry Johnnie. If you'd listened to me for a minute instead of always to Lucinda you'd have heard that long ago.'

'Issy! Issy, calm down at once!' His life was peaceful now that Lucinda had left. He had no intention of nurturing another virago. 'Now,' he continued placatingly, 'everyone quite understands that this is a surprise to you. It would take any girl a while to adjust to it. You need someone to talk to; not your sister though, I think definitely not Lucinda. Have you any other friends? Perhaps you'd like to invite someone to stay for a while?'

'Of course I haven't. You saw to that yourself, Papa. How on earth could I have any friends when everyone we used to know suddenly became not good enough for us any more?'

'Oh dear. Oh dear Issy, you really are a silly girl.' He smiled at her.

Isabella looked at her father in amazement. He was changing beyond her wildest dreams, softening in such an odd way; she could not understand it.

'Papa, I think it will be easier for us both if I say this simply. I shall never marry Johnnie, never. I have always said that and I mean it. I am sorry but there it is.'

'If we are talking about what is easiest for us both, Issy,

it is for you to give up this nonsense. You will marry him, and there is nothing more to be said. You are a silly girl. I see now that I spoilt you by letting you have your own way far too much. Well, we all have to come across authority in the end, my dear, and I, for you, am it. You will do as you are told and marry the boy. Not only your future happiness depends on it, but the livelihood of all my men at the brewery, and the workers on the Pencombe estates. All of that is your responsibility now, Issy, and you, especially, with all your high ideals, should be proud to accept it. Now go away, and don't disturb me any more, I have a great deal to get through today.'

'But Papa,' she said desperately, 'Papa, he tried to force me!'

'Force you, force you to what?' Her father was looking down at his desk again, transparently eager to get back to work.

'Force me to, to . . .' but what could she say?

'Go away, dear, that's a good girl. Go away now.'

She looked at him in desperation, fury at her inability to communicate with her own father welling up inside her. She pushed hard on the chair back and it swung violently round. It was still turning as the door closed behind her.

After she'd left the room, Eli looked up for an instant. What had the young devil tried to force her to? Probably he'd stolen a kiss and that was enough to send her into a tizzy. Well, thank God for Lavender. If he got down to work now, and went through these figures again, he would go to her this afternoon. He needed her to soothe him, he wanted to talk about the little lad. Good grief, girls were difficult!

Michael darted around the maid who had let him in at the front door. He wanted to enter his aunt's dining room unannounced.

'Good evening, Aunt Hermione, George, Adele, and I assume Mr and Mrs Macaul plus sons. How very comfortable you all look! I'm sure you won't mind if I join you; it looks as if there's more than enough food for just one more. Smithers, be a good chap and bring me a chair.'

The gathering around Hermione's silver-bedecked, pedestal-legged, mahogany dinner table had turned in surprise at Michael's unannounced entrance. Hermione's surprise turned to disbelief at the tone of her nephew's greeting. Such behaviour! She began to rise, but George forestalled her action.

'Yes, by all means come and join us, Michael. Smithers, fetch another chair and lay a place. I'm afraid you've missed out on a couple of courses, my boy, but there's an admirable saddle of venison here. I was just about to carve it myself, but on consideration I think once Smithers has you settled he can do it for me. Meanwhile I'd better introduce you. Even though you may appear to know our guests, I don't think they know you.'

'But I'm sure they must do, Uncle. After all, I must have been the topic of quite a degree of your conversation and I'm told often enough I have the beginnings of my father's nose. I'm sure Mrs Macaul at least must recognize that.'

'You miserable little . . .' Macaul senior was rising to his feet, his silver whiskers sparkling with indignation.

'No insult intended, I'm sure,' Michael continued, 'but you were engaged to be married to my father, weren't you, Mrs Macaul? I'm sure you see some family resemblance.'

Betsy dabbed at her lips with her napkin. She saw quite a remarkable resemblance to the young William; in fact although the boy was certainly better looking in the conventional sense, he was alike enough for it to have startled her. 'Yes, yes, you are very like your father,' she said. 'My husband wouldn't know that, or my sons, or, come to that, Adele.'

'Ah yes, but Adele and I are old chums, as you no doubt know.'

Macaul senior was still on his feet. 'What do you mean by that? How dare you bring my daughter's name into your conversation. She's never set eyes upon you in her life.'

'Now, now.' Michael was smiling fixedly.

'Shall I punch him in that splendid nose, Mark, or will you?' David asked.

'I think eldest first, then you can have a turn,' his brother replied, standing up and starting to unbutton his shirt cuffs.

'Please! Please, everybody, calm yourselves. This is my dining room!' Hermione could think of little else to say, she was so dismayed, so put out; perhaps she was dreaming, perhaps she should pinch herself.

'Now, now,' George said. 'Sit down, Randolf, you're making my neck ache peering up at you so. And an English lady's dining room is much too sacred to allow fisticuffs. Come on, Mark, sit down and have some more wine.'

'I'm afraid not, Mr Bullstone. That, that stuffed shirt just insulted my mother and my sister. We look after our women.'

'No, no, he didn't insult me, Mark, just sit down.' Betsy had recovered her equilibrium. 'He certainly didn't insult me because, however much I might not like to remember it, I was of course engaged to his father. As for Adele, she does indeed know Michael. George introduced them to each other here at Hermione's and they've been to one or two shows together. I didn't see any real harm in it.'

'Good God.' Randolf Macaul subsided into his chair. It

was quite obvious that he was completely unaware of his daughter's liaison.

It was Michael's turn to look surprised. But it didn't stop his power of speech. 'So, Uncle George, it seems I've underestimated you.' He looked wonderingly at George, who was still beaming quite expansively, though his mind whirled behind his small, deep-set eyes. 'Perhaps, if it wasn't quite such a widespread ploy as I imagined,' Michael continued, 'you might like to let us in on it, all of us.'

George was the centre of their attention, but before he had time to answer, Adele butted in. 'Nobody's asked me what I was up to, I see.' She looked quite affronted. 'I hope that you boys haven't been lulled into a false sense of complacency by the namby-pamby British girls you've come across. I have a mind of my own, you know.'

'Adele!' Betsy looked quite cross. 'It's not nice to be impolite to your hosts.'

'I didn't mean Hermione was namby-pamby.' Adele pouted, looking as if she quite obviously did.

Betsy huffed in exasperation. 'No, no, don't be silly. I mean that when you are a guest in a country you should try to understand their ways, respect them even if they're not the same as ours.'

All her children snorted, a joint orchestrated contempt for such ridiculously old-fashioned views.

'If you women will just hush up.' Randolf once more took centre stage. 'George, I'd like an explanation of just what has been going on here.'

Michael thought of adding that so would he, but contented himself with a sip of claret.

George was expansive, having worked out his strategy. 'What has been going on, as you put it, Randolf, was simply a matter of boy meets girl and they fall in love. It

272

was so charming I couldn't resist helping them along a little.'

'Poppycock,' said Randolf. He spoke for them all.

'I'll tell you what,' George moved to a different tack, 'I'll talk to you men after dinner, round the port. We'll thrash it all out then.'

'You will not,' his wife snapped at him, and he felt his defences wavering. She was very, very rarely angry, but this was clearly one of those occasions. 'I shall not allow my house to be treated like some second-rate club. The behaviour around this table has been quite atrocious. You, for one, Michael, I would have expected far better of. You were brought up to behave properly; your mama must be turning in her grave at this disgraceful behaviour.' She ran her baleful eye over the other members of the party.

Betsy rose immediately to the challenge. 'My children were also, as you put it, Hermione, well brought up. They are not usually given to unseemly behaviour. But you must admit, even apart from your nephew's performance, George has been most provoking. As far as I was concerned, it was simply a couple of evenings out in London. Suddenly George is bandying the word "love" about. Adele, you haven't said anything of the sort to me.'

'I haven't said it, because it doesn't exist, Mama. Oh, he's nice enough, really rather gorgeous in a sort of offhand way, but I like a bit more "go" in my beaux.'

'Thank you very much,' Michael drawled.

'Shut up!' Hermione said forcibly, surprising them all into silence.

George was the first to recover. 'Serve the meat, Smithers, then put the vegetables on the table and leave us. We'll manage to serve ourselves this evening. Don't come in to clear until I ring, understood?'

'Yes, sir.' Smithers was his most obsequious. He

couldn't wait to leave the room, then he could listen with all his concentration through the door.

They were all silent as he moved deftly around the table, each of them marshalling their resources.

'Well, George?' Randolf sat back, arms folded. He no longer had any interest in the food on his plate. The candlelight laid an expensive patina on the smooth planes of his broad forehead and patrician nose. Betsy sat very still, as she always did when her husband was on the verge of anger.

'Well, as you say, well. Now, where shall I begin?' George looked from one to another around his affluent table. They were drinking his wine, had eaten at least some of his food; now, instead of being mellowed by it, they were fuelled for the fray.

'As you have obviously realized I had a motive in putting Michael and Adele together. Yes, I'm afraid, Michael, that I did engineer your meeting. Fate isn't always as kind as it might be, so I gave it a helping hand. And I'm sorry that the pair of you didn't instantly fall head over heels in love. It would have made a lot of things simpler. You see, I felt I had two separate responsibilities that I could, literally, marry together. On one hand there is Pencombe. It appeared that was being saved by the Bradburys but suddenly that fell apart.'

'There's still Isabella and Johnnie. You know perfectly well I've made the entail over,' Michael said.

'I know that you think you've effected a cure-all by making your sacrifice, Michael, but it's not quite as simple as it sounds. You see, unknown to you, your father borrowed a considerable sum of money from me to buy the betrothal jewels. He had to; he has no capital reserves for that sort of thing, and the family jewellery was lost long ago.' He looked steadfastly at Betsy, who returned the look without blinking.

'Now, I'm not wealthy enough myself to give such a large sum away, so I only lent the money, on the condition of a security on the house and Home Farm. That was granted and is in my possession. So, your generosity in being prepared to give your brother all, Michael, was worth a lot less than you thought.'

'There are still the other farms on the estate: they are under a separate title.' Michael reached out slowly towards his glass, his eyes still fixed on his uncle's face. His fingers clenched around the glass stem as George answered, spilling wine on to the table.

'Yes, they are, and I happen to be aware that they are also subject to a mortgage.'

'That's a lie!' Michael pushed his chair back and got to his feet. 'That land is mine and I've never mortgaged it. I never would, even though . . .'

'Even though your father asked you, eh?' George continued. 'Well, you may have said no, but I'm afraid the mortgage went ahead all the same. It would take a court case to have it removed, one in which you would have to declare that you expressly refused to enter such an arrangement, and that your father, quite fraudulently, went against your instructions.'

Michael sat down with a crash, nearly tipping his chair over.

'So, now you may begin to see that in hoping for you and Adele to fall in love, I had the good of Pencombe in mind. I was also, by your union, hoping to discharge a second responsibility. Randolf has been more than good to me over the years. I have achieved no small success in my American investments thanks to his help. Now he intends to set up in Britain, he naturally needs a base for himself and his family; he also wants a suitable husband for his daughter. With a few strokes of the pen we could repay the mortgages, bring Adele's money into the estate, bring it back up to what it once was, what it should be. Randolf, you and your sons would have had an ideal retreat for when you are in England. Michael, you and Adele could have had a delightful life, two young, happy souls, a round of continual balls, dinner parties, wooing the rich and famous, boosting the Macaul connections, whilst breathing life back into Pencombe. I don't see how any of you can think that I acted in anything other than the best interests of you all.'

They were all quiet for a moment, thinking out their own reactions.

'But what about Eli Bradbury?' Michael asked. 'He has money, and the mortgages don't alter the fact that there's still Isabella and Johnnie. I don't see why exactly the same plan can't work around them.'

'Your friend Bradbury is very nearly bankrupt,' George replied. 'He's on the verge of going under in a big way. He can't pick up the kind of bills we're talking about.' Michael was too stunned to speak, and George carried on, 'How about you, Adele, how do you feel about all this?'

'Ah, my turn at last! What surprises me, George, is why you tried to make us fall in love. That seems rather naïve, if I might say so. I came to England to find myself a husband, I haven't hidden that for a minute. I said what I wanted: a title, a castle and an exciting way of life.' She ticked her requirements off on her fingers. 'It seems to me I could have been offered all that without bothering with this "love" stuff. All that can come later.'

'My God.' Michael looked at her in astonishment. 'I really can't believe it. A little while ago you were telling me I hadn't got enough "go". Now, I assume, you're prepared to change your mind for the sake of a financial arrangement.'

'Well,' Adele spoke slowly, as if explaining the mysteries of life to a child, 'you're the idiot who said you'd signed it all away, Michael. I'm afraid I thought you were just going to fiddle about, going to your nice cosy parliament, poking your nose in other people's business. I didn't know you could still be a lord: that makes it all quite different.'

'My God!' Michael turned to his aunt. 'I'm sorry, Aunt Hermione, I'm really sorry, but you must think it's pretty incredible too.'

'Yes, dear boy, I'm afraid I do, and George, I'm amazed at all of this. I do think I should like to retire.'

'Better than that, Hermione,' Randolf said, getting to his feet, 'we shall leave you. I think there's been enough said for one evening. Adele is obviously a touch overwrought.'

'Father!' She too jumped to her feet.

'That's enough, we're going home now, Adele, Betsy, boys. I'm sorry we haven't done better justice to your beautiful dinner, Hermione. Betsy will talk with you tomorrow. Perhaps you'll dine with us shortly? We'll try to make it a little less exciting though, I think. Come on, everyone.'

George saw them out. On the way through the hall, he put his arm through Randolf's, making him drop back from the others. 'I'll bring the boy round,' he murmured.

'I don't like the sound of all these mortgages,' Randolf replied. 'Putting money into a sound proposition is one thing; I'm not sure about this.'

'Now, now, I said I'd sort it all out. Samuel is happy to lend against Pencombe, he'll put everything you want to set up over here against it, including those mortgages. They'll seem a drop in the ocean by the time we're done. It's all worked out on paper. Call in on me tomorrow and I'll go through it with you.'

Back in the dining room, Hermione and her nephew were both sipping their wine, Michael slumped heavily in his chair. Hermione suddenly felt absolutely at one with the boy. She'd always regretted her lack of children and had been foolish enough not to realize that her brother's sons, bereft of a mother, could have benefited from her love and guidance over the years.

'Poor Michael,' she murmured.

'No, I'm not poor, at least not in the emotional sense,' he replied. 'I'm a bit shattered, that's all. I'm having my eyes opened rather too quickly, I think. I'm sorry, I know George is your husband and all that, but I'm sure that there is more in all of this for him than simply helping out the family.'

'Yes, I'm afraid I agree with you,' she said. 'And saying that's no disloyalty on my part. George is a business man through and through. I don't really understand what he does, but I do know that he sees things quite differently from the way we do. You and I, Michael, we were both brought up at Pencombe, though at different times and in different ways, it's true. And you, of course, went away to school. But our lives were so much more ordered than the lives of people like George, like I expect even Betsy, and Adele. You mustn't feel too upset by Adele this evening. She's a sweet girl, but a bit headstrong. And no one has yet taught her to think before she speaks.'

'Well, it won't be me who teaches her. I'm no longer the person to fit in with their plans. I'm afraid George's scheming came too late for that.'

Hermione smiled sadly at her nephew. 'Yes, I expect it did,' she said. 'He's not going to give up easily, though. And the Macauls have an awful lot of money. I believe it's going to be difficult for all of us for a while.'

'I can't get over Father, though. God, I just can't get over it.'

'If you mean the fact that he borrowed against your inheritance, then I'm sure it must be an awful shock for you. Still,' she gave a most uncharacteristic giggle, 'just think what a shock it's going to be for Johnnie!'

'Aunt Hermione!'

'I'm sorry, but he's still going to get a lot more than he would have, if you'd kept your rightful place. What on earth possessed you?'

'I've told you all about it, before.'

'Oh, you've told me all about the African business, and I agree with you, my dear. I've even signed a petition myself for the poor creatures. But you didn't have to give up your inheritance for that. You would have been in a position of influence at Pencombe.'

'I would have been a lapdog if I'd stayed.' Michael was shifting restlessly on his seat. This was beginning to feel like an inquisition.

'A lapdog, what on earth do you mean? Oh, I see, you mean that girl you were to marry, is that it? You really are much too fussy, child. I should have taken you in hand long ago.'

'I'm not a child.'

'Emotionally you are a child, an absolute baby. You wouldn't have Lucinda because she was a silly creature who wanted to tame you, you won't have Adele because she doesn't do the accepted thing and say she's madly in love with you. What on earth do you expect? The world isn't all flowers and love letters. Why, George courted me with those things, the flowers and the letters and things. I mean, he said he loved me continuously, and for months I pretended I couldn't remember his name from one meeting to the next. I used to be absolutely beastly. I was much too frightened to admit that I thought him wonderfully handsome, marvellously domineering, so I'd pretend, you see. But George saw right through me and wouldn't take no for an answer. That's how it is, Michael, you have to fight for what you want.'

'Bravo!' George had come into the room during Hermione's speech.

'I shall go too.' Michael stood up. He looked very earnest, very young. 'The problem is, Aunt Hermione, that there is nothing I want that is worth fighting for, not in the marriage stakes, that is. But don't worry about me, I shall pour all my energies into my political life; I shall learn to be devious.' He looked at his uncle, 'I shall learn to dissemble. And I shall learn to pursue my ambitions to success. I shall probably die a bachelor, very old, and with good fortune I might be very, very famous. They might even bury me in the Abbey for services to my country!' His eyes were very bright. Smiling, he bowed a farewell, and went out into the starlit night.

'Poor, poor boy,' Hermione said to her husband, 'he's so very hopelessly in love, poor, poor boy.'

'Who on earth with?' asked George, then his eyes lit up. 'With Adele?'

'Don't be stupid,' said his wife and went slowly upstairs to her bedroom, leaving George to congratulate himself on how well he was doing in pursuing the third and most important responsibility that he had not outlined to his guests, or even to his wife. His responsibility to himself.

There was no point in Lavender getting up in the morning until at least ten o'clock. It was so chilly outside, and they brought her a lovely breakfast, on a tray with legs that fitted comfortably even over her now very visibly swollen tummy.

The little blighter had now begun to kick regularly, every morning as she drank her first cup of tea. It made her laugh; he was so strong that the bedclothes jumped up and down. He had another trick too: he'd wriggle his little self round and stick his feet up under her ribs and push. The doctor had laughed at her claims of his strength at first, but then even he'd had to agree her baby was a natural athlete.

It made Eli so proud. On the rare mornings that he was able to be with her early, he'd sit, his broad hand resting ever so lightly on her tummy, then when he felt the movements, he'd light up with pride. He hadn't wanted to feel, not at first. But she'd persuaded him, and now wasn't he glad!

She wouldn't see him this morning. He'd told her that he was expecting a caller from the bank in London. They were coming down to go through his books. They were driving him to distraction. She let out a sigh, a mixture of compassion for her Eli and irritation at the silly bank. They didn't need to worry; Eli was going to move heaven and earth to make sure there was a great fat inheritance to be left for his son. She had got over not wanting to face up to the fact that the little lad would probably lose his father before he was fully grown. She had to accept that Eli was no longer a young man. In fact this problem with the bank was ageing him alarmingly.

She thought that the knock at the door was the maid, come to clear away her tray. The girl was a bit early, but it didn't really matter.

'Come in,' Lavender called out happily.

She'd forgotten all about Harold. For once, he had slipped unheeded from her mind. She had nothing to fend him off with, nothing. He stood, just inside the door, leering. He hadn't changed: he was still a weasel, cunning still sharpened his features. She hardly dared breathe, she was so alert, waiting for the rush she was sure he'd make. All her earlier nightmares about him harming the child inside her flooded back. She felt a sweat on her brow. She wanted to sit up, lean up off the pillows, but she didn't dare move, in case she sparked him off.

'Hallo, Lavender,' he said softly. 'You don't mind if I

281

come in, do you?' He slid forwards across the floor, sitting down suddenly on the round buttoned-backed chair that Eli used. Her eyes followed him; she was like the prey of the snake, mesmerized.

'I haven't seen you in ages,' he cooed. His voice was smooth, devoid of emotion. 'My, my.' He leaned forwards in his chair to look at her. 'You're really getting on, aren't you? You know, Lavender, sometimes I think how nearly that baby might have been mine, 'cept it wouldn't, I mean not really, would it? Just like it's not really old Bradbury's, is it? No, no, don't trouble yourself to deny it. I know all about everything, you know. I always was sharp. Ha ha!' His laughter was almost genuine. 'If you'd just managed to get me into you, then I would have been the poor fool looking forward to another man's leavings, looking forward so happily to paying for another man's bastard. Wasn't I the lucky one?'

Lavender was very, very slowly stretching out her hand towards the side knife on the breakfast tray. It was the only thing anywhere near a weapon in her reach. Not that it would do much, but it might slow him down while she screamed.

'I'm going away today, Lavender, that's why I came to see you. Going away to where they'll never find me. I've just got a little job to see to first and then I'm off.'

Lavender knew now he had come to kill her, then he was going to make a run for it. She sat forward suddenly. 'You won't kill me easy,' she cried, clutching the little pearl-handled knife in one hand, holding out the other with her long, ladylike nails curved as talons.

'Kill you, kill you indeed.' Harold had jumped to his feet laughing. At his sudden movement she'd flinched and she felt the baby kicking, annoyed at her tightening muscles. 'Now why should I put myself in jeopardy by killing a little slut like you, Lavender? What sense would there be in that?' He was walking round her room, peering at the trinkets on the dressing table, turning over her dressing gown hanging on the back of the door, feeling its fine quality.

Just then the maid's knock surprised them. He turned to look warningly at Lavender. 'Not yet, I'm not finished, Mary. I'll ring for you,' she called out from her bed, as calm as she could. If her life was safe, and that of the baby's, then all that mattered was her very new good name. No one should know Harold had been here.

'I'm going to be rich, you see, Lavender. My work's paid off at last. I'm getting my just rewards today, just as you are, Lavender, just as you are.' He walked to the very end of her bed to deliver his statement. 'You see I'm going to tell Eli all about you, Lavender. I know who the baby's father is. I bet it'll surprise you to know that your ex-lover and I are going into partnership in a new venture. We're thick as that, Lavender, thick as that.' He clasped his hands together to show how close they were.

'Thick as thieves more like,' she spat at him. Christ, she'd never thought the two of them would pal up.

'However you like it, Lavender, 'cause you're not going to matter much any more. The way I see it, I'll tell old Eli. It'll take a few minutes for it to sink in, I expect, especially since he's in for another rude awakening today. The thing is, his number's up. I've done my bit and all his clever figures won't save him now. He'll throw you off like the clinging limpet you are, Lavender. It'll be out on to the streets for you, and the condition your body's in, it's not going to pay any bills this time. How does it feel, Lavender, eh? It's cold out there today, going to be bitter tonight, I reckon. How does it feel to know you'll be out there? You and your little bastard.'

He stepped forwards suddenly, pulling the bedclothes back off her. The tray fell with a crash to the floor, to reveal Lavender sitting with her nightdress rucked up round her waist. Harold ran his greedy eyes over her fat, distended belly, down to the nearly hidden mound of hair.

'You're not pretty to look at any more, my girl,' he sneered, as she pulled the sheet back frantically. 'No one's going to want to get between those fat thighs.'

The door behind him opened with a bang as the maid rushed in. 'I heard the crash, ma'am, I . . .' she looked in astonishment at the stranger in the room, then at Lavender, red in the face, pulling a sheet across her nakedness.

'Get out!' Lavender screeched at him. 'Get out! Get out!'

He turned without another word and walked from the room. He felt better than he had for a long time.

'Quick, quick, help me get dressed. Hurry, I must hurry.' She scrambled into her clothes. Oh, it was such an effort, she was so clumsy, her legs and arms had become quite fat in the past weeks. She was gasping for breath by the time the girl was fastening the buttons down her back.

'Leave it, leave it now,' Lavender said. 'Run down and get me a cab. For God's sake, hurry, hurry.'

The brewery loomed up in front of her. She hadn't felt the chill air on her face as she'd dashed from the hotel into the cab's dark interior, and she didn't pay attention to the damp river mist swirling round the building. She leaned forwards on her seat, as far as she could go with the lump of her pregnancy working against her. She must be on time, she must reach Eli first. She willed the cab on, hurry, hurry. They pulled up to a halt outside the gates.

'Go on, go on!' she cried at the cabbie.

'Can't, there's a dray coming out. We'll have to wait.'

But she couldn't, there was no time, no time. She fumbled with the door, then it was open and she almost fell out, down on to the road. She started to run; she must get to Eli, Eli.

There he was, she could see his back, going into the office doorway. She ran, crying out to him.

'Eli! Eli!'

The dray was filling the gateway, fully laden with a load of brand new barrels piled high and wide. The drayman cracked his whip at the pair of shires, making them heave against their collars to tackle the incline coming out of the yard.

'Eli! Eli!' she cried again. But it was Harold, only a few yards outside the brewery gates, who saw her. He'd taken his time coming the long way down to the brewery from town. He'd been savouring the moment of his final victory. Lavender ran towards the narrowing space in the gateway; the leading wheels of the cart were almost there.

'Eli!' She could hardly get her breath now. It seemed as if her legs were weighed down with lead. Harold too was running, running to fend her off. He wanted his moment of glory all to himself. He wouldn't have her crying out her innocence, spoiling the look of defeat on the old man's face. They met at the very gates of the yard. He pulled at her arm, but she was so fixed on the office door that she hardly saw him. She shrugged off his grip, bustling forwards, tight to the wheel. He grabbed her fiercely, clutching round her, pulling at her cape.

'You won't go in there, won't!' he shouted above the sound of the wheels.

The drayman had his mind fixed on his job. He craned forward to peer around the blind corner out to the right: the way was clear. He cracked his whip again to make them 'git up'. They had to get round before anything came. The wheels spun on the mist-damp cobbles, the cart slewed. With a scream Lavender slipped, her cape catching in the spinning wheels; tightly together they tumbled, rolling, legs kicking at air. Harold shouted out, a deep short shout, not like his voice at all. Lavender saw the underneath of the cart spin past, she felt a sharp jerk as her hair caught on the turning axle. There was a flash of light, blinding, then it was deathly still and she felt no more.

The voices cut through the swirling fog. At first she'd thought she was lost, but then, hearing them, she knew she could follow the voices to safety. She had to concentrate hard, very hard to hear them, though. There were other things tugging at her attention. She must follow the voices, follow . . .

It was another day before they realized she could hear them. At first they thought the flickering of her eyelids when they whispered in the room meant nothing, but then Eli felt a similar twitching in her fingers. He started to talk to her then, telling her that she was now at Linstone, telling her that the doctor was sure she'd be all right after this enforced rest that her mind was compelling her body to take. Telling her, most importantly of all for her, for her peace of mind, that the baby was safe; miraculously the scrap of humanity inside her had refused to be shaken loose.

Lavender knew more than Eli told her, however. She had heard them when they thought she couldn't. Trapped within the darkness she had to face the fact that she would never walk again. When they'd started to say that they might have to take the baby away from her, for her own safety, that was when she'd managed to force her fingers to move. But then she'd also heard them say, thank God, that her pregnancy was too far advanced for abortion. She was glad then that the baby hadn't been truly Eli's. The fact that it had lived an extra month in her womb might make all the difference to its survival.

At night now, five days after the accident, there was a nurse sitting in her room. Eli had been forced to accept that he needed rest. The doctor had made it plain that if he wanted to be available to be a father to the child, then he would have to look to his own health. And he had so much to do, so many tangled chains of responsibility to keep under control. And after all, it seemed that Lavender had bought him a breathing space.

The bank's man had arrived as they were lifting her into the carriage and, more to the point, as they were washing away the aftermath of Harold's bloody destruction from the cobbles. Londoners are not made of stern enough stuff. He'd taken one look and vomited, bolted back to the station. Eli was saved for a day, not that he'd spared it any thought. And then the letter: he was to be given another month's leeway. He couldn't understand it, nor was he going to waste time thinking it out. The time he did spare for his books was revealing something he had never suspected. Where he himself was working to put a favourable light on the balance sheets, someone else had been working against him. And that someone could only have been Harold. Then there was the business of the clerk being in Lavender's room. The maid's description had fitted too perfectly for there to be any mistake, and Lavender had been so desperate to get to the brewery to speak to him. It could only mean one thing: he'd tried to get money from her as he'd known Eli wouldn't give him a penny. But he'd imagined that Lavender would hand over plenty to keep her Eli in business.

He told Isabella an edited version of it all. He told her in Lavender's room and through her swirling mists she heard enough of it to bring her peace. It was his interpretation of the facts that saved her, saved the baby. Eli was grateful to her, and she was at his home. The words drifted into her mind, so softly, so gently. He was going to marry her as soon as she regained consciousness, and the doctor said that this unconsciousness was only a safety measure that

287

her strong will was imposing. She'll surface when she's ready, he said. Perhaps he was right, for the day after hearing that Harold's menace was gone for ever, she woke with the dawn.

The nurse went through to wake Eli, thinking about the wife-to-be, and mother-to-be, come to that; the woman's condition was plain. Mind you, she wasn't one to query anyone's dates; she'd been around too long to lose a job over that. But that baby was going to come a clear month before they all said. Still, it wouldn't be the first one.

'Lavender? Lavender?' He tiptoed into the room. Good heavens, she thought, he really does look old.

'Hallo, dear.' She'd meant to sound strong for him, but it was only a whisper.

He sank down on the chair beside her bed, taking her hand in his own. 'I've prayed for this, Lavender, prayed. I can't say . . .' and then he was crying, burying his face in the blankets laid over her, his shoulders heaving. She managed to lift her other hand and stroke his hair. She hadn't realized how weak she was, weak like a kitten; but then think how quickly she would be on her feet. Of course, she wouldn't be, would she? Not if they were right. She couldn't feel any pain from her waist down. She felt bruised, aching everywhere on her chest and back and up her neck, but she couldn't feel a thing down there. That was what they meant, she supposed. She looked curiously round the room. It was beautiful. All mahogany furniture, maroon curtains, heavy ones, pulled nearly closed against the light of day.

'Open the curtains, draw them back for me, Eli.' She struggled, she wanted to sit up, but it was so difficult. The nurse saw and rushed to help; the old man clearly doted on the little thing, and she was expert at extracting gratuities from besotted old men. But she was skilful as well as cunning, and helped Lavender to sit, propped up by the pillows, without too much pain. The light streaming in the room showed how pale Lavender was, but also how determined; the weight she'd lost over the past few days highlighted the strength of her jaw, the almost hawklike nose. She would be a fierce old woman, if she lived that long.

Eli kept her to himself that morning. He felt jealous of her company, he couldn't stop prattling on, tiring her; the nurse muttered, but he shooed her away, and Lavender didn't mind. She'd been trapped inside her head too long and it was lovely to feel free again. That was the funny part of it. She might have felt trapped by this business with her legs, might have been desperate to get up, out of bed, to run around. But she didn't feel trapped at all, all she wanted was here, in this room. It was so nice, so comfortable, yet so, so special, so different from anywhere she'd ever known. Compared to it, the hotel room that she'd thought luxurious was a hollow shell. This was substance. And Eli, well, she loved Eli, it was as simple as that. She didn't want to get up and go out; there was nowhere for her to go, her world was here, holding his hand and being confident of the little chap, kicking merrily inside her.

Isabella had no idea how to feel, now that Lavender was truly with them. She'd gone through all the initial trauma of feelings of her father's disloyalty to her dead mother. Then she'd watched him suffer; that was awful, and she could do nothing other than suffer for him. He'd insisted that she went into that room with him and then she'd had time to look at this Lavender, this stranger who'd been thrust into their family. She'd had a fleeting glimpse as they'd taken her upstairs, but then there'd been blood running down her face and blueing bruises running up from her neck. Now, tidied up, lying as if asleep, she seemed tiny, in need of care. As for the baby she carried inside her, even Isabella had to admit to herself that it seemed God's will it should be born, after all that and no miscarriage. She'd even seen her father put his hand so tenderly on the sleeping woman's tummy and smile at the kicks he swore he felt. The doctor had looked compassionately at Isabella, but whether it was for her father's fancies, or his lack of decorum, she didn't bother to work out. But life was certainly turned upside down by it all. Everyone's life, that was, except Isabella's. Her father clearly still intended her to marry Johnnie. Now, when he spoke of the brewery he was making it plain that it continued only on the basis of the certainty of the Pencombe settlement.

Isabella was summoned in the early afternoon. So, Lavender was now actively among them. She thought hard what she should wear for her first visit to the woman, and eventually decided on a red, light woollen dress with a mandarin collar. It made her look older, Maude said. Very well, it might highlight the fact that she and Lavender were far, far closer in age than Lavender and Eli.

'Isabella, my dear, come and meet Lavender. It seems strange to say "meet", doesn't it, considering she's been living with us for a good week.' Her father was prattling on, so eager that they should be friends, yet how could they possibly be?

Isabella walked towards the bed. Lavender's hair had been left tumbling around her shoulders and she had a soft pink bed jacket around her. The bruises on her face were almost faded. But, Isabella realized, there was an expression in her face that Isabella could never match, a kind of knowledge. 'Hallo,' Isabella said, putting out her hand.

'Hallo, my dear,' said Lavender, and her eyes seemed to glow with a kind of softness. 'I've heard ever so much about you. Your father never stops going on about how clever you are, with your painting and everything.' Isabella darted a look of surprise at her father. 'He's very proud of you, you know. And I know he hopes you'll help me. I'll need a lot of help, you see, for I've never been one for the social graces.' She giggled, and her face crumpled; it hurt in her chest when she laughed.

'My dear, my dear.' Eli was reaching out to help her in an instant. But she put out a hand to keep him back.

'No, no, it's all right, I just need some air, and I need some woman's chat, not you moping around as if I'm going to go and kick the bucket every time I have a little cough. Now, clear off, go on, go away and write out some more figures for that dratted bank. Or go and have a walk in the garden; you look as if you could do with some fresh air, too. Go on, leave Isabella and me alone. There's a lot we can talk about. We've got to get to know each other, and we won't manage it at all with you fussing over us like an old mother hen.'

After he'd gone, Lavender allowed the nurse to ease her back on the pillows. She did feel very tired, and in considerable pain. Her chest was like a fire inside when she coughed. 'I'll have a little of that medicine I had this morning in a while, dear,' she said to the nurse, 'but leave it just a bit. I want to talk to Isabella, and it makes me so sleepy. You just go off and have some tea or something whilst I've got company. Go on, off you go.'

They had the room to themselves. 'There, that's got rid of them all for a bit.' She closed her eyes. Isabella thought she might be going to sleep, but she spoke again. 'You don't mind me lying back like this, do you, dear? But my eyes are stinging something rotten, and I feel as if I've been trampled by a horse, which of course, I have.' She went to give a laugh, but stopped. She knew, now, that the pain of it was too much.

'I'm sorry it had to happen like this for you, Isabella. I'd thought that we could manage it much more, more gentle like. It must have been a shock, and I'm sorry.' She was silent again, but Isabella couldn't think how to begin, how to talk to this stranger, who seemed to know her.

'And you've got your own wedding plans to look forward to. Your father's told me all about it. He's so proud of you, dearie, so proud.' Lavender paused, for, even with her sore eyes, she could see the look on the girl's face. 'It's not just me that's upset you, is it?' Realization came quickly to Lavender. 'I could hear a lot, you know, when they thought I couldn't, and I could hear your voice when you talked to your papa. I thought you were upset about me being here, but it wasn't that, was it?'

'You? You? No, of course it wasn't!' Isabella was too highly wrought, she tried to pull herself together. She shouldn't be talking like this to a sick woman, particularly not a pregnant one. 'I'm sorry, I'm very sorry, Lavender. I've had no one to talk to: my father won't listen, won't accept how I feel, my sister is determined I'll marry Johnnie. It's all locked inside me, I've had no one, no one, don't you see?' Her voice had risen quickly, on the verge of hysteria.

'But you have now, dear, you've got me. I'm not very strong today, but I'll be a bit better tomorrow, and a bit better the day after that. I'll be here for you to talk to, Isabella. After all, I'm not likely to run away, am I?'

Isabella had paused on the edge of abandoned emotion, but Lavender's reasonableness was like the cool wash of reason. She looked down at the figure on the bed, amazed. There the woman lay, broken beyond repair, but she was smiling at her, welcoming her confidences. Isabella felt horrid, horrid for having wished she would just die, horrid for wishing Eli would turn her out of the house.

'Come and talk to me tomorrow, dear,' Lavender murmured. She'd closed her eyes again. 'We can work it out, whatever it is, don't you worry.'

Later, as she slipped off to sleep she was smiling at the

thought that here was something special she could do for Eli: she could sort out Isabella and her little problems.

'I am very sorry to have to insist, Lord Montford, but I am afraid this is not simply going to go away.' The young lawyer was quivering with indignation. Whilst his lordship was a valued and venerable client of his father's practice, he was still subject to the laws of the land. He could not, as he had been proposing, simply ignore unfortunate pieces of paper, as he had called them, in his most imperious tone. Neither would pulling the bedclothes further up around his shoulders and embarking on a choking fit save his aristocratic sensitivities from what was clearly going to be most embarrassing for everyone concerned.

'I reiterate, Lord Montford, Mr Bradbury is waiting on us in the library. Obviously, if you feel unwell,' further coughs came from the bed, 'he will be only too happy to attend on you in here. But it cannot be put off any longer. Goodness me, they're fixing the date for the wedding down there! Your son is struggling to fit it in with his sporting calendar, but eventually they're going to marry. We have to clear this up, and it has to be now.'

Lord Montford stopped coughing in the face of his man of law's continuance; in any case it was making his throat hurt. He cast an imploring look up to heaven for deliverance, but it was inevitably cut short by the magnificent ceiling. Even the cornicing he so enjoyed was newly whitened, thanks to that man's money. All this fiddling about; there had to be something that could be done, nothing was irreparable, was it?

'Well.' His lordship had at least begun to utter, thank God for that, thought Perivale Court of Court, Court and Thumbles.

'Well,' his lordship continued, clearing his throat; he

293

may as well get it over, he supposed, then he could let himself get up. It was, truth be said, unutterably boring in bed.

'I assume you have some sort of plan worked out, Court? Something to put to Bradbury? Something that,' he paused to choose the right word; one had to be careful with these legal types; such a pity it wasn't his father, the older Court, who had a far more developed sense of decorum, 'something that will keep a modicum of a veil of secrecy over this little misunderstanding?' He blessed his lawyer with his most charming, beguiling smile, marred to some extent by the fact that he had not yet put in his bottom dental plate and the splendid twelve ivory teeth that it held.

'No veils, no innuendos; nothing but the entire, unvarnished truth, I'm afraid, otherwise you're going to find that he smells a rat, and these self-made men are very quick to react to that sort of thing, very quick indeed. He'll either throw up his hands in horror and run off to find himself another titled husband for his daughter, or he'll negotiate you over a barrel. I'm very sorry to have to speak so plainly, sir. Perhaps if my father was here he wouldn't. But I do have your best interests at heart. I never, ever, for one moment forget my responsibility and that, in this instance, is to represent you in your dealings with this man Bradbury. We must recognize him for what he is, and deal with the situation accordingly.' And recognize you for what you are, you awkward old devil, Perivale continued in his head. They were impossible, these aged jewels of the realm.

'Bring him up here then.' Lord Montford admitted defeat. 'But you'd better tell him I don't feel up to it.' That was quite true, he was actually feeling rather sick at the thought of an Eli Bradbury who might throw up his hands in horror at what, after all, had only been a very little mistake to begin with. Worse still was the thought of the brewer 'getting him over a barrel', whatever that meant.

Eli brought a breath of new life into the room. 'William! I am sorry to find you confined to your bed. You should have put off our little bit of business; another day or two won't matter, I'm sure.'

William darted a quick look at Perivale but the lawyer's expression did not waver. There was to be no last-minute reprieve. 'Ah, yes, Eli.' His lordship's voice faltered admirably. 'I think I will let Perivale here talk for me. I'm still quite weak, you know, quite weak.'

Perivale managed not to show his surprise at being addressed so intimately by his client. Instead he lowered his chin, and his voice, to deliver his oratory. 'Mr Bradbury, I am speaking on behalf of Lord Montford, and on behalf of his heir, who, whilst technically speaking is still his elder son Michael, is to all intents and purposes the younger son, Jonathon.' He paused to look again at his papers. He hoped Eli didn't have a heart condition. 'I have here the outline of the marriage settlement agreed between you and Lord Montford. It was drawn up by my father, and you have of course been party to all the details. My father, as you may be aware, has recently retired from the practice, owing to continuing ill health. In fact he is at present in Italy, for the warmer weather, and we have not been able to contact him. There are, it seems, a few discrepancies in this settlement.'

He could hear Eli rustling on his seat. He was obviously eager to interrupt, but that would not do, so Perivale pushed on, still staring hard at his papers. 'There are in existence two separate deeds that affect the settlement, that I believe cannot at that time have been in my father's possession. However, even if I had succeeded in verifying his awareness or otherwise of them, I do not at this present time see that it would affect their standing. I have, to the best of my ability, verified that they are still in effect, and therefore they materially alter the position, in law, of the Pencombe estate.' He stopped talking for a moment to allow Eli a word, but the brewer was saying nothing now until fuller facts were produced.

'The first document is a mortgage on all the lands, farms and holdings tenanted and otherwise of the Pencombe estate, other than the Home Farm and the house itself. It was granted initially in respect of the sum of eighty thousand pounds. The mortgage was written to encompass any further borrowings. It appears that interest was never paid on the capital and that unpaid interest stands at sixty thousand pounds. There is therefore an outstanding mortgage of one hundred and forty thousand pounds. However, I was eager to contact my father, for although those lands already belonged to Michael, having been in the trusteeship of his mother and passed to her eldest son on her death, the deed of mortgage had been signed by Lord Montford.' Perivale paused. 'Do you have any questions at this stage, Mr Bradbury, or shall I continue?'

'Why did Lady Montford hold them?' It was an odd question for Eli to ask, but the major issues he wanted to reserve comment on. He could see that the shocks weren't finished.

'The present Lord Montford's father arranged it so. There was some question of another part of the Pencombe inheritance being mislaid, I believe, so it was done to safeguard the entail.'

Lord Montford was flushing furiously: the jewels, the damned jewels; now look where that wicked woman had got him.

'Thank you, please continue,' Eli said.

'Very well, as I say, it was Lord Montford and not the Honourable Michael who signed the mortgage, but I doubt if it would be to the good of the family name to pursue the legality of that point. It is not exactly flattering.'

There was a short silence, while each of the three men in the room formed their own mental pictures of the result of dragging Lord Montford's name through the courts, along with his son's, Eli Bradbury's, *et al*.

'So, we will accept for the moment that the mortgage exists. Now, as to the Home Farm, and the house itself, we have this very recent mortgage.' He couldn't resist looking over at Lord Montford; this really was very naughty, all things considered. 'It appears that a mortgage was granted on that property for the purpose of the purchase of jewellery, pursuant to the engagement of Miss Lucinda Bradbury to the Honourable Michael.'

'What!' Eli had jumped to his feet. 'When was this?' He held out his hand for the document.

'I think it would be best if I finished my statement first, Mr Bradbury. I do not wish to make any omissions.'

Eli left his arm outstretched for a moment more, but then subsided back into his seat.

'I shall take your silence as consent to continue. Now, where was I? Ah yes. This second mortgage is very difficult. It is certainly legal and in effect. The property was in Lord Montford's hands to dispose of how he thought fit. The problem lies in the terms of the mortgage. I have the feeling that it was constructed in a hurry. It may be of course that the mortgagers did not intend what they have actually written. To put that more plainly, it may be that I, a stranger to the document, whilst interpreting it legally correctly, am not in possession of the, shall we say, emotional intent. For the mortgage is in fact between members of the family, at least by marriage. The mortgager is a Mr George Bullstone, who I am given to believe is the husband of Lord Montford's only sister. Therefore,

as I say, whilst legally speaking it appears a most dangerous document, possibly there is no real threat in it.'

'I don't follow you, Mr Court,' Eli said. 'To begin
with, what is the amount of the mortgage, and secondly
why can you not simply contact this man George and clear
the whole business up?'

'The potentially dangerous thing about the mortgage is
that there is no fixed sum. There was an initial advance
put at one hundred thousand pounds, the sum spent on
the aforementioned jewellery. But, it is in the mortgager's
discretion how much further can be advanced. In effect,
he is at liberty to pay any sums of money he thinks fit into
his lordship's account. I understand that there are considerable unsecured overdrafts at the bank that could be, shall
we say, infilled, by deposits. These further sums would be
debited against the mortgage, and it is at Mr Bullstone's
discretion when or indeed whether the mortgage can be
repaid. It is an extremely strange document. I for one have
never seen anything quite like it. But, as I say, it may be
that the strict legal interpretation was not in fact the result
they were aiming for. Indeed, if I could only contact Mr
Bullstone, I might be able to set your mind at rest.'

'Why can't you contact him?'

'Because his lordship will not allow it.'

'What!' This time Eli was up on his feet in earnest.
'Don't be ridiculous, of course he must contact the damned
man, William.'

'Please, don't call me ridiculous.' Lord Montford tried
vainly to hold on to his dignity.

'Not call you ridiculous? Good God, man, you're lucky
I'm not yet calling you scandalous, and dishonest, a dozen
other words that I won't bandy about until we've got to
the bottom of this.'

Perivale darted a look of 'I told you so' towards the bed.
On the open market the estate would fetch well over

£500,000, perhaps closer to £700,000. Paying back the mortgages would still leave over a quarter of a million pounds. But that wasn't what a man like Bradbury wanted: he was marrying his daughter, and his own wealth, to the glory of Pencombe, the splendour of its name. The brewer wasn't going to take any of these setbacks to his planning without a great deal of fuss. Here was the aforementioned barrel. His lordship was going to be unceremoniously 'got over it'; whether by Eli Bradbury or George Bullstone had yet to be determined.

Isabella knocked tentatively on Lavender's door. Yesterday's visit had been postponed, as Lavender had been too weak to do anything other than sleep. Waiting the extra day was difficult for Isabella; it was one thing to be without a confidante, but now it was almost more daunting to be presented with one. In any case, Lavender would probably see everything from Eli's point of view so Isabella was not expecting very much from this morning. Still, even the prospect of saying what she felt out loud was unnerving.

'Come in, come in,' Lavender's voice called out.

Her accent this morning was quite different. Eli had confided to his daughter that Lavender needed only to recover her strength to rediscover her newfound refinement. Isabella had felt suddenly sorry for her, having had to appear before her future daughter-in-law with her defences removed. Future daughter-in-law: the concept was almost beyond belief. Isabella turned the handle and walked in.

'Good morning, my dear,' Lavender greeted her. 'Did you sleep well? No, looking at you, I don't think you did, you've got rings under your eyes; you want to try splashing cold water on them. I've got lots of little tricks like that to help you make the most of yourself, you know. And I think we're going to have quite a bit of time together to chat. Your father popped in last night, after his visit to Pencombe. Has he spoken to you about it yet?'

Isabella shook her head. Her father hadn't been at breakfast.

'Oh, there's been a right old to-do. I don't know quite what, but something about deeds and mortgages. Anyway, your father's all set to go up to London this afternoon, after he's sorted some papers out. At least he's bouncing with energy now he's so cross. Come on, anyway, come and sit down beside me. I haven't forgotten you've come to tell me all about your love life. No, no, don't look so horrified, Isabella, it's just my way of talking. Come on, sit down.'

'I'd rather stand for a bit if you don't mind. I know it sounds funny but I think better when I'm walking about. I just feel so restless these days, sitting down makes me want to scream.'

'Well, you'll frighten nurse to death if you shriek your head off, dear, so walk about as much as you want. We'll have to do something about you being so tizzed up, though. It's not good to work yourself up into a state, it does bad things to a girl's insides.'

Isabella had to smile. Lavender was such an odd person, but quite clever in her own way. Isabella's system was very upset; it had never been like that before, before she was so frightened of her future.

'I'm trapped, you see, Lavender, that's what I feel. I think that's why I have to walk about, to pretend I can escape to somewhere, and I would, I would escape to anywhere, if there was only something to escape to.'

'You can't escape from yourself you know. And often, that's what a person really wants, to escape from the person they are, to become someone else, but it doesn't happen. I may be lying here in this lovely room, looking quite different from how I did a few months ago,' she patted her bulging tummy with a laugh, 'but inside I'm still me. I still have the same way of looking at things, still feel the same. No one escapes, Isabella. Not from themselves.'

'No, but you have escaped from being poor, haven't you? My father told me that. I want to escape from riches. Doesn't that sound silly? But I want to escape from everything that goes with them. The dreadfully dull, empty hours, when there's nothing to do, only pass the time. I want to escape from being the daughter of a wealthy man. I don't mean I don't love my father, I do, but I've become a part of his business. If we'd stayed as we were, then he would have been pleased if I'd married a nice, honest man and settled down and been happy. Now, I'm to be sold off. Don't shake your head, of course I'm being sold off. I'm part of it all now, even he says so, part of the plan for the brewery, part of the Pencombe estate. I've been told of all the people who depend on me, and it makes me squirm to think of it. If I was asked to go out and do something, go and work at something, do anything, that would be one thing, but I'm to become even more a creature of idleness, even more incarcerated in my ivory tower, even, even . . .' she stopped, at a loss for words.

'Oh, it's more than that, though, isn't it, Isabella? What you've to do is lie back and close your eyes and think of England.'

'What?'

'What I mean is what you're really frightened of is being a man's possession and having to do what he wants, in bed and out. Most terrifying for you, I expect, and what's getting you like this is the thought of what you might have to do in bed. I'm right, aren't I? Go on, don't clam

301

up, there's not much point. I can't help you if you don't let me.'

'I don't suppose you will help me. You're bound to side with my father, aren't you, after all you're his . . .'

'Don't say it, Isabella, it's not your kind of word. And anyway I'm not his mistress, I'm his wife-to-be and funny though it sounds, I'm also your mother-to-be. That makes you laugh, doesn't it? It certainly makes me and your pa laugh. But don't make it so difficult for me to help, because I do feel sorry for you. And don't toss your head about at that, there's nothing wrong in sympathy. Why don't you fancy young Johnnie, then? Your pa says he's a good-looking boy.'

'Because of lots of things, because I never loved him, only now I'm frightened of him too, because he tried to force me, that's why.' Isabella spat the words out, daring Lavender to laugh.

'What, forced a kiss off you? There's nothing wrong in . . .'

'Oh, no, he didn't just want to kiss me, he ripped my dress, and was forcing me, forcing me with his body . . .' Isabella was feeling hotter and hotter. 'And he said things about Michael, coarse, unkind things. It was Michael who saved me.' She finished, flopping down into a chair.

'That's what your pa said.'

'What? That Michael saved me? But I didn't think he even knew about Johnnie; at least he wouldn't listen to me when I tried to tell him.'

'No, your pa doesn't know about that, and I don't think he should, not right off. But he does know that it's Michael you're in love with, and there's nothing he can do about it.'

'I don't love Michael, I don't. You mustn't say that.'

'You do, my dear, and I'm sorry for you. There's

nothing that can change it all around again, it's all too late.'

The door opened abruptly as Eli entered. He was dressed, ready to go to the train. Isabella leaped to her feet and rushed out past him, running for the privacy of her bedroom. She wouldn't accept it, couldn't.

'Oh my God,' Eli said as he stepped towards the bed, 'what on earth has got into that silly creature now? She hasn't been tiring you, has she?'

'No, my dear, of course not. She's got a few women's problems at the moment, nothing that time won't cure. I'll ask the doctor to see her when he comes by later. Are you off, then?'

'Very shortly. I've got a few last papers to get together from the library. I just popped in to see if you'd like anything before I go.'

'I don't think so, dear, although, you know, I would quite like a book to read. Something light; you know the sort of thing.'

'Of course, of course. Nurse can buy you something in the village. There's nothing like that in the library,' he said and bent forward to kiss the top of her head. 'I shall miss you, you know. I'm going to be away until tomorrow afternoon at the earliest. I'd like to pick you up and carry you with me, my little dear.'

'A fine fool you'd look, Eli! Go on, hop off, and don't you worry about Isabella, I'll see she's all right.'

The nurse came in then, bustling around, chivvying Eli out of the room.

Lavender sat, puzzling over Isabella. She didn't want to do anything to upset Eli. He was her first consideration, but the girl was in a right state and that Johnnie didn't sound quite the little gentleman that Eli believed. She had to do something.

'Nurse, be a dear and get me some writing paper and a pen, will you? I've got a letter to send off.' The address was a problem, but he was going into politics, wasn't he, so she addressed the envelope to The Hon. Michael Montford, care of the Marquess of Salisbury, Downing Street, London. That should do the trick, she thought.

'Nurse, will you post this for me today, please; it's rather urgent.' The nurse slipped the letter into her needle-work bag. She would pop out before tea.

It was a short, pleasant walk to the village, where the general shop stocked all the day-to-day requirements of the local population, with haberdashery competing for shelf space with the blue bags of sugar and jars of fish paste. The nurse bought a novelette for the lady as the master had asked, and a nice iris-blue skein of wool for her own needlework. All the time her mind was busy with thoughts of how nice it would be to have a permanent position at Linstone, since she was obviously a necessary fixture in the household.

She returned to Linstone Park and, after giving her patient some tea, sat down in the bedroom and resumed her petit point. Lavender asked her if she had performed her little errands, and the nurse happily answered in the affirmative. In a while Lavender slipped into a doze, happy in the belief that her letter was winging swiftly to London. The nurse sat in blissful, oblivious dereliction of her duty, as the note lay hidden beneath the multi-coloured skeins of Berlin wool that awaited her infinitesimally slow attention.

Luke stooped down to put his fingers in the sticky, clinging mud at the very edge of the water. He brought the brown silt up to his nose. The very essence of the river was in the smell. He stared unseeing downstream towards a dull red dawn breaking over the village. He wanted to take it all with him, locked into his mind, but it was as if he had already left and the life of the water went on without him. To love a woman can be a dangerous affair; to have a river for a mistress is to invite rejection. There would be nothing to mark his having ever been here at all.

His luck had held; the sailor's body had floated as far as Maidstone before it was discovered. Nobody there paid much attention to where it had come from; it was just another nameless corpse to be buried with much speed and little solemnity.

Brownie whickered suddenly in her stable. It was time to go and, looking back at his river one last time, he went out on the high road to make for Flimwell. There he'd take to the forest and work his way down to the coast. It was a route he'd travelled often enough, and so had Brownie come to that. Only she didn't know that she would not be coming home.

Thomas Cade had it all worked out: a recompense for Luke's saving Lucinda from the flood. He had kept Luke one vital jump ahead of the magistrate who was gathering the smugglers in with his net. John was already in Maidstone gaol and others would undoubtedly follow. Thomas was a natural organizer: he'd even provided a prospective husband for Jenny. The new traction engine foreman, a man called William, fresh up from Brighton, was a big man, handsome, so Jenny proclaimed, and with excellent prospects.

They'd have a cottage high up on the weald and in a few years it would be overflowing with babies.

While Luke, he would be in alien France. It should have weighed him down, the thought of a land so strange, a way of life inevitably different. But the truth was, it didn't, not now that he'd left the river; that life was yesterday. France was a new, exciting future that Thomas Cade had provided for him. He could feel the money belt tight round his waist. There were one hundred gold sovereigns safe in there. Enough to buy wine, and to set himself up in business in a small way as an exporter. And Eli Bradbury was agreeable to marketing the wine in England. The thought of his new life made Luke kick Brownie into a canter. He wanted to be in the forest as soon as possible. He didn't fool himself; that bloody magistrate was out to make a coup of the capture of the complete run, and wouldn't want Luke slipping away.

He avoided the crossroads at Flimwell. He'd originally intended to say goodbye to Ned, who ran the pub at the crossing, and that section of the run. But if they were watching anywhere, that would be it. So he took a narrow path that led down through an old disused iron workings and then back, up towards the London Road. He got down from Brownie to cross the highway, and when he judged the way clear, ran across beside her, holding the bridle. He had a sudden urge to hide in the dying, rotting bracken. It was a primitive going to earth that his soul required. Brownie was shod, as she had to be for the journey, but he didn't like the way her steps rang out on the flints in the woodland track. He pulled aside, into a dell, and pulled his spare moleskin trousers out of the pack bag. A pity, he thought as he ripped them up with his knife, but presumably they sold trousers in France. He tied the cloth over her hooves and, checking the path, joined it again. He had a premonition that there was someone on the track ahead of him. He must be passing somewhere behind the pub now. He slipped off into the woods. The undergrowth, although beginning to die back, was still thick enough for cover. Brownie plodded quietly behind him.

He made a wide semi-circle to keep clear of the path that, had he only known it, was empty. He was about to step down, into the hollow left by the roots of a fallen tree, when the bird screeched out. It was a jay, and a cross one. Whatever startled it, startled Luke also. He stood, turned to stone. It was quite silent in the wood. The birds and animals took their refuge in silence. Luke very slowly placed his palm on Brownie's soft, warm face. It was as close as he could come to telling her to be quiet. They were right in front of him. Another few steps and he would have walked in amongst them: six of the excise men, dressed in brown so as not to stand out in the forest and moving off away from him.

Then he realized how close his detour had taken him to the back of the Three Keys; they were only a hundred yards or so from the pub. And that was their goal. If they were after Ned, then it probably meant they knew the names of the whole run. Luke had to get into deeper cover. He waited until he heard a shout – the sleeping publican had been rudely awoken – then he turned and slipped up on to Brownie's back. They'd be too busy for a while patting themselves on the back, and he'd got to get well off the route.

He went deep, deeper into the woodland than he'd ever been. Where once he would have craved the sight of water, craved the open sky, now he sought the deepest cover, the thickest growth of summer past. After a mad half an hour, twisting through brambles, skirting dew-ponds and continually barking his legs and elbows on the crowded trunks, he paused. He had to get his bearings.

It was a long time since he'd climbed a tree. Fortunately, there were any number to choose from, and a branchy oak gave him a relatively easy staircase towards the sky. He peered furtively above the bronzed canopy. The new bright future that stretched before him on the Continent was infinitely preferable to a rope round the neck. That was how he excused to himself what in other circumstances he would have called a panic-stricken rush.

The forest stretched around him, and he was lucky; he was still on high ground and had a good vantage point. He turned slowly. The branch he stood on was none too strong to take his weight. There on the horizon the land rose and fell as he knew. He must work through the forest, and wouldn't need to leave his cover until the last four or five miles. Then he'd be in country where he wasn't known: sanctuary, or near enough.

They stopped for Brownie to drink from a still pond and him to swig at his flask at midday. There was a watery sun trickling through the branches, and its height gave him the hour without his having to bother to take his watch out. He was feeling like a woodsman, and Brownie too was quick to learn, no longer stumbling over hidden roots.

The afternoon took them to the edge of the wood. Luke had climbed two more trees to check his direction and they were as close as they could get to the town. Hastings: here was a boat, here was the end of England. Here he had to leave the pony, his last encumbrance. They made their way down through the winding streets, towards the sea. The tang of it was on the air, gulls screamed overhead. Luke felt a clear, light-hearted joy. It wasn't given to many men to have a second try at life. They walked down alongside the beach towards the small harbour. The boats were high up, pulled well out of the tide, and it was here that he sold the pony, for too low a price, but with so little time he knew he had no choice.

'*Pride of the South*?' he asked a pipe-smoking sailor.

He got a direction pointed with the pipe, and a mumbling through the old man's gums.

The boat was identical to all the others, except that there was life on board. He called up at the figure standing above the gunwale. '*Pride of the South*?'

A heavily bearded young man peered down at him, taking in the dusty, travel-stained garments.

'Passage to France?' Luke asked.

The sailor nodded and told him to come on up. A wave of relief swept over Luke. His new life was about to begin.

It was the first time Lucinda regretted any of the happenings of the past few weeks. She eased the dress a little higher up her waist so that the last button could just reach its hole, but the bodice wasn't quite smooth any more. Her waistline was thickening daily. If only she hadn't become pregnant as quickly as Thomas had expected. Surely a month or two wouldn't have made any difference. Her father had acquiesced to the marriage without any actual proof of her pregnancy, so Lucinda could have been as slender as she'd wanted for the ceremony. Even though there was no one to see her in what should have been her glory today. She was wearing a pale lilac silk dress, edged with deeper purple and set off with fine cream lace. The lace was Honiton; it had been a present from Thomas and was beautifully worked with tiny shells clustered at the corners of the scalloped border.

She gave one final glance at herself in the mirror on the inside of the wardrobe door. A smile crept upon her lips. As she'd lain in Thomas's arms last night he had made her the most amazing promise of all. After the monument of business solidarity that he'd constructed in thin air, he'd told her his ultimate ambition. Men bought knighthoods, he'd said, his arm under her neck tightening; he would make her a lady his own way, through his own power. A self-made man, that was how he saw himself, with a wife who'd be an asset to him every step of the way, and whom he intended finally to reward with her rightful title, the one she'd thrown over to marry him. Lucinda had been sleepy, tired after their lovemaking; the words had soothed

309

her, seemed a part of love itself, but now, with the bright light of day polishing her pink cheeks, she bloomed in the memory. He would do it, too. He was no idle dreamer. Suddenly a shaft of wintery sun shone through the bright cleaned windows, her dress glowed; she was beautiful, never mind the tightness round the middle. She smiled widely at herself. To leave Reason Hill on the arm of the man she was already bodily wedded to might be a strange beginning to a wedding, but Lucinda knew she would be the most beautiful bride, never mind her father's diminutive Lavender, never mind Isabella.

Thomas straightened his necktie for the twentieth time. His eyes kept being drawn to the grandfather clock. The ticks were painfully slow; it must be running down. He pulled out his gold hunter to check yet again: the gold hunter watch that Lucinda had given him. All her love went with it, she'd said. He cupped the watch in his large hand. It was smooth, soft and warm, with the warmth that only real gold gives. It told the same hour as the clock. Time wasn't running slow, but Thomas's heart was beating fast. It was stupid, he kept telling himself, but his palms were sweating too and he ran them down the back of his trousers. He heard the rustle of her skirts on the stairs before she appeared. She was beautiful, quite perfect and smiling as she'd smiled when she'd come to him out of the flood. A smile that drew him towards her. He held out his hands to her, and she came slowly towards him. It was a moment they would both remember for the rest of their lives. For Lucinda he was the man she'd always dreamed of, strong, forceful, handsome and adoring. Thomas wanted to sweep her into his arms, crush her against him, bury his face in her sweet soft breast. Instead, they must stand apart, arrive unruffled for the ceremony. There was a ritual to be gone through, a making legal of all that had already been consummated.

310

It was only a short journey to the church, where Eli and Isabella would attend with a handful of villagers and of course Timmy, who would be going back to stay with Jenny for one more week, then coming home. Thomas had missed him. It would be good, he thought, to have the boy back at Reason Hill.

After the ceremony, Mr and Mrs Thomas Cade went back to Linstone. Eli wanted to give them his present there, and it was something, he said, that he wished to do on his own home ground. They went up to Lavender's room, on Eli's insistence. She hadn't been able to go to the church, but could at least witness her husband-to-be handing Lucinda a plain brown envelope. It was very quiet in the room as she unfolded the document and slowly read it. She passed it to Thomas without a word, but her eyes were glowing. They all waited as Thomas rapidly scanned the pages.

'You've done it,' he said at last, his voice trembling with excitement. 'Eli, you've managed it. I don't know what to say.' His voice was choked with emotion.

'It's all yours, my dears, unencumbered. The final title passes over from Lord Montford on Isabella's wedding day. We seem suddenly blessed with a lot of weddings in the family, don't we?' He reached out and squeezed Lavender's hand that had been lying limply on the bedcovers.

No one looked at Isabella. They were chattering suddenly, full of joy, plans and happiness. She wouldn't be allowed to spoil it. The marriage of Johnnie and Isabella would take place no matter what, even though they were all so aware of Isabella's feelings that no one had even suggested asking Johnnie to the wedding. Not that he'd have come. He was becoming fond of telling his drinking cronies that to attend one wedding, his own, would be enough torture for him in his lifetime.

After a celebration tea of salmon sandwiches, iced fancies and cook's very best fruit cake had been taken, Eli turned to Isabella. She hadn't said a word since the deeds to Reason Hill had been given to Lucinda and Thomas.

'Well, come on, Issy, time for your present for the happy couple. Bring it out now. I know they're dying to have it.'

Lucinda smiled at Thomas. She had everything she wanted now. Isabella's gift hadn't even crossed her mind.

It was Thomas who was delighted and moved. The painting of Timmy lying asleep had caught the child perfectly. He loved the boy like a son and now, safe in his pocket, were the deeds to the farm. Reason Hill would pass to Timmy. The rest of his sons, and he was sure there would be several, could have new farms bought for them: other parts of the Cade empire. But Reason Hill, that would always be Timmy's.

'A long time ago, Issy,' Thomas said, 'you said I might like to give you a commission one day. Well, on the strength of this I think you can look forward to several. You can paint all my children; this one is only the beginning.' He laughed. 'I'll have to build an extension on the house to give us more space for hanging all their portraits as well as housing the little brats themselves.' His laugh hung in the air, and eventually Lucinda's joined it.

'I think we had better be getting home, Thomas.' She stood as she spoke. 'It's been a tiring day, in my condition.' She stressed the last words and Thomas was instantly at her side. The newlyweds left Linstone where a quietness fell and Eli and Lavender were content to sit in companionable silence. Isabella in her room stared at the empty space where the painting had rested for so long. Timmy's sleeping form had given her company. Now the room was very empty, as she felt empty. She slowly changed out of the finery she had worn for the day. There was now another knot in the silken cords tying her to Pencombe.

'I want you to promise me something, Isabella.' Lavender lay back on her pillows. She felt weighed down now by her pregnancy, anchored to her bed more by the weight of it than by her wasted legs.

'You'll have to tell me what it is, Lavender, before I promise anything. Having Lucinda for a sister has taught me not to agree to anything before I know what it is.'

'Ah, Lucinda. I should think you two have had some right old fights. But it'll get easier now she's got a husband of her own. You wait and see. But we're drifting away from that promise I want from you. It's not a big one, but it is very important to me. In a few weeks, three or four, I shall ask you to take your father away, right away, to London or something, for the whole day. The trouble is, I won't have that much warning to tell you when, but you'll do it for me, won't you, when I ask?'

'What a funny thing! What are you going to do, run away from us or something? I don't think my father would like that. In fact I don't think I would like that.' Isabella smiled.

'I promise you, Isabella, I'm only asking you to do it for your father. It is something very, very important. I know I'm not very serious most of the time, but I do know what really matters in the end. Please promise me, please.'

'Yes, of course I will, if you feel like that about it.' Isabella didn't like it though. She felt a shiver like goose pimples run over her skin. 'At least it'll be a month until your time. I wouldn't agree to it then.'

'You're a dear girl, Isabella.' Lavender closed her eyes. She was so tired all the time now, so very tired.

Isabella stood quietly, looking out through the window

313

at the rain falling. It was chillingly cold now, and short sharp bursts of wind whipped the rain almost horizontal. It was bleak out there, but the bedroom was warm and snug. A fire crackled in the duck's nest grate. There were flowers, late chrysanthemums in a vase.

Lavender was no alternative to her mother, she wasn't trying to be. But she was a friend, an unusual friend, with clever, almost cunning ways and a very soft heart. She had to have, to love Eli so obviously; Eli who was daily becoming more owl-like. His eyes seemed to have grown rounder, his hair fluffier, and his face was certainly redder; he was working so many hours, long hours into the night. He worked in his study from dawn into the middle of the morning, then went to the brewery for at least four hours every day. Thank goodness he'd found such a trustworthy manager, at least that was what Papa called him. Isabella could judge for herself tomorrow, for the brewery was to be closed for the day. Eli was giving them a day's holiday to celebrate his wedding.

Eli was almost overcome with papers. His desk was piled high with them. There were copies of all the deeds involved in his current crisis. Then the fat leather-bound ledgers of the brewery and the rent rolls from Pencombe, the valuations of the estate. He alone could make them into a meaningful whole. But still, there was this one wild card, the fact that the mortgage on the house at Pencombe could be escalated beyond all reality, at any time and in a matter of hours.

Lord Montford would still not allow his representative to contact Bullstone, and when Eli tried to call on the man in London he had been refused admission. When he had pressed for a reason his lordship's brother-in-law had sent out a short note deploring Eli's treatment of Michael. That was nonsense; nothing Eli had done had effected the boy's fall from grace; it had been his own doing. No, it was an excuse, and as such, meant that the man was up to something. But Eli couldn't work on suppositions, so he was constructing his plans on the figures he had in hand. At present, it looked as if he was solvent. That was the initial hurdle for him to cross.

He had two propositions for expanding his business out of the narrow confines of brewing. One, and it was very small at present, was the importing of wines. He had an agent in France now, one Luke Jones, whose taste and business acumen appeared inspired. Three smallish shipments had arrived so far and sold well, at an excellent profit, and there was repeat business in the order books. The second, more nebulous scheme at present, was from Thomas Cade. He wanted to buy up hop farms, beginning with those at present tenanted from Pencombe, rapidly expanding out into the surrounding counties, and to radically modernize hop-growing on them. Planning to use his traction machines and a core of skilled workers, he had produced figures that brought the cost of a massive hop-growing organization well within their reach. That would give Eli a near monopoly in the south of England. He would set the standards, his brewery would thrive on the advantageous rates he could buy in at, whereas other breweries would be forced to pay his price for their hops. It was an ambitious scheme, bold like Cade himself. Eli was beginning to be inspired about it. But he needed the Pencombe valuations, needed them desperately. If the settlement came into effect, even with the outstanding mortgages, there was surplus security enough: a clear two hundred and fifty thousand pounds. He would have to buy out the existing mortgages himself, of course. No bank would accept a second mortgage as sufficient security for the kind of funding he had in mind. And he had to fund Lord Montford's endowment, but in exchange for the security of Pencombe it was all worth it. In time his grandson would inherit and Bradbury money and Montford lineage would continue for ever. He had plans that showed that with an investment of £50,000 in stock and equipment, he could nearly double the income from the estate in three years. That would double its value, making it worth at least a million pounds. Then, together with the brewery, he would be one of the richest men in England. He just had to see his way through this bad patch. At least with Harold gone, he was beginning to see daylight in the brewery figures. Another month or so and he'd have floundered with that devil at work in the books.

Tomorrow, he had to have time to compose himself for tomorrow. He had bought Lavender a wedding present, a magnificent brooch, diamonds set in gold in the shape of a hop leaf and fruit. He knew she'd love it. The thought of the brooch made him think of the necklace that had been the cause of the mortgage at the root of all this worry. After he'd left Pencombe that day he'd gone to Reason Hill, gone to say to Lucinda he must have it, must see what monies could be raised against it, only to find that she'd sent it back to Michael. Stupid, stupid girl, to let all that money out of her hands for a foolish gesture. Thomas had been stunned: he hadn't even known of its existence. If he had, then he would never have let it go, but would have used it to fund his own schemes, and again Eli would not have seen a penny.

He'd added up, at last, the expenditure that he had put into Pencombe. It was over one hundred and fifty thousand pounds. He must have been mad. He saw it now. Nobody in their right mind would have acted as he had. What a price for glory! Now Isabella had to be the key. It upset him, what Lavender had said, but it just had to be. Isabella would learn to love Johnnie; she'd been happy enough in his company before, before what? Before she

316

fell in love with Michael. Stuff and nonsense. Girls shouldn't fall in love where they weren't told to.

He stood up stiffly. He had to move about or he'd start feeling stupidly sentimental about the silly girl. This was all Lavender's doing, she'd undermined his determination. If it wasn't an absolute, financial necessity, then he'd be very tempted to let her have her way. But the figures proved it, they couldn't lie. He needed the extra quarter of a million pounds in the estate. The terms of the marriage contract enabled him to use the property as security, as long as he maintained and improved it. He had to give himself room to breathe while he put the brewery back on its feet. The marriage was the only way to get the creditors off his back. He flopped down again into his chair. Everyone had some cross to bear, Isabella was not alone in that. He set to work again, putting down on paper the framework of his financial plan that tied Isabella and Johnnie inextricably together.

Dr Groake came for his regular visit that evening. He was a kind man, gentle and understanding. Lavender looked upon him as a friend as well as a practitioner. And the doctor approved of Lavender; she was good for Eli, a man he admired, and so he was determined to do his best for her. That was why he spoke his thoughts first to her, and not to Eli, who paid his bills.

'I have been of a mind for some weeks now that the baby is going to come somewhat earlier than we are planning for.'

Lavender wriggled. She'd known this would come, but tried to wish it away. 'What makes you say that, doctor?' she asked in a small voice.

'My examination, the position of the baby, your own state of health. Yes, I am almost convinced. You haven't had a baby before, have you?'

'No.'

'Any miscarriages?'

'No.'

'Well, I just thought I'd let you know before I tell Eli. He'll be excited, I expect, not so long to wait as he'd thought.' He started to get up but the urgency in Lavender's voice stopped him.

'But, you mustn't tell him, mustn't. He's got so much on his mind at the moment, what with the brewery, Isabella and her marriage, and business; he's got plans to go up to London again. If he thinks I might be a couple of weeks early, then he'll get flustered, not want to go. But he must, he's told me he must. You can't tell him now.'

'It's not just a couple of weeks we're talking about, it's a full month. I think he should be prepared.'

'Look, doctor,' Lavender's voice was low, full of pleading, 'you've seen how he gets when he's worried; he's very red in the face, really worked up already. If you make him even more so, and his business problems get worse because he's not doing what he should, then what's that going to do for his health? You tell me. You wouldn't promise me then that he'd be here when the little chap arrives, would you? Not if he gets really, really excited. He's not a young man any more, doctor. You must promise not to change things for him. He's working everything out, expecting me to give him his son in two months' time. You musn't change it for him, promise me, please?'

She had tears in her eyes, and she was right, of course. Eli was clearly under intense pressure, a stroke was a distinct possibility. 'Very well,' he said after a while. 'Very well, I promise.'

She had them, she had the two precious, precious, promises she needed. She lay back happier than she'd been in weeks.

'Just one thing,' the doctor called back as he walked to the door. 'No one can promise you you're going to have a son, you know. It may well be a little girl.' He left the room, leaving Lavender thinking that doctors don't know everything.

Michael laid down his pen. He was so pleased with himself that he couldn't put his mind to composing the correct, formal acceptance that was necessary. He'd actually achieved something at last. The nights of scheming and the days of hanging about in draughty corridors, calling on aged generals at their fusty clubs, were over. He had a job at last. He picked up the letter from the Prime Minister's office again. The words on it were printed indelibly on his brain, but he couldn't stop re-reading them. He was to make arrangements, 'with all possible haste' to sail for South Africa, where he was to report, for the Prime Minister's office, on the prevailing conditions.

The private interview that the PM's secretary had given him was certainly thought-provoking. A cause, the man had said, very rarely lasted a lifetime. If Michael was effective, then the reason for his campaign would cease, and what would he do then? The question had taken him by surprise, but it was a fair one. Michael had had to look at himself clearly. Was he really a changed person, or was this a phase? Would he want to go back to living the life of a country gentleman once this was over? He'd had to think quickly but his reply had to be a true one; subterfuge would have been dishonourable, and also stupid. He now saw injustice where before he'd overlooked it. He now saw inequality where before he'd seen and accepted the order of things. His eyes had been opened, there could be no going back. So he told the secretary that he felt called to an active life in politics. It was a short statement that covered an immense change in him. Having made it he felt more complete, and yet empty, for he hadn't yet really begun to live his new life. He picked up the pen quite slowly, deliberately, for acceptance was an act of dedication.

Bill Bates, master brewer and manager of Bradbury's Brewery, put his hand up to his lips to cover his involuntary belch. It wasn't the done thing at weddings.

Mind you, this wedding was a rum do anyway. He ran his sharp brown eyes over the gathering in Lavender's bedroom, or perhaps boudoir was more the correct word, all decked up as it was with flowers and bows and things. He'd spent a lot of his time in the brewhouse wondering what the available daughter of the house might be like. He'd pictured the ideal girl, bright colouring, pert, a snub nose to make it really perfect, and a real little goer. She'd have to be, because in his happy imaginings she fell instantly, madly, head over heels in love with him and they ran away together, to return, man and wife. She would bring up the kids and he would carry on at the brewery. Eventually, in three or four years' time, when the old man retired, he'd take over. That's how it was meant to work out, wasn't it? That's how it worked out in the novels at any rate. But Isabella hadn't fitted the part. To begin with she was taller than he'd imagined, nearly on a par with his own five foot six, fair haired and more of a lady to look at than he'd expected. Mind you, he watched as Lavender caught the girl's eye and the two of them exchanged a conspiratorial look that made him suspect that there were hidden currents. But she wouldn't be one to run off with the paid help; not her, she wasn't the type.

The vicar leaned over Lavender in her bed and began the blessing. Bill had to put his hand up again. Drat the ale he'd had at breakfast; it had been too fresh, too yeasty, and these new trousers pinched a bit round his middle, which didn't help. The older sister now, he turned his eyes on to her, she was a right one. All flashing eyes and heavy breathing. Bill reckoned Eli must have been more than glad to get that bit of hellfire off his hands.

Ah, good, it looked as if that wrapped it up, and it was to be shaking of hands all round. Right ho, Bill wasn't one to be backward in coming forward. With any luck there'd be a slap-up lunch and that would make up for his having to take his day's holiday in the company of his employer.

Eli came up to him, pure joy in his eyes, and held out his hand. 'Thank you for coming, thank you very much. I won't forget it, you know.'

'My pleasure, Mr Bradbury, my pleasure,' Bill replied, and suddenly, seeing the old man's beaming face, suddenly it really was a pleasure.

Lavender's face was very puffy. Isabella looked down at her with concern. She would never have given her promise to get Eli out of the house for the day if she'd known what a difference these past few weeks would make.

'You will go, won't you, now, as soon as you can?' Lavender was fumbling in the drawstring bag she kept by her bed. 'Here's ten pounds, here you are, take it. Buy something for the baby; that will give you both something to think about. And please do just as you promised and stay away all day, please.'

'I really wish I didn't have to do this,' Isabella said.

'It's too late to change your mind now.'

There was only one sure way that Isabella could think of that would get her father up to London at such short notice. She rapped on his study door.

'Come in,' he called.

'Father, will you do me the most enormous favour? I want to go up to town. I've decided what to buy Johnnie for my wedding present to him, and I simply must go today, while I'm inspired. Please come with me.'

Eli looked at her in astonishment. All the tears, all the tantrums, suddenly this! 'I don't see anything too difficult in that, my dear,' he said. 'Just come with me when I go to the brewery this morning. You can do your shopping while I'm busy and come back with me when we've both finished.'

'No, no, I don't mean Maidstone, I mean London. I have to go to Bond Street, that's the only place where I'll have enough choice. Please, please come. You know Bill can manage perfectly well without you for one day.'

Eli was perplexed, he hated to be rushed into anything not of his own making. But if it really was a change of heart on Isabella's part, then it ought to be encouraged. 'Well, I'll go and see how Lavender is first,' he said.

'No, no, there's no need, she's asleep. I left a message with the nurse. Come on, if we go now we can catch an early train, and the sooner we're there, the sooner we're back.' That at least was true.

There was a bustle and fuss to get the carriage out quickly, and then they were off, heading for the station at Maidstone. There was a train to London every hour, on the hour. If they were lucky, they'd catch the nine o'clock. It was only as she leaned back against the leather, relaxing a little now that she'd actually managed to get her father out of the house, that Isabella thought about the money in her purse. Ten pounds. Three for the fare to France, and seven left over for food and essentials. She could escape to Margaret who was now in Paris; she could be there by tomorrow. She almost stopped breathing, it was such a shock. Escape was suddenly within her power. To leave it all behind, to join in with the others on their campaigning. A life so different from her own that all the hurts must fade away. She'd forget, forget she'd ever dreamed impossible dreams. Father would have Lavender and the baby. She wouldn't be leaving him alone. There was still the question of the Pencombe money, but her father was clever, he'd manage if he had to. Manage without her. She closed her eyes. Paris.

The train was at the platform already, steam billowing from its stack, and they hurried to get on board. She had the journey to think and to decide. Eli had buried himself in his newspaper, so there was no one to consider but herself. It was only three weeks to the wedding. One day less than that to the grand ball that was to be given on the eve of the ceremony.

The countryside was bleak; they passed brown field after brown field. At intervals there were the hop gardens, stripped of their vines, bare skeletons of their summer glory, shrunk within themselves to cope with the harsh winter ahead. Isabella felt like that, stripped of softness, with the worst yet to come. She couldn't go through with it, couldn't face becoming a chattel of a man she couldn't love or respect.

'Ah, ha!' Eli's voice made her start. 'There's a piece in here about Michael. He's to be sent out to the Cape to report for the government. He must be getting somewhere at last. At least it means there won't be any question of him turning up at the wedding. It says here he sails on the eighteenth, that's two days before the ball. I'm glad about that, I haven't felt happy about Lucinda seeing him again, not in her present condition; we don't want her getting excited.'

She would go away, she would go today. She closed her eyes tightly against the thought of Michael, back in Africa. He'd look for his Boer woman again. She would catch the boat-train. She'd escape from her father in London somehow.

As they climbed into a cab waiting in the rank outside

the station, Eli was delighted at how enervated Isabella looked. This must be it; at last she was getting excited about her forthcoming marriage. She was nervous as any bride should be. He'd go along with her moods for the next few weeks, and then it would be over. He felt a wave of relief. If the baby kept on time then it would only be another week after Isabella was off his hands before his son arrived. Eli couldn't wait.

It was overcast and dull in London, and all the shops were brightly lighted, displaying their wares to their best advantage. They walked from one end of Bond Street to the other. Isabella looked in every window that might suit her purpose. She told Eli that she wanted to buy a set of dress shirt studs for her groom-to-be. A nice thought. Eli was pleased with it and joined in enthusiastically, peering at neat circles of gold-rimmed mother-of-pearl, centred with seed pearls, and knots of gold encircling shining enamels. There were dozens of suitable sets. Not one of them found Isabella's favour. It was nearly lunch-time and Eli was flagging. They should revive themselves at the Ritz, he said. It had become his favourite lunch-time haunt, which he and Lucinda had visited often. Isabella begged to try just one more shop, a splendid edifice on the corner of an arcade. She looked slowly, painstakingly through leather box after leather box. Even the obsequious salesman began to fret. He too had wanted his lunch at one o'clock. But Isabella had a timetable of her own to keep to.

At last she admitted defeat and Eli made for the Ritz where he announced his intention of choosing himself and Isabella a celebratory lunch. As he began to pore over the menu, Isabella excused herself, saying that she wanted to tidy up after their rigorous morning. Eli sat back at leisure to decide between Scottish salmon or roast beef or possibly a fricassee of duckling. The waiter suggested something to drink while he made up his mind: a capital idea; champagne, he thought, they might as well do the thing in style.

A portion of Isabella's seven pounds had to be spent on a hansom cab to Victoria station. She sat forwards on the very edge of the seat in the cab, feeling so alone that it was painful. Around her, London, which had always seemed so welcoming, suddenly appeared threatening. She could still be found and stopped. She paid her fare and turned and dashed into the station. There was a queue at the booking office. She felt conspicuous on her own in such a public place. There was a short, swarthy-skinned man in the queue in front of her. He turned around to appraise her, looking her slowly up and down. It was difficult for her to avoid his eye, so she looked around, desperate for something to focus her attention on. There was the great black and white clock that showed it was only half past one. She had an hour at least before the boat-train left. What on earth would she do with an hour? The queue was shuffling forwards and at last the man in front of her was at the window. He was French: of course, that explained his attentions, the French were notoriously bold. She would have to be careful when she got to Paris until she reached Margaret.

'A ticket for the boat-train please,' she murmured, shy now she had to speak.

'Wot class?'

'Oh, I don't know.' Margaret hadn't said anything about class. 'Whichever is the cheapest, please.'

The man slapped a ticket down in front of her. 'Third class. Three pounds, twelve shillings and sixpence, please.'

'Oh!' She fumbled to give him the money. Twelve shillings and sixpence extra and she'd already spent two shillings on her cab.

'Next train five fifteen,' he said and looked past her, eyebrows raised in query at the person behind her in the queue.

'Five fifteen? But . . .' Isabella's fingers tightened convulsively round the ticket. 'Five fifteen,' she said again, 'I thought . . .'

'That's right, mid-season timetable, changed yesterday. Move on now, please.'

She stepped aside from the window, oblivious of the amused glances from those around her who'd seen the confusion. Mid-season, she'd never thought that Margaret's information might have been out of date. After all, the letter from Paris had only arrived a few short weeks ago.

But she had the ticket, the precious ticket at last. Where could she go? She wandered for a while, peering at timetables, skirting the book stand. She looked hesitantly at the trolley piled high with portable foodstuffs for travellers. She hadn't eaten since breakfast, but she couldn't spend her remaining money; she had no idea what other expenses she would have. She couldn't stand about like this; she could sense that other men were looking at her. She went to the ladies lavatory, where at least she would be safe.

There was an old woman in charge and a saucer on a little table where she received payment for her services. Isabella would have to give another precious coin for the use of the facilities. She closed the door of the little cubicle behind her with an overwhelming sense of relief. She leaned back against it. There was a lock between her and the world outside. What would her father be doing now? How long would he have waited before getting someone to check on her? She had gone quickly to the powder room at the Ritz, commenting to the woman who took the cloaks that she was just popping back to a shop in Bond Street, going to buy a surprise present for her papa. The woman would tell them that when they asked about her. With all the shops they'd visited that morning, Eli would spend a lot of time vainly looking for her, she hoped, she prayed. She jumped at the knock on the door.

'You all right in there?'

'Yes, yes, perfectly all right, thank you,' she called out. She heard the attendant shuffling away muttering her objections about how long some ladies took performing. She couldn't hide away in here much longer. She went out slowly, leaving her penny in the saucer, checking her hat in the mirror. Her eyes were far too bright, her cheeks too pink; no wonder people were looking at her.

She felt trapped, exposed, she must get out of the station. Making her way back to the entrance she had to thread her way through a throng of uniformly grey-coated children. It was an orphanage outing, the children categorized by their pinched faces, the too short haircuts of the boys and the darned black stockings of the girls. They were shepherded by two hard-faced harridans who in their turn were being grandly overlooked by a matronly woman in a vast black straw bonnet. 'Margate train, Platform 2 my little duckies, come along now, come along,' the woman called. The children's faces registered no change of expression, reacting to the urging of their benefactress like a flock of sheep. Isabella stood to watch them file off. Poor little souls, she thought, poor mindless, helpless little creatures. She suddenly saw how pathetic she was being letting a few extra hours' wait for the train panic her. She wasn't aimless, she had a reason, a future. She turned with a new resolution and walked out into the bright, hard light of London in autumn.

She couldn't afford another cab fare but neither could she loiter outside the station. A seat on one of the omnibuses careering past, that was what she needed. The crowded streets that had frightened her such a short time before were now welcoming. She would become part of

327

it, just another ant in the bustling ant-hill. A few steps from the station a short queue waited at a bus stop. Isabella took her place behind a young woman wearing a showy french-blue and maroon outfit and happily humming a music hall tune to herself. She had time to study her neighbour: the jacket the girl wore would have been elegant if it hadn't been for the red ruffles on the cuff and hem, and the skirt, too, had basic good lines marred by the three deep flounces that echoed the ribbon rosette adorning the pill-box cap worn jauntily on one side. Then Isabella noticed the girl's hands: they were pink, well scrubbed with short-cut nails, the hands of a worker. Of course, the girl was a servant, she'd been given the cast-off suit by her employer, since it was outmoded for a London lady of fashion, and then in her attic room, she'd added the frills, the flounces. Isabella smiled at the instant scenario she had created.

The bus arrived with a clatter of hooves, cutting off her thoughts but not her smile. She stepped up on to the platform and the conductor reached out a hand to steady her as they moved off with a lurch, pulling out into the mainstream of traffic. The girl in the blue suit walked easily to her seat, oblivious of the swaying movement of the vehicle. Isabella, unaccustomed to buses, had to clutch at the wooden seat backs to make her way to the empty place, where she sat down with relief.

'Where to, luv?' The conductor stuck his hand out for her fare, but she hadn't had time to think of a destination.

The girl next to her leaned over, a penny ready in her hand. 'Harrods, please.' she said.

Isabella clutched at the inspiration. Lucinda had talked about Harrods, so new, so bright and, fortuitously for Isabella, in Knightsbridge, a good distance from Bond Street where Eli would be looking for her.

The new store was fabulous, shining windows fronting

328

decorous displays stretched away from her, the great red building towering above. A steady stream of the elegant and their imitators made their way into and out of the commissionaire-flanked doors. Isabella let herself be swept along with them through the handsome portals, to be instantly enveloped in the heady atmosphere of affluence. She wandered, like the other browsers, lured from one area of enticement to another. The perfumery declared its presence from afar, wafts of pure rose beckoning her forwards. Business here, the serious transactions conducted by the rich for their pleasures, was being conducted in dulcet tones. It seemed that even the aged duchesses sniffing and sampling the pots and potions were a little in awe at the splendour of it all.

If life were perfect, then Isabella would buy some luggage for her trip, a neat leather case to fill with a travelling lady's necessities; as it was she would have to make do with looking. She asked her way to the requisite department from an elegantly morning-suited assistant whose splendour came close to eclipsing that of his customers.

Here she found, piled expansively, the brass-bound trunks and the leather portmanteaux that were attracting the custom of the wealthy voyageur. Here she also found Michael, tucking his wallet back into the inside pocket of his jacket. It was hard to see who was the most surprised, but Michael recovered to speak first.

'Issy! What on earth are you doing here?' he asked.

Isabella had to swallow before answering; the shock of meeting him had driven conscious thought from her head. 'Hallo, Michael,' she said, 'I'm just looking really, not buying. Just here to see . . .' she gestured vaguely at the opulence of it all.

Michael's instinctive expression of delighted surprise changed; her pause had given him time to think, time to remember. His face closed down as if shutters had been drawn. 'Here to choose your trousseau, are you? Or is it more luxuries to pile into Pencombe? Who are you with?' He looked around expecting to see a companion for her.

'No, it's nothing like that. I'm here on my own.' She paused. She had a feeling she was standing on the brink. 'I'm here to waste some time. I have three hours before I catch the boat-train. I'm going to Paris.'

'To Paris! Good God! With Johnnie? Already? You're going away with him already? Now, today?' Michael had coloured quickly, looked almost feverish.

'No, no, not with Johnnie.' She was wringing her hands. It was so difficult. 'I'm going . . . oh heavens!' she looked imploringly at Michael.

The assistant who'd been wrapping his purchase was standing deferentially to one side, interest in their conversation showing clearly on his smooth-shaven face. This was one of the perks of the job; the nobs and their affairs.

Michael turned abruptly to the man, reached into his waistcoat pocket and thrust the card he'd pulled out towards the assistant. 'Here,' he said, 'I've changed my mind. I won't take the case with me after all, send it to my club.' He took Isabella firmly by the arm and propelled her so forcibly away from the department that the salesman smirked. High emotion running there all right. They were always the ones to let love go to their heads, the thoroughbreds.

'Where are we going?' Isabella asked. She was pulling against him, trying to slow him down, trying to dictate the speed of their passage to something matching the sedateness of the other shoppers who had to step, somewhat alarmed, out of their way.

'We're going to Cadogan Gardens. The house there is shut up, closed down, no one's there. We can talk and not be overheard by those damned nosy layabouts.' He shot such a look of venom at a passing floor manager that Isabella blushed.

They didn't talk on the short walk along the streets, nor as Michael unlocked first the iron grille and then the massive dark green door that set off the red brick of the opulent façade. He walked ahead of her down the dim airless hall, dropping his keys with a clatter on the tarnished silver tray on the hall table. He did not look at his reflection that passed, ghost-like in the twilight, across the face of the gilt-framed mirror. The double doors he threw open ahead of them led into the drawing room. It, also, was dark. Isabella felt rather than saw the dust sheets, smelt the dry, bookish smell of disuse. There were three heavily draped windows in the wall opposite the door and Michael walked to the centre one to pull back the curtains, allowing a shaft of light into the room. Golden dust motes swirled up around them, disturbed by their entrance, and now Isabella could see the dated maroon and cream walls, the lifeless chandelier. She looked from one inanimate object to another, forcing her mind away from the intimacy of the moment. She would not allow herself to look at Michael, who stood so motionless, his hand still on the curtain, staring out at the street.

'Why are you going?' Michael's voice was low, he was speaking slowly, enunciating his words with care, concentrating on keeping the emotion he felt hidden.

'To get away, to get away from it all, from Pencombe, Johnnie, even my family. I need to get away from everything. I have to see clearly, to be able to act for myself.'

Michael turned, the light behind him masking his expression from Isabella. 'Why Paris?' he asked.

'I have a friend there. Margaret, you remember, I sent her your name. She's still campaigning for your women in the camps, stirring up support in France, bringing their conditions out into the open.' She had brought the Boer woman

331

into the room with her words, the one that Johnnie had told her about. She was in the room now for Isabella, invading their privacy, an insurmountable barrier.

'How long will you go for?' Michael asked.

Isabella hadn't thought that far; she had to run away from the woman in Michael's life.

'Perhaps for ever,' she said. 'There's nothing for me to come back for, nothing.'

Michael felt the tautness of his body fade, the impulsion that had been in him drain away. He wanted to sit down, to close a door between them; there was nothing to keep her here, nothing, she'd said it herself. Their silence hung in the air, a desolate emotion for a lifeless room. Isabella turned away from the figure in the window; she shivered, loneliness making her cold. There was a portrait on the wall in front of her. It was of a young woman, about her own age; she had a kind face, sensitive compassionate eyes and she was somehow familiar.

'It's my mother,' Michael said, for the first time since they'd met that afternoon correctly interpreting Isabella's thoughts. 'That was painted before I was born, when this house was in its heyday, when my grandfather was still alive.' His lips formed the words, but they weren't his thoughts. Isabella, her head tilted back to look at the portrait, looked very vulnerable. In a few seconds he could be beside her, telling her of his love, pressing her to him. But she had already said there was nothing for her in England, nothing.

The memory of a remark Hermione had once made surfaced in his mind. Lovers must press their cause, she'd said. 'If things were to change,' he said slowly, feeling his way, 'plans that have been made, I mean. If there was change at Pencombe, could you stay then?'

Isabella kept her eyes on the painting. What did he mean, plans change? 'I can't think of anything that could

332

make me want to stay there. I've never felt it could be my home.' There was nothing in Isabella's thoughts that could make it possible for her. She believed that Johnnie was the heir to the estate now. In Eli's endeavours to bring Isabella to agreement he had slid away from the reality that Michael had yet to complete the final transfer of entail.

Michael knew none of that as he went on, taking himself to the verge of a proposal that Isabella was unaware he was able to make. 'There is nothing then,' he asked, 'that the heir to Pencombe could do to make you love him?' She didn't speak, but the sudden drooping of her shoulders made him walk swiftly to her. 'Tell me, Isabella, tell me, is there any hope, any way?'

His eyes were so bright, so alive, his face so eager. She couldn't bear it, she felt ill, physically sickened at the effort he was going to, to make her love his brother. 'None, none at all,' she cried. 'I will go to Paris and get out of all your lives, away from all of you.' A band of pain tightened round her forehead. She ached to throw herself into his arms, longed for him, but all he wanted was to persuade her, as they all did, to sacrifice herself for their benefit.

Michael made himself take a step back; he wanted to crush her to him, to smother her objections with his lips. But memories of Johnnie forcing her, of her terror, stopped him. Stopped him from taking her in his arms, which was what they both wanted above all things but which the fates were refusing to allow.

Michael took up his position at the window again. Turning his back on the woman he loved, making his thoughts go to his imminent journey to Africa. Isabella's words came back to him. 'Perhaps' she had said, she would be gone 'for ever'. So would he; he would go to Africa and never come back; after all, there was nothing for him now in England, nothing.

* * *

Standing on the platform, thinking sadly of Michael, Isabella waited for the boat-train. Suddenly, unbelievably, she saw her father. His coat was flapping open, his hair flying back frrom his flushed forehead. My God, she thought, he looks demented. He was rushing forwards, rushing headlong towards Platform 5, the down line for Maidstone. He must be going home. Why so soon? Why wasn't he still looking for her? Then she saw Dove, running after Eli. He caught his master up and ran alongside him for a while whilst Eli talked at him, gesturing back the way he had come. Dove ran back, out of the station. Ahead of her there was a whistle of steam as the boat-train pulled into its platform. Over her head there was a sudden whirring of pigeons, disturbed from their perches on the intricate metal beams in the roof. She looked back. Eli was standing alone on his empty plat-form, leaning dangerously far forwards over the edge, to peer along the tracks. It seemed he couldn't stand still. He put a hand up to his forehead to push the wispy hair back from it.

Isabella was frozen. The softly sinking sound of steam beckoned her to her train. She could hear the doors opening, closing, banging, porters shouting. France was simply a few steps away for her. Concern flooded through her as she watched him desperately looking for his train, desperately willing himself to, to what?

It had to be Lavender. With an awful flood of realization she saw what must have happened. Lavender had done something awful; she had planned something for today, something that Eli was desperate to stop. What on earth was it? She saw him slip, and his foot went over the platform edge. He wobbled for a moment, then stumbled back, still far too close to the edge. She ran then, ran in the only direction it was possible for her to run, towards her father.

'Isabella!' He turned in astonishment. 'But how on earth did you get here? Where's Dove? Is he with you? Oh my God, my God.' He was utterly distraught.

She held his arm to steady him. 'What is it? What's the matter?'

'It's Lavender, the baby; the baby's coming and she's said, she's said they've to save the baby, even if it means her life, and I'm not there, not there to stop them. Oh my God, my God.'

As the train came slowly towards them, its wheels spinning backwards to slow it down, it gave a merry toot on its whistle. Isabella felt the horror of it then. That was what Lavender had planned all along. She must have had a premonition of disaster and had planned it all, planned it so that she could say what Eli never, ever would; to save the child's life at the expense of the mother's.

'I can't allow you to make this sacrifice, Lavender. Eli wouldn't want it.'

The doctor's voice was high with concern, and penetrated even the new, strong, overwhelming surge of pain. She had to wait for it to pass before she could reply, and even then the words squeezed out, between teeth that she couldn't unclench.

'Not your decision, doctor, not your right.' She stopped for breath, curling her hands into tight, sweating balls to fight the pain. 'You got to do what I say. Eli's not here.' She couldn't believe the pain. It was solid, like walls falling on her, crushing her. But the baby must live, must live perfect and whole; not like her, she was broken already.

The nurse was wiping Lavender's face, vainly dabbing at the rivulets of sweat that poured from her. 'Give him the word, dearie,' she murmured, 'give him the word, there's still time.' She'd been in on this kind of thing before, and it was always bad, always very nasty. Only before, it had always been the man determined to have his heir. New wives, it seemed, were easier come by than the scraps of humanity men went mad for.

Lavender clutched at the woman, anything, she needed something to hold on to. But nothing would change her mind, nothing. She knew what she was about. The doctor hadn't gone into detail but he had said that she wouldn't survive the shock of normal birth. He could only save one life, not both, and pleaded with her to sacrifice the baby to save herself. But it was her child, the son she had promised Eli, and the decision was hers alone. Then she started screaming. She couldn't hear the cries herself, the keening, howling that filled the house, sending its occupants into hiding with their hands over their ears. Making the girls cry and the men find excuses to go out into the open air. It was incredibly loud, the silence, when it came. And then, like a trickle into a still pool, the tiny cry of new life.

They were far too late. The drama played out, over and done. They wanted to show Eli his son, but he wouldn't have any of it. Take it away, take it away out of the house, out of my sight, he said. I'm too old for babies. For God's sake, take it away, and he locked himself in his study. So the doctor took the baby and the nurse off in his pony trap and went to Lucinda at Reason Hill. She sent for Jenny, who took the tiny, unloved bundle into her arms and held it close. The whimpering stopped against her ample breast; the tiny soul had found a home.

Isabella wandered the house, walked through the rooms, that suddenly seemed strange and empty. Eventually she came to Lavender's room, emptied and washed and cleansed to house the empty shell that had been so full of life. Lavender's face was drained, white alabaster. Isabella sat beside her, hour after hour, through the night. She

336

made the vigil of a friend, she prayed for the soul of the departed, that she had no doubt would wing its way to heaven, for God must welcome the truly selfless.

Isabella stared at her reflection in the full-length mirror. Her face was almost as pale as the ivory white silk of her dress. The seed pearls that had been embroidered in cascades over the shoulders ran down the bodice of the wedding dress and made her waist seem even narrower than it was. The lamps were burning in her bedroom, even though the curtains were pulled back to let in the morning light. Extra light was essential on such a bleak morning so that the two bustling seamstresses could ply their talents with their needles.

Marooned like a mannequin, Isabella was standing on a stool so that the deft fingers could work on the hem. Her view was limited to that framed by the mirror in front of her. A portion of chill grey sky was visible in the top right-hand corner. Rain rather than snow was carried on the wind, although a blizzard was expected, prophesied by the gardeners and grooms alike, but then they enjoyed the thought of the grand guests having to fight their way to the feast. The older seamstress was clucking again. Her eyes had narrowed earlier as Isabella stood for her to fasten the tiny fabric-covered buttons running down the fitted back. The girl was still losing weight, so the dress had dropped and the hem would have to be lifted yet again. It should touch the floor at the front and the sides, but not drape until the train at the back, those were Madame Penelope's instructions. There would be mothers of unmarried daughters in abundance at tonight's ball who would scrutinize the couturier's work with an eye to their own future requirements. Odd though it was for the wedding dress to appear on the eve of the ceremony, Madame, dressmaker to the high and mighty, had been quick to realize that her wares would, for once, be shown off to their full perfection. There would be no crowded church to cope with, no clambering in and out of carriages to risk her handiwork. So the greatest care and attention to the finest detail had been lavished and here this inconsiderate creature was fading away before their eyes. It was just as well that they had reached the day itself; any more taking in of seams and the detail of the bodice beading would have to be reworked.

'How about a nice glass of warm milk, my dear?' Madame Penelope swept into the room, fresh from supervising the packing of the 'going away' outfits. She offered the milk in the knowledge that it would keep the last bloom of youth on the diminishing figure. Madame had experience of dealing with reluctant brides.

'No, no, I'm fine, thank you.' Isabella didn't want a glass of milk, she didn't want anything. She felt numb, her senses were dulled, muted by an excess of emotion poured out in the last weeks. Now the wedding was so close that she was beyond sensation. This morning her face had lost its tightness, the lines of stress had faded, leaving her skin taut but smooth and clear, the dark smudges under her eyes heightening their blueness. Her hair was like spun gold, thanks to the continued attentions of Maude. She was like a fragile, porcelain figure, without life, without emotion. Guided by the seamstress she turned slowly around, the train of the dress falling in a cascade on the floor. Madame herself darted forwards to lift it, revolving around Isabella's slow pirouette, the looking glass reflecting them all left unregarded.

Safe, hidden in the regal blue and turkey-red petit point needlework bag that her mother had once worked, lay the phial responsible for Isabella's new found calm. Lavender had left a legacy to Isabella that no one save the recipient was aware of and Lavender would never have wanted. But the laudanum to dull an invalid's pain also dulled over-heated sensibilities. What Isabella did not know was how much she could take before reaching the point of no return.

Eli too had constructed for himself a fortress against his sensitivities. But where Isabella moved slowly, as if through water, he bustled, ever faster, ever more demanding, his body manufacturing adrenalin at an unprecedented rate. He'd insisted that the delivery of oysters for the ball stopped at Linstone en route for Pencombe. The squat barrels, draped with seaweed, crammed with the delicacies of the coast from nearby Whitstable, had been piled high in the cart. There had been frost on the load and he had fussed around demanding that the top barrels be opened and their contents poked and prised. He didn't want any problems; there was still time for another load before evening if need be. But the fresh tang of iodine had been undiminished by the chill; they were in perfect condition and eventually he let them on their way.

He sent Dove off to the bakers at Yalding. Their ovens were packed full of unusual wares. There were six, whole hundred-weight pigs, far grander than suckling, a centre-piece for the most splendid feast. They were crackling to perfection, Dove had reported. Following Eli's instructions, he'd slipped the master baker a five-pound note to make up for the fat spitting over the insides of the brick-lined oven. Where the master had complained, the boy who was apprenticed had nearly cried. When the pork was cooked, he would be put in to the ovens to scrape off the black crusty fat deposits and with the pressure of bread orders building up, he knew no one would be too fussy about how cool they let the ovens get. He'd have blistered knees and elbows by the time the day was out and no mistake, and he wouldn't get a crisp bank note for his trouble.

By lunch-time the panic in the house was too much for the two main participants. Isabella lay down on her bed and slipped into a doze. At last there were no future-searching dreams to trouble her. It was as if her mind had shrivelled to encompass nothing more than breathing.

Eli took a plate of cheese and bread to his study. His mind hadn't been as obliging as his daughter's. Thoughts crowded, collided, competed for precedence. He sat down heavily in his chair, then pushed the plate away from him, untouched. He had no appetite. Lavender was gone, and his desire for food seemed to have gone with her. The baby, the baby had gone too, safe and secure into Jenny's welcoming arms. She was a natural mother to the child, and William would make as good a father as a boy could wish for. Eli squeezed his eyes more tightly shut. They were stinging but he couldn't afford the time to cry, couldn't break down, not today. He had this dreadful premonition of disaster welling up inside him. If he hadn't watched Isabella's spirit fade over the last few weeks, then he would have been sure she wasn't going to go through with it. But it wasn't that, the girl hadn't got an ounce of spark left in her. She was a study in tragedy that it didn't do any good at all to dwell on. In a year or so she'd have a baby of her own, and Johnnie would be all her life. This marriage was best for her, best for all of them. Well, at least, best for all of them, and Isabella had never known what was good for her. Eli cautiously opened his eyes. The overwhelming urge to weep had faded. He had to fool his body nowadays. This was one of the lessons of old age he'd learned. To sneak around emotion, to ease activity on to tired, old muscles, never to allow degeneration to conquer will.

He had to find something to occupy his mind. Something to override the confusion. He got up and walked around his desk. Everything in the room reminded him of the business of the day. There were the brewery ledgers, the piles of Pencombe deeds, the papers that he'd worked on to formulate their salvation. The men at the brewery, their families, the men on the estate and their dependants, were all tied in to tomorrow, the final act, the marriage. Everything then became possible. The bank had agreed to fund the entire complex manipulation of funds, the brewery would look to expansion, there would be sound first mortgages on the entire Pencombe estate but they would be regulated, in Eli's possession. It was a clearing of the counting house. George would be at Pencombe tonight; he and Hermione had accepted their invitation to the ball as Lord Montford had prophesied. And George had communicated through his brother-in-law his willingness to negotiate. That had to mean he would accept face value for the Hall mortgage; Eli had a banker's draft for the full amount prepared and sitting in his safe. Even the Macauls had been sent an invitation; George had made that a condition of his acceptance and eventually Lord Montford had decided to agree.

Eli laid a proprietorial hand on the pile of deeds. It had taken a long time, and a circuitous route, but they were to be his, it was all to be his. And he and Thomas had plans laid that would turn the brewery into the cornerstone of an empire bigger than even the young Eli had dared to dream. If only Lavender had been here to share it with him. Looking around the room, he saw something he had been meaning to deal with. The photograph album that Isabella had given him still lay unregarded on the window sill. He had never thought of looking through it. Now, it was just the thing. He should look at it and then he could talk to Isabella about it. They would need some neutral ground over the next few hours.

He opened the leather-bound loose-leaf book with a burst of enthusiasm. At least this was something outside the closed, daily round he had created. But he was wrong. Here, the first of Isabella's offerings, was a photograph of the brewery. She must have taken it on a Sunday, for the tall iron gates were closed. The buildings behind loomed in a mist, sensed rather than seen. It was a view Eli hardly ever saw. It was almost derelict, in the absence of life. He shivered, touched by foreboding. He turned the page quickly, then drew in his breath with shock.

The photograph was another view of Maidstone. Isabella must have been in the park above the river. There were figures in the foreground, almost darkened silhouettes against the light sky that outlined the iron railings behind them. But they were not without features; they were recognizable. Eli's hand trembled as he touched the lifeless representation of life brought back from the dead. Harold, all his shabbiness captured by the camera, was in distinct contrast to his companion. His companion whom Eli expected to meet this very evening, his companion with whom Eli intended to conduct civilized, orderly business. George Bullstone, every inch of his polished perfection captured by the camera, every nuance of satisfaction in his face as frozen in action as his hand reaching for the package that Harold held out to him. The package that for Harold had brought death, for Eli near downfall and for George, for George, ultimate man of business, it had brought profit.

The sky outside was almost dark, storm clouds had brought night early. Isabella looked down at the carriage clock on her dressing table. It was four o'clock; she only had half an hour left at Linstone. Thirty minutes, thirty revolutions of the tiny second hand busily making its way round the white face before she would be packed in to the carriage with her trunks. Lucinda was going with her, and her father, and Thomas. There was to be no escape for the captive.

'You'd better go and get your own things ready, Maude,' she said.

'Oh, I couldn't leave you now, ma'am. Besides, I don't have much to do, I'm all packed. Been packed for days.' The girl giggled in her excitement. Dove was already ensconced at Pencombe, this was Maude's own last hour at Linstone, then she'd be joining her intended. Matrimony seemed to have been in the air recently.

'No, no, off you go, Maude. I'd just like a last few minutes on my own in any case.'

'If you say so, ma'am.'

Isabella turned the key in the lock. Then she tried the handle to check that the door couldn't be opened. She walked swiftly to the wardrobe, and reached down inside to pull out the work bag. She put her hand inside, pushing away the tangled threads. For a second she held her breath. She couldn't find it, but then her fingers touched the cold glass; the little bottle had worked its way to the very bottom of the bag.

The few drops she'd taken so far had not been too difficult to swallow. But she didn't think she'd manage to drink all the remaining bitter-sweet syrup at once without being sick. Fortunately there was the glass of milk that Madame Penelope had earlier insisted she try to drink. She'd hidden it in her bedside cabinet to put it out of the woman's sight; now she would drink it after all. The milk had formed a thin skin, so she ran a finger over the surface to pull it to one side. It was awkward, clutching the glass in one hand and the laudanum in the other. She smiled at herself for being so silly, and put the glass down on her dressing table with the bottle beside it. She found it easy to smile now; relief was flowing over her. She glanced up at her reflection in the mirror and smiled back at herself.

Her breathing was gentle, she felt so very calm. There was a tiny cork to cap the glass bottle. She'd put it back after the drops she'd taken this morning and she'd forced it almost too far in, but her nails were long enough to get a grip. There, it was out, but the cork crumbled to pieces in her hand; it was just as well she didn't need to use it any more.

Her hand was very steady as she carefully poured the liquid into the milk. She laid the empty bottle down. Her smile was fading now, she could feel her face stiffening. It was, after all, a big step to take. She stared again at her reflection. The neckline of her dress revealed just the beginnings of the swell of her breasts. Very slowly she raised a forefinger to her lips. She had kept her secret, it had helped her through today. Then delicately, hardly touching the skin, she ran the tip of her forefinger over the point of her chin and down her throat. She traced an invisible line down to the top of her bodice. Her skin was soft, smooth, warm. By tomorrow night it would be at the mercy of a man she feared. She turned her hand, running it flat-palmed over the swelling of her breast, down to her waist. There was nothing she could forbid him, nothing. She sat frozen, a quivering, consuming fear welling through her. She reached out slowly, her eyes held by her reflection, the fear in her eyes impelling her on. Her fingers closed around the glass. Her eyes were brimming with tears, the mirrored form began to tremble. Slowly, carefully, she raised the precious liquid to her lips.

'Ma'am, oh ma'am!' Maude's cry hardly interrupted her. 'Ma'am!' The door handle rattled noisily. The edge of the glass touched her lips. She was surprised how cold it was.

'Ma'am, ma'am, it's Master Michael. He's here, ma'am. Oh my God, he's coming down the corridor.' A thunderous knocking made the door behind her shake.

'Isabella, Isabella, open this door.' It was his voice. The

344

glass dropped from her nerveless fingers, crashing on to the edge of the dressing table, spilling its contents all over her dress. 'Open this damned door! What the hell's going on here? Stand back, girl, stand back.'

She sat transfixed, staring at the door she saw in the mirror. It was like watching life elsewhere. This wasn't happening here, to her. There was a splintering crash and Michael staggered into the room.

'Ma'am, whatever were you doing, ma'am?' Maude ran in, pulling at Isabella's arm, turning her round from the chaos of glass. She stuck a finger in the puddled milk, licking it cautiously, then pulled a face.

'Get out,' Michael said to her. 'Go away!'

'They said you'd gone,' Isabella said. 'They said you'd gone to Africa.'

'I damned nearly did. I would have sailed yesterday if I hadn't . . .' He shook his head, to clear his thoughts. 'But it doesn't matter, nothing matters now except, why? What's driven you to this?' Michael pointed at the smashed glass. 'What was in it, Isabella?'

'Laudanum,' she whispered.

'How much?' Michael asked.

'Nearly the whole bottle.' She gestured towards the green bottle, still standing on the dressing table. 'It's all spilled, I hadn't taken any before it spilled.'

'Christ Almighty.' Michael lifted a hand to his face, feeling very sick. 'It would have killed you, you know that?'

She nodded dumbly, as Maude came back into the room.

'You'd better come out of this mess. Come with me, I'll take you to your father.'

She sat in a chair in her father's dressing room. He came and sat beside her, holding her hand as they told him. She had no feeling any more, her emotion was spent.

'Is your dress dry, Isabella?' Michael asked.

She nodded.

'Then you can make the journey to Pencombe wrapped up in your cloak. We're late enough as it is.'

She looked up at him. 'I still have to go to Pencombe?'

'Yes,' he said, 'you do.'

'Hermione, of course, will chaperone Isabella for the evening.' Lord Montford, resplendent in white tie and tails, was at his most autocratic. This was to be his last evening as sole master of Pencombe, and there was to be no lessening of his role until, like Cinderella, he had to leave the ball. It was all a fairy tale. The great house was lighted to a fabulous brilliance by two thousand candles made of finest beeswax, their light reflected from the baronial furniture polished to a peak of perfection by a dozen village ladies who had wielded their best soft polishing cloths and tins of Dr Mctavery's Most Especial Polish.

All of this, as well as the orchestra playing so demurely on the balcony above the great hall, and the banquet spread invitingly in the state dining room, all of it was paid for by Eli, yet this evening his was a very minor role. His rank as nouveau riche put him far below the several dozen families of impeccable breeding who formed the apex of the gathering. Then there were the guests drawn from the long monied society of the county, those made rich by the sea, the land; there were bankers too, made rich by other men's avarice. The men wore elegant black evening coats, or if they had recourse to it, uniform as bright and gilt bedecked as possible. Their ladies made a great pageant of colour. Fashion had been interpreted liberally at this out-of-town event; cream and soft beige might be 'the thing' in the London salons, but the stone walls needed life, and life and colour in abundance perched on the gilt chairs with the bright red velvet seats, hired for the occasion. Every possible corner was crammed with flowers, swags of green with imported roses in red and white, ribbon-hung, arranged to perfection by Madame Penelope's minions. Roses also flanked the receiving line, piled on to and around a pair of magnificent mahogany carved torchères. The line consisted of Montfords and Bradburys. It began with his lordship himself, then Hermione who was wearing a gown of midnight-blue satin, then Isabella, then Johnnie in hunting pink and Eli. Michael had not been seen since making the journey over from Linstone in the Bradbury carriage.

Isabella shook yet another hand, accepted yet another stranger's effusive wishes for her future. She felt very conscious of how close she was to Johnnie; their elbows kept touching as they greeted their guests. He had kissed the back of her hand fleetingly when she'd first entered the hall but their eyes had hardly met. Where Isabella was too nervous to see Johnnie's own fear lurking, Johnnie had been quick to see hers.

He took the warm, compliant hand of Charlotte, wife of his old friend and shooting mentor, Mumbles Buthry. 'I can't believe it,' she whispered to him, in her breathy voice. 'Married man, dear boy, you'll be a married man.' She darted a glance at Isabella, who was far too virginal for a high-blooded man like Johnnie, she thought. 'We'll console each other, my dear, you'll see, we'll be great chums.' She squeezed his hand some more, in a moist fleshy sort of way and then was gone, another eager face taking her place. God, was it going to be like this, for ever and ever? The fear of boredom, his ultimate enemy, welled up in him.

The line was alerted by Hermione's involuntary intake of breath. The Macaul family had made its entrance. Cutting a swathe through the straggling queue of guests still waiting to be received, they made their way to the head of it. Not that anyone objected loudly; the men were too taken aback by the brilliance of the two American ladies, and the English roses were too busy making instant mental comparisons with their own outfits. Johnnie leaned forwards in the line. Adele was scanning the gathering, vivid, vivacious. Seeing the handsome young man in the hunting pink she gave a smile, showing her white teeth between her deep red lips. Johnnie smiled too and automatically reached up to straighten his stock.

The silver-bearded Randolf Macaul had reached the beginning of the line. Johnnie watched, his face creasing in mirth as the two men met. You didn't need to be a family historian to know who these visitors were. The two elderly men bridled at each other; custom dictated that they must shake hands, and they did so, but with such a stiffness, such a formality that it was more a ritual of challenge than greeting. Lord Montford's face was a study in stone. He had no choice but to raise the hand that Betsy proffered to him to his lips; she was good at engineering that sort of thing, but he hardly saw the girl who followed, or her two brothers. Somewhere deep inside he still had the heart of a young man. So this was the Betsy he dreamed about on unguarded nights, this product of the New World, with her gloss and shine. Yet, unmistakably, she was an old woman. He'd never really considered that she, too, would have grown old.

Isabella suffered the scrutiny of these new guests as she had suffered that of all the others. She wasn't aware of who they were, of their possible importance. She did fleetingly observe that the girl seemed to pause at Johnnie, seemed to take longer than usual. The two brothers she barely acknowledged, and they felt awed by her chill stillness. She was the nearest they had found to their own imaginings of the perfect English lady, which was odd since she was the brewer's daughter. And they'd been prepared to glower hatred at Johnnie, the brother of Michael. But he wasn't what they'd expected at all; he was like them, they instinctively felt, in search of a good time, a good chap. So they grinned rather shyly at each other and Johnnie's face relaxed. For a few minutes he looked like the Johnnie of old, before the war. A chap to hunt all day and drink all night, a good sort. But then the breath of fresh air was past. There were other self-important arrivals to be allowed to bestow their felicitations.

Johnnie's sigh of ennui was loud enough to be heard down the entire line. Lord Montford's nose twitched in irritation; his calf muscles were beginning to ache, as they always used to on parade. God damn, he hated parades. He abruptly abandoned the be-ringed hand of the wife of the constable of the county and with an indecipherable muttering made off across the stone-flagged room. He looked neither left nor right. He wanted a sanctuary. He would go to the billiard room. Michael was in there. Neither of them had any more part in this evening's festivities. They could have a quiet game of snooker and a glass of decent port and a cigar. He wasn't going to let the prophecies of doom from some damn doctor spoil his enjoyment of the extremely fine Havanas that George had brought down from town.

Michael and Thomas were in the billiard room having a quiet game, leaving the guests to their own devices.

Michael chalked the tip of his cue slowly. This game with Thomas was enlightening. It was proving two things: that Thomas seemed to have lost the killer instinct in his play, and that the Bradbury family, and that now clearly included Thomas, was concerned that Isabella might still manage to avoid marriage to Johnnie.

'She's a stupid girl,' Thomas said, leaning over the edge of the table to judge the line of the balls. It was Michael's turn to play. 'There are too many people dependent on this union for some silly fancy of hers to muck up.'

'What silly fancy?' Michael spoke softly. He was controlling the tremor of anger he felt from communicating itself through the cue. He struck sharply at the white ball, neatly dispatching a red into its designated pocket. He glanced over the table. 'Black,' he murmured and, squinting down the line of the cue, he potted that with the white spinning off a cushion.

'Oh, Johnnie got a bit carried away, tried to anticipate tomorrow and it gave her the willies. She'll have to get used to it when it's legal.'

Michael stood up, straightening slowly. He should never have signed away the entail, he could see that now. If that damned letter had only reached him earlier. Lavender, Eli Bradbury's so brief second wife, had scrawled an enigmatic little note, but it had made one point clear enough. The woman believed that Isabella loved him, Michael. And he'd nearly crumpled it up without reading it, thinking that the two-page epistle that was wrapped around it, the letter from the nurse, was a misplaced appeal for a job. Fortunately he'd felt a pang of conscience; as a budding MP he should be aware of constituents' problems. So he'd retrieved it from the basket, smoothed it out, and then it had become magically clear. The nurse had been instructed to post the enclosed missive a month or so ago, but it had been misplaced; he'd skipped through the rest, the reasons, the apology. All that mattered was there. Isabella was being coerced into this marriage, and it had been in Michael's power to stop it for she loved him. They could have married and he'd never have signed the final transfer. Now it was too late. Far too late.

'Michael!' Lord Montford stalked into the room. 'Pour

me a decent glass of port.' He peered around the smoke-dimmed room. 'And where are those cigars of George's? I can smell you're at them already. Ah Thomas, didn't see you there. God, this is the only safe room in the house. Women all over the place upstairs. Strange servants in the corridors. Half the guests I don't even recognize.'

'You might do better if you wore your glasses, Father.' Michael potted another red ball with a satisfactory clack of ivory. 'This table plays very well. I know it seemed a sin to alter it at the time, but it is a definite improvement.' His father snorted. Michael walked the length of the table, judging the position of the balls. There were only two reds left to play, then the colours.

Thomas studied the elder Montford son. 'You know, Michael,' he said, 'you've changed a lot. You've become calculating. Even your play is different.'

'I thought yours had changed too, Thomas.' Michael chose his target. 'I thought it had deteriorated.' They were silent as the red was satisfactorily potted.

Then Thomas laughed. 'I thought it had improved, but still you're much better than you ever were. More determined to win.'

Michael could have gone on to win the frame then; he was in an unassailable position. But instead he stood staring almost vacantly into the cigar smoke. Determined to win.

That was an odd thing to say to someone who'd chucked everything up. Determined to win. It was a pity life wasn't a game, a challenge to be thrown down, battled for and then finally won. But life wasn't as simple as that, or was it?

In the silence of the room, where they'd played out so many scenes of their lives, everything fell into place for Michael. He was laying the cue down, carefully, almost reverentially as Eli burst into the room. He was very red in the face, apoplectically so. 'Thomas!' he cried out. 'Thomas, God Almighty, it's that Bullstone man, he's gone mad. My God, he's pushed it up to four hundred thousand, he's got the papers here. My God.' He staggered forwards into the room, then leaned his weight on the edge of the table. 'I'm done for, done for, we're all finished.'

Thomas's face tightened. In the near gloom he became suddenly so much older. 'It's not finished, it can't be.' He almost whispered the words.

'It's that American family, they're in on it too.' Eli forced the words out, his breathing was laboured.

Michael moved to bring a chair up to him. 'Can you fill me in quickly, sir?' he asked. 'Just the outline, that's all. Thomas, come over here, fill in any bits that might get left out. Father, you'd better come closer. Quickly now, we don't have much time.'

Beyond their hearing the festivities continued, the orchestra playing the well-loved tunes. Isabella danced every dance. She was held by earls and merchants, soldiers of fame, and some of fortune. But she didn't dance with Johnnie because he didn't come to ask her and no one else seemed to have thought to arrange it.

Hermione clucked her annoyance; her younger nephew had disappeared as had the two Macaul boys. 'George,' she whispered, as a sudden, very disturbing thought struck her, 'George, I think you'd better check up on Johnnie. I wouldn't like to find he was brawling with those Macaul boys.'

But George just smirked knowingly; women could never understand men. Those three young fellows were out of the same mould, they might be gambling with dice, or sampling the serving girls, but brawling, not in best bib and tucker.

'Aunt Hermione,' said Isabella, who had been left temporarily at her chaperone's side during a lull in the music. 'Aunt Hermione, how long do I have to stay?'

'Here, at the dancing, you mean?'

'Yes, yes.' Isabella was desperate; another red-faced hero was making his leering way to her, another unknown name to be ticked off on her card.

'Well, until the end, of course. This is your evening, my dear, your party.' Hermione's aristocratic forehead creased briefly. Girls today had no stamina. She watched as Isabella was led out on to the floor. The girl and her partner made several false starts, and Hermione quite clearly saw the oaf's feet stamp on Isabella's satin slippers at least twice. Good Lord, she sighed audibly, young girls had no stamina, and young men no ability on the dance floor. Why, in her youth . . . She turned to look up at George who was in deep conversation again with the Bradbury man. He had a very unhealthy colour, that brewery fellow; it probably came from drinking too much of his own produce. Gentlemen should drink claret, not beer. Yes, Isabella's father looked quite unwell, choleric. If he didn't calm down he wouldn't live to see his grandchildren.

Michael found his brother in the stables, as he'd expected. He hadn't anticipated the company he was keeping, however.

'Hey look,' David Macaul drawled. 'It's your big brother, Johnnie. Come and see who's here, Mark.' He raised his voice to summon his brother who was further down the building, peering in at the hounds who were slowly getting to their feet at the unexpected night-time visitation.

'Will you step outside with me for a minute, Johnnie.' Michael was very correct, his tone moderate.

'Step outside.' The older American's tone was mocking.

353

'He wants you to step outside, young Johnnie, me lad. Watch out he isn't all set to punch you on your nose, he's got a thing about noses.'

The three younger men grouped together, Johnnie grinning at his brother. 'I think I won't accept your invitation, old chap. I'm a bit old for a brotherly lecture on the facts of life, thanks very much. My technique's already pretty well developed, so I'll pass up on any hints you picked up in the bush.'

Michael had him by the throat in an instant. He twisted the tightly tied hunting stock until Johnnie's eyes bulged. David came for him at a rush, but Michael kicked out, catching the would-be rescuer a crack on the kneecap that felled him with a crash, then Mark was on him, pulling him off Johnnie.

'What the hell is this?' Mark's voice came in gasps. The English brothers were almost impossible to part: Michael's grip was like iron, and still, although Johnnie's face was turning purple and his eyes closing, he wasn't trying to defend himself. Abruptly Michael let go, the fury draining from his grip.

'Johnnie, you bloody fool, Johnnie,' he cried, and flung his arms round his brother to stop him from falling, 'I nearly killed you. Christ, I nearly killed you.' The hounds began to call then. One started it, then the others joined in baying. They wanted food now that they were really awake.

'Go and shut them up, go on.' It was Johnnie who croaked out the words, and the two Americans gladly bolted the length of the building. There was too much emotion in the atmosphere, escape was welcome. They threw their energies into shouting the hounds down, making the noise unbearable.

Michael helped Johnnie out into the air. They could hear

354

the orchestra playing a waltz. 'It's such a bloody mess,' he said, 'and I caused it, I caused it all.'

Johnnie didn't contradict him. What was the point when it was all so true? 'You don't love Isabella, do you?' Michael asked.

'Good God, no, I'm terrified of her, terrified of her high ideals, her ruddy art; all that sort of thing scares me to death.' Johnnie pulled his jacket tightly round him in a vain effort to keep his teeth from chattering in the bitter cold.

'That's hysterical, really funny.' Michael laughed mirthlessly. 'She's frightened to death of you. She actually tried to kill herself to avoid marrying you.'

'Christ.' They stood silently for a while, then Johnny said, 'I'll make it all back if you'd like, the entail and that, it can't be impossible. Come on, let's go to the old man. Then you can marry Isabella. You wouldn't find that so bad, would you?' He turned and looked so plaintively at Michael, that Michael could have howled like the hounds.

Find it bad? My God, it was all he'd ever wanted. Isabella. Since he'd first seen her he'd been fighting it down, holding it back. He squeezed his brother's arm, smiled into his eyes and then stopped, frozen. But it wasn't the answer any more. Eli had made that clear; Eli was ruined, ruined by George and the Americans. The Macauls.

'What were you and those chaps doing?' Michael asked urgently.

'Betting.' Johnnie grinned sheepishly, 'They'll bet on anything, types like that. You were in the billiard room so we couldn't have a game. They're full of how red-hot they are at snooker now. They've been coached up apparently. They were bragging about how they skinned Lord Belzes the other evening, and he's a dab hand with a cue all right. Anyway, we put a couple of beetles on the lip of a bucket, betting on which one would fall into the water first. They're even more addicted to chance than me.' He laughed.

That was all it could be now, Michael could see, a death or glory gamble, all or nothing, and nothing would be worse than nothing, for to lose meant too much pain for everyone.

'Come on, Johnnie.' he said. 'Come on, we'll show them an English gentleman really knows how to bet; we're going to make them the wager of a lifetime.'

Supper was announced. Isabella was surrounded by her entourage on her way to the top table. She was aware above all of her bruised feet, and she could have cried with the pain of them, but instead she smiled obediently at Hermione's bidding towards the sea of faces. There were small, intimate round tables for the guests, while the long top table was only laid on one side. She thought fleetingly of the painting of the Lord's last supper – it reminded her of that – and suddenly a real smile touched the corner of her eyes at such a silly thought.

She really is a beauty, Charlotte Buthry thought suddenly, surprising and annoying herself with the thought. But still not right for Johnnie, not right at all, and with that consoling thought she very charmingly began the clapping that rose in a tribute as the bride-to-be made her way to the table.

As the party seated themselves it became clear that several of their number were missing. Dove was sending out frantic envoys; spaces at the top table meant disaster, a blot on his organization. He looked imploringly at Maude who was hovering on the edges of the gathering. It was Maude who proved the butler's salvation, for she had the bright idea of asking Lucinda if she knew where the others might be. That sent messengers running to the billiard room to summon the elders, and others to the stables to summon the youngsters. Yes, Lucinda was every inch a natural-born lady of the manor; it was a pity she'd have to wait so long now to get there.

The food was magnificent, every mouthful bursting with the flavour of fine fare, every confection a tribute to the art of the cooks and chefs who had worked so hard to provide the banquet. Where Isabella only picked at her portions, the guests more than made up. They fortified themselves with the velvety soup, then fell on the oysters; the great wagon-load that Eli had provided was consumed almost entirely. Then the celebration meats, the roasted pigs and venison pies; the salads, dainty morsels of lettuce, fine thin onions and tender carrots that had been grown under glass through the foul weather; then the pastries, brimming with apples from the local orchards, gilded with apricots imported in the summer and preserved in Muscovado sugar, dark and sweet. They drank the wines and wiped their lips on their napkins, then sat back. Contented as only good food can make a man. Now for the speeches.

When Mumbles reached under the table to caress the stringy thigh of the ageing countess next to him, he was not alone in his actions. Around the room looks were exchanged, trysts arranged with fluttering eyelashes. Port was being passed, nuts put on the tables. It took a while for the movement of the top table to attract attention. There was a rustling of amazement around the room. They were leaving, filing out: the entire family of Montfords, and the Bradburys and the Americans. Dove had given out his orders and the guests were quietly, courteously encouraged to keep their places. After a while they went back to their contemplations of each other, rather than of the party givers.

★   ★   ★

357

Michael stood at the door of the billiard room. He was checking them in, assembling the participants. As Isabella passed him, close on Hermione's heels, he reached out and grasped her wrist, pulling her out of the line to stand beside him. Eli looked at them. He seemed about to comment but then, shaking his head, followed the others.

At last Michael was alone with Isabella in the corridor, the suits of armour of his warrior ancestors forming a blind bodyguard around them. Michael still had his hand on her wrist. He pulled her slowly round to face him. She still seemed so distant, her eyes almost unseeing.

'Issy! Issy! ' He felt like shaking her into wakefulness. 'Issy, you must help me. This is it, this is the last chance for any of us. You must understand what I'm trying to do.'

'You mean I won't have to marry Johnnie?' All that had happened, all the drama of the evening: she hadn't been aware of any of it.

'There's no question of that now. There hasn't been for an hour or more.'

A flush spread up her neck. 'I don't understand, no one's said anything to me, no one's spoken to me about it.' Her tone was almost querulous; it was too sudden, all of it.

'Now listen to me.' He pulled her closer to him, put his hands on her waist. She was so thin, he thought, painfully thin. 'Issy, do you love me? You do, don't you, Issy?'

She nodded dumbly, hesitantly, then suddenly, as if she had torn down barriers between them, she relaxed in his arms and he felt the new warmth of her body against him.

'My dear, dear Issy.' He looked down at her so gently, so tenderly. 'I'd like to be able to say, right now, at this very moment, that I'm falling in love with you, but it wouldn't be true, because I've loved you for always. You were in my heart before I met you, in my heart before I even knew what love was. My dear, my dearest Issy.'

Very slowly he tipped her face up to his, then bent to kiss her.

The door beside them opened with a crash.

'What the hell's going on here?' It was Randolf Macaul, a man unused to being kept waiting.

'We're just coming.' Michael put his hand under Isabella's elbow to guide her forwards. She reached up behind her neck. She didn't know what he was going to do, but he needed her help, so she unclasped the locket that had been her mother's and handed it to him.

'For luck,' she whispered. He put it briefly to his lips then dropped it into his top pocket. Isabella stepped away from him, leaving him at the centre stage, everyone in the room waiting for him. This was his hour.

'Father, ladies and gentlemen, as you all know, it was intended that any business that had to be transacted before tomorrow's wedding would be finalized this evening. It is now eleven o'clock, and carriages are at two. We do not have much time, so I'll be brief.'

Isabella stepped back into the shadows at the edge of the room, wanting to catch every expression on Michael's face without having to guard her own.

'Despite the confusion, the deliberate confusion,' he continued, looking over at George whose face was wreathed in Havana perfumed smoke, 'the overall aims of this gathering are still the same. At the heart of this evening is Pencombe. The estate needs new blood, monied blood. A considerable sum has already been spent here by Mr Bradbury, Isabella's father, in anticipation of tomorrow's event. That has to be borne in mind as well as the fact that a contract has already been signed for the sale of Reason Hill. So here we have Pencombe, Johnnie and me. And Isabella, whose father has been badly compromised by all this, and then, of course, we have Adele.' He turned to look at her, as they all did. Her surprise was very obvious; she hadn't thought she had a part in any of this. 'Adele,' Michael continued, 'who came to England with the express purpose of finding a husband. A husband with a title, an estate, not necessarily money, because she has plenty of that, or at least her family does. That's right, isn't it, Mr Macaul?'

Randolf bowed his head in agreement and he smiled wryly; this was intriguing.

'Very well,' Michael went on, 'so let's suppose for a moment that this evening's scenario is played out the way certain amongst us have planned. Pencombe becomes part of the Macaul empire. That's what you intend, isn't it, George, using the leverage of the mortgage you hold on the Hall? And logically, Johnnie will marry Adele.' There was a chorus of surprise from those who hadn't yet worked that out for themselves. 'Well, that suits quite a few: it suits Johnnie and Adele, who I must say are perfectly matched, and it suits Mr Macaul and of course George. Yes, George. I'm sorry, Aunt Hermione,' he said, 'but for once it can't work out just the way he planned it.'

'Don't see why not, my boy.' George was his bluffest, heartiest self.

'Well, how's this to begin with?' Michael reached inside his pocket and pulled out a piece of paper emblazoned by the red of the Pencombe seal. 'This is Johnnie's signed and witnessed deed passing the entail back to me, and Adele and I are not a perfect match because I am, how did you put it, Adele? Lacking in "go".

'So there we are. But before you all look too glum and perhaps as a proof that I do in fact, possess the magic "go", I have a proposition for you. One that already meets with the approval of the Macaul heirs.'

'Sure, Pa, it's a cinch.' Mark Macaul was beginning to take off his evening jacket.

'Just hold on, son.' His father put a hand out to slow him down. 'What's this proposition then, boy?'

'A wager, to be played out in this room,' Michael answered. 'It has to be in here; everything important that has happened at Pencombe, the family joys and tragedies, has had its origins in here. And, just as inevitably, the game must be snooker, the pure distillate of all the other games of chance ever played on the table. The fact that my father had a hand in developing it in India is something that I personally am very proud of.' He looked at his father; it was true, he was proud of the old man, with a pride born of a love that tolerates faults. 'So, that is the challenge, three frames of snooker – no more, there isn't time – between the eldest son of the Macauls of Chicago and myself, eldest son and heir at Pencombe; the Old World versus the New. Our futures staked on this table, that symbolizes already the marriage of the old and the new. Whatever happens, whoever wins, it's the run of the game that will create a new heritage for us and our descendants.' Michael ran his hand caressingly over the smooth, new green baize. 'I'll wager this piece of paper I'm holding, the transfer of the entail, against the mortgages on the house and Home Farm.'

'How about the rest of the estate? That includes Cade's farm, remember.' It was George.

'Yes, well, that's where I'm going to be a bit awkward, Uncle George. You see, it was through you that that mortgage was effected, and you were perfectly aware that I was in ignorance of it. That makes you an accessory to the fact and you could be taken to court for it.'

'Stuff and nonsense, you'll not take this to court. You can't drag your father through a scandal.'

'You seem to be more sure of that than I am, George. Perhaps you're forgetting that, at this moment, I am being forced into an untenable position. In any case, I have

361

another little something that may persuade you. You're sure you don't want this the easy way?' George took his cigar slowly from between his lips, blew a perfect smoke ring, then equally slowly replaced it.

'Very well, I take your silence as an invitation for me to continue. Can I have it please, Eli?' He held out his hand, and Eli took an envelope from his inside pocket and passed it across. 'Thank you. Perhaps you should open this, George.'

George took the proffered packet, turning it over in his hands before untucking the flap. He pulled the photograph only half out. It was the one Isabella had taken of him with Harold in Maidstone. He held it closer to the light for a moment then put it back. He put the envelope into his own pocket. 'You can add the rest of the estate to our side of the wager,' he said.

Michael felt a sudden surge of adrenalin. They were going to accept after all. 'There is one last thing,' he said. 'I add this to my stake.' He laid down a cluster of shining stones that sparkled brightly on the green: the betrothal necklace that had begun it all. 'On the condition that you agree, if I win, to pay Eli back all he has already spent here, and also, and this is vital, you must tell him why you have been so viciously undermining his business. It can't have been just for spite; you're not like that, George, I'll give you that. There has to have been a profit in it somewhere. And knowing you, I should reckon it's a damn big one.'

Hermione's tutting at her nephew's swearing was the only sound in the room, as Mark began once more to take off his jacket and then started to roll up his sleeves.

The stakes were laid, Pencombe's future, Eli's salvation, the future of them all, against the white and red deed of entail and the shimmering ice-fire gems.

'If you'd choose a cue, Mark.' Michael gestured to the

rack of a dozen assorted ones, standing to attention beside the fireplace.

'Thanks very much. Case of choosing my weapon first, is it?' Mark grinned, as he ran an eye over the implements. 'Tell you one thing though,' he continued, 'if I were you I'd move this rack; they'll get warped by the heat.' He put a hand out to take the cue furthest from the fire then he walked to the table and laid it down gently, rolling it away from him, checking that it was straight. 'This one'll do me,' he said.

Michael walked to the rack himself and, feeling self-conscious, took the cue nearest the fire. He ran his hand along the length of it; it was warped, he knew that perfectly well, but he was happy with it, it was an old friend.

Mark was at the table now, running the palm of his hand carefully over the cloth, stroking softly downwards, then back, away from the black spot, against the nap. Michael's breathing had become very shallow, he watched as he would any combatant. His opponent was planning tactics, judging the field of play. The American squatted down, running his eye across the lie of the table. Some of this was for real, Michael knew, and some was for effect, but the signs were unmistakable: Mark Macaul was serious.

Isabella leaned back against the wall behind her. She put her palms flat against the cool stone; her hands were trembling and she didn't want anything to distract the force she was trying to will to Michael. She too was breathing slowly, consciously building reserves of energy. It didn't do to think of failure; instead she concentrated on victory, staring at the green cloth as if she could make it an ally.

Mark won the toss, the coin coming up heads as he'd called.

Thomas set the balls out, his broad farmer's hands

moving smoothly, not showing the emotion that was making his collar feel uncomfortably tight. The fifteen reds gleamed opulently in the lamplight: they were almost new and had an unmistakable gloss. He walked to the baulk end of the table to place the green, brown and yellow balls then he walked back, putting first the blue and then the pink on their spots. Finally, almost reverentially, he laid down the black. Then he turned to put the white ball into the hands of the man who, if he won, would carry off Reason Hill.

David stepped forwards suddenly, inspired to shake his brother's hand, pat him on the back and wish him luck. The Macauls all came forward then to crowd round their champion, the women kissing, the men back-slapping. Michael stood apart. Johnnie grinned briefly at him and that was all. The others in the room had their own ways of assisting fate: Isabella wasn't alone as she furtively crossed her fingers, but it took his lordship more effort, on account of his rheumatism.

The American moved to the table. He swiftly took up position, bending at the waist, the cue held perfectly parallel, clutching the butt some two or three inches from the end, his elbow bent up in an immaculate right angle: he was a perfect product of his coaching. Michael breathed out, emptying his lungs totally of air before inhaling again. He fixed his eye on the white ball on the table, a trick he had for keeping calm. He wouldn't let his concentration be broken, wouldn't let his mind ramble on to Isabella, to Johnnie. On and on his thoughts went, his eye following the play, his mind revolving, combinations, permutations of relationships, his adrenalin surging.

Johnnie had gone to keep score, standing on the left of the wooden plaque with the brass sliding scales and pointers. David moved around the room to stand on the other side of it. He was there to protect his own family's interests, after all, Johnnie was a Montford.

The white ball shot into the body of reds, sending them scattering as Mark made them all start by letting out a raucous rebel yell. George blew his nose very loudly with a great deal of white handkerchief. Stupid young ass, he thought, all the technique, all the careful foreplay and then to let himself go, silly ass.

But Mark had done the right thing. Michael had expected to have to wait. He stepped forward towards the table unbalanced and nervous. He bent down quickly, sizing up the shot he favoured as he went. There was a close enough line, if he . . . He struck the white ball below centre, the backspin imparted by his rushed shot slowing the ball as it ran. He was lucky it connected at all with the red; in any case, it only nudged the ball gently forwards, leaving Mark a beginner's pot for first blood.

He wasn't slow to take the chance, leaving the spot ball nicely lined up for an attack on the blue. 'Blue,' he muttered, almost under his breath. He made four or five stabbing little jerks, feints at the ball, then with a decisive movement of the cue he potted his target. The table was open. His earlier attack on the reds had spread them and the game was set up for a raid. David stepped forward to replace the colour on its spot. The next red popped in simply. 'Pink', he murmured, and in it went. Mark's score was thirteen on the board, unlucky for some, but not for him. He took another red, then the brown, a red and then the pink again. He was concentrating in earnest now; his score was up to twenty-five. There was time for a flashy 'double', the new rubber cushions propelling the ball smartly off the side, back the way it had come. So far he had been potting in the corner pockets. This time it was a middle for the red; it looked easy. He was smiling as he struck the white. The line was fine, just edge the red on the far corner of the pocket to tip it in, there! To his astonishment the red came off at a tangent, rolling about a foot away from the pocket. He narrowed his eyes and glared at the offending piece of brass.

Eli's sigh was heard by everyone in the room, like steam from a boiler. His face was very red, he felt sick with nerves. Michael had bought them time with his challenge, but it was only that. Eli didn't know if he could face failure. Hermione was studying him closely; she was concerned at his colour, the man looked most uncomfortable. She herself felt uncomfortable. It was her husband who had brought all this about; she was beginning to feel responsible for it all: Michael's desperate, pale determination and Eli's approaching apoplexy. She stirred in her seat; if only Michael could win, and win quickly.

He came to the table differently this time, more cautiously; it was something to approach with respect. The red that had surprised Mark was nicely positioned, an easy start for Michael. He bent very slowly to the table, squinting along the line of the cue carefully. He struck the white ball dead centre and it travelled perfectly to collide with the red and send it into the centre pocket. He stood up to look over the table; he must think tactics, tactics. But the black was appealingly in line for a corner pocket at the baulk end. He was playing against the nap so he must push it a bit, and he did. The black ball careered into the pocket; he'd hit too hard, but it was safe except for the white that shot across the table, bounced against a cushion and came almost instantly to rest. Damn, shots so tight up against the edge were tricky.

Isabella had pushed herself abruptly away from the wall: the sharp clack of the speeding balls was too much for her nerves. Even Lord Montford had to surreptitiously wipe the palms of his hands on his evening trousers.

Michael walked slowly round the table as Johnnie

moved his counter along, eight. Isabella was edging gently closer to her father; it wasn't a conscious movement but at every pause in the play she shuffled a little bit further. She put her hand on to his shoulder and when he turned, startled, she looked down at him; he looked very unwell. He put his hand over hers, it was damp. If this failed, he would be bankrupted, the shame might kill him.

Michael cleared his throat and all their attention was suddenly drawn back to the table. He had lined up on a red well down the table; the line was good, everything was fine except for the white ball, almost obscured from his view by the bulging, opulent cushion. He bent low, trying to steady the bridge of his hand that had to be right up on the wooden edge of the table. It wasn't secure, it couldn't be. He made a couple of feints, but it was no good, he'd have to try as he was. It was a miss-hit, inevitable. The ball made a desultory appearance on the table, rolling a sluggish few inches. A miss-hit, foul shot, four to his opponent and not only that but a very simple pot to follow.

Mark set to with a will. He played the well-placed yellow, then back to pot a red and the blue, then spinning himself back into position very neatly for a red followed by the black. The reds were harder to find now, but he accomplished a nifty double that took the full length of the table, then the brown, that brought his score past fifty. Isabella was unaware that her fingers were digging fiercely into Eli's shoulder, but the tightening band around her father's chest was causing him much more pain than her nails.

Michael was talking to himself now; he could play better, he knew it. He honestly believed that he could beat the American, but not with this intolerable pressure on him. He looked over at Isabella: her face was taut, her jaw white with the strain; she wasn't looking at him, her eyes were fixed on the table, mesmerized by it. As were all the others, all of those on his side: his father, Eli whose deepening colour was worrying them all, Thomas with his arm around Lucinda. They all depended on him, relied on him to solve it all. God! He looked up at the ceiling. How the hell could he calm down? A particularly loud clack of balls pulled his attention back to the table. Mark was straightening up. Clearly the play was now in Michael's hands, but Mark was smiling and it was easy to see why. He didn't need to say 'Snooker!' but he did, and his brother clapped loudly, to be shushed, though not very effectively, by his father. Michael had as good as lost the frame, and he knew it. He bent quickly to the table and made the requisite foul, hitting the pink ball with the white.

The penalty points were added to the board, and Mark stepped forward to polish off the eight remaining reds and an assortment of colours that boosted his score to ninety. He was now well set to begin on the set colour sequence and his position looked unassailable. He potted the yellow leaving himself straight on the green. With casual aplomb he hit the cue ball with just the right amount of screw to bring it back for the brown. He used screw too to bring himself into position for the blue. He was pleased with that shot, one he'd had difficulty with. If he managed the next tricky one, getting himself into position for the pink, then he'd be home and dry. He was on what he called to himself the 'family' side of the table: they were ranged behind him. He leaned over, beside the pocket that he considered to have cheated him out of the earlier pot. If he'd got that, Michael wouldn't even have had a look in. This was it, he had to hit the white ball with screw, twisting it to the right-hand side, to pot the blue in the pocket opposite him and then have the cue ball veer off right up the table, to rebound off the cushion and roll back, plumb for the pink. He held his breath, willing it to happen, and it did. That was it, they might as well pack up and go home; the pink fell, and then the black. This time his pa didn't quieten his brother, but joined in with the cheers, one more rebel yell.

Isabella bent down urgently to her father. She wanted to speak while the din covered her words.

'I'll stay with you, Father, no matter what.' She was loosening his tie as she spoke, shielding the actions of her hands from the others by her body. 'Rely on me, we can build things up again together, honestly.' She wished desperately they'd had more to say to each other in the past, more to work on. She had to convince him. 'Father!' she said urgently, trying to pull his attention back.

'Stand back!' It was Hermione. She pushed Isabella aside none too gently, but she was now very worried. 'Eli! Eli, can you hear me?'

'Yes, yes, what?' He felt confused, and hot, he needed air, but couldn't leave, not now.

'Eli! Have you got any tablets, anything the doctor's given you? Eli!' The damned woman was shouting at him, couldn't let him concentrate to fight the pain. Pills? What pills? Then he remembered and feebly tapped his waistcoat pocket.

'Thank goodness!' Hermione said and tutting ferociously she set about getting the small bottle out, tipping the tablets into her hand and gesturing imperiously towards the water that sat beside the decanters. It was Michael who fetched it, carried it towards them.

Isabella caught at his sleeve as he turned to walk back to the table. 'Whatever happens, I love you, you know that, don't you?' She whispered the words fiercely at him and he nodded.

He could see it all: if he lost then Eli would lose and Isabella would stay with her father, nursing, being companion to an ageing destitute wreck of a man. Michael knew all about duty and honour and how they could rule and sometimes ruin lives. He must win. He was calmer now, on a higher plateau than he'd ever been, and in a way at peace; he didn't have to concentrate to control his breathing any more. He ran his hand caressingly along the wooden shaft of the cue, then looked over at the Macauls. Adele shot him a smile of open sympathy. Well, she could save that for her brother, he thought, and so they began the second frame.

It was so easy. They played a few alternate shots that did nothing more than spread the reds around the table, then Mark's concentration slipped. He left the table open and Michael was not slow to take advantage. Everything worked: he hit straight when he had to, and put on topspin by raising his bridge more effectively than he'd ever managed before. When the position of play required it, he hit the ball neatly below centre to impart screw. He didn't falter. Johnnie didn't have to touch Mark's score once as his brother's mounted inexorably. The tension in the room defused as Michael progressed. It would be one frame each unless disaster overtook him. But nothing went against him. Even the pocket that had offended his opponent accepted his obliquely angled shot.

Isabella felt her father's recovery under her hand. She could sense his breathing growing calmer, his blood slowing. She glanced down at him whenever Michael stood back from the table. Eli was growing pale now, looking tired and old, but he had the strength to hold on to her hand, and, as Michael potted the last red, he turned his head to give her a little smile of victory. Michael cleared the colours in exemplary demonstration style. He could smile at his earlier nerves, and felt he could play on all night. The black, and it was over, a splendid frame.

He'd never played better. He stood back as his own side rustled in appreciation.

Thomas walked to the decanters. 'I for one,' he said, 'need a drink. Anyone else?'

'Good God, yes.' Lord Montford got stiffly to his feet. 'I'll have a brandy, a bloody big one.'

'Betsy, can I fetch you something?' Randolf was unctuous towards his wife; he enjoyed showing these Britishers that Americans see to their women first.

The ladies all had sherry, while the men took fortifying glasses of spirit, except for the combatants who had water. Michael sipped at his glass, studying his opponent over the rim, as he was studied back. The atmosphere in the room became charged again, only differently this time, the spectators scenting the kill.

'George!' Hermione tugged at her husband's sleeve. 'George!' she hissed. 'I want you to tell that man why you've been trying to ruin his business.'

George looked down at his wife, horror in every line of his face. 'Do what?' he said.

'You heard, George. You go and tell him now. It's disgraceful, my goodness. I thought he was going to die a short while ago.'

She jumped suddenly as Randolf's voice whispered, close to them both. 'You will not disclose anything of the sort, George. My business is involved here as well as yours. You do anything before this game's out and I'll make you wish you hadn't. And I mean that. I don't make idle threats.'

Hermione was quivering with fury. She rose with considerable dignity to her feet. 'Mr Macaul,' she began in a glacial tone.

Her brother barked across the room at her, 'Sit down, Hermione! Sit down and shut up!' he shouted. 'It's the off, you silly creature, shut up.'

She sat slowly, maintaining her hold of her husband's

sleeve. This was a dreadful evening, dreadful. She reached for her reticule, she wanted her handkerchief, but Lord Montford caught her eye, and the movement ceased. She sat very still as her nephew approached the table. Suddenly she realized with a shudder, there was no more putting off, this was the last ditch.

It was as he bent down, lining himself up, that Michael realized he was trembling. He gripped the cue tighter and that made it worse. He straightened up slowly, gazing down at the table, as if lost in concentration, hoping his opponent hadn't seen, but it was a vain hope. If this frame started like the last then Mark would win it. Michael stooped suddenly, hardly sighting himself at all and fired the white ball into the reds, then he let out a 'view halloo', the huntsman's cry that he'd loosed a thousand times in the field, and Johnnie joined in, the call blood-curdling in its enthusiasm. Michael grinned at Mark, follow that!

Michael felt his blood cooling; he'd been flushed at his inspiration, but the tactic hadn't worked. Mark bent to the table as calm as he could wish. But then he had all to gain, and nothing to lose; at least that's how it looked to Michael. He watched as the score against him began to mount. A red and the black, top score, bad start for Michael. Then a red and the pink, another red and the black again. The cue ball reacted to its master's command, running up and down the table, veering to the best position for the next shot, continuously, almost monoto-nously. There was the most awful feeling of defeat in the air. Three last reds were left on the table. Mark stood up slowly; he'd been ready to play his shot, then he'd felt the tremor pass down the wood in his hand. He was going over the top, he could feel the urge of victory, he'd got to slow down. He chalked his cue again slowly, made himself think back to the lessons at the club, that silly story about the guy who doctored his chalk with pepper to blow in his opponent's eyes.

Isabella would not give up, she couldn't. She forced her mind to think on, forwards to victory. There had to be time somehow, she couldn't believe in their defeat. She willed her thoughts on to the table. It had to come right for them. Mark potted the red, then called that he was going for the yellow; he wasn't going to try anything more difficult than he had to. Another red, easy, and it was the brown he wanted; he was at the baulk end of the table, leaning well forward to reach. He wanted the cue ball to come back, nice and easy, for that last red. He held his breath and smartly tapped the ball. The table was, after all, against him. A minute inconsistency in the nap of the new cloth was enough; the brown ball teetered close to the edge of the pocket, but nowhere near enough. Mark stood and gave a jerky little bow to his backers then ushered Michael forwards. 'Remember where to find the table, old man?' he said. It was the over-anglicized 'old man' that sparked Michael into action.

He squatted to check the lie of the final red. He was trying to work out the figures; had he got enough balls ahead of him? Anyway, he'd got to pot the red before he did anything else. He sighted sharply along the cue, his arm swinging back smoothly, a couple of feints, then he was off, the red winging to the requisite pocket. 'Brown,' he said. At least that was nicely lined up for him. He potted it and Johnnie started to move the score that had sat ignominiously still for what had felt like hours. Now for the essence of the game. Michael could feel the grim smile working at the corners of his lips, as he glanced over at the old man who was staring steadfastly at the table. Well done, Father, he thought; well done, old man, thank Christ you lot invented snooker. He had to master the art, be its true exponent to get the score in his favour.

Here goes, Michael thought, as he leaned forward, snooker!

Clearing all the colours on the table could only score him twenty-seven. He had five already, that made thirty-two, and Mark had sixty-three; there were an extra thirty-one points to make up to tie and thirty-two to win. Michael bent to the table. Of the men in the room, only his father now believed he could win. They'd snookered for hours out in India, becoming so engrossed in it that the boys who didn't play said it was close to an unnatural vice. He studied his son dispassionately: the boy could do it, but it would be damned tight. Michael studied his line, working out the sums as he drew the cue back.

'Thomas!' The sudden cry made him jerk up. Thank God, he hadn't touched the ball. It was Lucinda. 'Oh Thomas!' she cried again, clutching at her husband as she bent forwards in pain.

'Good God!' Hermione was on her feet in an instant. 'Not now, you can't be serious, Lucinda?'

It was quite clear, however, from her gasps, that she was.

'Is there a doctor here?' Hermione was assuming control.

'Dr Groake's here somewhere,' Isabella said, holding her father tightly. He had tried to jump to his feet, to go to his beloved Lucinda, but he was better sitting down.

'I'll go. Hang on, don't touch the board.' Johnnie was shouting his instructions as he bolted from the room.

Lord Montford was very quickly on his feet, he had something he wanted to say to his son. 'Michael, listen to me.' He bent close to whisper quickly, 'Pot the yellow and the green straight off, get them off the table.'

Michael was about to interrupt, but he was stopped. 'No, no,' his father continued, 'just listen. The Macauls have been working together on strategy so there's nothing dishonourable in my giving you a hand. You won't manage a snooker on all of them, so just do it on the high numbers. That's right, I know it is, I remember quite well. You can do it on the high ones. Try the lot and you'll slip up somewhere. Always happened, used to see it time and time again.'

Michael was concerned. What the old man said might well be right. But to take two balls off the table now, clearing them off for only their face value, seemed dangerous. The commotion at the far end of the room was clearing, Lucinda being almost forcibly removed by the doctor, Thomas was clearly distraught, unable to make up his mind whether to follow his wife or stay and watch their future unfold.

As he stood undecided in the doorway, Hermione called to him. 'Do come in and close the door, Thomas, there's the most awful draught, and stir up the fire, will you; there's a distinct chill in here.' They all looked at her, the Macauls, her own family. She was quite remarkable; it was strange how she'd almost been overlooked all these years. Her brother went to sit beside her, close to the fire that Thomas was obediently stoking.

Michael stared at the family group, unable to decide whether or not to follow the old man's advice. As the room settled he put his fingers into his waistcoat pocket to touch Isabella's locket. 'For luck,' she'd said. He pulled it out. It was made of gold, an oval delicately engraved with flowers. He pressed the tiny catch with his thumbnail and it sprang open. The surprise made him smile, for it was his own face that looked out at him, the photograph that Isabella had taken all that time ago, and must have kept. She was looking at him now, blushing at his discovering her secret. She'd kept it through everything, through all the time she'd thought she'd have to marry Johnnie, even

375

after she'd thought Michael had gone. He'd follow his father's advice, he decided. He had to win, had to.

He potted the yellow neatly, spinning the ball back up the table so that he could go for the green. Now, he took his time deciding on his line. He was still thinking on two planes, one tactical, and the other practical. He decided to take another swift step towards the end and pot the brown, and heard his father's intake of breath as he did so. He looked quickly at Isabella, to reassure her, but he could see from the bright brave smile on her face that she already thought they'd lost. The blue, pink and black balls were left. Michael smiled grimly. With the black and the pink still on their spots as he'd contrived, it was quite a straightforward matter to snooker his opponent. He tapped the blue ball with the white, sending it off down to the baulk end of the table; he had spun the cue ball off to the other end, and now the line of the black and pink effected a very neat snooker. He heard Mark's snort of irritation; he was eager to get the game over and stepped up to take his turn, glowering at having to accept the position and give away five points. He nudged the cue ball fractionally, trying to keep Michael snookered, but it didn't work; desperation makes for miraculous shots – at times. This was one. Michael effected a flying double that neatly hit the blue, pushing it behind the pink and leaving Mark snookered again.

There was a rustle round the room as the watchers began to appreciate what he was up to. Michael darted a look at his father, but there was no clue in that expressionless face as to what he should do, so he followed his own inclinations and potted the blue: he couldn't believe his luck with it would last for ever. He had produced fifteen points off that manoeuvre, and needed a further seventeen on top of potting the rest of the table. Now he had only the pink and the black to play with. As he walked round the table he noticed Hermione reach into her bag to bring out a minuscule notebook and pencil, and his aunt very carefully began to write down his points. She remembered now doing this for William, when he'd come back from India. Michael studied the table – two coloured balls; he must get the cue ball tucked in behind the black, on the far side from the pink. He held his breath as he bent. This was tricky. The white ball shot away from his cue; it had to strike four cushions, one, two, three, and by the final bounce it was going very slowly, just slowly enough to creep up behind the black.

'Christ!' It was Johnnie who'd spoken.

Mark stepped forward looking murderous. He went down behind the cue ball, his cue at a sharp angle and hit it with such venom that the black ball shot down the table, crashing into the pink, then the two balls careered to the edge, and, to everyone's astonishment, the black tipped up over the edge. It was something Michael had noticed the first time he'd seen the table, after they'd refurbished it; the new slate had made the bed shallow.

'Ball leaves table,' Johnnie said with a smirk as he added another six to his brother's score.

Twenty-four to go, Michael thought. Pot the pink for six and the black for seven; he had to pick up eleven on snookers. They placed the pink and the black again. Michael breathed in very slowly; luck had to be going with him. He hit the cue ball, one, two, three; he wasn't alone in counting out loud by the time they reached four. He'd done it!

Mark had calmed for this shot, he wasn't going to give another extra few points away. Let the bastard get out of that!

To get himself out of the snooker would require even more care than creating it, but Mark had hit fractionally harder than he'd meant to. In theory it was possible, but

377

only just. Michael had reached the stage in battle when overheated nerves cool. With mathematical precision he worked out the route of the balls, and the correct amount of swerve, and ran his hand for a final time along the wood; he'd been right to choose an old friend. He leaned over the table, and no one in the room breathed. Isabella closed her eyes, she couldn't bear it. He feinted twice, very carefully, methodically, then struck: the cue ball ran on its dictated path, collided with the pink then the two balls, like spinning dervishes, shot off on their appointed orders, creating another snooker.

'God damn!' Randolf Macaul punched the wall with his fist. 'God damn!' he said again. 'It's going to be a tie, after all this!'

Michael looked up suddenly. A tie? He hadn't worked it out like that. He looked over at the scoreboard; he'd been adding it up in his head and he must have made a mistake. Johnnie was looking desolately at the score, willing it to move for his brother.

Michael nearly gave in then; he wouldn't manage a tie break, his concentration wouldn't last, he was sure of it. But he couldn't take any more chances on this frame; he'd lose it here and now if he didn't pull himself together. He walked slowly over to where he'd left his glass of water on the side table and sipped, not touching the liquid with his lips. He was just trying to calm himself again. Mark was at the table. He looked annoyed but nothing more. He bent and played the necessary foul stroke and the penalty points were laid against him. Michael knew now what he must do. He potted the pink immaculately, bringing himself up to pot the black. The final ball of the frame sank to a ripple of applause. Michael felt his insides lurch; he'd spoilt it, ruined his chances.

Hermione was on her feet, clapping remarkably loudly for a lady. 'Well done, my dear boy, well done.'

He looked tiredly over at her. Poor thing, she couldn't be expected to realize he'd never manage the tiebreak.

She looked crossly at her nephew. 'Why aren't you more chipper, mm? My goodness, doesn't victory mean anything to you young people?'

'Victory?' Michael asked her almost in a whisper, 'victory?'

'Yes, here you are,' she said holding out her notebook. 'Everyone of your neat little manoeuvres all written down. I used to do it for William, didn't I, dear?'

Her brother was getting to his feet. 'Yes, you did, you were damned good at it too, Hermione. Let's have a look.' He took the flimsy book in his hands, running his finger down the figures. 'What's this, what's this here?' He pushed the page under Hermione's nose and she had to tip her head back to bring her eyes into focus.

'It's where the black left the table; seven points to Michael.'

'But he was on the pink, Aunt Hermione.' Johnnie came up to them. 'I gave Michael six for that, the value of the pink, you see.'

Hermione huffed officiously. 'My dear boy, don't you know anything? Value of the highest ball involved in the incident, and the black was that. Silly boy.'

Michael could feel the smile flooding over his face; Isabella was clinging to her father. She couldn't believe it, they'd won, they'd won.

'George! Tell that man at once. Mr Macaul, none of your nonsense now, if you please.' She was formidable in her authority.

George walked stiffly over to Eli and Isabella. 'It was business, you know,' he said by way of an explanation, the only one he had to offer. 'It was profit that motivated me; nothing personal, you know.'

'George!' His wife's voice spurred him on.

'There's to be a massive development, right along the river bank, some half a mile or more wide, back into the town. Your brewery is the key to it. You're on the access route; without your site they're landlocked by the river on one side and an embankment on the other. Drains, roads, all of it, has to come across your land, you can name your own price. You're on to a goldmine there, Eli.' His eyes were quick at the talk of money. 'You'll be a rich man, even if you never brew another drop in your life.'

It was very quiet then, very still, except for the far-off orchestra playing an unrecognizable waltz.

Michael put his hand out slowly to the pile of deeds that had accumulated on the table, empty now except for the two discarded cues. The spoils of victory. He picked up Johnnie's deed with its brilliant crest, the transfer of the entail. He held it up in front of them and slowly, with infinite care, tore it through from top to bottom. Then he tore the pieces again and again, until it was nothing but a scattering like snowflakes, drifting slowly to the floor.

'I don't want to be tied any more. I want to be free of the land, free of Pencombe, to live by my own rules, to follow my own ideals. Do you understand me, Johnnie, do you understand now?' he said and then he reached out for a final time to the table and picked up the necklace. 'This is all I want,' he said. 'The rest of it is yours.' He turned away, to walk to Isabella whose arms were held out to him, her eyes shining, bright as the jewels. He stepped into her embrace and they kissed gently before them all. It was very still in the room as he reached behind her neck to fasten the gold clasp. 'This was meant for you, always for you, my dearest,' he said. 'This is our real heritage.'

They walked out of the room together, away from the snooker table, out of the castle, out into the starlit night and into their future.

HERITAGE

COMPETITION
ENTRY FORM

*Win
the fabulous
£50,000 Heritage
Diamond
Necklace!*

A GRAFTON PAPERBACK

GRAFTON BOOKS
A Division of the Collins Publishing Group

It's a dream! Grafton Paperbacks, together with Ratners the Jewellers, are offering you the chance to win the unique Heritage diamond and blue topaz necklace. Made especially by Ratners and valued at over £50,000, the Heritage necklace is breathtaking in its exquisite beauty, timeless in its classic design.

All you have to do is answer these eight simple questions about **Heritage,** Heather Hay's enchanting new saga of love, ambition and wealth, and complete a special sentence. Ten runners-up will each receive £100 worth of Grafton Paperbacks of their choice.

Competition Rules

★ Answer the 8 questions and complete the sentence and send your entry form to the address below.

★ Only one entry allowed per person.

★ Closing date for all entries is 30 December 1988. The first prize will be awarded for 8 correct answers and the most original and imaginative sentence received. The judge's decision is final.

★ The winners will be notified by post.

★ Open to all residents of the U.K. and Ireland, excluding employees of Wm Collins Sons & Co Ltd and Ratners.

1 What colour are the gems in the necklace Lucinda is given on her engagement to Michael?

2 Who brought the letter from Margaret Cameron to Michael during the Boer War?

3 What had Adele come to England to find?

4 Who was selected by Randolf to tutor Mark and David in snooker?

5 Where did Lavender and Eli go for tea?

6 What was Lavender's legacy to Isabella?

7 What was Michael's wager and where was it held?

8 Who discovered the mistake in Johnnie's calculations?

Complete this sentence in less than 15 words:
'My ideal occasion for wearing the Heritage necklace would be

Please complete in block capitals
Name

Address

_____ **Tel. No.** _____

Send the form to:
Heritage Competition, Marketing Dept., Grafton Books, 8 Grafton Street, London W1X 3LA